futureproof

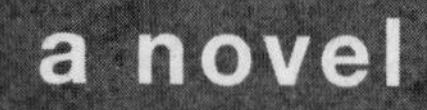
a novel

futureproof

n. frank daniels

HARPER PERENNIAL

NEW YORK • LONDON • TORONTO • SYDNEY • NEW DELHI • AUCKLAND

HARPER PERENNIAL

P.S.™ is a trademark of HarperCollins Publishers.

HarperCollins books may be purchased for educational, business, or sales promotional use. For information please write: Special Markets Department, HarperCollins Publishers, 10 East 53rd Street, New York, NY 10022.

FIRST EDITION

Designed by Joy O'Meara

Illustrations by Billy Jacobs

Concrete image from iStockphoto.com

Library of Congress Cataloging-in-Publication Data is available upon request.

ISBN 978-0-06-165683-5

09 10 11 12 13 OV/RRD 10 9 8 7 6 5 4 3 2 1

For all who seek and cannot find

The past is not dead. It isn't even past.

—**William Faulkner**

He felt as though he were wandering in the forests of the sea bottom, lost in a monstrous world where he himself was the monster. He was alone. The past was dead, the future was unimaginable.

—**George Orwell, *1984***

Now is the only thing that's real.

—**Charles Manson**

My mother gave me the Beatles albums when I was seven. They were her prized possessions. Not a scratch on them. She walked toward us, cradling the stack of records. Jonas and I were revving our Matchbox cars through the dirt at the end of the driveway. "You can play with these if you want," my mother said. "I don't have a record player out here," I said. She shrugged. "Use them like Frisbees." "But what about Mee-shell my bell?" my brother asked. He was four and his freckled nose crinkled as he squinted in the sunlight. Mother said, "God doesn't want us to listen to that song anymore." She walked away.

We pushed our cars around the black vinyl discs like racetracks for the rest of the afternoon, and then in the closing dusk we chucked the records up at streetlights. They fell back to earth, shattering on impact with the blacktop.

The next day we colored on the album covers with Magic Markers before shoving them under the couch. Sometimes I would pull them out for another look. I was proud of my artwork on the White Album. I liked to pretend that the band hired me to decorate because they couldn't think of anything themselves.

TRANSMISSION 01:

over the shirt, under the bra

September

Peckerbrook High—like every other high school—sucks. But Peckerbrook sucks for one or maybe two specific reasons in addition to all the other reasons high schools suck in general.

At Peckerbrook, every pupil is either "artistic" (as implied by its status as a Performing Arts Magnet School) or black. This isn't to say that there aren't black people registered in the vaunted arts classes. But in a school that is sixty-five percent African-American (a "vibrant and culturally rich community" is what the brochure says), only five people of color are involved in its arts program, which includes hundreds of students.

Most of us white kids are bussed in from the wealthier communities in the northern sector of the county. The rest of us have mothers like mine—women living in the squalor of the outer city limits who see their children succeeding where they never could, insisting that their sons and daughters are the next Brandos or Streeps or Barbra frickin' Streisands.

The black kids laugh at us "performing" white folk, then deal drugs right in front of the school, selling little bags of weed and crack after the faculty has gone home for the day.

Once I had to wait for my mother to pick me up (she was late, as usual), and these four crack-slingers walked over and just started beating on my head. A Samaritan in a BMW pulled up moments later and chased them away with an umbrella and his middle-class white-man authority.

My first day in drama this tall, unaffected Amazon of a girl sits beside me as I cocoon myself in a corner of the theater.

"You don't need to worry," she assures me. "All the drama people are cool."

I try smiling at her.

She is beautiful. She says her name is Tabitha. And unlike much of Atlanta, which consists of people who have transferred here from all points north, she has a *true* Southern accent—and breasts that round out the top of her shirt like an answer to prayer.

Class begins with a series of exercises where everybody lies on the floor and focuses on their breathing.

Breathe.

Listen to yourself breathe.

Then comes the "stress reduction" massage.

Tabitha scoots up next to me and asks if I'll "do" her.

"Do? Yeah . . . OK."

She lies in front of me and waits, eyes closed.

I touch her, allowing the palms of my hands to skim the linen of her shirt.

She asks if I am going to actually rub her back or just pretend.

"This part isn't supposed to be acting," she informs me.

"I know, I was just warming up," I say, trying to sound natural.

I begin at her neck, for real this time, kneading soft circles around the muscles and then down the spine and out to the shoulder blades, allowing my hands to pass over the contours of her body.

This goes on for some time before she begins moaning softly and I have to . . . *readjust*. With every moan I become more aroused and with every readjustment it seems she moans louder.

"Go under my shirt," she says.

I pull her shirt up to the middle of her back, just below the bra strap, and watch as goose bumps form. She is magnificent.

"Pull it up all the way."

"*All* the way?" I whisper.

"Yeah, all the way," she repeats, her head on her forearms, eyes still closed. She rises off the floor slightly so that I can get her t-shirt past her bra. I look around at the rest of the class to gauge how they are dealing with the striptease developing in their midst but no one seems to have the slightest idea.

"Does this feel good?" I ask, trying to keep my breathing in check.

"It doooes."

I swallow. "Good."

I continue rubbing, trying to be professional about it and all.

Then she pushes herself up onto her forearms, turns to face me. "Two things," she says. "I want you to take your index and middle fingers on both hands, bend them at the knuckle, then pinch and twist. It feels better when it hurts a little."

She lies down again and closes her eyes like before. I look at my hands and practice the twisting motion with my fingers before I go back to work on her.

"What was the second thing?"

"Oh, that's right," Tabitha purrs as I pinch her. "Unsnap my bra."

I want to make love to her.

"How do you do that?" Now I'm panicking.

"Just push the ends in toward each other and it'll snap free."

Finally the clasp loosens and separates. Her bra slips away and there I sit, straddling her bottom with a hard-on, her naked back begging me to touch it, to make love to it with my fingers. I can see her tan lines and how the sides of her breasts remain their natural flesh tone, completely uncorrupted by sun.

The more I rub the harder I get and I wonder if she can feel me through my pants. I *want* her to feel me. The tanned canvas of her back is mine for the taking and I imagine myself an artist of the highest vocation, sculpting her into immortality.

Her skin gathers between my fingers, and no matter how hard I pull or pinch, it always snaps back into place leaving a red welt, the only reminder of my concentrated ministrations. She moans with every twist, every pull. Her breasts protrude on either side of her prone body, pushed out slightly. There are no visible nipples or anything of that magnitude, but there *is* the definitive swell. It is the unmistakable sight of finality, fullness, completeness, the ultimate signifier of female perfection.

It occurs to me that I've never seen a real-life breast until that moment.

"Why'd you stop rubbing?"

I'm stuck, staring at her breast swells, my hands motionless on her back.

"Hey!"

"Huh?" I snap to attention.

She opens one eye and looks at me, shifts under my weight, and rises up just enough so that I can see her right breast fully rounded as it hangs suspended in the sweltering air.

She drops her arms out from under her and sinks back to the floor.

"Were you looking at my tits?"

I meet her upturned eye, ashamed. I've been distracted from the business of theater by something as inconsequential as a breast.

"No," I proclaim.

"Why not?" she counters, her eyes closed once again and a smile widening across her perfect face.

I've never gotten this much attention from anyone. And Tabitha has no qualms about using her sexuality to drive me batshit. She encourages me to take afternoon naps at her apartment. In her bed, no less. While she's *in* it.

After about the third day hanging out, it's obvious to both of us that I'd marry her whenever she might come around to that brilliant idea. So, because of my unabashed and unwavering loyalty to her, I've been awarded certain perks. Perks that most best-friends-of-the-opposite-sex-that-aren't-boyfriends wouldn't get. For example, I can sleep in her bed—but not have sex with her. I can't see her naked—but she'll lie next to me wearing only her panties and an XXL t-shirt that skirts just past her thighs. She'll wrestle with me and if I manage to pin her for some arbitrary amount of time she'll allow me to heft the weight of her breasts in my hands. And then I'll watch in excruciating pleasure as her nipples get stiffer beneath the fabric of her shirt, because she's turned on by the game of playing *me*. It's not a spiteful game, exactly, but one where she already knows the outcome and I am the kind of naive sucker who falls into all the little traps designed specifically to enhance her vanity. Yes, I'm *that guy*, the pathetic *friend* you always see in the movies, the nice guy who would give anything for his female comrade to finally realize that he is the one that'll make everything right.

She has her boyfriends and her pile-driver sex, but she always comes back to me to talk about how big a loser what's-his-name was.

"See, Luke," she's always saying to me, "*this* is why I don't ever want us to have sex. It would ruin everything."

"Are you saying that every time anyone has sex they're ruining a potential friendship?" I counter.

"No, not every time. I mean, there are people who have sex and love each other and get along great, I guess. But usually people are only having sex for their own amusement and it fucks up any real possibility."

"It wouldn't fuck *us* up."

She looks at me. She knows. "I can't do that, Luke. You know that."

"Then why do you keep messing with me like this, especially when you know I want to be with you the way Robert has, and Ron and Damien?"

"You mean you wanna *fuck* me?" She's sitting up now, pushing me off her. "Is that what you want? You want to be just another dick? Fine, I'll fuck you, Luke. Take off your pants."

She tries to unbutton my jeans. I grab her arms and, despite weeks of fantasizing to the contrary, try to *prevent* her from taking my clothes off.

"No, Luke, our relationship isn't good enough for you." She continues struggling with me. "You want my brain, my trust, my love, *and* my body, so I'll give it to you. I'll slide my pussy onto your cock and bring you to mind-numbing orgasm. I'm already slick and wet and ready for you."

Reverse psychology be damned, I am more turned on than I've ever been.

"But just remember," she continues as I lie helpless on her bedroom floor, her fingers nimbly working me out of my pants, "that as soon as you get this . . . you lose the brain, the trust, and the love."

"Why does it have to be like that?" I'm gasping with anticipation now, watching her hands, her heaving chest.

"Poor Luke." She shakes her head. "You're going to want me to stay at your house and hold your hand and act like we love each other the way *you* want us to love each other and I'm not going to be able to love you like that and then you'll see what I was talking about when I said sex would ruin us." She's so frigging self-assured. I hate that.

She's got me out of my pants now and I'm hard as all hell but Tabitha ignores my pecker in her hand, which really sucks or blows or whatever because I've always wanted to know what she thought of my size compared to her boyfriends'. She's staring into my eyes and squeezing me purple.

"Why can't we have all of it?"

"I love you more than I've ever loved anyone, honey. But I guess something's wrong with me. You're too *nice* or something. All the guys I'm attracted to are total dicks who I could never actually love. So maybe I'm just fucked."

I've resigned myself, yet again, to zero satisfaction. My hard-on rapidly falters.

I open my mouth to speak but close it just as quickly. Then try once more to get it out. "So this isn't true love, what we have?"

"I don't know what it is. I just know that I love what we have, exactly the way it is now. I want us to always have each other. And I know if we fuck, I'll change—and so will you."

"No—"

She shrugs. "And then whatever we had will be gone."

I feel myself going numb, the blood returning to other organs.

"Please let go of me."

"I'm sorry."

I stand and turn to zip up.

"You're right, Tab," I assure her. "You're always right."

"Where are you going?"

"Home."

"Are you mad at me?"

"No."

"I'm sorry, Luke. I love you and I wouldn't trade you for anything. I'm selfish that way, I guess." Something about her mouth looks like regret. Probably not, but I'll take it as such.

"Well, just don't stop letting me feel you up. I can't tell you how much that means to me," I say.

She smiles.

I stare at my feet in their socks, look up to meet her eyes.

"I love you, Luke." She puts her hand on my shoulder.

TRANSMISSION 02:

the horror!

October

The note Tab passes me during a particularly grueling period of Mrs. Hingleton's English class reads: "You want to do something crazy tonight? Get an alibi and meet me at my house by ten."

I am glistening with anticipation. An anticipation stymied only by the fact that I'm gonna have to sell some kind of bullshit story to my parents. They always have these totally self-righteous ideas about who is deserving of our "fellowship." Compounding the problem, my mother is positive that I'll screw anything in a skirt. She has no idea that I've been relegated to the little-brother/best-friend type. Of course, she'd never believe me if I told her this. I'm the next Brando. Looks and all. High cheekbones, the works.

The key to my going out is to get my mother separated from Victor. She's much more inclined to cave in after a few concentrated minutes of pleading, as long as no sex will be involved.

I gather myself, try to look as casual as possible, and move across the threshold from my room. Victor is sprawled on the couch in the living room, bathed in television glow and wearing only his underwear. I move past him nonchalantly and make it to the adjacent room without having to exchange so much as a grunted acknowledgment.

I slip into Jonas' bedroom where he sits with our mother, examining a textbook.

"Listen, Ma? I'm going over to Jason's house and we're gonna hang out, listen to music and stuff. I'll be back sometime tomorrow morning. He's a guy I met in drama class." I talk up the part about drama class because this implies that I'm actually getting into being in the *performing arts*, that my mother was right about that after all.

She sits there sizing me up, narrows her eyes.

"Sure, you can go. As long as Jason's parents said it's OK."

Jonas looks up at me. His envy is obvious, seeing as he's only thirteen and therefore in possession of far less privilege than me. I give Mother a long, appreciative hug, scrub the top of Jonas' head with an absent hand.

"Keep hittin' those books, kid. Maybe you'll get to be as smart as me someday."

"I'm already smarter than you," he says, punching me on the arm.

This will be the first time I've ever spent a night out with no parental supervision. The half-mile walk up the road to Tabitha's house is open and resplendent as the sunset riots out before me. It's as though God himself has condoned these preliminary steps into the world. Altogether it is the sort of autumn evening one remembers through the tang of wood smoke, when the leaves are all brilliant oranges and reds and the temperature is sheer perfection—

the kind of night when you can feel the rest of your life unfolding according to plan.

Tabitha is smoking a cigarette on the cement stoop outside her apartment. Her "friend" 8-Ball is on his way over to pick us up, she says. She drops the cigarette, stubbing it out with her slipper, and heads back inside to the bathroom. Her mom is watching TV in the back bedroom. She yells an acknowledgment to me and I yell back. Her mom is always nice to me in a pitying, I-know-your-parents-suck-and-you'll-be-lucky-to-get-out-alive kind of way, but I appreciate it nonetheless.

"I don't know why you have to wear so much makeup," I tell Tabitha. "You're already beautiful without it."

"I know you think that, but there's still the matter of the rest of the sane world thinking the same."

"Well . . . fuck 'em if they don't."

I smile at her mirror-face. She glares back, a lipstick half forgotten in her hand. "Please leave me alone for a minute so I can finish."

I continue watching her. "You're not wearing a bra, are you?"

"None of your business."

"Can I feel?"

"No!" She laughs and pushes me, narrowly missing my shirt with her lipstick. "Get out!"

I step outside the bathroom. "Do you think we have time for a quickie before it's time to leave?"

She slams the door.

Tab's friend 8-Ball talks a thousand miles an hour, punctuated by cackling laughter that makes you want to quit your job and follow him. And he's a maniac on the road. He cuts off other cars with complete disregard and takes hairpin turns at 60 m.p.h.

"He always drives like this," Tabitha yells over the blaring stereo.

"Do I look scared or something?"

Tab shrugs and looks away. "Maybe. Not really."

"Good. Because I'm not."

We screech into a parking lot, the bottom of 8-Ball's rust-bucket Ford scraping against the curb.

"We're heeeerrrrre," Tabitha intones in her best *Poltergeist* impression.

"We're where?" I ask. "This is the big surprise? A run-down movie theater?"

"It doesn't matter what the outside looks like, silly. It's what is happening on the inside."

"Good one, Tab. *'Don't judge a book by its cover.'* Great. Gee, I think I know that lesson. I remember it from A *Tale of Two Cities* in Hingleton's class. The picture of the guillotine on the front cover made it seem like the book would actually be interesting but it fucking sucked."

"Dude." 8-Ball turns to me matter-of-factly. "Chill. This is going to blow your goddam mind. I promise." He gives me a Cheshire cat grin that is more disturbing than reassuring.

In the parking lot kids sporting baggy pants are skateboarding, ramping off the cement staircases on either end of the theater sidewalk. As we approach the dilapidated box office I can see people milling around the lobby through a fog of cigarette smoke. One guy wears a foot-long Mohawk that sticks straight up. Another one has white makeup caked all over his face and lipstick smeared haphazardly around his mouth. There's a couple decked out in leather bondage gear making out in a dark corner. There are four comic book dorks playing ancient Atari arcade games against the wood-paneled wall.

It's a wild, beautiful circus, without the juggling. My eyes burn with all there is to take in. *These* are the people Victor always refers to as freaks.

"Well, whaddaya think?" Tabitha whispers in my ear.

"What is this place?"

"This, my young friend, is *The Rocky Horror Picture Show*."

As we walk into the theater, a guy dressed in red-and-black leather chaps is yelling from a stage in front of the movie screen.

"Rule number six!"

"SEX!" the crowd yells back at him in unison.

"SIX!"

"SEX!"

"Have it your way! Rule number seven: There is no rule number seven! Rule number eight! No sex with your date unless you brought one for me!"

I give Tabitha my "What an idiot" look.

"Just watch," she implores.

"Are there any virgins in the house?" the leather-chapped freak yells.

I look around the theater. Amazingly, only a few hands go up.

There is no way in hell I'm admitting to this guy that I'm a virgin. He looks like the demented ringmaster of a bondage circus.

"We've got a virgin right over here," a voice proclaims, not six inches from my head.

I glance at Tab and 8-Ball and shriek back in horror to find them vigorously pointing at me. 8-Ball is laughing so hard tears are rolling down his cheeks.

"I am not a virgin!" I yell in desperation, turning to Tabitha. Here sits a woman who at one time had her hand on my actual throbbing member. That has to be worth something.

"Not a virgin like that, Luke. A virgin at *Rocky* is someone who's never seen the movie."

I watch in dread as the Ringmaster approaches me with his little green-tinted sunglasses and a cast of willing lackeys following behind him. I'm led down the aisle along with the other unfortunates who've been ratted out by their so-called friends. As we are marched onto the stage I take solace in the fact that at least I'm not alone.

The crowd mocks us, chanting, "VIR-GIN! VIR-GIN!"

Two girls dressed like low-rent hookers approach the stage. One has reddish hair pulled up on top of her head and is wearing a black teddy that shows off her tits nicely. The other has dark, wiry hair that grows in all directions, a body that would stop a truck. I recognize her from school. She winks at me, which is comforting.

The "hookers" line us up across the stage, facing the crowd.

The first guy to be deflowered looks about my age and appears ready to shit himself. The crowd yells:

"Make him deep-throat a hot dog!"

"Have him run around the building naked!"

It is decided that he should have to receive simulated anal sex from the redheaded hooker. He does a piss-poor job of it. Barely a sound comes out of his mouth. He's obviously never taken any drama classes.

Then it's my turn.

With his bony fingers gripping my arm, the Ringmaster asks the crowd to hand down my fate.

The decree is announced.

I am to give the kinky-haired hooker simulated cunnilingus. The proclamation is barely pronounced and I find myself awash in relief. There will be no public speaking or fake sex noises. I just have to pretend to lick this woman from top to bottom, a scenario I've imagined about a million times. I stick my tongue out as far as it will go, like that one ugly bastard from KISS. The crowd cheers me on.

Twenty seconds later the girl lets go of my hair and I scurry back to the relative safety of my seat, feeling the blood drain from my face, the adrenaline really starting to kick in.

"Thanks a lot, Tab."

"Oh, you'll be alright, Luke. Wasn't that fun?" She flutters her eyes at me.

As the theater darkens for the showing of the film, small groups begin slipping off to poorly lit areas of the theater: guys making out with other guys and girls doing the same. A line of men snaking their way into the Women's Room and leaving minutes later with smirks on their faces as they zip their pants. After the last guy zips up, a trampy-looking woman emerges looking disheveled but grinning nonetheless, evidently proud of herself. She goes by the name Squirrelly because, she brags to anyone who'll listen, she "can fit more nuts in her mouth than a squirrel."

The debauchery taking place in the theater mimics the movie's ethos of "Live your life based purely on the pleasures that you can derive from it." My mom says Satanists have that same ethos, but then again, so did Walt Whitman.

In the movie, a couple gets a flat tire in a rainstorm and has to go to an apparently haunted castle for help. It is soon revealed that the inhabitants of the castle are two lesbians, a resurrected Elvis impersonator, and a flaming transvestite named Frank N. Furter.

Like some even more demented Dr. Frankenstein, Frank creates this buff-looking homo guy named Rocky, whom he can screw whenever he pleases. I think in the end somebody ends up being from a different planet. The movie pretty much sucks, even with the crowd yelling out ad-libbed dialogue over the actors.

I keep coming back, though, because these people, despite their moral depravity, despite their lack of social interaction skills, they accept everybody that shows up, no matter what.

There is a certain loneliness that hangs in the air, and we all feel it. We are all at home with it. Behind the façade of people being irresponsible and reprehensible and in all other ways completely morally bankrupt, there is a hopelessness that holds us together. This sadness is the glue between skaters and cross-dressing faggots, between the mohawked punks and computer dorks who've catalogued and categorized every episode of *Star Trek*, going so far as to speak to one another in Klingon. One night some idiot showed up wearing sunglasses and a wife-beater in fifteen-degree weather. These people don't function in any "normal" reality. They must stay holed up in their parents' basements, plotting revenge on the world five days a week, but on Friday and Saturday night they turn out en masse to mingle with their kind. I mean, the movie is a geek magnet. But despite these surface differences, they are there for you, whether you're the coolest dude on earth or a man trapped in a woman's body. Or vice versa.

And the girls. There are so many gorgeous girls—beautiful but fucked in the head just the same. I've begun to realize that fucked-in-the-head is my type. It just feels *wrong* to try to get with a regular, "college-trek" girl. They always have parents that want to size you up, explore your goals in life, find out what your parents "do."

I cannot talk to those kinds of people. I can't stand most of the people here, either, but they accept me and that's good enough, better than I can expect anywhere else. I usually sit in the corner of the theater, occasionally yelling out a line or two just to stay with the game and maybe messing around with Tabitha's breasts for as long as she'll let me before she's off to get laid by the next asshole.

Other than that I keep to myself and try not to make eye contact.

TRANSMISSION 03:

a promising career snuffed out in its prime

January

After months of rehearsal, my drama class is producing its first big production of the year. A circus elephant named Helga is cared for by an apprentice trainer named Red (played by yours truly). Red always mistreats the elephant, and then one day the elephant snaps and kills the little bastard. The ignorant hick town where the circus happens to be that night decides that the elephant must be prosecuted for murder. Helga is convicted and sentenced to death. There are protests against her execution, but in the end the elephant gets hanged by the neck from a scaffold.

It's a play for kids, a period piece in the vein of *Bambi* and *Old Yeller*, where the protagonist is an animal that has to die so the spoiled little brats scarfing popcorn in the audience will finally wake up and realize that life is full of absurd suffering and heartache.

The "elephant" in our production is actually three girls wearing gray sweat suits who weave their hands together so that their arms semi-resemble a trunk. I have to ride on their shoulders and get "thrown" from the beast during one scene. Without fail, I kick at least one of the girls in the head every time they lean forward to dump me onto the stage. We practice and practice but my foot inevitably comes up and levels one of them. Aside from that repetitive mishap, the three performances at our school theater go off without a hitch. We are given standing ovations every night. Terry, our theater teacher and the show's director, decides that our play is good enough to take to the state level.

The weekend of the competition I come down with a vicious case of the flu. I can't stop coughing, my throat is constricted and inflamed, I have a fever that won't break.

But the show must go on!

I try to stay positive and am helped considerably in that arena by the reality of there being only one dressing room at the high school where the competition is held. Which means, glory be and hallelujah!, we're all going to see each other *naked*—yet another of my long-term fantasies, about to be fulfilled. I've already seen Tabitha, of course, but now there's also the mouthwatering possibility of Katie and Nickie and Emily nudity on the horizon.

The excitement is short-lived.

As we unload our costumes and equipment, I find myself less invigorated by the impending promise of female nudity. It is slight consolation, the possibility of all those gorgeous breasts, because I feel like hell. Only the expectations of everyone else in the play keep me going. I have a small part, and I'm only in a couple of scenes, but what do they have if the guy that gets killed isn't there to get killed? They've got nothing! In the guise of hapless, moronic, doomed Red, I am integral. These are the words of inspiration handed me by

Justin Blackburn. He's the dashing actor who has landed the leads in our school plays for three years running.

So with my head spinning out, I struggle on, beating down my affliction for the good of my fellow thespians, for the good of our school. I've got my head in my hands, trying to remain conscious, sitting at a white table so bright it hurts to open my eyes. Emily Adams walks over and stands directly in front of me while a couple of other girls wrap her supple breasts in Ace bandages for her part as a prepubescent girl. Or maybe she's supposed to be a boy. Regardless, I open my eyes and there they are, right in front of me, two perfect, seventeen-year-old teardrop breasts. My stomach turns over on itself. I put my head back in my hands.

Terry approaches me as I stand in the wings waiting for my big entrance, when I'll demonstrate to the audience my utter lack of consideration for animal cruelty laws. She puts her hands on my shoulders and whispers, "You can do this, Luke. Some of the greatest performances of all time have been executed under incredible duress. You can do this!"

I am seeing three of her. Her voice echoes. Then she's pushing me out on the stage and for a moment I am terrified. I have to act angry and sullen, demonstrate an unhealthy level of self-confidence. I begin reciting my lines and immediately realize that I can't talk very loud, can't *project* my voice from the stage, from the depths of my diaphragm, as we have been over so many times in class.

This is a disaster.

This is a fucking plane crashing into a field full of lollipop-clutching tourists. I am the worst thing to happen to the stage since the invention of moving pictures. I want to run away and continue running, out of the theater, out of the school. Everyone will hate me and I will have ruined our chances at high school thespian fame, replacing it instead with a notoriety reserved for pedophiles and washed-up former child actors. But even if that scenario proves livable, I'll never outrun Darin Krenapter, the track star with one of the leads in this play. He thinks he's the next goddam Dustin Hoffman. His mom probably convinced him of it.

I tell myself that I *must* endure, I must find it in myself to battle this affliction. I look down at the floor, gather the power of all the sick-unto-dying actors who have gone before me. And then I stomp over to that "elephant" and smack the shit out of Kara's ass, she being the back end of our pachyderm.

"Listen here, you fat bitch!"

The audience begins murmuring.

"I've had it with your thinking you can push me around just because you're bigger and stronger and *fatter*," I enunciate. "I have opposable fucking thumbs! What do yooooouuuuu have? You walk on your toenails, for God's sake."

The audience is gasping.

"You're going to stand on that goddam ball if it means the death of me!" I inadvertently add some foreshadowing in my delusional state.

Kara, Darla, and Sarina, the triumvirate of girls that comprise Helga the elephant, stare at me in shock. I turn for a moment to stage right and Terry is flipping out, pacing back and forth and pointing violently at her copy of the script. I wink at her. This is the part where I climb up on the girls and violently assert my human mastery. But the girls just stand there looking at me in open-mouthed horror instead of shaping their hands into the form of a two-tier stirrup, like we've practiced ten thousand fucking times.

"Put your hands down!" I whisper. They comply. I struggle to maintain the strength it takes to scale the three actresses-as-elephant. I finally get there and let fly a snarl of dominant mastery.

At this point the girls run around the stage with me on top of them as I pretend to physically abuse them with a bullwhip. Then they stop and try to fluidly kneel down so that to the untrained eye it looks as though I'm violently thrown off and trampled to death.

But everything is out of whack.

I do the carefully planned roll off their backs, kicking both Kara *and* Sarina in their mouths. They dump me hard onto the stage. Kara kicks the shit out of me in retaliation as I lie there.

The crowd reacts with a smattering of bewildered applause as the lights go down and everybody scrambles around to prepare for the next scene. I am still floor-bound, my last remaining trace of energy sapped, and Darin and Justin run up with their fake beards hanging and drag me offstage.

"You're a fucking dick," Darin says.

"Thanks a lot, asshole," commends Justin.

Tabitha adjusts her corset and her bonnet, kneels down, and kisses me on my burning forehead. I lie there in the wings just offstage and hear the rest of them try to pick up the pieces, but it's too late. The crowd never roars for us like back home. My career in the limelight, under the hot glow of stage lights, is over.

TRANSMISSION 04:

fascists come in many forms

March

We're moving again.

I heave my 13" black-and-white television through the glass. It clatters on the driveway beneath my window. The sound of the freeway pours through now, crystal clear, into the realm of my fourth new bedroom in half as many years.

My parents have this absurd inability to find or maintain employment, so I've come to expect another relocation every six months. But I'm still resentful. You never think about money when you're a kid until there isn't enough for the basics. My parents don't seem at all bothered by the fact that my brothers and I are tormented daily by other kids at school because our clothing never matches. Paying my own way isn't a viable option, either, because Victor inevitably needs to "borrow" my twenty-hour, grocery-bagger-wage paychecks. Ever since I was old enough to stand outside strip malls and supermarkets collecting money for Jerry's Kids and their muscular dystrophy, my folks have been "borrowing" my money. And scamming unwary consumers for the balance needed "just to get by" for one more week.

A Short History of Scams

- Videotape rodeos and car shows; offer two-for-one deals (paid up front) on tapes that will eventually be mailed but never are.
- Register for college courses; receive loan money; never show up to attend classes.
- Place bid on residential house painting, using $20 investment for fake business cards; ask for up-front advance to pay for materials; never show up to paint house.
- Acquire cheap Halloween knockoff Alf costume (just like the popular TV character!); ask churches for small "love offering" to give kids "insightful message" using a beloved television personality that will give them the word of God from a source they can relate to.

According to my alcoholic uncle, I am powerless to conduct my life in accordance with my own goals and desires. I am powerless, and ironically enough, Uncle Sonny says, there is a certain amount of power in that recognition alone. He says that's the first step in overcoming all of one's troubles.

But I've got ideas.

I start screaming. I can't stop—what did Walt Whitman call it?—yawping.

I had to do it, you know. The window was painted shut. There was no other way to get through.

"What the fuck did you do, you little asshole?"

Victor was standing in the driveway when my TV landed on the concrete behind the half-emptied moving truck. Now he looms in my bedroom doorway, large and angry.

"Go fuck yourself," I say, trying to sound nonchalant and ballsy. The old man has taught me well. I have learned my insolence from the best.

He is cold, efficient, machine-like. He grabs me by the hair with one hand, smacks me in the face with the other. Blood flows, from my nose and possibly the corner of one eye.

"You think you're big and bad?" He's yelling in his best drill-sergeant bark with his mouth so close to my face I can smell his lunch.

I spit blood in his face.

He hits me again.

I'm pretty sure he slugs me as hard as he can this time, because I can't tell how long I've been down, and when I get up again my mother is in the room with my three brothers, she's standing in the doorway looking at me, and then he hits me again and she remains standing there and I get up and go back down and she begs him to stop and he waits for me to stand up again, so I do, and he hits me again and I fall again and then my two youngest brothers—Victor's children with my mother—start screaming and pulling out their hair. That's what they do in stressful situations. Jonas and I bite our nails down to nubs. Aaron and Adam pull their hair out until it's patchy.

I stand up one last time, just as Victor leaves the room cursing me. I can't see out of the one eye because it won't open. The taste of copper saturates my mouth.

"What happened, Luke? *What happened!*"

"Fuck you, Mom."

I'm stumbling, holding on to furniture and walls as I go, willing my feet to move the rest of me.

"Why do you do this to me? Why can't you just get along with him? He's the father of your little brothers! Do you want me to be alone? Again? Raising *four* boys by myself instead of two?"

I make it into the kitchen and slide her keys off the table. She follows me to the front door.

"Do you want me to be alone again like I was with you and Jonas? Is that what you want?"

I start the car and tear out of the driveway.

The mirror in the gas station bathroom is unkind, but at this point it looks worse than it feels, as the nerve endings have shut themselves down for maintenance. My face just feels inflated.

Dave works with me at Kroger. We're friends despite the fact that he's a skinhead of the Nazi persuasion. He always wears the same clothes: black jeans rolled up to the tops of his shins, a pair of oxblood Doc Martens boots with white laces (he says white laces indicate that white people are the best), some kind of rock-band t-shirt, and half-inch-thick red suspenders, which all the skinheads call "braces," presumably because that sounds cooler than "suspenders." He's been kicked out of school because one day he showed up wearing a t-shirt with a giant red swastika painted on it. He refuses to believe that I'm half Jewish.

"What the fuck ran into you?" Dave says. He has this great chipped front tooth that makes him look even cooler and more menacing than he seemed to me before we'd actually met, when the store manager had him train me in the art of grocery bagging.

"Stepdad," I say.

"Let's kill the fucker."

It hurts to smile.

"Can I stay at your place for a night or two?"

We go to his mom's house. He gives me a beer and then another and my face starts to feel less puffy.

We smoke a joint. It's my first time.

"I don't feel anything," I say, coughing.

"What? This is good goddam weed, man."

"What's it supposed to feel like? I just feel drunk and I felt like that before we smoked any grass."

He laughs in the middle of his toke and the smoke leaves his nostrils in spurts.

"Don't call it 'grass,' man. Only narcs, mothers, and old hippies refer to weed as 'grass.' Same with 'mari*juana*.'"

"Grass *is* what my mother calls it. And she used to be a hippie. That's what my uncle Sonny says, anyway. Mom always denies it, though. But still, whatever you want to call this . . . *weed,* I'm not getting anything off it."

"Some people don't get high their first time. Here," he says, pulling a pack of Marlboro Reds out of his bomber jacket, "try a cigarette. Sometimes that pushes you right to where you need to be." Skinheads always wear Air Force bomber jackets, even when it's hot as hell.

I cough on the cigarette.

"Look," Dave says as we sit on his back deck under the darkening sky, "my mom's outta town for three or four days. She's really cool so don't worry about being here or nothin'. But I don't want trouble from the cops 'cause you got that stolen car in my driveway. We gotta dump it somewhere."

"That's cool, man." I'm suddenly numb. It feels *good* not to feel.

"Where do you want to take it?"

"Take what, dude?"

"Your mom's car, man."

"Whatever. Wherever you want."

He starts to say something else but I interrupt him because I'm drunk.

"Why are you friends with me, dude?"

"Whaddaya mean? Aww, c'mon. Don't get all drunk on me, Luke."

"Seriously, Dave. I'm *Jewish*, man—well, half Jewish, anyway—and you come to school with a swastika on your shirt so I'm avoiding you like the plague, and then I start working at Kroger and you act all cool to me and we become friends and I finally say, 'Dave, man, I'm Jewish,' because I want to see if you'll stop hanging with me or even kick my ass—even though we like the same bands and have the same contempt for our fathers and shit."

"What's your point?"

"What's my point?" I can hear myself slurring but can't seem to make my tongue keep up with my brain. "You're a contradiction."

"So what do you want? You want me to kick your ass or something? Would that make you feel better?"

I think he's probably joking but can't tell through the haze of my inebriation.

"It'd make me feel better if you'd quit with all this Nazi bullshit, that's all."

"There are things that you can't understand about what it means to be a Nazi. Being a Nazi isn't just hating Jews and niggers, man. It's a brotherhood of white people trying to make sure their race is preserved and that all these bloodsuckers don't ruin this country for the people who founded it."

"But I don't count as a bloodsucker? That's real reassuring, dude. I'm glad the Nazi party makes exceptions for all us poor, run-down Jews."

"Well"—Dave grins, his chipped tooth gleaming—"that's more like *me* making the exception. Before I met Ralph and Bill, the guys who started this chapter of the Brotherhood, I had nothing to live for. But they showed me some incredible shit. Now I have goals and aspirations, something to *fight* for."

"Yeah, well, I don't get why one person's goals have to mean shitting on some other guy's."

"It's not as serious as you think, man. It's not like we're out doing drive-bys on the niggers or nothin'. Shit, they do that themselves."

I can barely keep my good eye open any longer.

"Hey, I want you to hear this new Four-Skins record I just got," Dave says. Even though we like a lot of the same bands, he always wants me to listen to his racist shit. The Four-Skins and the less cleverly named White Power are his latest discoveries.

Before the needle drops into the groove, I'm passed out on the leather couch next to the turntable.

• • •

The next morning we ditch my mom's car at the Pizza Hut next to Kroger. I call information and get my parents' new number. We've lived in Atlanta for two years and this is the fifth phone number we've had. Every time the phone company shuts it off my mother uses another of her kids' social security numbers to trick them into giving us a new account. Aaron's had a phone, electric, and gas bill all in his name. And he's only like six or seven.

"Hello?" There is a hint of hope in her voice when she answers. I know she's been worried about me. This makes me happy in a vengeful sort of way.

"You can find your car at the Pizza Hut by Kroger, where I *used* to work until your shitty husband made me quit my job." Victor forced me to leave with him in the middle of my shift so I could help them move to the new house. My mother managed, at least, to find another house in the same school district so I could continue at Peckerbrook with her beloved Performing Arts.

"Please come home, Luke. Dad is sorry for what he did. He was angry. You *did* throw the TV out the window. We can't afford to waste a good TV or to fix a window. You know that. You know how tight the money is."

"Fuck him. And stop calling him 'Dad.' He's no relation to me."

The week after my mother married Victor, he asked me what I wanted to call him. "You can call me Victor, or Dad if you want," he said. I didn't want to call him anything. A month earlier we hadn't even known him. Then, overnight, he lived with us, and was married to my mother, and we were moving to a new town. He drove my mother's car while she sat in the passenger seat.

"I'll call you Victor," I said.

His face stiffened. "That's fine. But you'd better make sure you know who's the boss around here." He stood up.

"I could call you Dad, too, if that's what you want."

"Whatever you want to do is up to you."

"OK. Dad."

I was looking at the floor when he clip-clopped down the hall in his loafers. He always wore holes into the center of the soles. He said they taught him to walk like that in the Marine Corps.

"You said yourself that you wanted to call him Dad."

"I changed my mind. And he's not the only one who's ruined my life. In fact, it's *you* more than him. Standing around and watching is just as bad as committing brutality yourself. Isn't that what you always said about the Germans, Mom? That the people that lived over there, the civilians, were just as guilty as the fucking SS?"

Hearing that, Dave runs into the room from the kitchen, making evil faces, pretending to kick my Jewish ass in slow-mo while I attempt to maintain my pissed-off composure on the phone.

"You're right, Luke. I should have stopped him," she mutters. "But I couldn't bear for him to leave us alone like Richard—like your *father* did."

"What does Richard have to do with any of this?! No matter what *Victor* puts us through"—I'm raging now—"it is somehow always better than anything Richard ever did. Victor is a goddamned angel compared to Richard. I never saw Richard beat the shit out of you. But I do distinctly remember Victor trying to strangle you when you were eight months pregnant with Aaron. Do you remember that, Ma? I do. I was nine years old."

She is silent.

"How do you think that felt to me? How do you think it felt to Jonas?"

"I know, Luke, I know." She's really bawling now. She always gets all snotty when she cries. "But I couldn't be alone again. Can't you understand that?"

• • •

Victor drops my mother off at the Pizza Hut in his p.o.s. Cadillac. It's like twenty years old and looks like every other ghetto hooptie: dented fenders and rust spots all over it, torn headliner. Victor likes owning it because he can tell people he has a Cadillac.

My mouth and left eye begin throbbing again. Dave stands beside me decked out in his full skinhead regalia. I *want* Victor to start something so Dave'll kill him. Dave wants an excuse, he says.

My mom steps from the Cadillac and Victor accelerates out of the parking lot, cutting the wheel hard right so the tires will screech. Mom runs over. Her mascara is smeared. She puts her arms around me and I return the hug limply.

"I love you, Luke," she says, pulling back, her arms on my shoulders, looking me in the eye.

I turn to Dave, introduce them. Mom tries to wipe her eyes without creating a bigger mess.

"Listen, man," Dave says, "are you sure you want to do this? Going back to live with that guy?"

"I have to. It's my mom, man."

Dave extends his tattooed hand. "You have my number. You call me if you need anything, OK?"

"Thanks, man."

As I walk to the car, my mother's arm around my waist, I feel the dread of return. Starting over again. A dog chasing its tail.

Dave watches us pull out of the parking lot, his arms folded, confident. He knows where he's going.

Back at the house, I slip into the half bath. My left eye is almost completely closed, my mouth and nose black and blue.

I jerk off into the toilet.

TRANSMISSION 05:

drunk in love

April

It's at *The Rocky Horror Picture Show* where the girl of my dreams is literally dropped into my lap. I'm watching the movie for the fifty thousandth time when this big dude, Jaeger (named after the shitty liquor whose t-shirt he wears religiously), places her right on top of me, legs on one arm, head on the other, her ass squarely nestled against my crotch.

Her name is Michelle. She sports a close-cropped pixie haircut and wears ten-hole Doc Martens with black-and-white-striped socks that come up to her knees.

"Do I know you?" I ask, attempting nonchalance.

"No," she says, sizing me up, "but I've been admiring you all night."

"Really?" I try not to sound surprised.

"Is that OK?"

She makes great eye contact, brims with self-confidence.

"You're the most beautiful woman I've ever seen," I offer, finally. Real smooth. Understated.

She looks away, puts her hand to her mouth, flutters her eyelashes. "Oh, you charmer! You want to sit with me and hold hands?"

We don't talk for the next hour and a half. And for the first time ever the movie ends too soon. As the theater empties for the requisite post-*Rocky* trip to Waffle House, she hands me a blue slip of paper, carefully folded over twice.

"Call me tomorrow, OK?"

"OK. Yes. I mean, of course. Yes. Of course I will." I don't know where to put my hands.

As she turns to leave I stop her.

"Hey, Michelle?" She turns back to me, expectant-like. "Why were you admiring me? I mean, I know that's a weird question, but what was it about me that you liked?"

"I don't know. Maybe it's because you were only here to meet me. A forlorn lover without anyone to love."

She blows me a kiss and disappears into the lobby.

I see her every Friday and Saturday night at *Rocky*. By our third weekend we've moved from hand-holds to full-blown making out, though I still can't muster a hand under the bra.

And then I know what I want. I'm not afraid. Michelle is the missing piece. She fills in the shallow spots and the empty areas, levels out the playing field of me.

"I feel like I'm falling in love with you," I say.

She readjusts in her seat, pulls away. "You're falling in love with me?"

"You *know* me, Michelle. I mean, I told you about my childhood bedwetting problem, not to mention the recurrence of said affliction in ninth grade, for God's sake."

"I'm just not used to guys putting labels on relationships. It's like they're afraid of not having a convenient way out. Maybe I've learned to feel that way, too."

"I didn't mean to push. Or label you."

She pauses. She looks at me. I love how she looks at me.

"But you're different, Luke," she says, finally. Yes! I'm *different*! "You're like this raw nerve of passion and naivete and that's what attracted me to you in the first place."

Her eyes are the best eyes God ever crafted. There is a softness in them, a genuineness that unfolds around me like velvet.

"I want to be your girlfriend, Luke. I want to love you . . ."

"But . . ." I continue her sentence for her.

"No but."

She is smiling now. "I just don't ever want to cause you any pain."

"There won't ever be pain between us, Michelle. I love you too much to ever be mad at you."

She kisses me, slow and deep. I melt again.

The next week goes by in slow motion. Tabitha is screwing 8-Ball now, her worst asshole to date. Yeah, he seemed all right at first but now has proven himself to be a total jerkoff. He harasses the hapless waitresses at Waffle House and expects everyone to laugh with him for doing it. Most of them do. And Tab spends her every free moment with him. She skips school to be with him, and we haven't spoken more than a couple of sentences in weeks.

All I have to tide me over until my next Michelle fix is my mother's wine stash and a new smoking habit I picked up with some guys from drama. We hotbox a couple Marlboros in the bathroom until the cherry is an inch long, then make for the theater, running down the hill whooping, our heads floating on a nicotine buzz.

• • •

On Friday night Michelle and I decide to skip *Rocky* and meet at Squirrelly's party. Squirrelly's apartment can only be accurately described as squalor. The carpet is stained with wax from long-dead candles, cigarette burns everywhere. Even the walls are dirty, handprints visible around every doorknob. Full-page photographs from magazines are taped to the kitchen cabinets, the walls, the sliding glass door.

Squirrelly, yelling into the phone something about hers being the *last* apartment on the left, you dumbass, not the first, hands me a pipe and encourages me through charades to take a hit. I get higher than hell this time and then stumble around the living room, laughing at dumb shit.

This guy Flick shows up with a rum-punch concoction. He hands me a plastic cup and splashes some in, saying, "Take it easy with this. It's harder than it tastes. It'll kill you so fast you won't even know you're dead." And that's how Flick convinces everybody to drink his World Famous brew. It's his calling card.

Squirrelly asks me for a kiss.

I laugh at the suggestion, more stoned than truly objecting, and drink, drink some more. Half a mouthful of punch escapes the cup, dribbles down my chin. Nobody notices.

"I'm serious," she laughs back. "You're the only guy in this room I've never made out with."

"Or girl, for that matter," Michelle interjects.

"Come on, it's just a kiss," Squirrelly says, fluttering her false eyelashes at me.

I look at Michelle and she nudges me toward Squirrelly.

She's a damn good kisser, warm and slow, suggestive of far more than just a kiss. As she lets go of the back of my head, I can feel myself spinning out.

"And if you think that was good," she adds, "you should try my blow jobs."

I laugh and look around to gauge the reaction from the rest of the room, their faces swimming past in a whirl of color, and they all concur, nodding and laughing. *Oh yeah, that's true, she can totally give great head.* Squirrelly's boyfriend Fred says, as serious as a news anchor, "It is true, man. She could suck a watermelon through twenty feet of garden hose."

Michelle is leaning back on the couch with a slight smile, her eyes half closed in her drunk/stoned euphoria.

"I've gotta take a piss," I say, already halfway to the bathroom door.

There's a girl passed out in the tub. I try to maintain balance, urinate as quietly as possible so as not to wake her.

8-Ball is in the living room, obnoxious as ever, when I get back from the toilet.

"You call that weed? Check this shit out!"

He hoists two fifths of gin and a huge bag of herb. "*This* is weed," he proclaims. "Moroccan kind bud." Moroccan kind. Sure it is. 8-Ball is so full of shit. Tabitha has admitted to me that his real name is Brad, of all things. And contrary to my first impression of him that night I went to *Rocky* and got devirginized, I've learned that he's the biggest bullshitter this side of my stepdad. 8-Ball—*Brad*—has spent a good amount of time and effort creating his own legend. He's always telling the story about how he used to be a Marine and was dishonorably discharged for spitting in a drill sergeant's face before taking a tank AWOL in Kuwait. And everybody buys that crap like it's on sale.

And then there's his toadie, Kyle. Kyle, like 8-Ball, wants everybody to call him by his military nickname. Kyle's nickname is "Rat," and it fits him well. He's only like five feet tall and has beady little eyes. He's always fruitlessly trying to pick up women by lecturing about military operations and weaponry. Of course, he's just overcompensating for his miniature dick, with his combat boots and his crewcut. People with crewcuts can't *stand* when somebody has long hair. I've been growing my hair out, trying to achieve a new look, and Kyle—*Rat*—always has to make some kind of smart-ass remark about how I look like Bozo or Krusty the Clown. As soon as he sees me stumble out of the bathroom, all stoned and stupid-grinning, he starts in on me.

"Check it out, 8-Ball," Rat yells, like a good sidekick. "It's Krusty!"

"Krusty has green hair, dumbass," I say, more a knee-jerk reaction than an attempt at direct confrontation. Rat turns a slight hue of red.

"What did you say to me, motherfucker?" He gets right in my face. Looking up into it, anyway.

Was that out loud? I can't believe I said it myself. The line between interior monologue and actual speech has been blurred and now nothing can keep the liquor from talking. I laugh in my own defense. *It was only a joke, guy.* But Rat isn't having it.

"I asked you what you *said*, clown."

"Leave him alone, Rat," Michelle says.

"You don't need to be getting all bent outta shape, Michelle baby. I'm not gonna ruin your little boyfriend's precious face, but I am about to kick him in his fucking dick. You don't know how to use it anyway, do you Bozo?"

"Fuck you, Rat," I hear myself say.

It's 8-Ball's laugh, I think, from behind me, that punctuates my brazenness. This pisses Rat off even more. He's red as my head. My red fucking hair. *I'd rather be dead than red on the head.*

And then all eyes shift from the confrontation in the middle of the living room, among the crumpled chip bags and empty plastic

Squirrelly emerging from the bedroom wearing only a long Fred follows close behind, zipping his pants.

“What the hell are you screaming about, Rat?” Squirrelly demands to know. “I have fucking neighbors.”

Rat looks at Michelle, who is standing beside me, touching my arm. He points his chin toward her. “Why’d you bring this little bitch?”

“Don’t call my girlfriend a bitch, dickhead,” I say flatly.

“I wasn’t talking to you, you dumb fuck. *You’re* the bitch. Though I bet you’d just love to suck on it, wouldn’t you, Michelle?” he says, grabbing his cock for emphasis.

“I’ll kill you!” I’m screaming now and don’t care if he has military training or not. Like my man Emo Phillips says, you might mop the floor with me but you’ll have trouble getting into the corners. At least there’s that.

8-Ball and Fred get between us. It feels good to nearly get into a fight. Especially with this asshole. And with quasi-chivalry on the line at that.

“You both need to leave,” Squirrelly declares.

“But he didn’t do anything,” Michelle says. “Rat said he looked like a clown.”

“Am I wrong?” Rat says.

“Look, just leave, man,” Fred says to him.

“Look at his hair! It’s goddam orange and girl-curly and sticks out in every direction!”

“Please, Rat.” Squirrelly touches his shoulder.

He stares at her in astonishment.

“Fine. But I’m gonna get you, Bozo.” He points at me, then turns around and goes to the door. He turns again as he walks out and points at me a second time. I give him a finger of my own. The door slams.

“Who wants to do some coke?” 8-Ball asks, breaking the silence.

• • •

Although this is the first time I've actually seen coke, I've watched enough reruns of *Miami Vice* with Victor to know it on sight. Michelle is first up to get her line. She sucks it up her nose like a pro with a rolled-up twenty-dollar bill, then sits back on the couch with her head cocked at a ninety-degree angle so as not to let any powder escape. After Squirrelly, Fred, 8-Ball, and some other girl have each snorted a line, 8-Ball tosses the baggie at me.

My head shakes of its own accord. "I don't mess with the hard shit, man. No offense."

"None taken," says 8-Ball, his bony face contorting with the high. "More for me. But don't say I never tried giving you nothin'." He laughs, then sticks two fingers in a glass of water and sucks the liquid up each nostril.

"Are you sure you don't want to try any, honey?" Michelle asks.

"Yeah, I'm sure." I turn to 8-Ball, who's hunched over the table cutting out more lines. "Do you care if I get into that gin, man?" I ask him.

"Go ahead. But you gotta get me a glass."

As I make our drinks, I yell from the kitchen, "Why isn't Tab with you tonight?"

"She had to go to bed early so she could go to a modeling agency in the morning with her mom or some shit."

"Better there than being with you," I mutter. I contemplate hocking up a loog for his drink but decide against it. He isn't half as bad when his little toadie bitch isn't around and he's not trying to ram his tongue down Tabitha's throat.

Michelle is back on her knees snorting another line when I return from the kitchen. I sit on the couch and slug my drink, get up and make another. Michelle doesn't so much as look at me. She never stops talking. Everyone is talking. I can't think for all the goddam talking. I keep drinking.

An hour later Squirrelly and Fred have retired to their bedroom once again and I am more drunk, stoned, and in all other ways fucked up than I've ever been. The room is spinning, my head is spinning. A half-full glass of gin slips out of my hand and falls to the carpet. I have to lie down. There's a perfect empty space in the darkened hallway.

Michelle and 8-Ball are still talking gibberish and loudly sucking up lines of white powder as my consciousness fades.

I sleep in blackness, one of those sleeps that has no dreams tethered to it. I don't know how long I'm out before the black is interrupted by vigorous shaking. I feel my head rocking back and forth, bumping into the baseboard of the wall.

"Please fuck me, Luke," a voice says. "Please fuck me. I need you to do this for me. Please fuck me. Please, Luke. Please."

I'm still drunk and my eyes won't focus.

"I need you to fuck me."

"Who? What do you want?"

Then she leans in close to my face and I can smell her cigarette-stale breath.

"C'mon. You're my boyfriend. You've gotta do this for me."

"Michelle? I can't do it. I'm too fucked up. Please. I promise I'll be there for you tomorrow. I have to sleep now."

She kisses me deep. I taste plastic.

"What's in your mouth?"

"The coke baggie."

"Why?"

"I had to make sure I got it all."

We look at each other for a moment. She can't keep her eyes on me for more than a half second at a time.

"I feel like hell and only your dick in me will make it better."

"OK." I tell myself I can muster the stamina, the centered mind needed for this. "OK . . . where can we go?"

"Right here."

"No way! There's people ten feet away in the living room."

"Then let's go to Squirrelly's room."

Moans are already emanating from behind the bedroom door. Michelle reaches for the handle.

"Wait! Are you sure they won't get pissed at us for interrupting them?"

"Trust me, Squirrelly won't give a shit."

As she opens the door to the bedroom the moans become louder. Squirrelly is on her back with her legs in the air, Fred is kneeling at the side of the bed in front of her crotch. I squint in the dimness of the room. His arm is moving back and forth. Guttural animal sounds are gurgling from Squirrelly's throat and Fred has his entire hand inside her, fist-fucking her. I've heard of such a thing but didn't believe it could really happen. The stench of smoke and sweat mingles with the sloshing sounds of fisting. I wrench myself from Michelle's grasp.

"I can't do this here!"

"Wait! We'll go in the walk-in."

She slips into the closet and pulls me behind her, slamming the door. We are enveloped in complete darkness. Her fingers immediately go to work on my fly. I reach forward blindly and try to cop a feel but she isn't there.

And then I'm enfolded in astonishing warmth.

I can hear her slurping, one hand jacking me up and down, the other pressed on my stomach. My head starts spinning and I collapse backward with a thud against the door. She never loses her grip on me, though, even as I slide to the floor, attempt to make my body prone. There are lumpy piles of clothing everywhere. The stench of mildew is strong.

"Does that feel good?" she says finally, the sound of her voice interrupting the rhythmic sucking noises.

"God, yes."

"Do you want to be inside me?"

"Oh my God, yes."

"Do you have a rubber?"

"No."

"It doesn't matter. I'm on the pill."

"I love you, Michelle."

"I know. Do you want to be on top?"

We tangle around each other in the thick darkness and then I feel her pubic hair beneath me. She reaches down and places me at the portal to lost virginity. I'm shaking so bad I can barely breathe.

"Now what?"

"What do you mean?" she says. "Just push."

I push. It is so warm and wet. She still has her shirt and bra on. I am momentarily regretful that I've never seen her naked, but it doesn't matter now. I lay my head on her shoulder and move my hips until I can feel the orgasm coming and I feel like I should be telling her I love her because surely this is what love feels like but I don't say it, I just keep saying "God" over and over and I don't stop until my breath is sucked out and I can finally breathe again. I roll off of her and hit the wall.

"Did you cum?" she asks.

"Yeah, I came. You couldn't tell?"

"I need you to fuck me more."

"I can't. I'm drunk. I can't even tell which side of my head, you know . . . which part is up—is on top."

She lies there beside me silently and at some point gets up to leave. I'm not sure when. I pass out again.

It's morning when I come to, still half drunk. The smell of sex and mold is strong. The living room is trashed. Michelle is passed out on the couch. 8-Ball is rummaging around in the kitchen.

"What's up, Minute Man?" he says, cackling with laughter. "Michelle was just overjoyed about your *performance* last night."

"What do you mean?"

He laughs harder and with more dedication.

I sit next to Michelle and stroke her hair. I like to tuck it behind her ear. She's so beautiful in the light, the morning sun streaming through the window, dust particles illuminated like tiny floating paint chips.

She wakes and looks at me through half-closed eyes and smiles.

"Do you want to walk to the store with me?"

"Sure. Do we need cigarettes or something?" She rubs her eyes and sits up.

"Yeah. And I want coffee. I still feel drunk."

"Me, too."

8-Ball comes into the room.

"We're going to the store on the corner. Do you want anything?"

"What are you gettin'? Some Minute Maid?"

"Very funny, 8-Ball," Michelle says. She gives him a look.

"Wait, I know, why don't you pick me up some Minute Rice. Or maybe just let me have a minute of your time. All it'll take is a minute."

"Let's go, Luke," Michelle says.

I don't know whether to feel hurt or happy. At least she still wants to hold my hand. And the day is gorgeous. It's cold and we can see our breath, but it's the refreshing kind of cold after a long night. The sun is warm on our backs and our shadows are long. Michelle jumps high in the air and her shadow lands on mine. I do the same to hers. We spend the next few minutes chasing each other's shadows, laughing, playing. Then we're holding hands again, surrounded by the morning quiet, the sound of passing traffic somehow far away, the returning birds chirping in newly budding trees lining the sidewalk.

"Why did you tell him I only lasted a minute?"

She doesn't answer.

"I mean, it had to have been at least two or three." She doesn't laugh.

"I don't know. I was just—really frustrated and horny. And then you finished so fast and passed out and I was drunk and coming down hard." She pauses. "So I went out there and took out my frustration to anyone who'd listen." She looks down. "I'm so sorry, Luke. I would change it in a second if I could."

I don't say anything. What can I say? A lifetime's worth of sexual anticipation blown in a one-minute wad.

"Look, I'll tell you honestly, Michelle. I've never had sex with anyone before. Last night was my first time and I'm so glad it was with you. So I guess that's why . . ."

"I know."

"You know?"

"Yeah."

I hold the gas station door open for her and we go to the coffee machine. It smells like morning.

"How did you know?"

"It's about the easiest thing in the world to spot a virgin, especially if you're going out with one," she says with a giggle, loud enough for the whole frigging store to hear.

A construction worker looks at me and chuckles as he turns down an aisle.

"I'm not a virgin, though," I say, just as loudly.

Michelle gives me the raised eyebrow. "I know you're not. I was there, remember?"

We pay, light our cigarettes as soon as we step out the door.

"How is it so easy to tell?"

"I don't know. You just *know*. You get a desperate vibe off all boys who've never made it back to the womb."

The sun is in our eyes now, our shadows behind us. I turn around and walk backward so I can watch us next to each other, holding hands in silhouette. My hair is longer than it's ever been and it points outward in all directions.

"Do you think you could give me dreads?"

"Dreads? Yeah. I could definitely give you dreads. I did it for Brian once. You know Brian, right? The gay guy from *Rocky*?"

"That narrows it down."

"The redhead. He wasn't always gay. I took his virginity, too."

"Do you have some kind of thing for doing redheaded guys or virgins?"

"I guess both."

I lean over and kiss her on the mouth, one of those kisses that says thank God you're mine now, thank God I have you.

We attempt all methods of dreading. There are many different food combinations that will make hair stick together. Peanut butter and egg whites, for instance. I decide against these options because of the inevitability of eventual stink. I put my head on the sidewalk in front of the apartments and Michelle scrapes her boot across clumps of my hair, back and forth on the cement. This option is quickly vetoed as too painful. My hair isn't long enough to facilitate a boot scrubbing. We end up going with the most tried-and-true method of dreading (though longest to execute), in which clumps of hair are gathered together and back-combed vigorously, thereby producing a frayed, knotted, tattered dreadlock; impossible to remove without shaving the whole head. The transformation is permanent. There is no second-guessing, no looking back.

I spend the rest of the morning and afternoon on the couch in Squirrelly's apartment, sitting on the floor in front of Michelle as she painstakingly installs dreads on my whiteboy head.

"Now you look more like Sideshow Bob than Krusty," 8-Ball says, cackling. Michelle giggles. I go to the mirror, try to change my voice so I sound like Frasier from *Cheers*. "Lilith, I told you that Diane was just an innocent, childish—obsession."

By the time the sun is setting I have a new shadow and it's darker than ever, more *me* than I've ever felt. I am totally, completely, irrevocably individualized.

Flick gives me a ride home. I ready myself for the inevitable parental explosion that will follow my having stayed out all night without permission.

When I key the lock to my bedroom's exterior door, Victor is sitting on my faux-leather recliner, watching my TV. I recently leased an entertainment system from Rent-A-Center for a hundred bucks a month. It'll be paid off by the time I'm thirty-four. Victor spends as much time as he can in front of my Zenith because it's newer and bigger than the one in the living room and it has cable. I paid for the cable with the money I made bagging groceries after school and on weekends when I still worked at Kroger.

"What the fuck did you do to your hair? You look like a faggot," Victor says.

"And you look like a fat piece of shit with no job," I mutter as I go to the toilet.

"Where were you last night?" he asks over the din of my urine splashing in the bowl.

"I got stuck at a party after *Rocky* and nobody would bring me home."

He doesn't answer.

"I have to do some homework. I'm way behind," I quickly follow up, attempting to change the subject.

"That's not my fault," he says.

"I'm not saying it's your fault. But I have to catch up if I'm going to pass these classes."

"So."

"So I can't concentrate if my TV's on."

"Sit in the kitchen, then." His voice is gruff and more contemptuous than usual. I remind myself that at least he's not making a big deal about last night, then collapse in a chair at the kitchen table, attempting to work out the subtleties of Richard Wright's *Black Boy*.

Jonas comes in the kitchen and opens the fridge. He sits down with two glasses of Coke and pushes one toward me.

"Where did you go last night?" he whispers.

I tell him about the previous night's adventures, without the drug or sex parts. Jonas is my biggest fan. I'm always reminding him of how the world is outside of Victor's command, that it won't always be like this. He says he wanted to leave with me that first day we moved here, the day I got my ass kicked and stole the car. I don't say anything, but secretly I wish I'd thought of that then.

Mother comes into the kitchen. I tell her there's no way I'm ever going to read this book in time for class if I can't have a minute alone. "Can you please get your husband out of my room?" I say.

She says I shouldn't call him that.

"But isn't that what he is? Would any of us even know him if you hadn't married him?" I say.

TRANSMISSION 06:

enlightenment occurs on multiple levels

May

Tabitha calls me a few weeks before school lets out. We don't talk much anymore. She says she's moving out of state with her mom and she'd like to see me before they go.

She's sitting on her stoop smoking a cigarette when I walk up. She looks tired, but more in a sleepy way than a worn-out one. She's still beautiful.

She stands, leans over to give me a hug, one of those hugs you know is supposed to be a good-bye hug because it's prolonged. It feels somehow uncomfortable.

She kisses me on the cheek. Then I do the next logical thing and try to kiss her *for real*. I dare her to leave without kissing me just this once, before she's gone forever.

Tabitha pushes me off the porch steps and I land in the bushes.

She stands there looking down at me and says, without the slightest hint of irony, "I thought you were different."

Before I can respond, she goes inside, slamming the door behind her. I lie there in the bushes trying to think and then go to the door, which is locked. I pound on it and yell that I *had* been different at one point and she changed all of that.

"It was *you* who did this, Tab! *You* are the one who made it like this."

The next week she is gone. She leaves her phone number and forwarding address taped to her front door. I put the page in my pocket and walk back down the hill to my parents' house.

Dragon*Con is coming up. There's a slight amount of consolation in that. And there's always Trizden, my best friend from the *Rocky* crowd. He keeps things straight when nobody else seems capable.

Dragon*Con is an annual summer event that, for most of the attendees, is a way to meet all the B-movie and Sci-Fi/Horror actors they've adored for years and could only have wet dreams about actually breathing the same air as. But for Trizden and me it's an excuse to wander around on a three-day drinking and drug binge looking for ass. I mean, I'm not looking *for ass*, per se, but it's still nice to look *at* some ass, even if I won't be indulging in any besides Michelle's. Ironically enough, there is also a Young Republicans convention on one of the lower levels of the hotel. I can see the hilarious possibilities already.

Now, while there are more than this city's fair share of gimpy, introverted nerds at Dragon*Con, there are many others like us, who are cool and only here to get wasted (and the Young Republicans, who are here to learn how to become more snottily self-assured of their moral rectitude). Michelle and Trizden do have a certain affinity for *Star Trek*, but, I mean, everybody's got their own issues. And on the plus side of that dork coin, Trizden has some kind of insider dork connection. He got us the passes for free. The passes don't cover a room, they only get us into the convention. He hands us flyers that detail when and where all the main events are taking place. There are autograph signings and Japanimation screenings, live bands and a speaker symposium featuring that "Tune in, Turn on, Drop out" guy from the '60s that my mother told me about one night not too long ago while drunkenly reliving her hippie days. We decide that we won't be throwing down the two hundred bucks a night to rent a room. We'll stay awake, hopefully assisted in that pursuit by a healthy dosage of LSD.

A black guy approaches us as we walk to the elevators. He asks if we know anything about the role-play gaming schedule. There will be a whole bunch of losers here playing real-time games where they pretend to have god-like powers and run around acting like they're saving the world from other losers just like them who, conversely, want to destroy all that is pure and good. This is called role-playing. And it isn't just three fourteen-year-olds sitting around in their parents' basements playing *Dungeons & Dragons* anymore. There are scores of different games for every kind of desperate imagination.

The black guy is obviously into the vampire sect of role-playing. We can tell because he's wearing a set of "handcrafted" eyeteeth that look like fangs.

"Nice teeth, man. You pick up many girls like that?" I ask.

"You'd be surprised," he says.

"You can't be serious."

"Hey, Luke," Michelle interjects, slugging me in the arm, "there is nothing more romantic than a vampire. He is one with the night. He has superhuman speed and strength and must search infinitely for his perfect bride, the one who will spend the rest of eternity with him. You can't get any more romantic than that."

"One with the night?" I say.

"What did you say you were doing later?" Blacula asks Michelle, leaning down to kiss her hand. He lingers over it in that way really suave guys do in movies based on Jane Austen novels.

"I don't think so, man," I say.

"Just kidding, dude," he says. "My name's Splinter."

He offers his hand and I hesitate, but then shake it anyway.

"I'm Luke. This is Trizden, and my girlfriend here, whose hand you've already acquainted yourself with, is Michelle."

"Michelle's a great name," he says.

Is she blushing?

"Dude, are you still hitting on my girlfriend?"

"Sorry, man," Splinter says. "I'm like my name: I get under people's skin." Great. A guy with a catchphrase. I grab Michelle's hand and pull her toward the elevator.

"Jesus, he's touchy," Splinter says to Michelle.

"You should see him drunk," Trizden says.

Trizden, Splinter, Michelle, and I spend the rest of the day people-watching. These people want to be watched. They are dressed in superhero costumes complete with prosthetic pectoral muscles and bulging codpieces. They are wearing makeup that looks like it took hours to apply. They have alter egos with names like Cthulu the Wanderer and Cable the Mysterious. Just being around them makes me want to get high. But Trizden keeps saying we have to put off any kind of serious intoxication until dark.

Trizden's a great friend to have around when you're fucked up and need a watchful eye to keep you out of trouble. I've taken to calling him Animal Mother, in reference to the Kubrick movie *Full Metal Jacket*, one of my all-time favorites. Because Trizden's definitely an Animal Mother, always taking care of us when we're out of our minds.

We decide to peruse the tables in the main conference room on the seventeenth floor to see which washed-up actors are offering autographed 5" x 8" snapshots—for a small fee, of course. In the far left corner is the dude who played Spider-Man on a short-lived TV series during the '70s. Then there's Tom Savini, who among the gore crowd is some kind of god for his innovative special effects techniques. Nobody can show a human face being sawed in half lengthwise more realistically. In one corner is the British guy who did the voice for C-3PO in *Star Wars*. There are infinite lines to see all these people. To the faithful they are immortal. They have found their niche. But there's no way in hell I'm standing in line for an hour so I can pay five bucks just to shake Swamp Thing's hand (ten bucks for an autograph). Michelle and Trizden say they'll wait it out, so I take off with Splinter to find some real action.

We stop at the bathroom and he asks me if I want to hit a joint. Usually I hesitate at engaging in illicit drug use in public, but as soon as we open the bathroom door we are hit with a wall of the previous occupants' pot smoke.

"Dude," Splinter says, firing the joint, "there's nothing to worry about here, man. There's no cops and the fifteenth through seventeenth floors are completely reserved for Dragon*Con attendees. This is our playground."

"Can you hook up some Acid?"

"I'm working on it," he squeaks, holding in a hit.

We exit the bathroom happy and red-eyed just as some Young Republican is on his way in. He's holding a bag full of T-shirts.

"Want a shirt?"

"What do they say?"

He holds one up. There's a cartoon of a regal, all-powerful eagle swooping down over some cowering Arab caricatures wearing turbans and sporting push-broom mustaches. It reads OPERATION DESERT STORM in a military font.

"Didn't we already win that war?" I ask.

"Of course we already won. It was one of the fastest, most overwhelming military victories in the history of warfare."

"What's the point of the shirt then?"

"The point of the shirt is to take pride in your country, take pride in the greatest military the world has ever known," the Young Republican says incredulously.

"Fuck taking pride in this country," Splinter says. "We never would have been trying to 'liberate' Kuwait if not for all their fucking oil."

I laugh and then Splinter starts laughing, too. Laughing and laughing. Idiots laughing in the face of political discourse.

We grab two shirts just as the guy pushes open the restroom door. I know what's coming so I grab Splinter's arm and hurry down the hall.

"Jeez!" the Young Republican yells after us. "Why can't you people do this shit in the privacy of your own rooms?"

We bust out laughing. Again. Klingons and Wookies stare at us as we stagger past.

"Hey, man, do you have a permanent Magic Marker?" Splinter says.

"Do I have a permanent Magic Marker? Let me check in my ass."

"Come on, dude, I'm serious."

"Ask that dork over there."

"Which one?"

Laughing and laughing.

We finally procure a marker and Splinter writes IS BULLSHIT in block letters beneath the OPERATION DESERT STORM logo. On the back he scrawls, I DON'T SUPPORT OIL WARS. I opt for the much more succinct FUCK above the logo.

We pull the shirts on and head back to the autograph tables to find Michelle and Animal Mother. They're talking to a girl with a shaved head. She has incredibly large brown eyes, like Sinead O'Connor. She's wearing punk garb: black-and-white-striped tights, fifteen-hole combat boots, black leather jacket decorated with safety pins and snide buttons with slogans like PROMOTE WORLD PEACE: KILL EVERYONE and I'D RATHER BE MASTURBATING. Trizden's already positioning himself for the conquest, hanging all over her. I've seen him do it about a thousand times at *Rocky*. There's nobody more successful with women.

"Luke, this is my friend Michelle," Michelle says. "No relation."

"I don't do this just to look like Sinead, and I don't have cancer," says Skinhead Michelle, cutting off all obvious first-impression commentary. "Cool dreadlocks," she says to me. "Funny, you don't look like a hippie."

"Why, because I don't stink like patchouli?"

"Well, there's that, and also because you seem far less laid-back than your typical hippie," she says.

"Well, I'm not a fucking hippie."

"See, totally un-laid-back," she says. "That's cool."

"Nice shirts," Trizden says.

Splinter turns around, does a curtsy. "You like?"

"Courtesy of a generous Young Republican, though I'm sure he'd shit a brick if he saw how we improved on the original design," I say. "You guys get any autographs worth mentioning?"

"The guy who played Wicket the Ewok."

"The midget?"

"Yeah."

"Dude, there was this midget in the MARTA train station once with her kid and it was so weird because the kid was, like, normal size," Splinter says. "The woman was no more than three feet tall, bossing around a fully grown eleven- or twelve-year-old kid. Totally fucking bizarre."

"I love your fangs," Skinhead Michelle tells Splinter.

Trizden moves fast. He's not gonna lose this one.

"Oh, Splinter, I heard the Vampire role-players are meeting on the fifteenth floor in twenty minutes for a strategy session," Trizden says.

Splinter heads straight for the elevator. "I'll catch you guys around," he yells over his shoulder.

"Bring back some Acid, dude," Michelle yells, leaning on me.

"So," I say, pushing back against my girl. "What's on the agenda tonight?"

"Let's find some liquor," Michelle says.

"That's the sexiest thing you've ever said to me," I tell her.

"You're gonna hang out with us, right?" Trizden says to the skinhead girl, using his puppy-dog eyes and annoying, upper-register vocal intonation.

"Sure, if you don't mind." Evidently Sinead has chosen to overlook the fact that Trizden is wearing one of those *Star Trek* tricorders on his shirt.

Trizden and I lead the search for alcohol, the girls trailing behind us.

"Are the Vampires really meeting in twenty minutes?" I ask.

"Of course not."

I shake my head. "That's just wrong, Mother. And all for a piece of ass."

"First of all, stop calling me Mother. Second, you would have done the same thing. Besides, *I think I love her*," he says, an allusion to my falling in love with every girl I meet.

"Touché, dickweed."

• • •

Many Dragon*Con-ers have rented rooms and brought massive supplies of alcohol with them. The catch is, they are only willing to give free liquor to those of us with vaginas, so we repeatedly send in Michelle and Skinhead Michelle to fetch us bourbons and rum punches until slurring is our primary dialect.

I bump into Splinter on one of many trips to the bathroom. He's coming out of a stall, a plume of smoke following him.

"Dude?" I inquire.

"Dude!" he assures me.

We drunkenly embrace.

"I am so fucked up."

"Me too."

"I bet I am more than you," Splinter says with a twinkle.

"Way? No way. You got some Acid?"

"Fuck yeah, dude. I'm seeing fucking angels. I've got a whole sheet. Two bucks a hit."

"Consider five of 'em taken off your hands."

"Sold. Let's go back to my home base."

"You sprang for a room?" I'm incredulous. Suddenly my new best friend is rolling in drugs and high-end hotel rooms.

"A room? No way. At $250 a night? I've just got the shit stashed under a trash can on the sixteenth floor."

OK, maybe not a room, but still good.

We head for the elevators. "Hey, where's your girl?" Splinter asks.

"I don't know. I left her right outside the bathroom where I ran into you. She was with Trizden and that skinhead girl but when we came out they weren't there."

I push the 16 button and the elevator doors immediately reopen.

"Damn, I didn't even feel any movement," Splinter says. "I must be totally wasted."

I wait for the doors to close again, then hit 16 once more. The doors immediately open.

"I think we're already on the sixteenth floor, dude."

We look at each other, laugh uncontrollably, step back out of the elevator.

"Oh shit!" Splinter points to our left. I wheel around. A maid is emptying the trash can as we speak.

"Stop!" Splinter screeches, running toward her. "*Parada!* That's Spanish for 'Stop,'" he yells to me over his shoulder, laughing as we run toward the frightened maid. I can feel the alcohol coursing through my veins, but am still newly invigorated regardless.

We've been tripping for . . . how long has it been now? Three hours? And we still haven't run into Animal Mother or the Michelles. So we're sitting in some guy's suite watching three girls dance to techno music in the dark. A glowing black light makes everyone's skin and eyeballs look creepy.

"Hey, Splinter?"

"Yeah, man?"

I momentarily forget what I was going to say because, as I lean forward to look at him, three of my dreadlocks drop down into my face. I jump back in split-second reaction, sure that someone has thrown snakes on me. But then I realize it's only my dreads and they look beautiful in this light. They have lives of their own. I lean over, look up, trying to see and admire every lock, how they each appear unique and perfect.

"What the hell are you doing, man?" Splinter asks.

I'm languidly moving my head back and forth, feeling the weight of the dreads pull my scalp in one direction, then the other. Every molecule of my skin reacts to the weight of their pull. I love this feeling. I sway to the thumping beats.

"Dude? Hello? Are you still with us?"

"Yeah, I'm with you." I'm caught in the rhythm of the music, the pull of the dreadlocks. I sit up suddenly, throw the dreads behind me with one head jerk.

"Why do all black guys own one of the same four dog breeds?"

"I don't know. What are you talking about?" Splinter says.

"No matter where you go: New York, Chicago, D.C., Philly, here in the ATL, black guys only own one of four different breeds of dog."

"And which breeds are those?" Splinter asks.

"Think about it: pit bulls, Dobermans, Rottweilers, and Chows. If they do own a different breed, then it's a mutt. That's just my experience, anyway. I mean, didn't your family own one of those kinds?"

"No, man."

"Well, there goes that theory, I guess."

"What do you mean? You think I'm black? I mean, not that there's anything wrong with that, but I ain't black, dude."

"You're not? What about your skin? And the fact that you smoke Newports?"

"Man, you need to chill with the stereotype shit. I'm only half black. I'm half Puerto Rican, too."

"Shit."

"Does it make you think less of me or something? That I'm a half-breed?"

"Hell no. Why would that matter, man? 'I do not look down on niggers, kikes, wops or greasers because here you are all equally worthless,'" I say, quoting Drill Sergeant Hartman from *Full Metal Jacket*. "Everybody's a goddam half-breed. I'm half Jewish, and that's just the half I know about."

"Shit," Splinter says, "I know a black guy up in Pittsburgh who owns a fucking poodle."

"You don't know any black guy that owns a goddam poodle. A black guy wouldn't get caught dead with a poodle."

"I'm crappin' you negative," Splinter says.

It's dumb luck we find them. Animal Mother and Skinhead Michelle just happen to stumble out of an elevator as we're walking by. He says he needs our help. "I'm too drunk and stoned to stand up," he whines. Sinead appears slightly less damaged.

I've never seen Trizden so incapacitated. The whole idea of him out of his mind—Animal Mother in need of care—is disconcerting. But he's laughing, so at least there's that. Nobody wants to be around a weepy drunk bastard when everybody else is trying to have a good time.

We shuffle past a conference room where old-school Japanimation is being shown through the night. A guy is leaving the room as we pass by and says to his other friends with plastic pen cases in their cowboy-shirt pockets, "That's when cartoons were cartoons."

"What the fuck are they now, Broccoli?" Trizden yells drunkenly.

"Very funny," the guy says.

"God, I get so tired of people saying, 'That's when cars were cars. That's when baseball was baseball.' It's all still fucking baseball," Trizden declares.

"You're right, dude," Splinter says thoughtfully. "It *is* all baseball."

"Where's Michelle?" I ask.

"Oh, I forgot to tell you, man. Rat and 8-Ball were at the GWAR show. That's the last we saw of her," Trizden slurs.

"What do you mean? The last time you saw her she was with *them*?"

"No. Well, I wouldn't say *with* them, but she was in the pit and so were they. 8-Ball had tried to get her to go with them earlier, said that he had a bunch of coke, and she said she was waiting for you. But then, once the GWAR show started she just kinda disappeared."

"Do you vouch for this?" I ask Sinead. I'm really tripping hard now. The world is crashing down around my ears, my head spinning out of control.

"She was jonesing for some blow," Sinead confirms.

"I have to find her," I tell them.

"We'll go with you," Trizden says.

The beauty of LSD is that any time I think about the possible worst-case scenarios of this Michelle situation (Rat's pounding her from behind and she's blowing 8-Ball while they take turns snorting fat rails of cocaine), the upside almost immediately distracts these conscious, soul-destroying thoughts into blissfully "tripping" from one harmless distraction to another:

"Look, you guys—Lights! *Lights!* They're magnificent, aren't they?"

"Dude, that's a potted plant."

We happen into several different rooms, each suite renewing the need to search out any possible signs of Michelle. She's never there, though. I drink some more. Every room offers more alcohol, but I can't get drunk when I'm tripping no matter how hard I try. The Acid part of my brain cancels out the drunk part. I wonder aloud if I should try driving to test this theory. Trizden refuses to let me use his car.

"But I have a license," I explain.

Animal Mother never has bad luck with women because he never allows himself to fall in love with them. But I'm not that smart. I *want* to fall in love. I want that *feel*ing. And right now the woman I love is sitting in some kind of Oriental spin-fuck chair being double-teamed by two military rejects who have a bag of coke.

At some point my despair levels out and I resign myself to the tragic yet somehow comforting fate of the lovelorn and cuckolded. We all end up just sitting on the floor, leaning against a wall in a hallway. In short order Trizden passes out with his head in Skinhead Michelle's lap.

"I like your shirts, guys," Skinhead Michelle says after a long silence.

"Thanks, man," Splinter says. We both look down at our shirts to see what we're wearing.

"Oh, yeah, fuck Iraq."

"I don't believe we should be fucking anyone, personally," Skinhead Michelle says. "I think we're only in Iraq for our own selfish interests and I figured that's what you meant by the slogans on your shirts."

"Yeah, well, that probably is what we meant when we made them, originally. But right now I couldn't give a fuck, to be honest," I say. "I'm tripping my brains out. I don't even know what time it is, but I've eaten at least eight or nine hits since last night. And now my fucking girlfriend, who I am totally in love with—the slut—is at this very moment fucking two army rejects just because they could offer her a little cocaine." I'm rambling but honestly *do not give a fuck*. "So to be honest, I wish there was a goddam war right now and they were right the fuck in the middle of it. Call me selfish."

Skinhead Michelle uncrosses then recrosses her legs, moving Animal Mother's head to a more comfortable position. "Well, I guess I can understand that," she offers.

Splinter is soon bored and says so, asks if I want to wander around some more, but I'm done. Done in. I say I'll catch up with him later.

"You wanna smoke a bowl?" I ask Skinhead Michelle.

"Sure."

We brazenly smoke right out in the hallway. I feel better. Less obsessed. Philosophical.

"You know how the hippies in the '60s thought they were changing everything, all these stupid kids that had no real idea what they were doing or why they were doing it, dropping out of high school and making their way across the country to San Francisco?" I ask Skinhead Michelle. She is absentmindedly running her fingers through Trizden's hair.

"Yeah, my parents were hippies, too. Now my dad is a securities broker and my mother has worked for IBM for the last seventeen years."

"My mother was a hippie but she never got a real job when all the hype died down. Just married a lazy retard."

Skinhead Michelle hands the bowl back to me, delicious pot smoke leaving her nostrils and surrounding us.

"Look," she says to me. Her voice takes on a sentimental, soothing quality. "I know how fucked up you're feeling right now. But you have to look forward, always. You think my parents are any better than yours? I never see either of them. Our entire relationship is based on some bullshit schedule they've designed around their careers."

I don't say anything. I look at her eyes. Never leave her eyes.

"Luke, nothing can stay the same forever. What you have to remember is that everything you do will one day add up to a specific, perfect you—the you you were meant to be. Everything we have done in the past, everything we will experience in the future will add up to the sum of its parts, at age thirty and thirty-five and forty and seventy. We have to consciously operate with that knowledge every day. That's what I try to do anyway."

And then I'm crying and then I'm being kissed on the forehead by Skinhead Michelle and then I'm running down hallways with no direction or destination in mind. Free fall. The fastest way to freedom.

The sun shining in my eyes wakes me. I'm under a black linen-covered catering table. There are only short flashes of memory as I wander around the now quiet hotel. In my head I see snapshots of myself stumbling into people. I hear their condemnations. I faintly recall sitting somewhere on the higher floors, overlooking the mezzanine in its patterned tile whiteness hundreds of feet below. And crying and crying. I know that much happened for sure. Crying definitely occurred. Crying until snot mixed with drool and hung in long strings onto my t-shirt, turning the irreverent antiwar logo into a pond of spittle.

I don't know where anyone is. I don't know what floor I'm on. There is a maid vacuuming an empty room. I speak to her repeatedly and she finally turns around. She is Hispanic, looks like she won't understand English, so I'm talking loudly even after she switches off the vacuum cleaner. She says, with no hint of accent, that she can hear perfectly fine, tells me I'm on the forty-seventh floor.

"Forty-seven," I say. "That's how many dreadlocks I have."

The goddam elevator takes forever but I finally reach 17, the main Dragon*Con floor. The doors open and nobody is there. There is nothing scheduled today except good-byes. Everyone is gone.

Lights blur and swirl out of the corner of my eye, Acid residual. My stomach is an empty pit, gnawing me away from the inside. I lean into the conference rooms. They too are empty, save for multicolored flyers still tacked to the walls. I take the elevator down to the lobby. The table that had been the main security monitoring station is abandoned. I sit and wait for five or ten minutes before a disheveled man, wrinkled and dark-circled, drags himself past holding a trash bag over his shoulder with brown fur pushing through the top of the bag.

I go over to the bulletin wall and study a poster that proclaims

The Biggest Dragon*Con Expo *EVER*!
July 14–17, Houston, Texas

There will be people from this Dragon*Con at that one. There are people who follow this shit around like it's the Grateful goddam Dead. Losers.

I roll up the poster and aim down the corridor at the man who just walked by with the Wookie in a bag.

"Hey, man!" I yell. "Whatcha got in the bag?"

The sound of my voice is like an air-raid siren in this dead place.

The man stops and turns around looking bewildered, pointing at himself as if to say, "Me? What do *I* have in *my* bag?"

"What-do-you-have-in-the-bag?" I say, over-enunciating every word.

He lumbers toward me slowly. "What do I have in the bag?"

Then I start to laugh because it's just so funny that this guy would walk all the way back over here to answer the questions of a dreadlocked asshole yelling at him through a fucking rolled-up poster.

He realizes he's been had, tells me I'm a dick. I laugh. He knows nothing. No pain. No despair.

More people begin exiting the elevators. I turn my attention to them. Any distinguishing characteristic is singled out and duly noted by megaphone for all within earshot.

"You need to shave! Everywhere!"

"Kmart is a notoriously *un*cool place to buy clothing!"

"It's just a fucking movie, Obi-Wan!"

After about twenty minutes of this, Splinter appears looking only slightly better than I imagine I do. He doesn't say anything at first, just sits in the chair beside me and watches with amusement as I continue berating all the losers. People might not like the way I've taken over this security table and used it for my own personal thrills, but fuck them, I thought of it first.

A woman approaches dressed in some kind of cheap Wonder Woman–imitation costume. Splinter says he'd like to take this one. I gladly hand him the megaphone.

"Hey, you! You're fucked!" Splinter yells.

She stops in her tracks, like a cartoon, arms and legs frozen in place, in odd configurations, trying to figure out if this epithet was directed at her. She does the finger-pointing-at-herself thing.

"Yes, you," Splinter yells, despite the fact that she is only fifteen feet away. "You're fucked!"

Her face falls. "I'm not fat," she says.

"Not fat, *fucked*. You're fucked! You're FUCKED!"

We're laughing again. Our asses are on the floor. Marvel Girl runs off to find the real security, the non-victimizing kind.

Minutes later real security shows up. They hold flashlights in front of their crotches in that threatening, tapping-the-palms kind of way. I ignore them at first, finish a blistering diatribe directed at an asshole wearing Birkenstock sandals. Then I redirect my yelling at real Security. They don't understand that this must be done. This is Reality Check.

"What, you couldn't get on with the *real* cops?" I yell at them. "Hiring practices too stringent?"

"Sir, if you yell at me through that thing again I'm going to be forced to eject you from the premises," the black guy says.

"Is it because I'm black?" I say through the rolled-up poster.

He glares at me. I can tell he wants to bust that flashlight across my skull, but at the same time, I don't really give a good goddam.

Splinter laughs on. Then Sinead comes to the table with Trizden. She says her name is Michelle.

As I look at her I'm reminded of my incredible failures. She is wholly representative of failure. She is my shortcoming. She is my end. Transferred from one woman to another, of course. To all women.

"This is what it feels like to be destroyed, ruined for all intents and purposes," I proclaim through my makeshift megaphone. "Fucked in the ass without even the goddam common courtesy of a reach-around!"

"You and the fucking *Full Metal Jacket*," Splinter says.

The two guards come up behind the table and they each grab me under an armpit and I keep yelling through the poster and now everyone is watching so I ask them what is so fucking funny and then I realize nobody else is laughing.

And then the plug is pulled.

One of the guards yanks the poster out of my hands. It sounds so strange, to go from magnified and sort of godly sounding, the man behind the curtain, to just some guy yelling indiscriminately at whoever catches his eye.

I suddenly feel penitent. I ask to be let go. I'm much better now. I've just been up too long.

The guards say nothing, place me neatly on the sidewalk outside the front door of the hotel.

I had expected to be thrown, like in the movies.

TRANSMISSION 07:

acts of desperation

June

I've been staying with Animal Mother since Dragon*Con. He thinks he needs to protect me from myself. After a couple of weeks I decide I'm ready to see Michelle again but she doesn't show at *Rocky.* I'm kind of relieved that she doesn't, actually, but find myself asking Trizden if he'll run us by Waffle House in case she turns up there.

I can see her through the window as we pull into the parking lot. She's sitting in a booth with Rat and 8-Ball. Everything looks yellow.

I stay in the car. I can't face her in there with those two snarling fucks sitting next to her. On the other side of the window Rat points at me, sneering. Michelle slips out of the booth and comes outside. She has such a great walk.

"Where've you been?" she says.

"Where have *I* been?"

"Yeah, I've been trying to call you at your mom's house since Dragon*Con and she doesn't know where you are. She's really kind of frantic. You should call her."

"What happened at Dragon*Con?" I say. "Why did you disappear?"

She looks down at the sidewalk for a long while.

"You fucking bitch."

Her eyes leap to meet mine. "Why are you talking to me like that?"

"Because you fucking betrayed me! You screwed those two assholes. I mean, of all people! You knew I hated them!"

She doesn't say anything, only looks at me with tears in her eyes, tries to touch my face. I pull away.

"And now you're sitting there with them! I hate you. You've killed me. I *loved* you. Do you understand, Michelle, I fucking loved you. I still love you now. And I hate you. I fucking hate you."

She turns around and starts back inside. I scream and run as hard as I can across the parking lot, lower my head, hit the dumpster, crumple.

• • •

I'm lying on an inflatable mattress next to Trizden's bed. There's a song playing on the stereo, something about a triangular man meeting a particle man, the triangle man beating the particle man.

I can hear them fucking and it sounds disgusting, the slurp and suck and squeak of sighs and prone bodies. Skinhead Michelle and Trizden. Right there, on the bed, beside me.

I listen for a while, wonder if they think I'm sleeping, wonder if they care whether I am or not.

She's moaning. He is moaning. It must feel good. Their flesh slaps together in rhythm.

I debate whether it would be bad form to stand up in the middle of their session and leave the room. That would definitely indicate that I've been awake the entire time. An embarrassment, maybe more for me than for them. After three or four more minutes of humping I decide I don't care if they know I'm awake, rush out of the room with the door slamming behind me.

I go to the freezer. Animal Mother always has rum or bourbon in there. I pour some, mix with Coke, down the glass, pour another. And another.

After pissing, I look in the giant bathroom mirror above the counter, pull off my shirt. I am skinny and pale, skeletal.

I yank open the drawer beside the sink and grab an unopened package of razors.

Michelle used to do this one thing. She would release her anxiety by cutting her arms with razor blades. She couldn't stand to be bottled up inside. She couldn't stand to live festering. Her arms were testament to this. They were covered in dull pink slash scars, clarifying why she always wears long sleeves and belying the popular image that she has everything together, she has that confidence. But I know better. She is an actress. She is a fucking charlatan.

I break the razor open with my pocketknife, pull out a single blade. It is small and inconsequential. I decide to go for the chest. It's whiter than all the rest of me—a perfect canvas. I draw the blade across the right pectoral. There is nothing, no sign of change. But as I stare at my chest in the mirror a small red line appears, less than an inch long. The slash is shallow, the blood slips out in tiny bubbles spread unevenly across the length of the cut. I go again, on the other side. I push down harder this time. The razor feels no more severe than cutting paper, feels like a paper cut, gets under the skin in a way that is more annoying than painful.

This is easy.

I go again, on the stomach. Then again, on the right shoulder. The left. I keep cutting. It becomes rhythmic, ritualistic. I don't have to hold my breath anymore. I stop periodically to look at my new self and I am rewarded handsomely with a vibrant display of slowly dripping red slashes evenly distributed across my torso. Nearly symmetrical. I contemplate trying to fit my t-shirt back over this rawness I have exposed, my true self. My skin and my heart in ruins. Unending, unendurable pain. Agony tearing at me from every side.

I am finished. I am *finished*.

And I'm still not drunk enough. I'll *never* be drunk enough. You give your heart and you trust and you give and give and give and then, like that—a snap of the fingers—it's all taken away.

We are begging to be killed, begging to be crucified, sacrificed on the altar of dead love.

I stumble into the kitchen, leaving small spatters of blood behind on the carpet, blossoms of the dying tree of me. They will help me find my way back, bread crumbs on a woodland path. I yank open the freezer and drink straight from the bottle, the bourbon spilling from my mouth and setting me on fire as it courses down my chin to the open places in my chest. I'm so hungry. The liquor only makes me hungrier, just like when Jesus was hanging fron cross and asked for a drink and got a sponge full of vinegar for His trouble, which probably made Him about fifty times thirstier. Those motherfuckers.

Every time I read that story I hold out hope that it will magically change, like a spiritual Choose Your Own Adventure, and this time Jesus will have decided to get up off that cross and destroy *everything*, just eviscerate everyone for miles around. That would show those pricks they were wrong. If He had just allowed them to put Him on that cross, a seemingly inescapable death for any mere mortal . . . and then, at the darkest hour, summoned the great power He possessed—and just *scourged* them all with His great fury—my God—none of us would be in the predicaments we're in now. Everyone would have known the truth.

My soul is a hollow fucking husk, dried and withered in the sun, whisked away by the wind and scattered.

Everyone would have known what was required of them, what we could expect in return if we followed through and were faithful. But He left us here instead, without any answers. There are no more burning bushes, clouds opening up, or dictates being handed down from above in God's own handwriting. We are stumbling around down here like fucking kittens in a knife drawer, mewing in the darkness.

I am howling these radical ideas and others aloud when Animal Mother stumbles out of his bedroom, squinting in the light. I'm sobbing with the snot running down and everything, mixing with the blood, everything.

"What the fuck did you do? What did you do?" He's screaming and frantic, which sucks because I have just been getting into the groove of this thing, this desperate longing and vivid despair, and he's acting like it's the end of the fucking world.

"I can't live like this anymore, Mother. I can't live anymore—like this."

"Oh my God! Oh my God!"

"Why are you screaming, man? It's not that big a deal. I'm fine. I didn't do the fabled 'suicide cuts,'" I say, making the fabled suicide cut motion up the inside of my wrists. "I stuck with the far more common 'cry for help.'" I show him my wrists to prove that there are, indeed, no vertical slashes running upward from the wrist to the elbow. It's all superficial. Crying for help.

"You fucking assholes," I slur in Trizden's and now the skinhead girl's direction. "You fucking assholes that think every suicide is an unanswered cry for help have no idea what it means to despair your very existence. Those people didn't give a fuck if you found them 'just in time' or not. They just wanted to be left alone so they could find out the truth about this whole 'religion' thing. You know? Who was 'right'?" Every time I get to a quotation word I do that thing people do where they put their hands up and make imaginary quotations in the air. It always looks like you're smarter that way.

"Who was right, that kinda thing," I continue. "Buddha vs. Jesus, for example. Winner takes Vishnu. Loser goes to hell. Hell has to be involved somewhere because I can't stand thinking that Hitler gets off that easy. Or Saddam Hussein, whenever he dies. Or that little asshole George Mickelson down the street in seventh grade whose fucking Grizzly Adams dad always had dead deer carcasses hanging off the swing set in the backyard. You know? With their windpipes poking out of these massive gashes in their throats, tongues lolling, bellies emptied of all matter, black holes, their eyes staring at you no matter where you stood."

Trizden hasn't been listening for the last of my reminiscences. He's on the phone to my mother. She shows up an hour later with

Victor and I'm in the car for about five seconds before he's telling me I'm nuts and they've decided to have me committed.

"I'm not going anywhere I don't want to go."

"You'll do what we tell you you're going to do or you can get right back out of this car."

"You couldn't afford to have me committed if you wanted to, you fat fuck."

He reaches over the seat and backhands me. I taste the blood gathering in my mouth. My mother starts crying again. I jump out of the car at the next red light, my mother pleading after me.

I call Trizden from a gas station pay phone, spitting wads of blood between sentences like it's tobacco juice.

Animal Mother retrieves me. He's always good like that. As I stumble back in the door of his apartment, I notice that my t-shirt sticks to me in many places. Pulling the fabric off the wounds hurts more than it did to actually inflict them.

I pass out sitting up in the recliner. I have the leg part extended out, though, so at least there's that.

Flick comes over the next night with his psychotic girlfriend Lydia. Actually, they're both pretty fucked up. When I met him, Flick was a "normal" guy. He used to give me rides to *Rocky* and we'd drive around in his brand-new Ford Escort (Turbo!) listening to The Dead Milkmen's *Beelzebubba* and that first Violent Femmes album, the classic one, and bang our fists on his car's headliner in time with the drumbeats. But at some point Flick had a psychotic break or something. He began composing rap lyrics about how "The Man" was keeping him down, even though he was somehow distantly related to the former Attorney General of the United States Edwin Meese. The Man was in his own family.

Flick met Lydia one night at *Rocky*. She's one of those girls who has a completely different outward appearance than what her personality might suggest, a librarian type who happens to be into whips and sadomasochistic sex. And while Lydia isn't a librarian by day, not by any stretch of the imagination (she's a cashier at Bi-Lo), she still maintains the stereotypical late-night side of the cliché, with the leather dominatrix outfits, complete with garters concealed underneath calf-length house dresses.

She and Flick were immediately drawn to each other. There was no latency period, no honeymoon phase or whatever you want to call it. That first night, Flick and Lydia sat in a corner of the lobby all night and gave each other eat-shit looks, like they'd known and hated each other for years. Archenemies. Nemeses. Later I asked Flick how he knew her and why they hated each other so much and he said they didn't hate each other, they were in love, love at first sight.

"Why the hell were you slapping the shit out of each other, then? You know, if it's 'love'?"

"You wouldn't understand this, man. You wouldn't *get* a love that runs so deep that people have to inflict pain on each other just to be able to withstand remaining under the enormous burden of that love" is what his answer was. Seriously. I couldn't make this shit up.

The night after my razor blade episode, Flick and Lydia come over. Splinter has already been called up as reserve support systems for me in my time of need. We're all laughing, joking with each other, trying to avoid, at all costs, the subject of last night, when Flick and Lydia start in with the slapping. Right there in the middle of the living room.

Now, when I say slapping, I'm not talking about the run-of-the-mill foreplay tapping that we all know and love. I'm talking about the hauling off—the reaching way back and walloping like you're trying to kill a leprechaun—kind of slapping. Red marks are imprinted. Welts.

The four of us can forget trying to hold a conversation because every few seconds another *CRACK* echoes across the room and that kind of thing just can't be ignored. It's worse than a mother beating her loudmouthed kid on the MARTA train. And then Flick and Lydia take it up a notch.

Lydia reaches into her duffel bag and pulls out a bullwhip, leather tassels on the end and everything. She cracks Flick in the side of the head with the handle. He reaches over with both hands and starts to choke her and we're all wondering if somebody should do something because maybe this time it's gone too far. But then Lydia starts laying into him with the whip handle and *then* she says she's so fucking turned on that he has no other choice but to fuck her right now.

She turns toward us. We're sitting there trying not to act like this is the wackest shit we've ever seen. "Do you guys mind?"

"Fuck yeah. Let me see you fuck her, Flick," I say.

Flick tears Lydia's clothes off of her faster than Animal Mother and the guys can get out of the apartment. They're tripping over each other to keep from witnessing this. I wish I could say I'm moral enough to do the same, but I've been drinking from the moment I woke up, called in sick to work on account of going crazy, and I'm ready to see some crazy-ass fucking.

They smack each other some more, Flick banging her on the ass with the whip. I slouch back in the lounge chair and drink more, and then I realize I'm really quite drunk, actually.

They get quiet after a while and I lean up a little to see if they've finally killed each other or something because they are never quiet.

They're both looking at me, grinning.

I am suddenly very afraid.

Flick says, "Luke, I want you to fuck my girlfriend. Wouldn't you like to have sex with Lydia?"

"No way."

"Why not, Luke? Do you think I'm ugly?"

"Of course not. You're totally hot. If you weren't so fucked in the head I'd be all over you."

"Please, man, she wants to take care of you," Flick says. "You know, with the Michelle thing and everything. Lydia and me, we want to give this gift to you. To help you get through this."

It's the old "fucking away your sorrow" angle.

"You've already seen *me* naked, if that's what you're hesitating for," says Flick.

"Yeah, there's that, but it's also that I ain't into that whole 'gettin' the piss smacked out of me while I'm doing it' angle."

"Sweetheart, I would never dream of doing something like that to you," Lydia reassures me. "The hitting is strictly between us. We'd never try to pull someone else into that. We're actually really happy that we are the only two people we know that like that kind of thing. It makes what we have more . . . *special.*"

"That or more fucked up," I say, weakening, anticipation rising.

"So you'll do it?"

Finally, a woman begging me to screw her. I guzzle the last of my drink and slam the cup down triumphantly.

"I'll do it."

Lydia's on me in a flash, takes my pants down to my ankles, puts my dick in her mouth. She blows me for a while and then says she wants me inside her. I turn around to see if Flick's about to bash me in the head with a baseball bat or something but he's still sitting calmly on the couch rubbing his crotch and nods his head at me for the go-ahead on the actual fuck action.

I tell her I'd go down on her, too, but she has to understand that

I just witnessed Flick shoot about eight loads in her. She says she doesn't hold it against me.

Then I'm fucking her. It feels like putting my dick in a bag of peach compote, really pretty gross, what with the whole Flick cum factor, but I don't give a shit at this point. I keep going. She is looking at me like no one ever has. She is so beautiful, her body a perfect receptacle for all my unquenchable suffering and shame. She is a willing martyr. She is showing me more love in these moments of raw unspeakable sluttiness than Michelle showed me the entire two months I went out with her. Lydia has given me her body so that I might find relief, a reason to live, to go on, to stake out another day. Her fingers glide along my torso, working their way delicately over my scabbed-over cuttings. She is tender with me. She knows everything.

Luke, I say to myself as we move together (pumping pumping pumping), all that came before now was just a warm-up for real life. Nothing should ever be reason enough to discontinue the searching out of the beauty that exists in the world. I will never hold back again, I will never believe that in order to live I must close down as some do after they've been destroyed by another's actions (faster faster). I will continue to throw myself across the train tracks of love and pray I'm not cut in half. And even if I am, I will sew back together. I *know* this. I will take every experience into my consciousness fully, as though it were my last. I will eat life with a fork and a knife, and when those utensils aren't available I will tear pieces off in chunks and swallow whole (she's yelling now, screaming). I will not lie down and die. Not for anyone. I am alive! I am banging a beautiful woman! She loves me! Right now, at this very moment, no one else exists in the universe but the two of us. We are one and the same. We are the same! We are the very essence of humanity. We are boiled down together, melted into each other. There is no differentiation between her and me. The same blood flows between us. We trade life force. We feed off each other. We are the same! (cumming cumming cumming CUMMING)

I collapse on the floor, the moth-eaten carpet. Lydia lowers her body over me, leans in to my mouth and kisses me. I bury my hands in her cascading hair and caress the tops of her earlobes. "Thank you. Thank you, Lydia."

They are quiet as they dress. I make no move to get off the floor.

"We're leaving now, Luke," I hear Lydia say.

"OK." I feel drunker now, somehow, in the afterglow. "Thanks, you guys."

Then I hear Flick say, "You never kiss *me* like that, you fucking bitch."

"You don't deserve to be kissed like that," Lydia says.

The door slams, shaking the apartment.

TRANSMISSION 08:

revenge is fucking sweet

July

My bedroom looks like a tornado touched down. There are food-encrusted plates scattered around the recliner. I become angrier by the second as I look around the room. Every poster I had pinned up in various angles and in triptych montage according to subject matter has been yanked down, *crumpled*, and tossed across the room.

There can only be one jerkoff at fault.

He has intentionally desecrated my stuff, my every representation of high school and teenage life encompassed in a few well-cared-for pieces of paper. I had set lists autographed by three different bands. I had a first-edition Spider-Man signed by Todd McFarlane. It's all gone. How could my mother marry a monster like that and continue to be married to him even now? How could she see the aftermath of his fury, taken out explicitly on my sacred ephemera, and not immediately gather one or two changes of clothes, pack the kids in the car, and get as far away from his obviously psychotic ass as possible?

I call Jonas into the room. I already have the words prepared, the "What the fuck happened in here?!" exasperation built up to unprecedented levels. But I pause to hug him and he hugs me back and then we're both squeezing the shit out of each other. He looks genuinely pleased to have me back, glowing really. I cannot wait until he's old enough to escape from here with me.

"What happened?" I ask, trying to sound calm.

"He just went nuts a couple of weeks ago," Jonas says apologetically. "He said one of your posters was obscene."

"Which?"

I scan the blank walls, trying to remember everything the way it was.

Jonas blushes.

"Which one?" I demand.

"It was a drawing of The Cat in the Hat . . . he had a . . . a boner. A boner with a sock on it. And it said, 'If you're gonna dive in the hive, better put a sock on your cock.'

"I'm sorry I couldn't save any of your stuff. He just *lost* it. We were sitting in here watching a movie about Navy SEALs and during a commercial he started looking around the room and stared at that one for a while, got up out of the chair and stared at it. Even after the movie came back on he just kept staring at it and then he ripped it off the wall and tore it to pieces." He looks down, nudges a crumpled poster with his foot, wipes his eye with his sleeve. "He didn't say anything. He just started walking around the room tearing everything off the walls."

"I can't wait until you can get out of here and come with me." I want to kill, I want to smash fucking everything. I want to fucking smash fucking everyfuckingthing. "I can't let this stand, bro. I don't give a shit if he kills me. If I let him get away with this he'll think he can walk all over me, do whatever he wants. He's always spewing this bullshit Marine talk, about there being repercussions for every action; well he's gonna see some repercussions."

I light a cigarette.

"When'd you start smoking?"

I tell my brother I've *been* smoking in that way that says, "Where the hell have you been?"

"What are you gonna do?"

"Jesus, Jonas, don't sound so frightened, man. I'm not going to implicate you or anything. What am I supposed to do? What? Am I supposed to act like this hasn't happened?"

"No . . . but I don't want him to hurt you again."

"He won't," I say, exhaling. "And even if he does, it'll be for a good cause."

He starts crying, which irritates me for some reason.

"What are you crying for? Aren't you sick of living in fear of this fucking guy? Aren't you tired of having to tiptoe around him? I can't take another second of you or Mom or anyone else playing the condemned around him. Victor's a goddam tyrant. He's a monster. Don't you get that?"

He doesn't say anything, just nods, tears streaming down his cheeks, a low whine escaping his throat.

"It's gonna be OK. We'll get through this like everything else."

We hug again and he helps me push all the poster refuse into a pile. We gather the nasty glassware and take it to the sink. I drop my handful of dishes as loudly as I possibly can without actually breaking any.

Victor opens the door to my room at 9 p.m. and ambles in like he owns the place. He turns on the TV, the volume so loud it's distorted.

I pretend to be reading a book, as though nothing he can do will make me incite him to further violence.

After about ten blaring minutes of a *Magnum, P.I.* rerun, he turns the volume down. And then, when he least expects it, I reach beside the bed and palm one of his old beer bottles. I'm on my stomach when I grab it. I turn my head back toward him. He's seated just to the right of the foot of the bed. I bring the bottle up, wing it at him as hard as I can, and watch it burst in slow motion across his head. His yelp is filled with surprise and anger more than pain. He knows he's been had.

He stumbles toward me, still clutching his current beer in one hand, the other hand over his face, blood spilling to the carpet. I grab another empty bottle, stand on the bed, and as he reaches for me with his beer, I clobber him across the left ear. He's screaming now, snatching furiously in the dark. He finds me and drops his beer on my bed. I look down to see it spilling out, darkening the comforter, and in that moment he grabs my arms and throws me hard against the outside door. He can't see, though. He can't finish. I fling the door open and run out into the night. He stumbles after me. I come across the side of the house, to the front yard, the headlights of passing cars momentarily lighting the lawn before it returns to darkness, a strobe light in slow motion. I start hollering. The front door opens and my mother and brothers look around for the source of the noise in the darkness. And then there we are, squared up in the passing headlights. His drunkenness cancels out his weight advantage and years of combat training. He lunges at me and I jump out of the way, turn and kick him in the ass as hard as I can. He goes down and then it's just like skinhead Dave told me. Once you get a motherfucker down, you make sure he stays down. You kick him until he doesn't move.

I kick Victor hard in the ribs, hear the wind rush out of him.

Then I take my boot to his face a few times for good measure. He doesn't move anymore after that.

Should I relish these moments? Probably not. But I do. I can't stop kicking him. I'm dancing like Ali and destroying like Tyson. And there's so much to kick, the fat bastard. He's worthless and bloody and heaving. He never asks me to stop, though. He doesn't beg. And soon I'm tired of kicking him and I can hear Aaron and Adam crying and they're hiding their faces in my mother's dress. I look over at Jonas and he's clearly invigorated. I smile, bend over to catch my breath, hands on knees. Victor is moaning.

I grab my suitcase, still packed, and my duffel bag filled with tapes and CDs, shoving my copy of *Black Boy* in at the last second. When I leave for the gas station to call Trizden, I'm so proud I'm beaming. I am born again.

TRANSMISSION 09:

friends lend each other helping hands

November

I couldn't hack it in school anymore, dropped out with less than a semester to go after promising my mother I'd eventually take the G.E.D. For now, I've embarked on a career in telemarketing. Flick got me the job. We sell credit cards over the phone to college students who don't know any better. It sounds like free money to them and it's a totally easy sell.

I go to work for monotonous eight-hour days, come back to Animal Mother's and smoke up, drink a few rum and cokes. It's an ongoing cycle of working and self-medicating after work. But there's still the excitement of girls and the possibility of getting laid. That makes it all worthwhile. And going to shows.

I always go to concerts with Trizden. He's one of those guys whose life aspiration is to stay on top of the newest music. He always knows more about every band than you could ever know, and six months before you know it, at that. This kind of shit is intuitive to him or something, because no matter what band you think you know about first, no matter how early you think you get in on the ground floor of liking some group, Trizden has been there first. And yet, despite this, he somehow always gets laid. Women couldn't give a good goddam about music, I've found. Most of 'em only care about Led Zeppelin, dance music (but only if you're listening to the dance music in a club), and the newest pop hits played ad infinitum on the radio. So the fact that he knows that Big Black's *Songs About Fucking* is a seminal post-punk record made by the guy that produced Nirvana's *In Utero* is little inducement in getting women to like him. But see, that's the key to staying cool. You have your elitist snobbery and all, make fun of the underlings who think they know something about something when they really know shit about shit, but you don't ever extend those same standards to the girls you're interested in. You'll almost always be disappointed, Trizden the Animal Mother has learned.

Since the beginning of time Triz has professed a love for Nirvana. He's had *Bleach* since it first came out. He had tickets to see them at the Masquerade when they weren't shit. He didn't get to go, he says, because he had the flu that night. But now they are here again, they are in Atlanta at the Omni, where the Hawks play. He has given me a ticket to see them for Christmas. Splinter is going with us. All three of us have general admission tickets, so there are no seats. We will be able to mingle freely in the pit, a roiling mass of bodies moved by music.

For the concert Splinter and I have obtained an eighth ounce of coke, an eight-ball, in the parlance of our times, and are planning to snort the whole thing before and during Nirvana's performance. We're gonna cut a few lines in the parking deck outside the venue and the rest we'll put in a couple of snuff inhalers (known in these circles as "bullets") so that we can stay geeked up during the show.

Trizden doesn't want to have anything to do with the shit. He doesn't take to drugs too keenly now. He says they're for losers, as though he has room to talk. Splinter and I have been dabbling in cocaine recently and Trizden thinks we're pathetic wasteoids because of this. But after the last Acid trip I had, I'm all about trying new shit. I can't keep this tripping bullshit up when it's making me want to blow people's brains all over the living room wall.

Animal Mother leaves us to our own devices in the parking deck and says he'll meet us on the right side of the stage. Splinter and I snort three fat lines each. By the time we get situated and climb out of the car we're soaring, smoking cigarettes like they're air. I pull the bullet out of my pocket and admire the vial at the bottom, filled to the brim with white powder. This is going to be a great night. "All signs point to this being a great night," I say.

By the time Nirvana takes the stage after the two opening acts I am completely fucking gone. I've been snorting coke out of the bullet for an hour and a half. Splinter and Trizden and I stood in front of the stage through the first bands' sets as well as another half hour of bullshit standing around and geeking and smoking cigarettes and waiting before Kurt and company finally took the stage. The set decoration is incredible. There is an angel placed right in the middle, the same one that's on the *In Utero* album cover. At times Kurt stands in front of it wailing on his guitar and he appears to have wings. He is a fucking rock *god*.

The pit is a mess, there are kids flying everywhere, a boiling cauldron of teen angst and aggression. I periodically duck down and snort two or three bumps of cocaine out of the bullet, stand up reinvigorated and throw my body carelessly into the fray. They tear through all the classics, "School," "In Bloom," "Lithium," "Drain You," "Milk It." And then I run into Sharon.

Sharon is Trizden's latest underage girlfriend. She is a redhead, cute as a fucking button, great fucking tits, and not even out of tenth grade yet. We stay close throughout the arrhythmic moshing and Kurt is screaming his goddam brains out and then we're kissing and all over each other, smothering in sweat and catching each other's breaths. The guitars are shrill and visceral, the drumming is tribal and banging harder than hell. Sharon snorts a bump of coke from my bullet and then we are practically screwing right there in the pit. I've got my hand under her shirt and she's grinding herself against me and this is the best fucking show I've ever been to. This is rapture.

Then Kurt stops the show right in the middle of "On a Plain" and says that he saw that, he saw that fucking guy feel that girl's tits as she was crowd surfing. He wants that guy taken out of here, he says. He says that people like that guy are fucking raped in prison for a reason and they deserve it. They have no respect for women, he says. The crowd is mostly silent. Splinter and Trizden are lost somewhere out there. Sharon and I are still slobbering all over each other in the silence. She continues moaning as I finger her. Then Kurt starts up again, recommences with "Territorial Pissings," and the crowd is destroying everything again and Sharon is yanking on my dreads again and biting my bottom lip and I have no worry in the world, I'm so high on the music and the cocaine and the kissing that I could die right now and not care ONE FUCKING BIT.

Once they exit the stage everyone starts screaming louder than they have all night. We know it can't be over yet because they haven't destroyed everything, instruments are still intact all over the stage. The band finally comes back and plays another song or two and then they begin the inevitable destruction by bashing holes in the drums with the mic stands followed by the impaling of the speaker stacks and then Kurt is grinding his guitar into the fucking monitors and then he's standing on his guitar and it is making the shrillest, most decrepit sounds we've ever heard and then they all take turns throwing one of the smaller monitors up in the air, trying to knock the mirror ball above the stage from its mooring and then Kurt does it, isn't that classic? Kurt dislodges the mirror ball from twenty feet above him and it crashes to the stage in a glittering display of broken glass and we are still screaming, the crowd is screaming, and both of my hands are down Sharon's pants, the right hand in the front, the left in back, and she has her arms wrapped around the back of my head, pulling on my dreads, and I have still more coke left for later. The monitors, what's left of them, are buzzing, moaning monotonally as Kurt and company leave the stage and we file out of the auditorium.

Sharon kisses me again at the door, sucks extra hard on my bottom lip, tells me not to tell Trizden, says, "That was fun, wasn't it?" and puts her finger to her lips in a "keep quiet" motion before disappearing into the departing crowd. I duck behind a trash can, suck up another four bumps, am still smiling when Splinter and then Trizden make their way through the door. Trizden punches me in the arm.

"Thanks for ditching me in the pit, jerkweed." He's always got one grievance or another. He's temperamental. Like a woman.

TRANSMISSION 10:

destroying your town to *save* it

April

The riots are in full swing in L.A. and everywhere. The news is having a field day. Cities all over the country are erupting in violence and looting. Splinter keeps insisting that we go downtown and fuck some shit up, but I don't know—it seems like a good way to get incarcerated for a long time and for no discernible reason. He goes anyway and returns to Animal Mother's that night with a brand-new set of golf clubs.

I don't see the point, though. I figure, why shit where you eat? It makes no sense. These looters aren't going after the oppressors by hitting up the rich neighborhoods. They're destroying their *own* backyards. It makes no fucking sense. But I've realized that this is what The Man wants. He *wants* us to kill each other. This makes The Man happy. Why expend money and manpower on keeping the poor people down if we'll do it ourselves?

I tell Splinter my theory a few days after the last rioter has gone home. We're sitting in the square in Little 5 Points. All the whacked-out hippies and punks and social outcasts of the Atlanta "scene" hang down here. Every store in the area has some variety of "X-treme" hair dye and sells t-shirts emblazoned with underground rock band logos. We come down here for a slice of pizza, with a side order of rabble-rousing from tripping hippies of the left-wing political persuasion.

"Dude," Splinter says, "have you not seen *Do the Right Thing*?"

"Of course I've seen *Do the Right Thing*. What's that got to do with anything?"

"What's that got to do with anything? Do you forget that Mookie—"

"Don't even. I *know*," I say, cutting Splinter off mid-sentence. "Mookie starts the riot after Radio Raheem gets killed by the cops and he initiates the burning down of the pizza parlor. That made no fucking logical sense."

"Of course it made sense, man. The Italian assholes that ran that fucking pizza joint gave no respect to the black people and it was a predominantly black neighborhood. That's fucked up."

"Fuck that, man. They were pissed that Sal wouldn't put any pictures of black people on his wall. And why should he have to put pictures of them on his wall? Like he said, it's his goddam restaurant. And if they want black people's pictures on a wall they can open their own fucking restaurants. Even *Black Boy* says as much. That's the great thing about that book. It's equal opportunity pissed at *all* the idiots."

"That's easy for Sal to say. He already has a restaurant. The black people don't have shit."

"Well, I'm sure at one point Sal didn't have shit, either. It's called *work*. If you want anything in life, you have to work for it."

"Nobody's ever let the black man get nothing. They'll let 'em work for $5.15 an hour and that's about it."

"So the Italians had it easier?"

"I don't fucking know if the Italians had it easier or not. I'm just saying nobody is going to give a black man a loan to open a fucking Pizza Hut."

"Maybe not, but what's that got to do with burning the fucking place down? Just because they can't get a loan to open their own pizza joint, they gotta burn another guy's restaurant down?"

"Yes. They do. Don't shake your head at me, dude. Look, if you are living in fucking squalor and always have to keep coming back to this asshole Italian every time you want a fucking slice of pizza . . . that shit just rots with you. It turns your insides out. This motherfucker has moved into your neighborhood and opened the restaurant you never had a chance to open in the first place. Would that not piss you off?" He hocks up a loog, spits right past my head into the bushes.

"Yeah, it would piss me off . . . but I wouldn't feel like I had to burn his whole goddam place down because of that fact. Ruining his livelihood isn't going to make me any better off."

"That's the problem with you nonrevolutionaries," Splinter says. "You can't see into the future at all. You can't see that until some eggs are broken . . ." He lights a cigarette, squints to keep the smoke from his eyes. ". . . there will be no progress made. What this country needed was a good dose of chaos. Re-level the playing field—let everybody start off equal." Splinter kicks back, lets his head hang over the side of the bench, takes a long, proud drag from his Newport.

"Oh, yeah," I say. "You're real fucking revolutionary. You and your revolutionary golf clubs."

"One less white dude is going to take up acres of perfectly good land so that he can play a stupid game. Land that minorities could be moving onto."

"What, are you going to use them?"

"Fuck no, I'm gonna sell 'em at a pawn shop."

"You idiot. White people will get 'em anyway. I don't know any fucking Mexican golfers."

"Maybe so. But at least Titleist didn't get the money from 'em. As far as I'm concerned, that's a victory."

"You're an idiot."

"Fuck you, dude. Tool of The Man."

"Me?"

"Yeah, you. You fucking buy into all that bullshit they sell. 'Don't fuck up the neighborhoods. Don't trash the stores.' They keep us poor folk down by making us take the little piece-of-shit carrots they dangle in front of us," Splinter says.

"And it's so much better when we destroy that much, isn't it? Now, instead of having a goddam convenience store where you can get milk or a beer in the middle of the night, there's a charred shell of a building and no way to get a fucking pack of cigarettes because we decided to show everybody our anger by ruining our own neighborhood. That makes no fucking sense."

A hippie reeking of patchouli asks if we have a cigarette. He takes mine, the nonmenthol.

"Nobody in power will ever relinquish that power willingly, my friend," Splinter continues. "We, the downtrodden, must take it." I hate it when he calls me "my friend." I ruthlessly counter his ignorance.

"By rioting we're showing The Man that he does, in fact, have as much power as we feared. And more. We're showing The Man that we, the poor, are fucking animals, that we deserve to have nothing."

"Because everything we have is worthless!"

"Fuck that. The people that *make* something for themselves, that bust their asses in one bullshit job or another, are the ones that will make it, that will rise above."

"I never asked for a handout. I wanted a hand *up*," Splinter says.

"You're so fucking cliché."

"Maybe so. But at least I get laid more than you."

"My ass."

"I wouldn't touch your ass with Flick's dick."

"Fuck you."

"No, my friend," Splinter enunciates elegantly, "fuck you."

I smack him upside the head, snap him out of his illusions of moral victory.

"Ow, fucker! You're a fucker!"

We stop talking to watch a hot hippie girl walk by. In typical Little 5 Points hippie fashion, she's not wearing a bra and sports only a wife-beater in the crisp spring air. Her nipples are hard. We can see everything. A moment passes, a fresh moment with just a hint of breeze.

"I love spring," I say.

"Me fucking too," says Splinter.

TRANSMISSION 11:

blow jobs and broken souls

June

I'm staying with Splinter at his "aunt's" house so that we can spend the summer hanging out. Our chief goals will be to get

1. laid
2. wasted.

Splinter's aunt is a total nutjob. She used to be his uncle. *She* used to be a *he*. She's totally mannish, has the jawline, the muscular arms, the bitchy faggot attitude.

"You knew her when she was a he?" I ask Splinter at the picnic table behind the apartment. We go out there every morning around 11 and smoke after we wake up. This morning we have a little weed, too.

"Yeah. Her name used to be Eddie," Splinter says, like it's nothing.

"Is that not fucking weird to you, man?"

"It was at first but now I guess I'm used to it. It's just like being around Eddie—except now he always wears dresses and has tits."

I shake my head. "I don't know, man. That shit freaks me out."

"Why, dude? So Aunt Tina used to be a man. Tina used to have a dick and she now has a manufactured vagina . . . yeah, you're right," Splinter says with a laugh, "that *is* fucked up. But I never liked him either way, so it makes no difference to me."

"My point is that she changed an integral part of her humanity. Altered forever. That would be like getting the words 'I hate children' tattooed on your forehead or something."

"Yeah. I know, man. She's fucked up. But she says she was born a woman, just didn't come with the right parts."

"She's some kind of fucking aberration of nature. Like a turtle with two heads. Or the lobster boy we saw in that magazine Lana had, with the claws for hands and everything? Goddam! Let's get out of here," I say, stubbing out the joint. "I want to see if Lana is up at the mall yet."

"What is it with you and her? She's blown everybody in the fucking food court," Splinter says.

"As long as she hasn't blown you, I'm good. She's a beautiful, amazing person."

"Whatever, dude." Splinter lights a butt as we walk to the bus stop. We pass it back and forth. I hate menthol cigarettes.

I first met Lana when Trizden and I went to see the industrial/metal band Ministry. Of course, Trizden was taking a step down from his musical snobbiness in order to attend such a mainstream metal concert, but he was a good enough sport to come along, and with only five or six mentions of how lame Ministry is. They were offhanded comments though, leading me to believe that he's secretly a Ministry fan. Mainstream motherfucker.

The concert hall was all chaos, loud and people everywhere. The band came onstage with four or five guitarists playing grinding chords in unison and the whole crowd lunged forward. The noise was more brutal than it ever sounds on the albums. The singer had long black dreadlocks and his microphone stand was made of a goat skeleton.

Halfway through the set Trizden yelled in my ear that he had to take a piss. I yelled back that that reminded me that I wanted a beer. We wove our way through the crowd toward the back of the hall where a girl was leaning against a wall outside the bathrooms. She was talking to a guy who was trying to walk away. She was grabbing his jacket, pleading with him not to go. He wrenched his arm away from her. She started yelling something but I couldn't make it out because it was so fucking loud. I went to her. Tears were coursing down her cheeks. Without the slightest pause she talked to me as though we'd always known each other. I liked that. And I liked that she was crying. Not that I liked that she was in obvious mental anguish but because it was such an open display of vulnerability, frailty.

From what I could gather over the din of the concert and her own broken explanations, the guy was her boyfriend or ex-boyfriend or something significant like that. She didn't know if they were over for good or not. She hoped they weren't. God, she prayed that they weren't over because she loved him so much. She loved Corey so much. Even though she betrayed him with Ricky, his best friend, she wanted him to take her back. She used to go out with Ricky before she went out with Corey. So by screwing her boyfriend's best friend, she was sort of reconciling with her ex, even if it was only to roll around in bed for a while. But Corey wanted back what was once rightfully his alone and she was unable to give it back because she couldn't travel back in time and make it to where she never cheated on him with his best friend. She couldn't make that fact change and he couldn't live with that being the case. Her heart was torn in half and she couldn't just turn off her love. Love doesn't do that. Love doesn't just come from some kind of faucet you can turn on and off at will.

She confessed these things through interrupting sobs. I noticed that she produced far less snot than I do when I'm emotionally destroyed. I'm far less attractive than usual when I'm destitute and hate the world, but Lana was somehow more attractive than any girl I'd ever known. She was small and vulnerable and I wanted to comfort her.

I touched her cheek, pushed a tear to the side, tucked her hair behind her ear. She had the smallest, most perfect ears. She looked at me with her eyes welling. I wanted to make love to her. Badly. I *needed* to make love to her. I wanted to drown all her sorrow, suck it all into me. This was the Lana I met and fell in love with unconditionally, regardless of her penchant for food court blow jobs.

I reached down and held her hand and she told me her life. The music was so loud. Everything was in slow motion. We were underwater. We were saved. "You'll never believe," the dreadlocked man onstage was screaming over the grind of guitars.

TRANSMISSION 12:

tripping in a field full of daisies

July

I'm tripping right now. We're all tripping. After a full day of loitering and bumming change at the mall, ten or fifteen of us headed to this girl Chris's house. Her parents are out of town and her older brother is spending the night at his girlfriend's.

Lana is acting weird and distant. I can't tell if this is because she is tripping, because I am tripping, or as she claims, because she is feeding off the energy of all the others who are on LSD like we are. The Acid is really fucking good. Two tabs in and I can already tell the Acid is really fucking good.

Chris has a massive backyard, filled with trees and life. Everyone is laughing, making their way from one person to another, asking how they are doing, if they saw this or that amazing thing.

Lana is about two hundred yards out in the darkness, literally hugging a tree.

That doesn't seem cliché to me.

She is completely and utterly *earnest*. She looks like a little woodland sprite, overcome by the beauty of nature. All of us out here are woodland sprites. We are running around in the grass and breathing in the crisp air.

This one guy, Dylan, he's some kind of surfer import from California. He has captured the interests of everyone with his radical beliefs on life. He shows a few of us how good it feels to punch tree trunks, does it a couple of times, hard, brings his scraped knuckles into the light to show us the release. His knuckles already appear bruised but somehow beautiful. I decide against trying it, though. I'm very cautious and opposed to pain unless I'm mentally destitute and without hope.

I approach Lana but she's in the middle of one of her little episodes and won't make eye contact or even acknowledge my existence. She is so beautiful and abused.

My Lana, communicating with a tree. All I want is for her to understand that I understand her. She is hurting. This is why, as Splinter said so basely, "she's blown everyone in the food court." But she only did that because she wanted to give them a pleasure that she can't achieve herself. Not a physical pleasure, necessarily, but a transcendent one—the pleasure people reach only by being selfless and self-sacrificing. I find her more beautiful *because* she's blown everybody in the food court. It makes me want to be with her more. I want to take care of Lana. I want to reach out to her and have her take me in, fold me under her wing as I fold her under mine.

Lana, my beautiful Lana.

I am doomed to a lifetime of yearning. I will never know love or life the way it is meant to be lived. I will never know true fulfillment—only unquenchable desire. Why is it that every time I take Acid I have to realize these things? I can't have fun without feeling guilty for being alive—for leaving my brothers at Victor's mercy. I have abandoned those in need in order to pursue fun in a fucking field. I am not the type that loves. I am the type that fucks. I have intentionally burned myself with cigarette lighters, put the hot metal to my arm and seared in agony as my flesh lit up in heat and pressure and I could feel myself leaving this hellish place, could feel myself transcending the Garden. They know I don't really belong here with any of them. I am outside of their realm. These people, these kids here, they will go back home to their cul-de-sacs and tell their parents to fuck off and still make it to college in time for initiation to this fraternity or that sorority.

We are crowded around this television set watching cartoons, and then after that is done, even more pathetically than the last thing, we are watching two guys play fucking video games. Laughing. We are watching *somebody else* play video games.

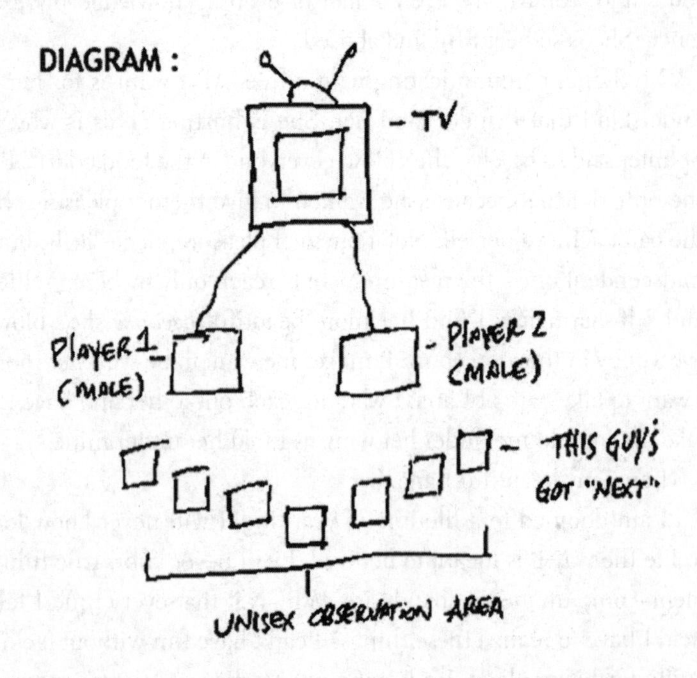

They are in control of our every thought and emotion. We passing through, merely biding our time until our lives slip th our gnarled old fingers, these self-inflicted scars disappearing in the sands with our souls because in the end we were never really here in the first place.

We were never here.

We are a blip, a mass of energy dissipated in a matter of moments, a flash in the pan, a twinkle of the eye, a prehistory lost in the passing of millennia, the minutiae of nothingness, a blink, an afterthought, a shallow stream evaporated in the first light of day. We are the misunderstood. We are the unclassified the oversimplified the target market the failing demographic. We are all already dead, the untalented, the ugly, the wasted, the underused, making way for the new. We are the bleeding. We are the profusely complaining, the overfed. We are the holes. The empty. The vacant. Carved out and hollow. Blankly staring. Echoes. Not ourselves. Not anyone.

Lana approaches me at around 3 in the morning. She is visibly tired. My eyes feel wide as plates. I ask her again if she wants to trip, because she looks tired. She says no. I tell myself I've already fucked this whole thing up with her.

But then she says she knows that I love her and she loves me, too. She tells me that this is why she's never given me a blow job. I tell her, you know, I never wanted a blow job but I probably would have taken one if you'd offered because you are so fucking beautiful and fragile.

"Did you not want to give me one because I'm ugly?" I ask.

And she says it had nothing to do with that, not at all, you are beautiful—(*I am?*)—yes, you are, and it had nothing to do with anything aside from the fact that I knew you didn't want that from me, she says. I knew you'd never approach me like that and just from that alone, that respect for me, I knew you were different.

"I was?" I say.

"You *are*," she says.

Well then why am I always so fucking broken? Why am I always shattered from the inside out, trying to hold this goddam thing together by the nails?

"Let's walk outside," she says.

We leave everyone to their video game watching. Lana takes my hand and we walk to the tree she had embraced for a good hour earlier in the night. She places my hand on it and asks me what I feel.

"Close your eyes," she says. "Tell me what you feel."

I tell her I feel a tree. She says that that's all you have to feel is a tree. Because that's all it is. It's just a tree, Luke. It's just a fucking tree. My eyes are still closed and I'm crying and realizing that she is right. All it is is a goddam tree.

She finds my lips and we kiss and then sleep under that tree and when I wake she is still there with me, my arm curled around her shoulders, her face pressed to my chest, the sun blinding me.

TRANSMISSION 13:

phone love

August

I've been talking to Lana on the phone every night and she's been telling me everything. She says that she is in love with love itself. Perhaps it's not Corey she needs after all, because she thinks her heart might finally be cutting loose from him. But at the same time, she says, he was the only one that *ever* understood her. He was the only one who listened to her. He was the only one who appreciated thunderstorms as much as she does.

"I like listening to you," I say. "I like thunderstorms."

She says she's coming to Trizden's next party to see me. My palms are sweaty with anticipation. But when she shows up at Animal Mother's apartment, she's with Corey. He's alright, I guess, but what if she's told him that I've been talking to her all this time, what if he knows that I'm *that* guy, the guy that conveniently presents himself for the hot chick when she needs a shoulder to cry on? After all, I *am that guy.* But it doesn't matter. I still yearn to be near her.

I decide I'm going to be honorable. I will go right up to Corey, shake his hand, tell him I've heard a lot about him (all good, of course), and wish the two of them the best together. And then I will go to Lana's house and sneak in her bedroom window and tell her she was right all this time. She was right about me, about life, about everything.

Corey's sitting on the floor, leaning against the back of the couch. The room is completely dark except for a shaft of blinding light blaring through the kitchen entryway. I can hear Lana's chipmunk giggle squeaking under the front door, where she's out on the porch with Splinter and Animal Mother smoking cigarettes.

"What's up, man?" I say to Corey. He is totally bombed, his eyes sliding closed. He turns toward me, slowly, and grins.

"Hey, dude," he slurs. "What's going on? Luke, right?"

"Yeah, dude! Lana told you about me?"

"Oh, yeah. She thinks you're a great guy."

"Well, I'm just trying to be there for her when she needs a shoulder—I mean, when she needs an ear."

"That's cool, dude. You got any weed?"

"I was just going to ask you that," I say, even though I wasn't just going to ask him that.

"Well, look man, my friend Tom is supposed to hook up a fat sack tomorrow. We'll stop by and get you totally zonked," Corey says.

"Sounds great."

Sitting there on Trizden's crumby carpet I realize that Corey really is a good guy. He's the kind of guy that people are drawn to.

Lana laughs her way back in the door with a cigarette and slides down beside Corey. She tries to hold his hand but he can't be bothered.

• • •

Corey shows up on a Tuesday with this lug of a guy named Tom. Tom says his band opened for Soundgarden once. Tom's a pathological liar, Corey informs me. We get stoned in Trizden's bathroom.

The next day they come by again and we smoke up again. Animal Mother gets pissed. He quit smoking weed and wants everybody else to quit too.

Tom pawns his video game system and we buy another bag of weed. I tell Corey I think the world of Lana. He says I should be careful. "She just uses people for whatever she can get off 'em and then throws 'em away," he says. "But other than that, good luck."

I call Lana on the phone every night after that, without guilt. For two weeks everything is going great, I'm plotting out the rest of my life with her and all—and then she drops the bomb.

Her mom is moving her out of state, way up to Bumfuck, Ohio, where she'll straighten up by living on her uncle's farm. No matter, I tell her, we'll talk every day, even in Ohio. I will not abandon you, I say. And I keep my word. The phone bill is obscene. Animal Mother threatens to kill me.

But then I have an idea.

I heard somewhere that car dealerships make hundreds or even thousands of long-distance calls a month and because of the great call volume they never check the long-distance log; they just pay the bill. It's almost too easy. But I'm desperate and so I call the operator one night and tell her that I need to make a long distance call and charge it to my residence (that is, the car lot, though I obviously don't tell her that), and just like that she puts me through. I talk to Lana for three or four hours a night at the expense of Henry Taylor Toyota or Big Jim Slade Ford. Every night I choose a new lot from the phone book. There are literally hundreds of car dealers in the metro Atlanta area. The plan is fucking flawless. And I do it guilt-free, too, because money should never be an obstacle to love and these greasy car dealers are loaded down with cash anyway.

Hearing Lana's voice every night is what I live for. Every moment at work I think about her perfect voice. I keep a 5" x 7" photo of her at my telemarketing phone station. Corey won't even talk to her, so now she has pretty much let him go, even though it kills her to say that, she says.

Animal Mother says she's going to mess up my head. He says he can tell these things. I tell him he's just jealous. He says that could not be further from the case. But that's what everybody says when they're jealous and don't want to be jealous.

TRANSMISSION 14:

ohio is for lovers

September

Corey's friend Tom is going with me to see Lana in Ohio. I bought this piece-of-shit 1980 Ford Fairmont for three hundred bucks and Tom has graciously volunteered to pawn his guitar to help with the gas money. He says he doesn't have anything better to do so he might as well take a trip.

"You're sure Soundgarden isn't going to need your band to open for them?"

"Fuck you, dude," Tom says.

Before we're out of Georgia the radio fritzes out. We ride in silence, which is excruciating at times and makes the miles go by in slow motion. Tom has a bag of weed, though, so at least there's that.

By the time we make it to Lana's uncle's farm eight or nine hours later, it is already dark. Lana is standing on the porch, waving and all smiles, when we get to the top of the driveway.

The house looks like it was put together by drunken narcoleptic elves. The windows are all different sizes and seem to be located randomly, with no discernible aesthetic consideration. The siding is peeling and falling apart. The porch is covered in dog shit.

"Spanky's old," Lana says in defense of the shit piles. "He doesn't like to walk down the porch steps at night."

Lana's uncle is in the kitchen. He is just as she described him. He looks like a total pervert. He has white gunk caked around the rim of his mouth and beneath that is an unkempt and graying beard. He's egregiously fat, his gut lapping over his belt buckle, and when he talks you can hear the phlegm rattling around in his throat. I find myself clearing my own throat, hoping that he will do the same. He doesn't take the hint.

Her uncle says Tom and I will be staying in the bedroom next to Lana's. There are sleeping bags on the floor, his phlegm says. I hug her hard and she says we'll talk in the morning. I sleep on top of the bag with my clothes on because who knows what could be nesting in there.

The next morning we drive around the town with Lana pointing out the so-called sights. It has to be the most boring place I've ever been. Everybody hangs out at Dairy Queen.

On the way back to her uncle's place, the car runs off the gravel road leading to the house, Dukes of Hazzard style, and we all scream as we're momentarily airborne before the car lands on some sapling trees. I realize as we scramble up the embankment that Tom and I might just be stuck in Ohio forever, because there's no way a tow truck will be able to reach the car way down there in the brush. It dawns on me that I am *happy* about the possibility of being stuck in this godforsaken place, because Lana lives here now.

But then her uncle brings his tractor down and pulls the car out with a tow chain as easily as if it were a toy. We check the fluids and find there's a small hole in the oil pan, but other than that it's good to go.

"You'll just have to keep checking the oil," Lana's uncle says, the white around his mouth clinging to itself. "School starts tomorrow, so you'll need to be getting going in the morning." He hitches up his pants under that giant belly and creaks back into the house.

That night Lana says to me, she says, "Luke . . . I just want you to know—I mean, I think you should know—that . . . that I still love Corey." I have sex with her anyway. She comes to me in the night and takes me to her room. Her body feels perfect in my hands. It makes me love her more.

"I want to be inside you like this forever," I say.

"I know," she whispers. Then she tells me that she doesn't deserve me, that Tom approached her after I was asleep the night before and she let him finger-bang her but, she assures me, "I didn't do anything to him."

"You let him finger you? *Finger* you?" My throat tightens. "Why did you let him finger you?"

"I don't know. He seemed needy."

"Needy?"

"Yeah. I don't know how else to put it. But I just wanted to tell you before he did," Lana says, her voice cracking.

"Well, you're too late," I say. "He told me this morning that you're a slut and let me smell his fingers to prove it."

"Do you think I'm a slut?" she says.

"Can we do it again?" I ask.

On the way home Tom crawls under the dash to mess with the radio wiring.

"You know, that guitar was my prized possession," he says.

"So you said."

He touches the wrong wire and shocks himself. I laugh appreciatively. He knew Lana was loose, just like Corey said, and that's why he wanted to come with me all the way to Bumfuck, Ohio. That's why he pawned his piece-of-shit, two-dollar guitar. He'd planned all along on getting some off her, too. It didn't matter that I was talking about loving her and shit like that. Fuck no. It's every goddam man for himself.

And then it is so silent in the car that I can feel myself going crazy. I can hear it, the approaching insanity. It sounds like that "Jabberwocky" poem my uncle Sonny used to tell me just to freak me out when I was a kid. The Jabberwock with his blade going snickersnack.

The miles drag by in silence. And we've smoked all the weed so there's nothing to take the edge off. Snicker. Snack. Snicker-snack.

Corey greets me with a joint at Animal Mother's the next morning.

"She fucked you over, didn't she?" he asks, more a declaration than a question.

"I don't want to talk about it."

"Let's hit this. It'll make you feel better."

I look out the front window to make sure Trizden's already gone to work. We blow the smoke into the bathroom exhaust fan.

"Dude, bitches like Lana are a fucking dime a dozen," Corey says. "They don't mean shit in the big scheme of things. They always say things to make a guy feel good and they pull the right strings, but when it comes down to it—they're only in it for themselves."

"You mean like your dickweed friend Tom?"

Corey's eyes widen, the smoke still held in his lungs. He exhales loudly. "Tom? Tom fucked her?!"

"Fingered."

"God, she is a total whore! She always told me she couldn't *stand* Tom."

"Evidently she can stand his fingers just fine."

"I'll bet Ricky was just the tip of the fucking iceberg, man. I'll bet she slept with fifteen or twenty people in the ten months I went out with her. She was always telling me she loved me and she couldn't live without me and shit but the reality is she can't live without dick. What a total fucking slut."

"I wish I could hate her," I say, seriously wishing I could hate her. Because that would be so much easier.

I hit the joint hard, angry. It chokes me.

"Damn, G, don't kill yo-sef! Shee-it," Corey says, in mock ghetto-ese. He's always pretty good at lightening the mood.

"Wait here, I've gotta go to the kitchen," I say.

Hell, yeah. The bottle of Jack, still in the freezer where I left it. I take a monster swig. It's cold and thick, smooth going down. I bring the bottle to Corey. He chugs some.

"That bitch wanted me to smoke fuckin' banana peels," I say.

"What?!" Corey tries not to laugh up his hit.

"Yeah, dude, I told her I wanted to get high, told her we had a little money to buy some weed, you know? And she comes back up the stairs with a baggy of fucking shriveled-up, black banana peels. 'I read about this in *The Anarchist Cookbook*,' she says."

"So—"

"What?"

"Did you smoke any?"

"Hell, yeah, we smoked all of 'em!"

Corey laughs uncontrollably. Like he hasn't been in the same position.

"What? We were desperate, man. I can't tell you how fucking boring it was up there. Couldn't fuck her or anything until her pervert uncle was asleep."

"So they don't get you high?"

"Banana peels? Nah. I don't know if they were cooked wrong or what. A total waste of time."

Corey hits the joint again, passes it to me. I watch him slowly exhale. The smoke moves in sleepy, languid circles until the exhaust fan catches it and then it is gone.

I call Lana a few days later. Her uncle answers and says she can't talk. She is on "phone restriction." Goddammit I need to talk to her. To tell her that she was right. God, how can this sixteen-year-old girl know so much about everything? Lana says it's because she has an old soul and my soul is brand-new. Mine is just learning to comprehend life, she says, and hers is on to the upper levels of understanding. Maybe this is why I chew my fingernails to the nubs. I'm careening blindly through this thing and hitting every possible obstacle on the way through.

The next morning I call Lana again. "Look, I know she's on phone restriction and everything, but I have to talk to her. Please. Please. It'll just take a minute."

He says she isn't home. "And she won't be home for quite a while because she's in a hospital," he intones, "a *treatment facility*, where she'll get some help and hopefully some medication. But I'll give her the message." He hangs up and I listen to the dial tone and then the machine-gun stutter of the off-hook sound for so long it becomes music.

Everybody of our age and disposition ends up in treatment at one point or another. It's a rite of passage for the suburban fucked-in-the-head set. Usually when you have a friend that disappears into the bowels of drug treatment or incarceration or military school or whatever else parents can come up with to fuck up your life, you never hear from them again—just rumors about them having sex changes or becoming born-again Christians.

This gay guy I knew from the *Rocky Horror* days named Evan was seriously the most feminine man I'd ever seen and his parents sent him away to this camp that "deprogrammed" homosexuality out of kids under eighteen. We never heard from old Evan again, but there were two primary stories regarding him. One was that he had escaped and fled to Europe and had finally become the woman he'd always said he should have been. The other slightly less triumphant yet entirely possible ending for Evan was that the brainwashing had worked and he was now a certified Bible-banger. He wore neckties, the stories went, and chose as his primary line of condemnation the practice of homosexuality. Regardless of what the truth was, though, he was dead to all of us except for the legends.

And now I'm thinking Lana's going to be in that same boat. We'll hear stories of shock treatment and her biting her tongue off and choking to death on it, being chained to a fucking slate-gray slab and screaming for hours on end until she has a brain aneurysm—all really stereotypical mental hospital stories.

Those of us that do make it back from the storied institutions tell tales of our parents ruining our lives by sending us to "Peach Ridge" and "Windswept Meadows." They could be the names of apartment complexes if you didn't know better. But we know all about them. These places are revolving doors. They drain our parents' health insurance and then turn us loose more fucked up than we were before.

I am an anomaly among most of the kids I meet, though, who count days spent in treatment like tours of duty. Institutionalization is our Vietnam. And in some way I'm ashamed of never having been shipped anywhere, a draft dodger shirking his duty, squatting in Canadian parks and bus stations until the shit blows over.

TRANSMISSION 15:

time flies when you don't care much about time

February

I'm living at Animal Mother's house again. I got kicked out of Splinter's because his transsexual aunt said I ate too much of her cold cereal. No regrets, though. It's good to move around. It's what I'm used to, the urban nomad.

Corey and I just finish smoking a joint in the bathroom when a knock comes on the front door. I'm fumbling around, frantically waving my arms back and forth, saying "Oh, shit!" and "Fuck!"

"What the hell are you doing, man?" Corey says. I remind him for the ten thousandth time that Animal Mother has been going ballistic on me for smoking pot in his apartment.

"Yeah, but why would he be knocking on the front door of his own apartment?" Corey says.

Then my paranoia hits even higher levels as I realize that nobody's supposed to be dropping by. I creep across the living room to the door, the knocks still coming. Through the peephole I can see a girl with long blonde hair walking back across the parking lot in the distorted fish-eye view, which makes me feel even more stoned. But it's a girl, so I open the door.

"Were you looking for somethi— someone?"

She turns around and walks toward me. I cringe instinctively just in case she's Federal B.I. or something.

"Is Trizden here? I'm Andie." She sticks out her hand and vigorously shakes me.

"Trizden? Oh, you mean Animal Mother! No. No, he's not here right now." She has huge green eyes.

"Are those your real eyes?" I say. She keeps looking at me.

"Do you guys want to match me on a joint?" she says.

Inside, she pours a large bag of weed out onto the table, at least an ounce. Corey rolls. I never learned how to properly construct a joint, which is a good thing because it saves me a lot of work.

"So how do you know Animal Moth— How do you know Trizden?" I ask.

"Oh, we've known each other for years now. Used to go out, I guess."

"'Used to go out'?"

"Well, I guess I'd call it that. A lot of sex was involved." She winks at me. "You guys should come over to my house sometime. I only live about a mile from here. My girlfriend and I know how to have fun." She winks at Corey, I think.

We get very, very stoned, some of the most potent weed I've ever smoked.

At some point Andie gets up to leave.

"Here's my number," she says, snatching my hand and scribbling on it. "You guys should drop by sometime. We'll have fun."

Corey and I are still on the couch watching reruns when Animal Mother gets home.

"I thought I told you not to smoke marijuana in my house anymore," Mother says.

He has become one of *them*, a non–pot smoker who refers to the drug as *marijuana*.

"We didn't smoke."

"Bullshit, man. You smoked marijuana in my house." He keeps saying it like that. *Marijuana*. "I can smell it. Do you think I'm fucking stupid?"

"Fuck this shit, dude," Corey says. "Let's get outta here."

"Yeah, you need to get out of here," Trizden says.

"I will," I say.

And then, as we walk out the front door, he says, "And don't fucking come back here unless it's to pick up your shit."

"I fucking won't."

"Good," Trizden says. I can hear a touch of sorrow in his voice. It makes me feel regret.

I turn around outside the door.

"Oh, by the way, this girl Andie came by earlier and said she wants you to call her. Can you give me directions to her crib?"

TRANSMISSION 16:

getting a girlfriend is easy

March

I officially move in with Andie on my fourth visit to her house. I'd been staying in Corey's basement but he was getting increasingly sketched about the situation, said his parents would freak if they ever found out he had a friend living in the basement. So I asked Andie point-blank.

"Can I move in here with you?"

She stared at me, expressionless.

"I'm litter-trained and I don't eat much."

She said, "Well, Luke . . . you *could*, but I don't think my boyfriend would appreciate that much."

"You have a boyfriend?"

"He drives a tractor trailer," she said. "He chews tobacco."

I got up to leave, feeling stupid.

I was at the door before she added, "Sure, you can move in."

"What about your boyfriend?"

"Oh, that? I was just kidding. Seriously, I just wanted to see what you'd say." She smiled at me, turned back to the TV.

I went outside to get my belongings. They'd been sitting in the backseat of Corey's car for the past two weeks.

I came in the back door, set a duffle bag and my box of music on the floor, tossing my weathered paperback copy of *Black Boy* on the bag.

"OK. I'm moved in."

"That's it? That's all your stuff?"

"I travel light. This is the only shit I really care about anyway."

"You're not just going to love me and leave me, are you?"

"No, he won't do that," Corey said matter-of-factly. "He's in love with my ex-girlfriend."

That night, Corey decided to go home for the first time in four days. His father's a preacher. That's probably why Corey's always conflicted about everything.

Andie and I got stoned and then I grabbed her hand, pulled her behind me into the bedroom. She looked at me, hesitating, so I kissed her, struggling to unfasten my belt with one hand. We began pulling clothes off and then we were naked, rolling around on her bed, tugging at each other in the darkness. As I was about to enter her, she stopped me with her hands on my hips and whispered something about having slept with Corey one night after I'd already passed out.

I hesitated for a half second.

"I don't care," I said. "He's my best friend."

She looked into my eyes, grabbed my ass, and plunged me inside her.

• • •

Andie and I are in her bedroom with her bitchy yet hot friend Jessica. Someone knocks on the window. We know immediately that it's Corey because he never uses the door, he always knocks on the window. His friend Hank, from West Virginia, is with him. Hank says that his boss is looking for another man to help on a hardwood flooring crew.

"What's up, dude?" Hank says.

"Would you care if I called you Henry?" I ask. "That's such a great name."

"Why would you call me Henry?"

"'Cause that's what Hank is short for, isn't it?"

"My name's not short for Henry. It says 'Hank' right on my birth certificate."

"Just straight up 'Hank,' huh? You West Virginians do everything your own way."

"Damn straight."

We pass the bowl around, pack it again. I ask Hank for the specifics about the flooring job.

"Seriously, dude, how much would he start me out at?"

"Depends. The more we put down, the more you get paid."

"When can I start?"

"Monday."

"I'm in."

"Don't think this is like anything you've known, I can tell you that. This job'll break you in half and then build you back up a *real* man."

"Shit, I'll drink you under the table right now, West Virginia."

"Yeah, but can you lift a bundle of eight-foot boards with one hand?"

"Just tell me where to meet you on Monday."

• • •

The job installing hardwood pays by the square foot. The faster we work, the more money we make. Telemarketing is for losers and rejects anyway, and now the opportunity to learn a trade has fallen into my lap. The last time someone straight up offered me a job was when Trizden said he could get me in with the "characters" clique at Six Flags, where you're in a Bugs Bunny or Marvin the Martian costume all day, getting kicked in the nuts by bratty little kids but with the occasional opportunity to feel up a hot MILF. I passed on that one. But this is different. As long as I'm willing to bust my ass, the money will roll in.

And get this:

Andie's family owns the house we live in so we pay no rent. Her grandmother is the matriarch of a large brood of boys who are partners in a plumbing, heating, and air business. Andie's dad is the oldest brother and therefore has the most control over what goes on in this giant industrial park of ten or fifteen tin buildings with giant bay doors. It stretches down most of the road, and although you'd think I did well by hooking up with this girl, she really doesn't have much of anything to do with the family. She's treated like a pariah by all of them, including, if not especially, her dad. He got her mom pregnant pretty young and they got married so Andie wouldn't be illegitimate. The marriage didn't last. Her mom was a prolific pillhead with severe mental problems, so her dad ended up with custody of Andie from the time she was a small child and then he remarried. The elder Andrew (Andie's named after him) decided the best way to get his troublesome daughter out of her stepmother's way was to let her stay in this run-down house, smack in the middle of the industrial complex, rent-free. She's lived here since she was fifteen.

But I'm not knockin' it. It's the most space I've ever had to live the way I want. I can smoke or drink or get fucked up whenever I feel like it. And I get to see my best friend all the time. Because Corey and I both live here, really, if living somewhere means you sleep and eat and take showers in the same place for a number of days in a row.

TRANSMISSION 17:

a lesson in performance art

April

Corey and I take turns fucking Andie. Well—I shouldn't really say "take turns" because it's not like I have her every second Tuesday of the month and he has her every third Thursday. We'll all three get stoned and drunk, and then one of us inevitably ends up making out with her while the other plays video games. I don't know why I'm not more jealous because I'm usually really possessive. But it feels good not to care. Andie doesn't sound like she makes any more noise with him than she does with me. Or maybe she does. I always wanted her friend Jessica anyway. Which is pathetic in its own right because Jessica can't stand me. But she's totally hot, with short blonde hair and a Volvo. She's got a serious set of tits, too, so there's that.

Jessica comes over while Andie and Corey are fucking this one day. I'm sitting in the living room, sulking. She stares at me as she walks through to the kitchen. "What's wrong with you?" she asks.

She really *is* a bitch. But I still want to bang her. No matter how much an attractive woman mistreats you there's still that part of you that would let bygones be bygones if she'd only let you give her the high hard one.

"I'm fine," I say, my voice coin-flat. She stands there looking at me for a second and then cocks her head as an especially loud cry comes out of Andie's room. I try to act like I don't hear anything, but Jessica, bitch that she is, says, "Oh, she's screwing Corey today. Must not have had what it takes last night, huh?"

"What the fuck's that supposed to mean?"

She walks down the hall to the spare bedroom and I hear the door click shut with an echo. That click alone makes me livid because it's just like Jessica to nonchalantly close a door in that way, that gentle door closing that burrows under a guy's skin. I want to run back there and grab her and fuck her until she begs for more and then walk away like it ain't a thing, let the door click shut behind *me*.

Out of Andie's room, the noises keep coming. This is where it always starts, when I need release. And no amount of weed or bourbon or Acid is going to let me out of the cage.

I get off the couch, move to the bathroom.

Jessica leans in the doorway just as I'm opening the medicine cabinet and asks if I'm going to make her wait all day.

Seriously. She says that.

I stand there looking at her. She takes my hand and pulls me into the bedroom, pushes me down on the tiny bed. She drags her hair across my face, lets her lips skim my features. I try to breathe.

"You want a drink?" I ask her.

She looks up at me from where she was kissing my stomach, her body suspended above mine, a diamond-encrusted crucifix dangling between her breasts. "Sure. Grab a couple for us."

I *run* to the kitchen and back.

"Have you ever had screwdrivers?" I ask, handing her a full glass.

She swallows, her nose crinkling. "I had a few at Georgia State when I went there a couple of years ago," she says. "Is this the first time *you've* had screwdrivers?" she mimics.

"No," I laugh, "and honestly, I can't stand the taste of pure vodka anymore because once I was at this party with this dude 8-Ball, and he bet me all the money in his wallet—twelve dollars—that I couldn't drink half a fifth of Absolut in less than two minutes. So I was trying to impress him and chugged the whole bottle."

Jessica nods. Her eyes are still fixed on me.

"Long story short, when I came to later, this girl Tera, this goth chick, she's standing there in her black dominatrix outfit and she's blowing cigarette smoke in my face. We're outside and I'm naked, Saran-wrapped to a tree."

Jessica's finished her drink, ignoring the rest of my story, my nerve-induced story, her fingers toying with my belt loops. She kisses my stomach some more and then pulls my shirt over my head, kisses me on the mouth. She is ravenous, running her fingers over the scars on my chest and then she's sucking me like it's her job and next she's climbing on top, my shoes still on and my pants around my ankles and then she's putting me inside her.

I can still hear Andie in the next room moaning and for some reason it's bothering the hell out of me. So I tell Jessica I want to change positions and we move around a bit and then I'm on her in missionary, where I like to think all my best work is done, and she is gritting her teeth and looking up at me and holding her legs open at the knees with her hands and telling me to fuck her harder and I do, goddammit I do, and she's growling, *growl*ing like a fucking animal and I can't pound her hard enough.

And even though she's doing everything I ever wanted a girl to do in bed, even though she's a hot little rich girl, even though she is hungry for more, the fact that Andie is in the other room fucking Corey is turning my insides out and I hate that this is the way it is—but it is.

I look at Jessica sprawled there, naked and heaving, and pause for a moment—Andie and Corey still echoing around the hallway—and then I stand up and shuffle out of the room, my pants around my ankles.

I stumble into the bathroom, tear open the medicine cabinet, watch my reflection shimmer and disappear around the corner as the door swings left. The mirror only covers about half the allotted area in the door because a few weeks ago we were all tripping and Corey decided to take a can of hairspray and shoot it at the mirror while we lit the vapors with a Zippo. The flames danced on top of the mirror and we could see our reflections framed by the trappings of a Miltonian hell, all blue and orange with a hint of red. The fire was magnified on the glass and our LSD-soaked eyeballs were transfixed by its dancing. Then the glass popped like a gunshot and all that was left of the mirror was a thousand shards scattered across the floor and this one crooked piece that managed to hang on to the cabinet door, the brown cardboard exposed where the rest of the glass once was.

I stare at my chest in the half-mirror shard. Still pale and clean. There are no visible scabs from the last cutting. I grit my teeth and drag the tiny blade across. The pain is more immediate than last time.

I feel release.

The burrowing mental anguish is rejected, smoothed out and soothed by this very real action. That's why they used to do it in the olden days: bloodletting to release the demons of the mind and body.

Jessica leans in the open door, wearing only a camisole and panties. She doesn't say anything, just looks at me. I cut again, feel the sting, repeat. Red lines canvass my chest and I pause for a moment to reflect, wholly experience the trouble slipping out and away, let my mind come back down to that place where it doesn't feel like everything is fucked. Jessica goes back to the bedroom. Her belt buckle jingles as she pulls her pants back on.

I make one last slash from sternum to navel, let my hand fall into the sink. Then this roll of duct tape calls to me. Who knows why it's lying here on the bathroom floor. We don't have different decorative themes in every room. We're poor and carefree. We can store our duct tape anywhere we damn well please.

I tear off a foot-long piece of tape and slap it across my mouth, wrap it around the back of my head. Then another. You really *can* use this shit for anything.

Jessica comes back to the door, pulling her hair up with a red velvet scrunchy. "You are one *fucked*-up screw-job, you know that?"

The blood drips from my chest and plinks on the vinyl floor. I continue pulling loud strips of duct tape from the roll and wrapping them around my face until only my eyes and nostrils are left exposed, and when I look in the mirror I am a bleeding *machine*, a cyborg, a robot encased in skin. I can hear my heart beating and the Cure CD in the stereo is nearing its end as I stumble to the bedroom door where the noises of fucking still emanate strongly and I imagine Corey is nearing his nut.

I open the door and there they are, naked and sweating, humping on the mattress and box spring that lie on Andie's floor in the middle of the room. Corey is behind her, both of them shadows in the dark room. I stand there looking at them, Andie glancing back at her ravager. Then I go for him, in mid-stroke, before he even has a chance to realize I'm in the room, and knock him off the bed.

Corey is shorter than I am by about five inches, but he's one of those guys who's got all kinds of natural muscle tone and weight about him, so I'm pretty sure that he can easily kick the shit out of me, especially when you consider that my pants are still around my ankles. But he doesn't. He stands up.

"What the fuck did you do, man?"

Andie pulls a sheet over her nakedness even though I've fucked her at least two or three more times than Corey.

I struggle with the duct tape covering my mouth, try to pull it off quick so it won't burn, but it still hurts like hell.

I tell Corey that I can't stand him fucking Andie anymore because I think I love her.

"You love me?"

"I don't know. I can't stand you screwing Corey anymore when I'm around, though. That's it. I'm sorry, but I just can't take it."

I'm getting teary now because this is not what is really going on at all. I can't love this woman. I'm not even that attracted to her. But she has this charisma or something that I want to have dedicated to me alone. I want her to stop being so unattached to everything around her that she doesn't even care if I'm in the next room screwing her best friend.

I mean, Andie came on to me first. She liked how I drove a stick shift. Once I gave her a ride home in Flick's car, a five-speed, and when she got out of the car she told me that my driving had gotten her really hot. She shut the door and walked into her house knowing I was sitting there watching her and stewing in my own juices, just wondering how I was supposed to take that kind of statement.

But that's how Andie is. She's always throwing out innuendo and suggestion and then acting like she's been talking about silverware or some mundane shit like that when you decide you want a piece of her for real. Standing naked in a room with two or three other people is nothing. It's telling somebody else what scares the piss out of you that makes for the real shit. But Andie is above all of that. Nothing scares her. She doesn't seem to have any specific hopes or dreams. She's just this girl I know that will give me everything, but always leaves me feeling like I never had anything to begin with.

And I haven't had this much fun since . . . well—ever. And shit like that doesn't come along too often. Shit like that has got to be explored.

I take a step backward into the living room and shut the door (click), pleased with the reaction my little piece of performance art has garnered.

See, I hadn't realized until recently that doing shit most everyone else would consider "crazy" can be seen by other people as art. Saw it on cable.

TRANSMISSION 18:

floors for the affluent

July

Johnny, my boss, is a total dick and more high-strung than a paranoid schizophrenic in a wax museum. On the brighter side, though, I now know how to rack out a floor and nail it down *fast*. Hank has taught me all of this. He's from West Virginia and all, but he's not as ignorant as you'd think. He quietly absorbs Johnny's almost daily fits, all the while slowly stockpiling tools so that one day he can start his own flooring company. He's already promised to take me with him when that happens—hopefully sooner than later. I mean, because this guy Johnny—*fuck*.

One day last week he showed up at the job site right after lunch and we were thinking, there's no way he can bitch about anything today. We had almost two hundred feet nailed down and another four hundred aside from that racked out. But as soon as Johnny walked in the door he threw his thermos across the room, acted like we just gangbanged his wife. He was pissed because we had tracked mud in the half-built house. A floor man always keeps his shoes clean, Johnny said. Look at my shoes, he said, do you see any mud on them? I told him he didn't have to walk three hundred feet through the mud to plug in the goddam extension cords at the power pole.

"I don't give a shit," Johnny said.

It really makes no sense that we have this same goddam argument all the time. It's the contractors who decide which subs do what and in what order. *They* are the ones to blame. They don't pour the concrete driveway until the house is almost finished. It's a logic that defies description because if it rains for twenty days straight and you have to walk from the road all the way up the sludgy fucking driveway twenty times to get the tools in the house, that's what you have to do. They don't put the driveway down until last because they're afraid it'll get oil spots on it. And God forbid the buyers of a new home have to have a driveway with a little goddam character. They want to believe that petal-slippered elves put the house together.

"And while we're in a complaining mood," I said to Johnny on that day last week, "how about you coming around on the breaks?"

"Breaks? What the hell are you talking about?" Johnny screeched in his high-pitched, psychotic Mr. Rogers Southern twang. Hank, ever dutiful, got dutifully back to work.

"I'm talking about taking at least two ten-minute breaks during the day," I said. "To catch our breath and boost employee morale."

Johnny turned his back to me and walked into the next room. I followed him.

"It's fuckin' hard putting down floor in eighty-five-, ninety-degree heat all day without a break."

"If you want a break, work at McDonald's," he said. He picked up a stapler and began nailing, the noise of which effectively ended the conversation, if it can even be called that. Regardless of how hard you try to please him or at the very least make it impossible for him to bitch, he always zeroes in on something. You just want to find a mute button and turn him off. Hank and I have laughed at that scenario over a lunchtime joint on more than one occasion, and we've decided that it would be worth significant money to watch Johnny's frantic gesturing, the veins popping out of his male pattern baldness head, with no sound coming out of his mouth.

It isn't all bad, though. Sometimes, on good days, Johnny will be out running errands and we'll have the whole room racked out, the wood just lying there like a puzzle, waiting for us to nail it in place. And then we're off, flying across the floor with our staplers gliding over the boards, our mallets swinging faster than John Henry, the sweat rolling, our muscles all aflame and struggling, but invigorated and somehow more alive.

We hold speed competitions to make the work less grueling, see who can nail up the most floor in the least amount of time. It takes our minds off of the fact that we're slowly ruining our bodies, our backs and our knees, so that somebody with more money can live comfortably. It's that whole Machine of Capitalism Oiled by the Blood of the Workers thing.

I tell Hank this but he shrugs it off.

"It's either this or the mines," he says. "At least here I can breathe easier. In the mines it's always pitch-black and freezing cold, even in the middle of July. You go in before the sun comes up, leave after it's down."

"Well," I say, "we deserve better. This is what they're always going to hand us if we are willing to accept it."

"Who is *they*?"

"I'm talking about The Man, dude. Obviously. The people in control are always going to try to maintain that control at any cost. Which means that your people, the people of Appalachia, have been getting fucked in the ass without even the common courtesy of a reach-around for years. There've been *billions* of dollars made on coal over the last century, and yet the people that have existed—or rather subsisted—on that land for years are still living in the fucking third world. No teeth. No education. All that."

"I'm just trying to make a living," Hank says.

"Yeah, and you're lucky you got out of the mines while you still had some lung left that isn't already blackened."

As if on cue we both go into a blistering rendition of Metallica's "Blackened," Hank holding up his hand in the time-honored devil's sign, with its two evil fingers.

"It's just like in Bosnia," I continue after our musical interlude. "These goddam talking heads in their ivory fucking towers aren't going to do anything to help those people being slaughtered." I'm a lot more educated about tyranny and things of that nature now. We listen to NPR every morning and afternoon, to and from the job.

"What does that have to do with the mines?" Hank asks.

"What does *what* have to do with the mines? On both counts we're talking about people being fucked over simply because they don't have the might to stand up to the oppressors that come along and try to use them for their own ends. I get so tired of this shit. Don't you?"

"I'm keeping my own head above water, man."

"Jesus, Hank, that's exactly what they want you to do. They want all of us to be so downtrodden that we have no choice *but* to be completely distracted by our bullshit lot in life."

"We've gotta get some more of this floor down, man. Johnny's gonna go off if he sees how little we've done."

"Fuck it, I give up."

"Do you wanna take the front end of the room or the back end?" Hank says.

TRANSMISSION 19:

appearances deceive

November

I smoke joints now like they're cigarettes. I have my own car. I don't live with my parents. I don't have to impress anybody. Some days, though, I can't muster the energy to take a shit.

So when I wake up this one particular morning, I decide that I am going to do something positive this week. I don't know what it is yet. I've been pretty much busting ass at work and then coming home and getting as fucked up as possible before doing it all over again the next day. But that's about to change. This is the beginning of the new me. I am going to get out there, goddammit, and I am going to make my life exciting and possibly even worthwhile.

This is the crap I'm telling Hank while we rack out the latest floor.

Then Hank says, "I have cancer."

I don't know how to respond. He's only twenty-one years old.

"Maybe you should try eating some fucking greens once in a

while," I offer. Hank refuses to eat anything remotely resembling a vegetable. He claims that all he's eaten since he was a kid is beef and pork products with a side of something potato-based.

Oh, and corn. He'll eat corn once in a while. But nothing green.

"And maybe you should stop smoking those cigars, too. Or at least cut back," I say. Hank, being from West Virginia and all—those people just don't hold themselves up to normal standards. He never tries to look cool or do shit that other people would think is cool. He doesn't go to clubs, and only demonstrates affinity for about five hard-core metal bands and Johnny Cash. His idea of the perfect day is cooking meat on a grill followed by chopping down saplings with a machete. Or seeing who can lift a two-hundred-pound rock and carry it the farthest. He always beats everybody at that event. Nobody can even come close to matching his strength. He prides himself on it. That is the law of the Appalachian Mountains. The strong survive, the weak are decimated and left to die without honor. In this way, he has already conquered everyone he left behind in West Virginia. He always wanted to be a woodworker, always had a love for the craft of turning a tree into a piece of man-made beauty, sculpted and formed into something more than what it used to be in the wild. We tread on this wood every day as we transform it into floors. Hank has conquered the trees. Hank has risen above. And though he'll probably never admit it, he has saved himself from the definitive doom of the mines. All that comes after is cake. Cancer or not, he's busting ass as hard as ever, strong-armed and ox-tough, and I just can't swallow it, that even this very minute he's being ravaged from the inside. There are no signs. He could still stomp the life out of me without thinking twice about it. All six feet, 220 pounds of him.

The only outward physical indication that something might be going awry with his body is that he has three semicircular bald spots at random points on his head. He says these have appeared because of the stress he is under. That's what the doctors say anyway. He says he feels no stress.

"It's just another steel-cage match, man," Hank yells across the room to me over the buzz of the screaming saws.

"What is?" I yell back.

"This fucking cancer, man. A steel-cage match between me and the cancer. Only one can win."

"How do you plan to win?"

"How can it beat me? I sit in fire for recreation. I sit in *fucking* fire."

There was this guy on the news about a month ago. I think he was a soldier. They kept showing the footage over and over. You could tell he was a soldier because, although his torso and head were completely uncovered, naked, he was wearing these desert camouflage pants. He was in perfect physical condition, big as a wrestler. Muscular. Hair close-cut. He was being dragged through the dirt streets. There were beanpole-skinny black people all around him, spitting on him and kicking him, and he made no move to stop them.

His eyes were closed. His arms were above his head, making rivulets in the dust as they dragged him along by his feet.

And there wasn't a mark on him. There was nothing visibly wrong with him.

He was being dragged along and stomped on, his arms splayed lifeless.

He didn't have a mark on him.

Their feet branded him. They were spitting.

He was dead.

They showed these images again and again, more than a minute of footage, and every time it replayed I thought that this time the soldier would get up and grab some of them, ten at a time, grab them and strangle the life out of them.

His naked arms made rivulets.

He was naked.

He was dead.

There wasn't a mark on him.

TRANSMISSION 20:

making crack is *easy*

February

Mom and Victor allow Jonas to spend the night, seeing as it's my birthday and all. He's been drinking every weekend with his skater friends from school and he knows how to hit a joint like a pro, too. Smokes cigarettes, the whole thing.

First to show up for my little birthday soiree is this girl Jenny, who I knew back in high school. She says she goes by Jenn*ifer* now. She used to date this asshole who couldn't stand any of the performing arts people. He was always calling us fags. So it was a surprise when I ran into her last week and she was clearly flirting with me. She gave me her number and kept touching my arm and everything. It was while I was birthday shopping for Andie. I told Jenny that, too, that I was shopping for my *girlfriend*, but like my uncle Sonny says, some women want you more than ever if they know you're already tied down. That's when they want you the most. Women *want* to steal a guy from his girlfriend. They see it as a challenge.

And now here's Jenny—Jenn*ifer*—at the door. I had to call her. She was too intriguing to not call.

She hands me a gift bag at the door, puts her hand behind my head, grabs a handful of dreads, kisses me on the cheek, dragging her bottom lip across my mouth. I feel myself stiffen. Andie comes out of the bedroom and I introduce them. Andie looks annoyed.

A half hour later, after Jonas and Corey, Splinter and everybody else have shown up, even Animal Mother (despite the rampant ingestion of intoxicants sure to take place), Shayla knocks on the door.

Shayla—I *always* wanted to bang her. She went to Peckerbrook High, too, but I never spoke three words to her then. She probably would have ignored me even if I had. And now she's sitting in my living room.

"I told her about the party," Trizden says, winking. Maybe he hasn't completely lost his coolness after all.

Shayla slides up beside me as I'm sipping a frosty beverage and whispers in my ear. "My birthday present to you is an *orgasm*." She actually says that.

I turn and look at her. She's all sultry and shit and my mind is racing through all manner of possible ways that this thing could actually happen. And every possibility ends with Andie kicking me in the nuts.

I look her in the eyes. She has the greatest eyes. "I'd love to. God, Shayla, I'd love that more than anything. But this is actually, you know, my girlfriend's house and she probably wouldn't appreciate that much." I try to make it perfectly crystal fucking clear: I want to have sex with her, for hours on end, but . . . I nod over at Andie in the kitchen.

"That's too bad," Shayla whispers. Winks. Licks her lips before moving across the room and sitting directly in front of me, her legs crossed, her panties visible beneath her short skirt, her hand on one knee.

The rest of the night I try to soothe my epic sexual frustration by drinking heavily, which works to some degree. But then Shayla starts making out with my brother, which culminates in her fucking him in my room, on my bed.

Andie's happy, though. A potential Luke suitor has been taken out of the equation.

It's around this time, as Jonas is getting laid in my room, on my bed, when *Jennifer* says she can get us some coke. She says her dad deals it.

Andie loves cocaine. She says she used to do it all the time before I moved in.

I give Jennifer a ride home, which ends up taking more than two hours. Before we pull into her driveway she's blowing me. I am a horrible person.

I get an eight-ball from her old man for a song.

Andie is passed out in the bedroom when I finally get home. Beneath her, a pen still clenched between her fingers, is a notepad that reads:

Dear Fuckhead,

Fuck you. I can't believe you left me for that little tramp. If I was any stupider I'd stay with your retarded ass. Leave me the fuck alone when you get back here and let's get back to me being the bitch you know and love to hate.

FUCK YOU!!!!

I put the pad down and a wave of panic crashes over me. She could just toss me aside without a second thought and that would be it. I'd have to move back in with my parents, because Animal Mother won't touch me now that he's on this anti-drug kick.

Back to the car again, my fourth or fifth wind kicking in by this point. I drive to the gas station down the street, the one with the $3 roses. I buy her two of them with some crumpled dollar bills and change from the floorboard, sneak back into the bedroom where the nearly inaudible clock radio is playing that Rolling Stones song "Angie." I wake Andie by tickling her cheeks with the roses and singing the song in a whisper, except putting her name in place of the girl in the song. She looks at me half asleep, one of her contacts sliding down her face.

I ask myself if this could possibly be worth it, and then I think about all the other impossible shit that is the alternative to living here and give her a hug.

"You save me from everything," I whisper. "You make *possibility*."

She stares at me with zero expression. I can't tell if she's going to throttle me or kiss me.

"Will you be my girlfriend?" I say.

She hugs me back. Squeezes tighter.

Not a week later Jennifer's dad shows up at our house holding a knapsack. He asks if we'd like to do some coke with him. He's like forty-eight and he gives off the sketchiest vibes. But then he pulls out a Ziploc baggie *filled* with cocaine. He asks for a dinner plate and dumps all that coke onto the plate. It is a *pile* of cocaine, I'm talking about a fucking *Scarface*-sized mound of cocaine—a mashed potato mountain in *Close Encounters of the Third Fucking Kind*, this-means-something-sized mound of cocaine.

Jennifer's dad cuts out three huge rails. We snort them and then he cuts out some more and we snort those, too. Then he asks if we want to freebase the shit with him. Andie and I don't know what this means but we're like, sure, we'll freebase it. We don't give a fuck how he wants to do it, we'll take the ride. Because despite all the jabbering away that we're doing, cocaine-inspired nonsense, there is always this little piece of our brains saying *more.* This is the most annoying thing about doing cocaine. I can't just fucking enjoy it because as soon as I get a good amount up my nose there are only four or five minutes where I actually feel really good. My stomach has butterflies in it, my head's in the clouds. But after those initial few minutes pass, I can't think about anything else but *more.* I have to have more. And fucking Jennifer's dad is taking fucking forever to prepare the freebase.

He takes a tablespoon full of coke, sprinkles in some baking soda, and boils it in a pot on the stove. That takes all the impurities out of the cocaine, he says, leaving only a small rock of pure narcotic, which floats to the top. He takes this rock, about the diameter of a dime, breaks it into pieces and hands us each a glass tube with pieces of steel wool shoved into one end.

We watch him to see what to do next.

He puts his little rock in the tube and lights the bottom of the glass beneath it. There is a loud crackling sound as the coke is melted and turned into a gas and then he sucks in really hard and holds it for a minute, then blows out a puff of smoke that smells like the smell in my head after these hours of railing cocaine.

I hit the pipe and feel the helium smoke enter my lungs. It is incredibly powerful, instantly removing the teeth-grinding anxiety, the need for more. And then, when I let the smoke out, feel my lungs constrict, I am in heaven. I am fucking flying. This is the most incredible shit ever. It's like a dream. I have never felt more alive or more unstoppable. I feel like I could run a goddam marathon or kick the biggest motherfucker's ass, save a baby from a burning building, catch a stray car by the bumper before it goes flying off the end of an unfinished bridge.

"You like sucking that glass dick?" Jennifer's dad asks Andie.

"Fuck yeah," she says.

Are they flirting? I don't care. I need more.

She is looking at him expectantly. He is in command of the dinner plate.

Andie doesn't acknowledge me now. She doesn't take her eyes off the plate. She needs more. And there is still more than half the original amount left. I get up, pace the room while Jennifer's dad makes more crack. I look at the clock six or ten times. It's 11 p.m. This could go on for hours. We could be here until morning. And we are.

The sun comes up, loud beams of light pounding through the living room window. Andie is noticeably drained. There is soot on her fingers and on her face, on the tip of her nose. I'm covered in it, too. There is very little cocaine left. Jennifer's dad is finishing the preparation of the last of it. I have chain-smoked three packs of cigarettes in twelve hours. I have moved from the couch maybe six times, and then only to piss or pour more alcohol, which only takes the edge off slightly and doesn't render any of us drunk. We haven't eaten a thing since yesterday afternoon.

But at least there's this last hit. I just need one more and then I'll worry about eating and everything else. Jennifer's dad, dickhead that he is, has been divvying more and more out to himself and Andie, and I've been thinking about kicking his fucking ass but that's not even a possibility now. My lungs hurt. I am so tired.

After the last hit, which wears off in less than a minute, I'm ground up and hating everything. Jennifer's dad takes a taxi home, has Andie walk him to the door. He's probably telling her that his daughter blew me in the car on my birthday and now they're setting up a time to meet and do more coke together and fuck each other.

It doesn't matter. Everything is shit anyway.

I gobble six aspirin. Andie comes in the room. She is crying, saying that she feels really bad. I tell her I do, too. We try to lie down, sleep it off, but our bodies aren't in agreement. We are forced to remain awake. We have to live out the affliction. And yet, even while our heads are throbbing and our limbs are aching, we both know that if someone offered us more tomorrow, we'd do it in a heartbeat.

"Let's promise each other we'll never do this shit again," I say.

"OK," Andie says. And then she's crying again. "I feel like I'm dying," she says.

"Me too," I say.

We lie on her bed and lie there and lie there. Eventually sleep comes. We don't wake up until two days later and I have to go to work.

When I get home there is only a note on the coffee table and the cat purring on my lap as I read it.

Andie's gone with Jennifer's dad. He "needed" her to come with him to pick up some more blow.

She is gone all night, though she does call at around 2 a.m. and tells me that she is scared, that Jennifer's dad has taken her somewhere south of the city and won't bring her back until he's done with his business. She is taking small breaths. I know she's coked up.

"Are you fucking him?"

"I have to go," she whispers. "I'm afraid of what he'll do if he catches me on the phone."

She gets home around 5 a.m., her eyes big as saucers. I think about asking her if she's fucked him, but can see she's in the throes of withdrawal and decide it doesn't matter.

I pretend I'm asleep when she finally comes to bed.

She clings to me.

She's still got black soot all on her nose, lying there with her clothes on. I look at the wall for the next two hours, and then it's time to get up for work.

TRANSMISSION 21:

strangers passing

March

I'm seeing Richard—my bio-dad—this week for only the second time ever. I'd never actually seen his face until I was in ninth grade because after they split up, my mother had thrown away every picture, discarded every remnant of his existence. Regardless of his mystique, despite the fact that he was in every way a phantom, I still maintained fantasies that he was a fighter pilot or a knight, somebody who would one day come roaring up in a cloud of dust and lower his mighty redheaded vengeance on Victor.

Black-haired, black-hearted Victor resents my and Jonas' red hair, perhaps more than anything else about us. He's always referring to us as my mother's "little golden-haired boys." Our hair is a constant testament. It clangs around in Victor's head, rings the story of my mother's previous attachments to the world.

I came out of my room that day when I was fifteen and there he was, my *real* father, kneeling on the hardwood in the foyer with my little brother. Jonas looked up at me and grinned as big as I'd ever seen him grin. And even though I had never seen this man before in my life, I knew it was him. His hair was red, just like ours. And, like ours, it was curled in thick tangles. I'd been holding out hope that Richard was like McMurphy from Kesey's *One Flew Over the Cuckoo's Nest*: fiery-haired, full of life, a guy that stuck it to The Man. But aside from hair color, the man in the foyer couldn't have been further from McMurphy. Despite his height, 6'3" or 6'4", his presence seemed somehow diminutive. He was barely there. I could feel his bones beneath his shirt as we hugged. My dreams of one day growing out of this body and into a Charles Atlas type were crushed like a ninety-eight-pound weakling at the beach. That day realities were permanently altered. The father I had imagined would be ready to raise his children. Ready to save the day. I knew as soon as I saw him that this guy couldn't save shit. He had the look of someone worn down long ago, a ghost of something real.

Jonas was only about thirteen then, and he was a lot more willing to let bygones be than I was. Part of me wanted to punch dear old dad in the face. Who the hell was he, after all? I was only just meeting him for the first time, the man who was responsible for half my gene pool. Beyond that, it was good to finally know what the old man looked like, I guess. Everybody said I favored him, but I didn't see it.

We zipped around Atlanta on the MARTA train, just the three of us. We ate pizza and ice cream and rode a glass elevator up the side of a building. I kept catching Jonas looking at him out of the corner of my eye. We could have looked at him all day.

We traded *Saturday Night Live* anecdotes. "Remember the one when . . ." type stuff. He laughed like I did, at the same parts, and

I wanted to love him just for that reason alone. But I couldn't. He'd been gone for too long.

And now he is back again.

We're meeting him at the airport. Jonas and Andie are with me when he comes out of the gate. His hair is all grown out and frizzy. He looks just like he did in that picture he gave us the first time we met, the one where he's at the tennis court before Jonas was born. He looks more tired now though.

He hugs Jonas and me, compliments me on the dreads. I can tell he's trying to relate and it annoys me. *See, even our hair is similar!* When we get to the car he asks if we know where to pick up a bag of "grass." Jonas pulls one from his pocket. We toke up going down the highway.

We spend the next four days at Andie's smoking a lot of weed and laughing at dumb shit. When we turn in for the night I get all stoned and introspective, in light of the current situation. A guy travels nine hundred miles to see his estranged sons. They spend the whole time smoking up. It makes no fucking sense. Father is reunited with children after years of separation. They get high together. I don't know. It's anticlimactic. Rick is turning into just another guy in the Rolodex. He no longer possesses the aura that the *idea* of him held before we actually met. He doesn't elicit any kind of real sentimentality out of me. He hangs out, smokes weed, enjoys a few drinks now and then, laughs about stuff, always uses a phone card when making long-distance calls, reenacts dialogue from old *Saturday Night Live* episodes, eats little, complains less, doesn't take sides in petty arguments, doesn't discriminate against minorities, remains politically left wing, laughs about stuff, tells of famous rock legends he's seen in concert (The Doors, Bob Dylan [three times], Led Zeppelin, Janis Joplin), never pees on the seat, stays clean shaven, cleans up after himself in the kitchen, takes pictures with a Polaroid camera he bought just for this occasion, always puts the toilet seat down, works in a record store back home in Philadelphia, never asks to borrow money, always pays his way when we stop for a burger, pays for me and Jonas to see a live band, argues (with spirit) over the top five bands and movies and TV shows of all time, laughs about stuff, smiles a lot, carries around a small backpack, gives no indication of mental aberration or abnormality, has never remarried since leaving our mother twenty years ago (though still lives with the same woman he left our mother for), doesn't understand why kids these days are so promiscuous because even in the hippie heyday of free love there weren't this many STDs and unplanned pregnancies, gives no indication of ever having been evil, presents no sign of ever having hated his children, presents no obstacle to probing questions regarding the past, posts no objection to drunken epithets hurled his way, offers no defense for past actions, stays upbeat, calls when he says he will, embraces warmly, laughs contagiously—and yet . . . as he waves from the airport hallway and then boards the plane, I know I don't know him.

Jonas and I stand there until he's out of sight, then head back to the parking lot before the plane takes off. Neither of us says anything. I turn up the stereo.

This is nothing.

This is what it feels to be in limbo.

And here is the final proof, this riding down a nondescript highway, listening to cheesy shit on the radio and crying about it. I look over at Jonas from the corner of my eye because God knows I don't want him to see me crying, and his head is turned to the passing traffic, and as we're flying past a semi I can, just for a moment, see his face reflected in the window and there are tears streaming down his cheeks.

The buildings flip past like shuffling cards.

TRANSMISSION 22:

passages

April

We're tripping—Andie, Corey, and me. It's a rare *day-trip*, which comes with its own set of virtues.

We've just gotten back from the gas station, where it was unanimously voted that I'd be the one to go to the window to ask the attendant for a pack of gum, Wrigley's Spearmint, the Plen-T-Pack with the seventeen sticks. There's nothing better than gum when you're tripping.

I get up to the window and the lady says, "Can I help you?"

Only then do I fully realize the magnitude of the task before me. I'll never be able to get all the information out: "Wrigley's Spearmint Plen-T-Pack, please."

So I'm just standing there and trying not to laugh and she's looking at me like I'm crazy and I can feel my eyes getting wider and

I can see the individual dust particles settling on the lenses, the air drying them out, tears beginning to form because I can't even bring myself to blink—

She asks me if I want something or am I just going to stand there. So I say, as concisely as possible, "Gum."

"What kind?" she asks.

"Gum," I say again.

She looks at me for a minute, sizes up the situation, decides she'll make it easy on us both, grabs a pack of Wrigley's Spearmint, of all things, and holds it up to the window. I nod my head. It isn't the big pack, but I'm excited because she randomly (intuitively?) reached for the kind we wanted.

We're all loudly, happily chewing away by the time we get back to the house. Andie suggests we watch the Nirvana *Unplugged* video that Corey taped a few days earlier off of MTV. He turns on the tube and is about to pop the tape into the VCR but Nirvana *Unplugged* is already playing on MTV.

"What a crazy coincidence," Andie says.

As they go to commercial, one of the talking heads interrupts and solemnly says that if you haven't heard yet, Kurt Cobain has been found shot dead in his Seattle home. There is video of the electrician who happened upon Kurt's body and saw his suicide note lying in a flowerpot filled only with dirt, the pen stabbed through the paper.

That's it for the news, they say. We'll be back with any updates as soon as we get them, they say. Then *Unplugged* comes on again. We're sitting there on the couch. The name of the song they're playing now is "The Man Who Sold the World."

I run out onto the back porch and let go. I can't stop crying. He was the belligerent front for all of our insecurities.

Andie comes up behind me, puts her arms around my waist and doesn't say anything. I am truly grateful for her at that moment, maybe for the first time ever.

We watch the constant MTV briefings for hours, the inevitable retrospectives, the professional analyses, the promptings to call this number if you feel like doing something to yourself because you are so very upset by this news. Then we get in the car, tripping and everything, and drive far south, into the country. The trees flicker in the breeze, the sun is warm.

It doesn't seem like this day should be any worse than any other. It's beautiful, really. Maybe that's the Acid. But what's missing is not readily apparent.

Andie holds my hand. Corey starts crying. The road sounds comforting under the wheels, the solidity of tires and speed.

When we get home the answering machine light is blinking two messages. The first message is from Andie's dad saying we need to pay the electric bill or he's going to let them turn it off next time they call asking for the money. The second message is Trizden. He's saying that Kurt Cobain *blew his fucking brains out.* He sounds angry. He can't ever let himself be sad. He can't ever be consumed.

"Looks like I need to find myself a new hero," he concludes. As though by saying that he can undo all of this.

We play Nirvana all the time for the next two weeks straight, through all the vigils and the readings of his suicide note. Fourteen- and fifteen-year-olds are cutting themselves, scratching his name onto their arms with razor blades. It is in the midst of this when Andie announces that she hasn't had a period in weeks.

We go to Eckerd and I gank a pregnancy test. As we're waiting in the bathroom the allotted ten minutes, Andie sitting on the toilet, me leaning in the doorway, I already know what it's going to say. It has to be like this. She is going to be pregnant. She is going to be pregnant and we're going to be fucked because everything is upside down. The signs are all so fucking obvious. Nothing was ever going to be OK. Nothing ever was.

One baby says to another, hey I'm lucky I met you
I travel through a tube and end up in your infection

Andie holds the test stick up to the light.

"I'm pregnant," she says, like she's reading a newspaper.

TRANSMISSION 23:

scratch marks

May

I get home from work exhausted, covered in heat rash and filled with anxiety. Every passing day, every passing minute, every second, there is a child growing larger and more incomprehensible inside Andie's belly.

Johnny wasn't too bad today at the job, seemed downright jolly by comparison to his typical self. And still, a child grows in Andie's belly.

This is never far from my mind.

Is there a difference between suffocating and smothering?

Andie sits around getting lazier and more psychotic. She's had employment a couple of times in the past two months, but her initiative always ends hours after she starts the job with her calling and begging me to come get her. "I can't do this," she'll say, her voice tight. "I can't be around these people. I feel like

I'm going crazy." The last time this happened she called from the side of the road more than seven miles from where I'd dropped her off for a telemarketing gig. She had no recollection of how she'd gotten there.

Something has to change.

I tell Andie that I will help her pay for an abortion, that I will take care of it within the next couple of weeks. She agrees to the plan.

We call to schedule the appointment. I hand her the receiver when they answer the phone at the clinic.

I tell her that I'm moving back home with my parents and taking Sativa the cat with me. *I'm moving back in with my parents,* if that's any indication of how bad things have gotten. Because she's always sleeping when I get home from work. She sleeps all day and then stays up smoking weed and watching TV long after I go to bed and I've pretty much gotten sick of having to clean the house and make my own dinner while being the only one bringing in any money.

I went to Trizden the Animal Mother first, of course, but he wouldn't have any part in helping me. He doesn't want to get involved again.

The last thing we do before I leave is divide up the socks. We always wash our socks together and then throw them into a drawer and wear them indiscriminately until they're all dirty again.

We dump out the basket on the coffee table and take turns picking.

"Is this really necessary?" Andie says.

"It is if you want any of the socks."

"Don't you care about me anymore?"

"Of course I care about you. What's that have to do with the socks?"

"I don't want you to leave."

"It will be better when I leave. Then we won't always be up each other's ass and wanting to kill each other."

She starts to cry again. "It just feels like this is the end," she says.

"Why does it feel like the end?" I try to sound compassionate, human.

"Because you're taking half the socks."

We look at each other for a moment and then we're both laughing through tears. I can't help it. I'm crying, too. I pull her close to me.

"If you want I'll just buy some new ones," I offer.

"No. Just promise you'll always bring our socks back together."

"I promise."

Living back home is not as bad as I thought it would be. Victor leaves me alone, for the most part. He actually had a job for a while there, painting for a large contracting company. But then he fell off of a forty-foot scaffold into an empty swimming pool and fucked his legs up. Now he's waiting for the insurance settlement to come through, the one that'll make him rich beyond his wildest dreams. And even if he's still not working for his family, at least he had to physically fuck his body up for the free money that's about to come their way. That gives me slight consolation.

Victor's a lot happier now than I ever remember him. He knows it's only a matter of time before he is compensated for his injuries. He stares at TV most of the day in the front room and sometimes I go sit in there with him, watch the news. There has been all kinds of coverage about some new occurrence of genocide in Africa. The footage shows black people chasing after and killing other black people, including women and children. They have no guns. It is all done with axes and machetes. The reporter says that the estimated death toll is 800,000 in two months.

"Fucking stupid niggers," Victor says. "They kill themselves if you let 'em."

"Why doesn't anybody stop them from doing this shit?" I say to nobody in particular.

"Fuck 'em," Victor says.

A man is being interviewed with an interpreter. He says he and two of his children barely escaped with their lives, that his wife and five other children were all murdered. He says a man who was one of the town leaders was married to a woman who was part of the targeted minority ethnic group. The leader, in order to set an example for all the others, brought his wife and children out one by one and decapitated them, each in turn, with a machete.

"I knew then we had to flee," the man says. "But it was too late. By the time I got back to my home, they were all dead. Only the children I had with me, my two eldest sons and I, managed to escape."

He does not cry as he says this. He has probably told the story a thousand times now, has probably told it so many times it almost seems like it hasn't actually happened to him, like he is simply recounting a terrible dream.

He brushes a fly from his forehead.

It's dark when I arrive. I told Andie I'd stay with her the night before the procedure.

"I'm nervous," she says.

"I am too, but this is for the best."

"I know." We're both whispering.

"I mean, we're just kids ourselves. We can't be responsible for another human being. You know?"

"I know."

I'm stroking her hair in the dim Christmas lights of our—*her*—room.

"If we had a baby now it would ruin our lives. We wouldn't be able to do anything. We'd be stuck doing bullshit work, living in run-down neighborhoods, becoming fat and worthless. And how can we offer a child anything when we haven't got anything ourselves, right?"

"You're right."

"Why do you seem so upset, then?"

"I don't know." She leans on her elbow facing me. "I'm just scared. I don't know if it's going to hurt. Or hurt the baby."

"It won't hurt it. The doctor said you're only five or six weeks along. He said it's only the size of a nickel or a quarter. I'm sure it won't be able to feel anything. It won't even know it ever existed."

"Yeah. But *I* will." She shakes her head, slumps back down on the bed, rolls over to face the wall.

"It's going to be OK." I rub her arm.

"Do you love me?" she asks, trying to choke back sobs.

"Yes, I do. And I'll be with you through this whole thing." She pulls my hand over her face. Her tears are hot and wet on my palm and fingers.

We drive past the gray-brick clinic once before I turn around and go back down the alley to the parking lot behind the building. I am surprised to see that there are no protestors outside. My biggest fear about this whole thing has been that there would be all kinds of crazy-ass religious zealots wielding picket signs and spitting at us, maybe even a nutcase with a shotgun. But there's not another human being in sight. Must be the political off-season.

"Are you sure it's open?" Andie asks as we climb the stairs to the entrance. I pull on the door and it swings wide. The inside is clean, with a black and white tile floor, but it has the same kind of gray pallor hanging over it that the outside of the building emits. Andie squeezes my hand.

A nurse behind the desk leads us back to a room furnished only by a metal chair with padding on the seat, a table with stirrups, and an odd contraption in the corner that looks like a miniature washing machine.

The nurse looks only at Andie as she speaks.

"I hope you had a chance to read over the pamphlet, but in case you didn't, I will quickly go over the procedure you are about to have. If you have any questions, I'll be glad to answer them then, OK?"

Andie starts to say something but it gets tangled in her mouth. She clears her throat and tries again. "OK," she whispers.

"The procedure you are about to have is called *vacuum aspiration.*"

She points to the machine in the corner and Andie sits down, still squeezing my hand.

"With this machine, the doctor will quickly, in five to ten minutes, empty your uterus. But first I will need you to get up on this table—"

Andie stands up to get on the table.

"Not yet, darling, just let me finish telling you what is going to happen with the procedure and then you can get up there." The nurse smiles at her with a gentle tilt of the head and continues talking.

"I'll need you to get up on this table and let me inject your cervix with a numbing agent. This numbing agent will allow us to insert a plastic . . ."

I look down at Andie as the nurse performs her speech and I can see that she is closing down now, I can see it in her eyes. She is ready to go through with this. She is closing everything out, shutting down emotionally and in every other way. She will do what they tell her to do.

". . . It creates suction to remove the uterine contents. Again, the entire procedure should take less than ten minutes to complete. Do you have any questions?"

I look at Andie. She is staring at the table.

"OK, then let me get you to put on this gown. Take off your pants and underwear and I'll be back in a moment."

Neither of us speaks. The only sound in the room is the rustling of Andie's jeans and the tinkling of piano whispered through the overhead speaker. She climbs up on the table and lies back, holds her arm across her eyes.

The nurse returns minutes later with a tray on a cart.

"Let me get you to put your feet in the stirrups, honey."

She snaps on some white latex gloves pulled from a dispenser above the machine, then takes a large syringe from the tray.

"Just let your knees fall to the sides, sweetie. It's easier on both of us that way."

Her face disappears beneath the gown. Andie squeezes my hand, winces in pain.

"It's OK, you're doing fine," the nurse's voice says. She stands up, places the syringe back on the tray.

"We're going to let the anesthesia work for a few minutes," she says, looking at Andie, "and then the doctor will be in to complete the procedure in just a little bit." The indiscernible song playing over the intercom sounds louder now.

The doctor comes in, makes no eye contact with Andie or me, but gives a gruff acknowledgment with his back turned as he hooks a tube up to the machine.

"I need you to stay as still as you possibly can," he says as he turns the contraption on.

It hums.

He is short and balding, wears glasses, has a pinched face. His forehead furrows and his breath whistles through his nose. He disappears under the gown and Andie squeezes my hand again and the sound from the machine seems to pick up in intensity.

Andie cries out, digs her nails into the meat between my thumb and forefinger. "*Oh, God,*" she cries, and I look down at her and she looks at me and there are tears streaming down her face. "It hurts," she says.

"I need you to stay still," the doctor says, the unmistakable tinge of impatience framing his voice.

"She says it hurts," I tell him.

"Of course it hurts," he says. "It will be over in just a few minutes."

There is blood and other matter visible in the plastic tube as it makes its way back to the machine. I am crying now. We started this thing. We fucked each other all over her house, on the kitchen table, in the hallway, in the tub, on the bathroom sink, on the floor in front of the bathroom, on both couches. We never tried to keep this from happening.

My arm is numb from Andie's grip, blood slowly trickling down my hand to the fingertips.

And then it's over.

The doctor pulls the tube out, tells her to try to make herself comfortable, says that the nurse will be in shortly.

Andie convulses in tears, moaning, her body quivering. She wraps her torso around my arm, holds herself up on me.

"We killed our baby," she sobs. "We killed our baby."

The Muzak is playing loudly now, a song that I actually recognize but can't quite place because of the bastardized format. It's so loud it nearly drowns out the despair. And then I can tell it's "Angie."

"We killed our baby," she's whispering.

I don't say anything. I wipe my eyes and nose on my shirtsleeve.

On the way home I stop at Arby's to get Andie her favorite Jamoca shake.

She doesn't want it, she says.

I throw it out the window as we exit the parking lot and it splatters all over the trash can and sidewalk.

Our socks are back together by the end of the afternoon.

TRANSMISSION 24:

my big screen debut

June

!EXTRAS NEEDED!

A MAJOR HOLLYWOOD FILM PRODUCTION IS NOW SHOOTING FORTY MILES SOUTH OF ATLANTA FOR TURNER NETWORK TELEVISION (TNT). THOUSANDS OF EXTRAS ARE NEEDED ON A DAILY BASIS! YOU CAN BE ONE OF THEM. APPLY IN PERSON AT . . .

"We're so there, dude," I tell Splinter. We will be actors. We will be paid scale.

We call everyone, but only Jonas is interested in throwing off the shackles of his workaday life and joining us on the mission. Andie can't participate because she's actually secured a real job. She went to a doctor following the procedure and got some kind of antidepressant prescription that makes it possible for her to interact with others, even strangers. She works at a car wash. It's not the most prestigious of occupations but she likes it well enough.

The next day at work I tell Johnny, much to his chagrin, that I'm taking a few months off. I try to convince Hank to come with me, explain to him that he'll only live once and other inspirational shit like that. He refuses, despite my oratorical skills, which I like to think of as more than substantial. He's been cancerous for months now but shows no signs of surrender. He's still strong. I tell him to hold my job for me. He laughs demonically. I punch him in the arm.

The next morning Splinter and Jonas and I pack up Jonas' hatchback and head south. The car is flying through the 5 a.m. darkness past cow pastures and isolated gas stations. The call time is 6. Once there, we are directed with flashlights to parking spaces in a field.

We walk about a half mile to a grouping of circus-style tents. There are hundreds of others just like us. They are eating biscuits and instant oatmeal out of Styrofoam cups, chasing the dream of Hollywood stardom. Or at least escaping the regular life of a no-talent hack stuck in a cubicle all day. I can't decide which group I want to belong to. Both choices sound pathetic.

We grab some food, then stand in line for sign-in. There are postings everywhere saying that it is essential for us to get in this line so that we can get paid at the end of the day.

"Dude, this shit pays *every day*," Splinter marvels. We are significantly stoked by this revelation.

After that line, the next lineup is for wardrobe. We are each outfitted with a crappy version of a Civil War soldier's uniform. We are to portray imprisoned Union soldiers. They give me a hat big enough on top that I can fit my dreadlocks inside of it.

By the time we get into the makeup line the sun is up and we've stopped shivering. After they smudge up our faces to make us look "dirty," we are directed to a large clearing where there are already hundreds of other disheveled-looking extras. There are men standing in front of us with long beards wearing gray uniforms far cleaner and less tattered than ours. They are, we discover, "professional" Civil War reenactors.

One of them yells in a booming voice that we are the scumbag maggot prisoners of the Great South.

"You will all line up double-file in divisions of one hundred," he booms in military cadence. Then another guy takes over the direction. We wonder if this is part of the movie.

"There is to be no talking among the ranks. If we hear any talking among you, there will be severe penalties."

"What is this bullshit?" Jonas says.

"No shit, dude," Splinter adds.

"It's obviously the Stanislavski-Strasberg Method acting approach." My drama background finally allows a real-world application. Who'da thunk it?

Most of the reenactors are actual vets who can't leave Vietnam behind. They all acknowledge their fallen Nam brethren by boycotting the shoot the day "Hanoi" Jane Fonda tours the set with her media-mogul boyfriend Ted Turner, whose network is financing the whole shebang.

To make up for the lacking number of extras (the prison supposedly held upwards of twenty thousand men at one time during the Civil War), the set crew has created hundreds of cardboard cutouts. These cutouts are life-size photographs of extras that are moved around the set to serve as background bodies. They are kept far enough away from the cameras so that anyone outside the know won't realize they aren't moving.

The entire set is a scaled-down model of the original real-life Confederate prison camp Andersonville. And it could actually function as a prison. There are literally thousands of twenty-foot-high tree trunks that wrap completely around a one-hundred-acre enclosure.

During the first few days of shooting all the extras are jockeying for position. We try to anticipate where the camera crew is going to move next. We want some face time on-screen, if at all possible. I make it onto celluloid the first day.

It's during a shot that takes place at the crummy little rivulet that runs through the center of the compound. It's supposed to serve as the place where all the prisoners get drinking water and wash their clothes. The director wants the audience to have a firsthand understanding that the water that ran through the prison was polluted. This is my face time—though I can't actually call it "face" time because the shot is taken from behind me. But in that one shot, at least, I am the focal point. And as an added bonus I am—get this—*pissing*. I shake it off, tuck it back in and everything.

But I don't actually piss. That's the best part. It's all *acting*. I'm on-screen for no more than seven seconds before hobbling out of the picture to demonstrate how sickly I am (more acting).

The director yells "cut" and actually takes the time to tell me, insignificant extra, that I provided very convincing urination. I am fulfilled. I don't care that it wasn't actually my *face* portrayed, because at that one point, for those seven seconds, I am the Everyman of the film. I am the example of the filth that people had to live in. Pissing in the drinking water.

Splinter tells me that I'm only slightly blowing the importance of my scene out of proportion. He always yanks me back down to earth, the fucker.

"You're a fucker," I tell him.

"Let's go smoke a joint," Jonas says.

Inside the prison compound, Andersonville proper, there are hundreds of makeshift tents, known in nineteenth-century dialect as "shebangs." The shebangs are constructed by set crews, pieced together with thick cloth canvas and sticks. They are perfect hiding places for getting high, which Splinter, Jonas, and I use to our fullest advantage. And we soon discover that we are not alone in our quest for enlightenment while at "work." All over the set there are little tribes of hippies and pot-toking nonpacifists as well who take turns smoking up and then standing watch outside the shebangs, making sure the coast is clear. Because these Hollywood types aren't stupid. They know that anybody here is a loser looking to make a fast buck. Who else could take three straight months off from real work to make a piddling seventy bucks a day? And so, by progression, they know then that every extra who can get away with it is going to take cover away from the unrelenting sun. But this is far from the only reason for our retreat into the tents. Movie shoots are fucking boring, we soon learn. They shoot each scene using only one camera, and then they put that one camera up on a crane and shoot the same scene, again and again, with numerous takes. By the time they finish one scene, every one of us extras knows the lines better than the actors themselves. One scene that'll end up on-screen for two minutes, at best, takes an entire day and a half to shoot. This is monotony in its purest sense. And under the central Georgia sun at that.

But we are getting paid to basically stand around looking pathetic. Normally we do that in our real lives and get paid far less to do it. And we really only take breaks every once in a while to get high. Any time the assistant directors get on the bullhorns and say they need everyone out of the shebangs for a particular shot that pans across the compound or whatever, we are there. Loyal, waiting, and bored.

TRANSMISSION 25:

hollywood leads to girls and hard drugs

July

For the next two weeks we're doing night shoots on the film. We are instructed to arrive on the set at dusk since we'll be "working" until 3 or 4 a.m. every night. On the second night Corey comes down to the set. He has pretty much dropped from sight ever since he started dating this girl Janine. She is actually an old friend of Andie's. They both attended the same summer camp for troubled girls back when they were fourteen or fifteen. Like Andie, Janine has mental issues. Corey loves her, though. He says that she helps him stay straight. He rarely comes by Andie's anymore because he says all we ever do over there is get high. I don't know what he's expecting us to do at Andersonville. It's not any different on the set. I don't tell him that though.

We sneak inside one of the bigger shebangs, where Jonas rolls a fat joint (he's a pro now). Corey skips on it the first three times it goes around. On the fourth pass he hits it and immediately steps out of the tent, walks around it (we can see his circling shadow), then comes back just in time to hit it again. He mutters that he'll see me around and disappears.

When we run into him later he's tripping so hard that he thinks the cardboard cutouts are real people.

"They won't stop following me around," he says. "Everywhere I go I see this same guy. He has no neck. He has no fucking neck! His eyes follow me everywhere and when I run to a different area he's already there."

"He's like Pepe Le Pew," I say, for fun.

Corey laughs and Splinter asks where he got the Acid.

"It's not Acid, man," Corey says. "It's fucking mescaline. It's so pure I can feel the blood in my veins."

"Is that a good thing?" Splinter asks.

"*Yes.*"

Corey pulls out a cigarette cellophane with five tiny pellets in the bottom.

"That's mescaline?"

"It looks small, but this is seriously the cleanest high I've ever had. It's so fucking pure and good."

"What happened to wanting to stay clean and the straight and narrow and all that shit?"

He puts his finger to his lips. "Shhhhh."

"Where'd you get that stuff, Corey?"

"Some guy. I don't know who. I can't remember, actually."

He hands me the cellophane.

Within thirty minutes we're all tripping. Hard. We edge closer to the action. Despite the multiple takes and the dialogue repeated ad infinitum, the shit actually seems real. The assistant directors corral all the extras together and tell us to prepare for some simulated fighting. The "bad" prisoners are going to lead an assault against a band of "good" prisoners who have been attempting to curtail the bad guys' strong-arm tactics. Or maybe the other way around.

Bloody conflict ensues. Rubber clubs and knives are used. But even after the director yells "Action!" none of us can stop laughing long enough to appear as though we're angry and ready to kill for our freedom or beliefs or whatever.

It occurs to me in the mescaline haze that my dad once spoke of a war protest he and my mother had attended back in '69. It's one of the few times he ever said anything about what it was like when they were still in love. He'd said they were in D.C. at the Washington Monument. They were tripping, smoking weed, being peaceful, as was the general hippie tendency. Then these cops came up on horseback and started running down all the peace lovers gathered there. They were assaulting and arresting anyone who looked even slightly "revolutionary" (that's the way Richard said it). He said that one of the cops grabbed hold of my mother's dress and was trying to yank her back out of the car they had jumped into for escape. They barely got away.

I mentioned this incident to my mother once in passing and she denied it ever happened. She can never admit that she ever did anything halfway exciting with Richard. Though she has said that she danced onstage with Jim Morrison at a Doors concert. Richard wasn't there that time though, she said.

"What are you thinking about?" Splinter asks me.

"My parents. My dad told me about a coupla times when they were being stereotypical hippies, opposing war and not bathing and loving the one they were with and all that."

"Like when?"

"Once they went to a 'Love-In' or some shit at the Pentagon.

He said there were thousands of them there, all wearing flowers and what-have-you. Have you ever seen the video footage of the hippies putting daisies in the soldiers' gun barrels?"

"I don't think so."

"Well, that was the same time, I think. Anyway, all these hippies, thousands and thousands of them, completely encircled the Pentagon and using the 'Power of Love' they levitated the building. Supposedly, I mean."

"Did it really come off the ground?"

And that's when I see Larry.

Larry as in "I'm Larry, this is my brother Darryl, and this is my other brother Darryl." From the old *Newhart* show. I used to watch that shit religiously after we moved to an Atlanta campground following our last eviction and my parents got backslidden and left the majority of their extremist religious beliefs behind (Mother's occasional outbursts of divinely inspired revelation not withstanding). This was back when they decided that God actually *did* approve of television and wanted his children to own large TVs. With many channel selections. And yea, verily they bought a thirty-two-inch TV and had cable installed upon it.

"Look, you guys, it's Larry!" I whisper reverently, nodding in his direction.

He's leaning against the deadline fence, smoking a cigar.

"Who's Larry?" Jonas says.

I do my best Larry impression, try to make my voice sound like I've just swallowed bugs.

"From *Newhart*?"

"Yeah! That's him!"

"God, he looks old."

"I've gotta get him to say, 'I'm Larry, this is my brother Darryl, and this is my other brother Darryl.' I can't believe that's fucking Larry!"

I approach him, try not to seem like a crazed fan on drugs.

"Hi," I say, my right hand extended in a gesture of warmest friendship.

"Hi there," he says, taking my hand limply.

Fuck yes! Even when he's just talking to regular people his voice sounds exactly like it did on *Newhart*.

"I love your work on *Newhart*. You were so funny on that show."

An expression crosses his face. I'd almost call it one of annoyance. He is an actor who cannot live down the role. I ignore the look and move on to the business at hand.

"Will you say that line for me?"

"What line?"

"You know, the line from the show that you'd always say when you came on."

Larry looks at me hard for a moment, then turns his gaze back toward the set hands preparing the next scene.

"No," he says. "I don't say that line anymore."

What does he mean he doesn't say that line? That fucking line made his career. He'd be just another washed-up character actor out of a job without that line. He doesn't grasp the ramifications of his own fleeting fame. Does he honestly *believe* that when people tune in to this movie and see him they are going to be like, "Oh, look there, dear! It's [whatever his real name is]"? Of course they aren't going to say that. They're going to say, "Holy shit, it's Larry!" If they recognize him at all.

"You don't say that line anymore?" I ask him.

He doesn't answer, doesn't look at me. He shakes his head no.

"Ooooh-kay."

I turn on my heel, head back to my boys.

"Did he say it?" Splinter asks.

• • •

Splinter, Jonas, and I meet this couple at Andersonville. They seem cool, though probably older than us by a few years. The guy, Brandon Stickney ("I'm Brandon Stickney," he told us by way of introduction, shaking our hands violently), is always joking about people smoking crack. Which is kind of odd because his girlfriend Sherri is a total fucking junkie, of the Heroin persuasion. She's twenty-eight, fairly attractive, pretty good body. Good sense of humor, all that. The topic turns to drugs, as it inevitably does when you're a Head and are trying to find out who else is. I mention that I've always wanted to try Heroin, but that you hear all these negative things about it in the media and high school health class and everything so it's like this really taboo thing. And all the little lily-white suburban kids look at you like you're nuts if you mention it.

But Sherri doesn't.

Her face lights up when I tell her of my secret desire. She asks Brandon Stickney to run to craft services and grab her a cup of juice and a cookie and then she tells me that the only reason she's even at Andersonville is to get away from the junk. She pulls her left sleeve up and shows me track marks like I've never seen before, except in that one Jane's Addiction video where the naked woman has scabs all over her body from shooting dope.

Sherri assures me that the health class videos are all scare tactics. She says that crack is pretty much the only drug that you want to do more of as soon as you get it in your system. Heroin's subtler than that, she says.

"Can you tell me where to get it?" I ask. "I've been asking around about it for the last six months and nobody knows where it's at."

"That's because there's only about a six-block radius in all of Atlanta where they sell it. I'll take you there. Once. *One time.* I don't want you getting hooked. I'll take you once and get the hookup. But two conditions: You can't mention anything to Brandon and you have to buy me a bag."

"That's cool. I don't have to be blindfolded or anything like that, right?"

"I'll take you just this once." She gives me her phone number and tells me to call her when I get back into the city.

When Brandon Stickney returns we try to act nonchalant, but he can smell betrayal. He acts different, doesn't tell any jokes about seemingly normal people being crackheads. He doesn't say anything. He just stands there drinking his juice from a wax paper cup.

I tell Andie about the Great Discovery as soon as we walk in the door. Then we all rush around cleaning the house, throwing out our old soft drink cans and paper plates, making the beds, everything. We swore to each other that if we ever tried Heroin it would be a one-time thing. Just to see what it was like. The house must be clean and perfect for this One Time.

We get the house cleaned in an hour and then I call Sherri. She gives me directions to her house.

"Come by yourself," she says. "I don't want all these other people knowing where to buy it. And it isn't a good idea to bring five or six people to the ghetto anyway. That freaks the niggers out."

She's already waiting outside when I pull into her driveway.

"Where's Brandon?" I ask her.

"He's inside," she says, then, seeing the look on my face, adds, "Don't worry about it. I told him I was taking you down there just this once. He's letting me go one last time because he knows I want to clean up. We're moving to California in a month, so it doesn't matter anyway."

In the ghetto, or "The Bluff," as she calls it, there are run-down buildings and broken glass everywhere, like in that Grandmaster Flash video "The Message." It's right by the Georgia Dome, the newly constructed home of the Atlanta Falcons.

We pull up next to a three-story brick apartment building with all the windows boarded up. Sherri tells me to wait in the car. I give her the money and she goes in the side entrance. In place of a door there leans a piece of plywood that has to be slid back in order to gain entrance.

The windows are completely fogged up in the T-Bird. I can't see shit, and I'm starting to freak because there are people all over the place and headlights bouncing around and you never know when a cop is going to show up.

In moments Sherri comes back out. "That nigger Pooky says it's cool for you to come in and wait. He has to go down the block to get the stuff."

"Why do you call him a nigger? I thought you were friends with him."

"Rule number one down here: Everybody that has any connection to the dope game is a nigger. All of 'em will try to fuck you over, I don't care how long you've known them."

"So you're not a racist?"

"No. Not at all. When I say 'nigger' it's only because these motherfuckers down here are tried-and-true *niggers*." She sees that I don't grasp the logic. "You know, a nigger. Someone who'll fuck you over at the drop of a hat if they think they have the slightest chance to get away with it. Every white person down here is nothing more than a mark for these people, OK? That's why they're niggers."

"OK."

The room is completely dark except for a single candle. The place reeks of kerosene. A mattress and box spring sit on top of cinder blocks. A woman is hitting a crack pipe on the bed. Sherri introduces her as Joyce. She exhales some crack smoke and flashes me a toothless smile.

"Do you want a hit?" she asks, extending the pipe to me.

"No, thanks."

"So, you guys doing OK?" Sherri says.

"Not too bad," Joyce says. She speaks remarkably well for someone with no teeth.

"Joyce is a pretty name," I say lamely, an attempt to join the conversation.

"Thank you," she says, looking up from the pipe she's repacking with another rock. She looks at me in the darkness.

Pooky slips into the room, says that the bags are small and he couldn't do anything about it. You've gotta take what they give you, he says.

"Is that your Christian name?" I ask Pooky. He gives Sherri a stare of annoyance. "This nigga witchoo?"

"Thanks, guys," Sherri says.

"Pooky's a fucking dick," she says when we get in the car. "That nigger fucking went down to the dealer's house, bought half the bags we paid for, and then split them up so that he'd be able to pocket the rest of the money. See? A true nigger."

"So you're saying that we only got thirty dollars' worth of Heroin for sixty dollars?"

"Yeah, but you won't know the difference."

"So, we'll still get high?"

"Definitely. God, I'd give anything to have zero tolerance again. I remember when I first started getting high I couldn't do more than half a bag."

"So we're definitely gonna get high?"

As I speak, Sherri is climbing over the bench seat to sit in the back.

"What are you doing?"

"I'm fixing."

"Now? Can't you wait until we get to my house?"

"No. God—damn, this is some good shit."

• • •

Andie is sitting on the bed when we hurry in the door. Sherri is more shuffling than walking, and her voice sounds deep and slurred.

She has brand-new needles for all of us. Insulin syringes. She says you can get them downtown at the Eckerd on Ponce for $1.99 a ten-pack. If Eckerd isn't open you can buy them in the ghetto for three bucks apiece. "Not that you'd need to know that, 'cause you guys won't be doing this anymore after this," she says.

Splinter, Jonas, and I crowd into the bedroom with Andie and Sherri as she stands at the dresser and begins a demonstration of proper Heroin injection.

"Here's whatcha do, guys," she slurs. "Cut the tops off the baggies, cut the tops off." She snips the zipper locks off the tiny baggies with Swiss Army Knife scissors. She dumps the contents of one into a spoon we have at the ready. The handle has been bent so as not to allow spillage of the precious brown powder.

"Step two: Draw water into the work, up to about the forty mark—that's what junkies call syringes. In junkie terms, syringes are called 'works.'"

"We aren't planning on being junkies so we'll keep calling them syringes," I say.

Ignoring me, she continues. "Slowly squirt the water into the spoon. You don't want to go too fast or else the water'll blow the dope right out of the spoon. Just go real slow, letting the water mix with the dope."

She is relishing this lesson. She is reliving her romance with the junk. She takes her time, letting her adoration manifest itself. I am hungry just hearing her voice, how she loves what she's talking about.

"Take your lighter, hold it under the spoon, just until the liquid starts to bubble."

She sets the spoon on the dresser.

"Then you pull the plunger out of the work and stir it all up with said plunger until there is nothing grainy left. All that should be left in the spoon is a dark, milky solution. God, I sound like I'm teaching a fucking science class. But look at how perfect that shit looks."

We all lean in, stare at the teaspoon full of murky liquid.

Sherri drops a small wad of cotton in the spoon, slips the plunger back in the syringe, places the needle on top of the cottons and sucks up all the liquid. She is just going through the motions now, not talking. For a moment I wonder if she's going to shoot the bag herself.

She holds the syringe upside down, flicks it with her fingernail so the air bubbles will rise to the top. Then she pushes the plunger up slightly until the air is gone. "All that's left now is a full shot of liquid heaven," she says. "Who's going first?"

"I am," I say.

Sherri hands me the syringe.

I am sweating and scared. I move slowly backward until the bed hits my legs and then I sit down, still looking at the syringe, holding it in front of me, a sacred object. I can't stop staring at it. My fingers are quivering.

"Do you want me to hit you with it?" Sherri offers.

"Just stick it in me and I'll do the rest," I say, offering my right arm to her.

She drops to one knee in front of me.

"Damn, you don't even need a tourniquet. Your veins are perfect for shooting dope. It took me months to get to that point. Veins popping out all over. A born junkie."

"Just stick it in already."

She holds the needle parallel with my outstretched forearm, slides it effortlessly into the vein. I'd prepared myself for a shock of pain but there is none.

"Let me do the rest."

"You have to pull the plunger back first to make sure you're in the vein good," Sherri says.

I pull the plunger out slightly and immediately a plume of red appears in the chamber, languidly mixing with the brown dope-water.

"Now push it in?"

"Just push it in. You'll be high as hell before you even get to the bottom."

I compress the plunger slowly, watch the liquid disappear into my vein.

Sherri was right. I can feel it before the plunger makes it even halfway down. The Heroin rushes over me like a slow, warm wave. It starts in my legs and within moments my entire body is enveloped in a velvet warmth like I have never experienced. I am floating. Every part of me is separate and yet whole.

I am perfect and alive.

I lie back on the bed with the syringe still poking out of my arm but I haven't the energy or the care to remove it.

I am in love.

I am alive and I am in love.

I am home.

I can't imagine being so powerfully addicted to something that you'd blow a guy just so you can get more. Sherri says that these things happen, though.

So we've been extra cautious with our Heroin use, though Jonas hasn't been as careful as the rest of us. Jonas does the shit all the time, it seems. When we meet him at Lollapalooza he's already high on smack, sitting out on the lawn under the sun with his pupils pinned, listening to L7. He doesn't start puking his guts out until A Tribe Called Quest takes the stage.

Heroin has that nasty side effect when you first start using, but it isn't a bad kind of puke, if you can believe that. The puking actually makes you feel higher than you did in the first place. Like you're exhaling all the bullshit in your life that might otherwise bring you down. It's all very symbolic and somehow contributes to the high. Out in public, though, it just looks bad. And it's for that very reason that Andie and I have decided to bypass the H and take a couple tabs of Ecstasy. We haven't done E since O.J. offed his wife and ran from the cops in slow motion.

"Do you think O.J.'s guilty?" I ask Corey during the Beastie Boys' set.

"What?"

"Do you think O.J. is guilty?"

"What the fuck are you talking about?"

I sigh, annoyed. The Ecstasy hasn't kicked in yet. "Do you think O.J. Fucking Simpson killed his wife or not?"

"I don't know, dude. Maybe."

"What do you mean, maybe? Haven't you watched any of the news about it?"

"I was trying to watch the Beastie Boys."

"Jesus, what is it with everybody? So fucking apathetic. Nobody has an opinion. And you weren't watching the Beastie Boys, anyway. You were fucking lying there with your eyes closed."

"Whatever, dude. Fine. I was *listening* to the Beastie Boys." Corey closes his eyes again, drapes his arm across his forehead.

Nearly everybody here is half dead and lifeless from sitting in the sun all day. Then the Ecstasy starts to kick in. The Beastie Boys are jumping all over the stage and they look like they're in another time zone, so far away. And then they're admonishing the audience for its lack of enthusiasm but, I mean, we've been sitting out in the sun for fucking five or six hours and it's ninety degrees out here.

"Come on, Cincinnati!" Ad Rock implores us, by way of insult, after a particularly weak round of audience participation in the whole hand-waving, call-and-response thing that rap groups learn in Hip-Hop 101.

Jonas is sitting there with some hot little punk girl. Corey is drunk and passed out on the lawn.

"What's your name?" I ask the girl. Her hair is only about an inch long, spiked up and dyed pink. She's wearing a studded dog collar.

"I'm Karen. I'm your brother's girlfriend."

"You're Jonas' girlfriend?" I say to her. "I've never seen her before, dude," I say to him.

"I've never seen *you* before," she says to me.

"How long have you been going out?" I ask Jonas.

"About—an hour and a half," Jonas says.

It's dark outside and cool now. Andie and I are thoroughly fulfilled and just as thoroughly fucked up. During several of the Smashing Pumpkins' songs we even have a moment or two when our hands touch and our fingers snake themselves together. As one of the security guards looks the other way we sneak into the seated section under the pavilion and find a couple of empty seats. Everyone stands on their automatically folding plastic seats to get a better view, but when we try to do the same we quickly realize that our balance is totally screwed up by the Ecstasy. If the weight is even slightly disproportionate between the front and the back of the seat the goddam thing tries to fold up and dump you backward. It's really disconcerting and undermining to an otherwise good high.

Billy Corgan is singing about how he and his lover are Siamese twins attached at the wrist and the lights are beautiful and I can feel my heart beating full of love for Andie and the rest of the world in general.

It is a rare moment and I'm staying in that moment for as long as possible. I have found my place and it is radiant and safe and good.

TRANSMISSION 26:

a ship comes in, an inevitable return to slow asphyxiation

August

It's finally happened for my mom. After years of struggle and avoidance of real work, she and Victor are filthy rich. He hasn't worked in months because of his swimming pool accident ("I can't cut the grass—the insurance adjusters are always watching, Barbara!") and now the insurance company has settled for a whopping $80,000. That's more money than either one of them has made in the entire twelve-year history of their relationship.

They call and invite me to dinner with the rest of the family. Mom tells me not to bring Andie. I bring her anyway. It's free steak, after all.

Victor is in the best mood I've ever seen him. He's laughing and joking with the waitresses.

"Did you see my new car out there?" he says.

"Which one was it?" I try to sound enthused. I don't know why. I've never seen the bastard happy before unless he was pulling a scam. And maybe this is just an extension of that: the most successful scam of his life.

"Red Porsche. 944. That little baby can take a corner faster than any car you've ever driven."

"You bought a Porsche? Where're Mom and Adam and Aaron gonna sit?"

"They've got a car, too. Tell him what you've got, Barbara."

I look at my mom. She can't stop smiling. She's covering her mouth with her hand so that the food she's chewing doesn't fall out. She throws back what's left in her wineglass, coughs a little, clears her throat.

"It's a BMW."

"You have to see it, man," Victor says. "Top of the line."

"Do you guys have any money left?" I am incredulous for some reason. As though somehow they might've been more fiscally responsible.

Victor holds up his left hand. Handcuffed to him is a metallic silver briefcase. It looks like the kind of case they always show in the movies about the president having to push the Button from a secret location in case of nuclear war.

"You've got all the money in there?"

Victor nods his head and smiles, forks a piece of steak into his mouth.

"You're carrying around $80,000 handcuffed to your hand?"

"Less the price of the Beamer and the Porsche. It's not like they're brand-new or anything," Victor says. "Oh, and look at this."

He holds up his right hand, his fork hand, and waves his fingers in my and Andie's faces. There is a huge diamond ring gleaming on his pinky, set in yellow gold.

"Wow," Andie says. I look at her for a moment and can't decide if she is actually impressed by this vulgar display or is just being the typical sarcastic bitch that I know and love.

"And this," Victor says.

He looks around the restaurant a couple of times to make sure no one is watching, then pulls out a black pistol and sets it on the table in front of me. Aaron and Adam start oohing and aahing. Evidently this last piece of booty had not yet been revealed to them, either.

"Is that loaded?" I ask.

"Hell, yes, it's loaded. Do you think I'd carry around this much money without a way to make sure no one can take it from me?"

"Most people use banks for that very reason."

"Fuck banks. If I carry the cash on me there's no way I can ever lose it."

"Unless you spend it all."

Victor regards me for a moment, glances away, then lets his eyes come up sharp. "I know what's eating you, Luke. You're wondering where your share is. But *every*body's getting paid tonight. We're all getting what we deserve," Victor says.

"Yeah, look how much we have, Luke," Adam says. He and Aaron both hold up crisp, new $100 bills.

"Let me have those, boys. You're going to lose them," Mom says.

"Oh, they'll be all right, Barb. Just let them enjoy their money," Victor says.

I look at Jonas. He isn't saying anything.

"What about the rest of your life? In a week you're not going to have anything left at this rate. Have you guys even thought about, I don't know, buying a fucking *house*?"

Victor stops smiling for the first time.

"I will discuss all of this with you—but I will not tolerate profanity."

"You swear like a goddam sailor all the time."

He looks at me sternly.

"You, alright. I learned it by watching you," I say.

"We're already taking care of the house," he says around a fresh mouthful of steak. "Your mother is about to close a deal."

"You wouldn't believe this house, Luke," Mom chimes in. "It is so beautiful. It's an antebellum mansion with columns out front and everything! We're putting a down payment on it this Monday."

"What about the rest of the payments? How are you guys going to afford paying for a mansion for the next thirty years?"

"You don't need to worry about that, son."

I hate it when Victor calls me "son."

I take a bite of my baked potato. Everyone is chewing.

Nobody says much of anything for the rest of the meal. By the time Victor asks for the check I figure it's a safe time to make an exit without creating a scene. People usually walk out of restaurants after they finish eating. This is completely normal.

"I guess we're gonna go." I slide out of the booth and stand in front of the table.

"It was good to see you again," my mother says to me, ignoring Andie.

"You, too, Ma. You guys started school already?" I say in Adam and Aaron's direction.

"No. We're going to after we move."

"You're not enrolling them in school until you *move*? How much more school are they going to miss, Ma?"

"That's what I keep asking her," Victor says.

I look at my mother for a minute while she downs the rest of her wine. She finishes and doesn't look at me.

I extend my hand to Victor.

He squeezes hard.

"Thanks for coming out," he says.

"Thanks for having us," I say. Then, to Jonas, "Are you gonna come over tonight and drive me and Splinter to Andersonville?"

"No. I'm going over to Karen's mom's house for a while."

"I'll see you on set, then. Be good, you guys."

Andie and I hurry out to the parking lot. There's somebody right behind us, I can hear footsteps echoing ours.

I turn around and it's Victor, the briefcase still fastened to his wrist. For a moment I wonder if he's going to shoot me and then tell the cops that I tried to steal his money. But he doesn't draw his gun. He's asking me to wait and then he's walking us over to a red Porsche. He gently sets the briefcase on the hood and fingers the combination.

"I forgot to give you the money I owe you," he says.

He opens the case and there are bundles and bundles of money and for a split second I actually contemplate grabbing a handful and running. It's not like it isn't owed me. But that's probably what he wants me to do, what he *expects* me to do. He's probably itching to blow somebody's brains out.

He flips through a small stack of hundreds and hands me three of them. Three $100 bills as repayment for years of embezzling my paltry after-school paychecks. Three hundred bucks for taking my entire savings in tenth grade. I had $843 that time, nearly my goal for a car. And now he's offering me $300. I take it and don't say anything.

Then he says, "Oh, what the hell," and hands me two more hundreds.

"What about the eight hundred bucks you took from me back when we lived on Housitonic Street?"

"I don't remember that."

"Sure you do. That fight when you almost cut your toe off on my bed frame?"

His face darkens. Aside from the beer bottle incident, the bed frame debacle was his lowest moment in the ongoing battle of My Childhood. He'd tried to kick my ass and I was just ducking and covering to keep him from getting the money out of my hands, and then we were wrestling around on the floor and he somehow cut the fuck out of his pinky toe.

"That money was to help out our family. You were a part of this family, weren't you?"

"Yeah, regrettably I was. But what the fuck right does that give you to take my money? It's the parents' responsibility to get a goddam job and support the kids, not the other way around."

"Let's just go," Andie says.

I stare at Victor and he stares back at me and then at Andie. I start walking back to the T-Bird, sure that he's aiming that black pistol at my back, that my head's going to explode and I'm going to crumple to the ground any second, dead.

But we make it to the car. Andie crawls across the seat and puts her head on my shoulder. I whip the T-Bird out of the parking lot and can see Victor walking back into the restaurant as we drive off.

"You wanna go get high?" I ask Andie.

"You mean . . ."

"Yeah. I just want to smooth out a little."

"OK. Yeah. I've been hoping that you'd say that."

The *Andersonville* set has reached serious tedium levels. I don't know if it's the inescapable need for change that chases me around at all times or my semi-frequent Heroin use, but I now dread driving all the way down to this goddam set every day and I swear to God—if I have to look at mud and ratty fucking tents another day, I'm going to lose it.

But then, Divine Providence! The crew chief announces that we extras will be a major and integral part of the shots over the next few days. They are going to be shooting this massive execution scene, when five or six guys are all "hanged" simultaneously from a scaffold. The way they do this, he explains, is by running metal cables down through the nooses that connect to harnesses the "condemned" actors will be wearing under their costumes. If anything goes wrong and the cable doesn't catch or something, the nooses are all rigged so that one end will immediately pop free the moment any pressure is applied to them.

Splinter, Jonas, and I decide that we'll have to take Acid for this shit. The believability level of a six-man hanging will be increased nearly a thousand percent while under the influence of psychotropic chemicals. This will be an experience nobody in America gets to have in our modern era. We will take drugs and convince ourselves that we are witnessing the real thing. The director will yell "Action!" and then somebody'll pull a lever that will drop them all at one time and we will watch them die for their sins, their bodies twisting in the wind. It sounds morbid but what the hell, you have to take advantage of the opportunities given to you.

The day of the hanging we are all stoked. The sun is just rising and the sky is pink at the edges.

We gorge on a breakfast of chewy, untoasted bagels and cream cheese. I eat a couple of danishes and a bowl of oatmeal, too. I have to stock up on energy because once I'm tripping I can't stand eating anything. Food tastes like Play-Doh when I'm tripping.

As we trudge down the dirt road to the set, I hand everybody their hits.

"We should probably wait until we get down there before we take it," Splinter says.

"Yeah. Who knows how long it'll take them to get everything ready."

The hanging scaffold is set up in the center of the compound. We duck inside a tent to take our drugs and then come out feeling ready to watch people (pretend to) die. The Acid won't kick in for another forty-five minutes or so. Hopefully they won't do the actual hanging scenes right away because we'll still be stone-fucking sober, watching people *filming* other people being executed, cameras everywhere, with no hope of make-believe to enhance the experience.

But, of course, in true unceasing filming fashion, there are all kinds of preliminary shots to be done:

First, the scaffold in all its menacing grandeur; then the crowd of people gathering around to watch and talking among ourselves (they tell us all to say "Gobba gobba gobba" in hushed tones so that it sounds like we're discussing the events about to take place). And then they shoot the scenes leading up to the execution, where they bring the condemned men up to the scaffold and get shots of their reactions as they struggle to maintain composure in the face of death.

It takes at least two hours to do all of this, so I'm tripping really hard even by that point. And then they're filming the shot of Larry from *Newhart* who wouldn't say his trademark goddam line during the night shoot. He's playing the guy who has to freak out when it truly hits him that he's only got a few minutes left to live (there's always one of them). He's begging them to let him go. He's saying he'll be good, he'll do better if they just give him one more chance. He's too young to die, he screams, as he's wrestled to the ground and blindfolded.

By the time they get all of them on the scaffold, it's well after noon and we're at the peak of our trips. I am more in character now than I've ever been while working on this movie. I imagine the actors as having really committed the acts of treachery and murder that have been depicted earlier in the shoot. My insistence on the gravity of the situation seems to rub off on Splinter and Jonas.

The Acid is doing its job.

We *live* in this world. The cameras have disappeared. It is 1864. We are bedraggled and oppressed prisoners in the shittiest prison ever built. Those assholes on the scaffold have bills to pay. We are, all of us—even the condemned—Union soldiers, and those sons of bitches up there took advantage of the rest of us, killed some of us for the good shoes we had, the salt pork we carried on us when we came through the gates of this godforsaken place. And now they are going to pay for their transgressions with their lives.

The appointed executioner asks them if they have any last words. Only one of them speaks, the ringleader. He's a large man, missing a front tooth. He laughs in the face of death. His laugh sounds just like Victor's. He says he'll see us all in hell.

The hoods are put over their faces and the nooses around their necks.

There is a long silence when I can feel everyone's breath holding expectantly in their chests, can hear all of their hearts beating. We are anticipating the pulling of the lever, the dropping of the bodies. The six men all stand silently as well, even Larry. Their hands are tied behind their backs. Their boots are black and shiny.

Then the lever is pulled and the noise it makes is like a gunshot and it all happens in slow motion after that.

The two-foot-wide plank drops from beneath them and they fall a short distance, maybe a foot, before they are jerked into place at the same time by the neck. The bodies move and turn, the legs kick. The big man with the tooth missing takes the longest time to die. He fights it the whole way.

Then they are all lifeless and twisting slowly, their heads slumped over and pulled up at the neck. Nobody yells cut for at least a minute after the initial drop.

It is completely silent. We are all wondering if they're really dead. Perhaps the cables didn't work, the breakaway nooses caught in place.

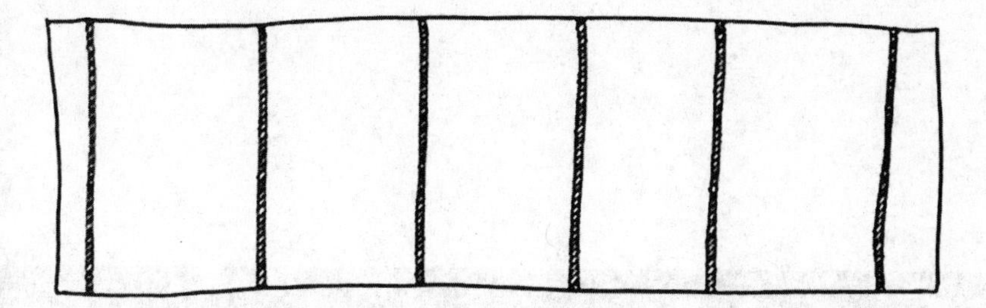

"That was creepy," Jonas whispers.

"That was totally cool," Splinter rasps.

We look up at the scaffold and all of the actors have taken off their hoods and are smiling and laughing, some lighting cigarettes as they hang there, nooses still around their necks, breakaway-rope handcuffs on the ground beneath their feet.

As filming winds down, a sense of desperation wends its way through me. Once this movie is over it's back to Andie and mind-numbing drudgery, back to Johnny and backbreaking hardwood floor installation. No more lazing about the Andersonville compound and meeting the new people who filter in every day and are brought up to speed by all of us "pros" on the mechanics of what it means to be a full-time movie extra. No more sunrises over cow pastures or hot coffee sipped out of Styrofoam cups. No more hanging out with Splinter or Jonas or Corey on a day-to-day basis. The boring routine of everyday normal life is fast approaching.

But Andie can't comprehend the situation. She's been working at a car wash, accepting loose change for tips, while we have been a functioning part of the Hollywood mystique. It has been our job to appear bedraggled while our spirits soared, heady with the rarity, the magic of it all.

And now it's over.

TRANSMISSION 27:

saying "fuck it" because it's tuesday

September

Andersonville ends in rain. Jonas and that girl of his, Karen, are totally up each other's asses all the time. All they ever do is shoot dope now. He came down to the set with Karen a few times and they hid out all day, picked up their checks, and headed straight for the ghetto.

Andie is always pushing me to "just pick up a couple bags," and when I won't do it she says that she *needs* a bag, that she can feel her insides peeling away when she doesn't have just a little bit to mellow out with. I usually cave at that point and we jump in the car and speed down there, our works hidden under the carpet beneath the front seat.

We'll have two works and two spoons and we'll inject each other at the same time and then kiss and let the wave wash over us, let the dope take it all. It never fails us. It works every time.

• • •

I rotate back to the post-Andersonville world with some difficulty. Johnny is still a dick but he's happy for my return to the hardwood crew. Hank now sports a giant incision scar across his throat, Colombian necktie shit. He said they had to remove his thyroid. He's proud of the scar. It gives him evidence. Nobody can think he's been faking it all this time.

"They took a tumor out of my neck as big as my fist," he whispers enthusiastically. His voice is completely gone. They tell him he'll probably never be able to talk again. There is no nerve activity in his vocal cords, they say. They are paralyzed. So he whispers. We now laughingly refer to him as "The Floor Whisperer."

"Why didn't you call me when you got that surgery?" I ask him.

"I didn't have a fucking voice to call you," he whispers.

"You couldn't call me before you went in for it?"

"You stopped working for Johnny. I hardly ever saw you. You were dead to me."

"I was *dead* to you? Dude, I live twenty minutes away from you."

He shrugs. I can't say I've done much to keep our connection up-to-date, either. I never really do with anybody. It's all random reconnections if there's ever one in the first place.

"So does that mean that your parents up in West Virginia are dead to you, too?"

"No," he whispers. "You can't just stop talking to family. But other people come in and out of a dude's life all the time."

"I just thought we were closer than that." I finish my sentence yelling over the racket of his nailing. He's gone back to stapling the fucking floor down mid-conversation. I bend over, grab my mallet, my stapler, start banging away.

I'll never get used to this shit. I'll never be satisfied doing this work. I can still nail faster than Hank, I can pull up a wall almost as efficiently. But I can't imagine being thirty, forty years old, and still on my knees, sweating, back aching, one forearm bigger than the other because the right arm is constantly swinging a mallet, right calf muscle gigantic because that leg is used for kicking the boards into place just right so that we can fly through another upper-middle-class home before heading directly to the next one. I'm making only slightly more money doing this shit than I was pulling in at Andersonville, and every time I think about that it burns me to the core and I want to grab my mallet and hurl it through every fucking window in every fucking house in every artificially contrived "community."

But I stay bent over, break that monotony with kneeling. Always some form of supplication, some form of prayer whose answers come in little baggies of dope bought in the Bluff with ever-increasing regularity. Those little baggies make all this workable, they make this life of blue-collar slavery with no chance of advancement livable, excusable.

I get out of the shower with my back aching. Andie hasn't returned yet with the dope. Round trip, it takes about forty-five minutes to get down there and back.

We've got it down to a science. I call her after work, and she gets a twenty out of the coffee can, then drives the T-Bird to make the pickup. Using this method, I feel like hell for maybe an hour and a half, tops, after the workday is over.

I'm pulling on sweats in the bedroom, my dreads still dripping, when I hear Andie open the door, back from the latest mission. By the time I make it from the bedroom to the living room, Andie's already bent over the coffee table, spoon out and everything.

I've got the work filled half full of brown dope and my breathing is shallow and rapid. This is my favorite part. The anticipation, when your mouth is watering, when you can almost *feel* what you're about to feel.

I've got the syringe between my teeth so that I can use my free hand to smack the vein in the crook of my right arm to prominence. I look over at Andie, who is now slumped deep into the couch, bliss pasted to her face, expressionless and barely there. I'm sliding the needle in and pulling the plunger back to watch the blood register. I push in slowly and in moments everything sounds like a 45 record spinning at 16 rpm. I can see lips moving at the same speed as before but the words come out like sludge. It's all slowed down and bearable now. Andie pushes herself up and stumbles toward the bathroom to puke. She pukes every time.

It feels like the final curtain every time I walk into these houses and see the same gray Sheetrock, the same towering piles of hardwood in corded bundles, the same insurmountable summit to climb just to make a buck, only to have to do it all over again the next day.

So I decided a few weeks ago that I can't come to this job anymore without a little assistance. Nowadays, after unloading the tools, tromping through mud, whatever is needed to get the preliminary shit out of the way, I head to the basement with my little junkie kit. Every day I bring a prefilled syringe with me, carefully prepared each morning at the house before Hank picks me up.

Today we will be finishing a floor that we began yesterday. It's a twelve-hundred-footer. The wood is all racked out for the most part, set in its design. All we'll have to do is run the air hoses to the compressor and nail like bastards all day long, swinging our godforsaken mallets. While Hank is on the phone confirming with Johnny that, yes, we will get it done today, don't worry, we won't let you down, I slip out the back of the house. This one doesn't have a basement, though, so I have to shimmy into the crawl space to fix myself. It's a pain in the ass, and it goes against my every survival instinct to put myself in such a confined space, where any number of rats or insects are making their homes, but it's just too risky to try fixing inside. If Hank ever found out I was doing this shit on the job I'd be fucked. He smokes a couple of bowls every day, but weed is a far cry from injecting opiates.

I pull the work out of my lunchbox from its hiding place beneath the two ham sandwiches slathered in mustard. An enormous racket begins inches above my head. It sounds like the house is collapsing around me, the noise overwhelming. Then comes the unmistakable sound of rhythmic nailing. I look up, still gripping the syringe between two fingers, and can see the staples appearing one after another through the plywood subfloor. They are poison darts, aiming for the kill.

I push the needle into my arm and try to ignore the sound of impending doom. It is loud. It is chaotic. It is destroying me. This whole fucking job is death. This is what killed Hank. *This* is how he got cancer. He was minding his own fucking business, trying to make a life, and now look at him.

I push the plunger down, feel the sounds, the chaos, feel the distress dissipate from the air around me and fade into the background. I suck them all in, all the slamming, the pounding mallets, the din of wood locked into place with methodical exactitude—and turn them into fuel. That is how to win. That is how to stop feeling victimized. Take the adversity and make it your bitch. Struggle harder, take leaps of faith, walk away.

Walk away.

I snap the tip off the syringe and toss it into the dirt far beneath the house, then come up for air.

"Hank," I yell. He looks up at me from his bent-over stapling position.

"Hank, I'm leaving!"

He stops nailing, stands up straight.

"Why are you bleeding?" he rasps, pointing his mallet at me. I look. There is a line of blood creeping down my forearm. I try to wipe it away but it just smears and more appears in its place.

"I'm outta here," I say, ignoring his question.

"You're leaving?"

"I can't take this shit anymore."

"How are you gonna get home?"

"I don't give a fuck. I just can't do this anymore. I can't stand waking up in the morning."

"I'd give you a ride but Johnny'd kill me if I left the job."

"I know, dude. I'm not asking you to give me a ride. And it's no hard feelings or anything like that. I just have to get my life straightened out to the point where it's at least semi-bearable."

We do the handshake/embrace thing and then I walk out into the sunlight. I turn around and go back. Hank's already nailing again. I tap him on the shoulder.

"Do you have a cigarette, man?"

"I smoke cigars."

Fuck. I have to have a cigarette right after fixing. And I'm miles from any gas station.

"I guess I'll take one of those."

He hands me the cigar, a Swisher Sweet with the plastic tip. These are the same I used to smoke during high school, in my room with a stolen cup of my mother's fruity wine.

"I hope we stay in touch, man," I say to Hank. He nods his head. We won't stay in touch. We both know it.

"Keep fighting that fucking cancer, man."

"I sit in fire," Hank says.

TRANSMISSION 28:

absence makes the heart

October

Andie and I actually had to detox for a few days there, locked in our room. This was the point when we realized that we had one hell of an addiction going on. Andie bitched nonstop, wanted to pawn the VCR and anything else not nailed down.

Everything opens up when you hit a real desperate withdrawal, when the body's been without the fix for more than a day or so: assholes, sinuses, tear ducts, Andie and I both running back and forth to the toilet for two or three days straight. Like having the flu except about ten times worse, because no medication can take the edge off the symptoms. We just chew on ten or twenty aspirin a day and then, on the fourth day without a hit, the symptoms finally begin to subside. But not enough. I call my mother.

"Luke! You have to come down and see the house. It is so beautiful! We can drink some tea."

"That's exactly why I was calling you, Ma. Give me directions."

Not five minutes after arriving at my mother's giant new house, I hit her with it. I need to borrow money.

Her face falls.

"Victor left. He took all the money with him. All I have now is this house and that fricking BMW," my mother says.

"He left? When?"

"Last week. We got into an argument about the way he was spending the money and he just got into his car and left. He didn't even take any clothes with him."

"That son of a bitch. God, why did you ever marry that motherfucker?"

"Hey, don't say that around your brothers. If it wasn't for him they wouldn't be here."

"Yeah, well, if you never married him you wouldn't know that they *could've* been here."

"The same can be said of your father," she says. She always does that, throws Richard in my face like he's my fault.

We move inside for the tea, and while she's fixing it Andie and I step into Aaron's room so he can show us his new comic books. I got him started collecting a couple years back. Adam's more into basketball and non-nerdy shit like that. I tell him that I'll look at whatever he collects, too, though.

I'm flipping through one of Aaron's books when I notice the fifty-dollar bill lying on his dresser, probably what remains of that crisp $100 he had that night at the restaurant.

I have to take it.

It'll just be a loan. I'll pay him back. He'll understand. And if not I'll just deny ever snagging it. Deny everything.

• • •

Victor pulls into the driveway just as I'm slipping my brother's cash into Andie's purse. My mother runs out on the porch and waves to him like he hasn't abandoned anyone, but has only just returned from a ten-minute trip to the grocery store.

He slides out of the sports car wearing an expensive-looking suit. He laughs at something Adam says to him, and I'm reminded of how much he looks like Saddam Hussein. During the war my friends always used to comment on how my stepdad was creepy, how he was always laughing like he was jolly and shit but it seemed that he was really plotting all of our deaths. My mother says that he has this way of talking to people that makes them put their guards down so that he can get in their good graces. She says that was why she married him after only knowing him for three weeks. But I don't see the appeal. I'll humor him on occasion, though, pretend to find his anecdotes amusing. Like now.

He jokes about us trading cars for a day, I tell him my T-Bird will smoke his little German piece of crap. Jokingly though. And then he wheels around, looks in the driver-side window and starts flipping out.

"Where's your mother?" he asks.

"I don't know," Aaron says.

"There she is." Adam points down the street.

My mother is walking away from us quickly, cradling something in her arms.

"You better get her back here with my briefcase, Luke, or I swear to God I'll shoot her," Victor says, his hand on his hip, indicating that he has his legally concealed weapon at the ready.

"Andie, come with me," I yell over my shoulder. Mom looks back and when she sees me coming she starts into a jog. I look back at Victor and he has his gun pointing at us, brazen as fuck. What a total dick.

This is just like the time he kicked the shit out of my mother when she was still pregnant with Adam. When the ambulance and the cops got there he told them that she'd had a psychotic breakdown and they carted her away still crying and snot-covered while the neighbors watched. She didn't come home for a week, and even after that she stayed married to him. He always finds a way to come off looking like the good guy.

"Mom, what are you doing?"

"He's not leaving me with nothing, Luke. I have to take care of these kids and I'll be goddamned if he's going to just pop up with his fancy suits and his flashy car and then leave again with all the money. There's no way."

"Ma, he's got a gun. You have to bring the money back."

"I don't give a fuck," she yells, crying.

"Barbara," Andie says, "you have to think about Aaron and Adam and what their lives would be like if they didn't have either of their parents. If he shoots you you'll be dead and he'll go to jail."

Then Andie hugs my mom and my mom actually hugs her back, drops the silver briefcase to the ground at her feet. I scoop it up, leave my mother and my girlfriend to their emotional woman thing. Victor reholsters his gun as I walk back toward the driveway holding the case.

"Your mother's crazy," Victor says.

"Why do you even come around? Why do you keep showing up if you're only going to leave again? You throw this shit in her face and then expect her to take you back whenever you're ready. It makes no sense. *You* make no sense."

Victor tosses the briefcase into his car and gets in next to it.

"*You* try living with her, Luke."

He pulls out of the driveway and in a pathetic/hilarious attempt at being cool, he throws the car back into first gear so as to facilitate a high-speed, tire-squealing exit, but instead it just stalls at the stop sign.

Jonas runs up to the T-Bird as soon as we pull up to the car wash. Jonas says that he found us a job laying floor with some guy named Lou. I've had a pretty hard time getting another job. There's nothing out there that pays as well as hardwood, unless you consider these bullshit sales jobs where they lure you in on empty promises of commissions you never reach. Fuck all that. As much as I hate the backbreaking tedium of floor installation, at least I know that if I put the work in, the money will be there. And Jonas says that this guy Lou wants us to start on Monday.

The mood in the car is festive. We have plenty of money and we're about to get high.

"Where's Karen?"

"She's waiting for me to pick her up. I figure I'll surprise her with a couple bags of dope. That always gets her going."

"Me, too," Andie says.

"Throw in that *Cuban Linx* shit."

We always listen to either Mobb Deep or Raekwon or maybe Nas's *Illmatic* when we go downtown to score. It gets us in the mindset, tales of urban gunslinging and dope dealing. It's a mental mindfuck, an inverting of our heads so that we are on the dealers' level. Because these dealers and their runners will eat you alive if you let 'em. The music doesn't take away from the stress of it, though. Just the thought of heading into the ghetto gets me wired. Half the time I have to stop and take a shit at the Burger King before we turn left into the Bluff on Proctor Street, or else I'll ruin my pants.

"Turn down Griffin Street," Jonas says.

"Griffin? Who's down there?"

"I've got a badass connection. He always has fat bags and can get girls *and* boys." "Girl" is street slang for cocaine, "boy" for Heroin.

We pull up to the corner and immediately three niggers circle the car. Jonas lowers his window about six inches.

"Where's Alex?"

"I got Alex's hookup," one of them says.

"Fuck that, man. Where's Alex?" Jonas says. I'm impressed. I've never seen him so aggressive.

Another guy strolls up, light-skinned and clean-cut, not wearing a do-rag or all scarred up. Most of the runners are dope fiends themselves, so they're always skimming off the top. But this Alex guy looks like a businessman. He tells us to drive around the block.

By the time we circle back three minutes later he has all of it: eight boy, six girl.

It is a damn good day. You can *taste* the goodness. We have a full dope-load and a few bags of girl to go along with it, to make us that much hungrier for the smack.

By the time we get back to the house my hands are sweating nonstop. It's been five days since I've gotten high—forever. Before we make it inside, Corey and Splinter pull into the driveway. We set up on the kitchen table.

"Where've you guys been?" Splinter asks.

"Hooking up," Andie says, stupidly.

"You've gotta hook me up, then," Splinter says.

"You got any money?" I ask.

"Hell, yeah, dude. But even if I didn't you'd still be hooking me up."

"Yeah, my ass."

"How much do you have?" Splinter asks.

"I guess we can give you a bag," I say.

Andie has already gotten all of our shit out by that point, the spoons, cotton, water, everything.

"Give me my bags," Jonas says.

He mixes a bag of coke with a bag of Heroin. Speedballing.

"Be careful. I don't want to have to take you to the hospital. When did you start doing that shit, anyway?"

"Don't doubt it till you try it," Jonas says.

"Do you wanna try it that way, Andie?"

"Sure. I'm up for anything."

We mix ourselves some speedball and then shoot. I immediately feel the difference from straight smack shooting. My body wants to go up and down at the same time. And then it begins to alternate between the up feel of coke and the down of Heroin and I'm on a splendid roller coaster where every high and every low is just as perfect as the feeling that came before.

"Who the fuck discovered *this* shit?" I say.

"It feels so *fucking* good," Andie says.

I decide I have to puke and head to the bathroom, feel better as soon as I finish the Technicolor Yawn.

My arm is leaking blood beneath the sleeve. I can feel it dribbling down my elbow. All bets are off. Nothing stands for anything. We are lost in the moments that slide by, grabbing whatever we can on the way down.

I wash my mouth out and when I come out of the bathroom Andie is standing there and I kiss her deep. Her mouth is warm. Her breasts heave against my chest. Then we separate and she looks at me with her head down slightly and I wipe my mouth with my sleeve.

I want to take her right there and pound her until she can't see straight. So I do. She writhes and curses and begs for more. She's like some kind of porn star now, nothing like the melancholy bitch she used to be. She has given up on love, I decide. She has given up on attempting anything meaningful or heartbreaking.

But the body shuts down the sex parts when you're high, and coasts on endorphins for a good while. I realize these things after trying (to no avail) to fuck Andie.

She pulls my face to her chest and slips one breast and then the other out of its prison of lace and grants my mouth her pink nipples, one then the other. I push her down on the bed and she pulls her nightie past her hips and I try to enter her from behind but I can't stay focused. And then I'm pushing on her with only limpness and pathetic will.

I go to the bathroom to piss, ashamed. Can impotency set in this early?

I stand over the toilet with my limp dick in hand, the urine hiding in the recesses of my bladder. Nothing comes out. I have to pee so bad but nothing will come. It's right there on the spouting and it won't make that final leap to the toilet. Because who does this shit, anyway? You can't pretend you lead a normal life, get up at 6:30, go to work, bust ass, come home, and shoot bags of cocaine and Heroin. People just don't do that. It ain't natural. None of this shit is normal. None of it. It's all a fucking pipe dream without a single hint of nobility to it.

I turn on the sink faucet and wait until the tap is warm, run the water over my prick for a good ten minutes until, finally, the piss is coaxed out and down the drain. It turns the water yellow. The vitamins I take every day to supplement and replace lost nutrients make my piss bright orange. I shoot Heroin and take vitamins. The water going down the drain is rust-colored. Nobody fucking does that. This is not maintainable. None of this is going to pan out.

TRANSMISSION 29:

adventures in pharmaceutical construction

November

Working with Jonas has proved rejuvenating. We haven't spent this much time together since we were kids and having him around has made it easier to adjust to working with two total strangers. Andie always says that she doesn't know how I ever meet anyone. I can't talk to women until after they approach me, and even then it's like one-track-mind shit. Not just sex, though. More like—cutting to the chase. Because I can't stand the mealymouthed bullshit that passes for small talk. It bores me and I'm terrible at the sport.

This guy Chris that we work with and Lou, the guy who runs the crew, all they do is cut to the chase. Lou's a lot older, in his forties. He has a mustache like I guess every guy that age does. I call him Mr. Mustache sometimes, in reference to the Nirvana song, and he seems to be cool with that. And Chris, with his unabashed love for porn, isn't too bad either.

Lou, who moved to Atlanta from Detroit twelve years ago, used to be a junkie. He moved here to get away from the shit. If that isn't a sign then I don't know what is. I talked it over with Jonas over lunch our third day on the job and we decided it would be alright if we told Lou that we are non-habit-forming, occasional smack users. Except we didn't actually tell him. We just stopped wearing long-sleeve shirts. The inner-elbow bruising and scabs proved fast billboards for our favorite pastime. Not an hour into the afternoon Lou lit a cigarette and said, pointing with the lit butt between two stubby, calloused fingers, "Where'd you get those marks on your arms?"

Jonas looked at me and I lit a cigarette of my own. All of us standing around smoking. Within minutes we had the tools packed and were headed to the ghetto. Lou said it was just this once, for old time's sake. A junkie for ten years and clean for twelve, and still thinks he can walk away after a single shot? Who does he think he's fooling? Nobody who's ever had a habit can come back to this shit for a weekend visit. It doesn't work like that. I know this already because I can't keep my mind off it even now . . . and it's only been . . . how long has it been? Regardless, it's harder than fighting a straightjacket to get back out.

We go to the Bluff and head straight to Alex, then circle the block at his command.

"This is like a fast-food drive-through," Chris says, amazed.

"Yeah, but the service is a lot better," Jonas says.

"And I'd take this any day over a Big Mac," Lou says, with complete sincerity.

"What about a Whopper?" Chris says.

"What are you, fucking *Pulp Fiction*?"

"Royale with cheese," Chris says.

After the shoot-up in the Krystal parking lot, we drive back to the job and for the first time in a long time, I am into the work. The dope makes it bearable. I am efficient. I am a machine. It is not a test of will every time I lift the mallet or drop to my knees. The smack has alleviated all need for conscious thought. I function purely on intuition. I forge the straightest line between two points. I move from the front of the rack to the back, effortlessly. I am a machine. The dope heightens my perception. The world slows down around me. People have this misconception that a junkie becomes slower, more languid in his environment, but really it's the opposite that's true. We slow the world down *around* us. Like Spider-Man, observing everything in slow motion, then executing decisions with complete, machine-like efficiency, the mind telling the body what to do before it even knows it's doing it.

And when I pause to light a cigarette and catch my breath, I look at the others and they are all machines, too. We are all silently working, not saying a word, bringing everything together in perfect time.

Well, Jonas and Lou and I are. Chris doesn't shoot dope. He only drinks prolifically. But he did say that next time he wanted to get a couple bags of coke—a couple girls.

"You know, for snorting," he clarifies.

TRANSMISSION 30:

christmas brings out the best in everyone

December

I have this enormous, gelatinously mushy soft spot for all things Yuletide. I still wear the sleigh bell that Animal Mother gave me back in the day, when we first met at *Rocky*.

He, Splinter, and I started this tradition where we'd wear a sleigh bell around our necks starting the day after Thanksgiving straight through to Christmas Day. People said it was a retarded thing to do but we didn't care. It was a tradition that *we* started. It's *our* thing.

I still do the whole *It's a Wonderful Life* bit and everything, too. I love *The Grinch* and I fucking love *Christmas Vacation* with Chevy Chase. I love all the goodwill that is automatically activated when this time of year rolls around. I love plastic snowmen on lawns that'll never feel the cold dust of real snow, and I love lights slathered across the roofs of suburban houses in the gaudiest possible array.

This is Christmas and I love every second of it. It's the one time of year when I can find a nondrug avenue to release my anxiety. On Christmas I can see proof that the world is not as horrible as it normally seems. And this year is no different. I'm using the holiday to try once more to stay the hell off of dope for a while, because it's getting to that point again where I can't function without it.

Mom has cordially invited me to attend Christmas at Victor's parents' house in Arkansas. There's no way in hell, I told her. So she said I could stay at their antebellum mansion with my girlfriend for the holidays. Mom's given up on protesting my relationship with Andie, much like when Vietnam went on for another five or six years after all those hippie protests petered out. They finally realized their smelly asses weren't accomplishing shit. The Man in charge only backs down on *his* time frame.

So we're getting ready for Christmas, for the trip to Mom's house, and Jonas and Karen are both high and kind of out of it. They sit in the corner nuzzling each other and making general annoyances of themselves with their self-absorption and their nodding off in the middle of sentences. It reminds me of Kurt Cobain, how he used to tell interviewers that he had narcolepsy in case he nodded off midsentence. And everybody believed him.

It wasn't until I started shooting dope that I realized what a perfect cover story he was fronting. Nobody ever noticed the pinned pupils. Nobody questioned why his face was covered in acne or why he was always scratching his nose. But now, when I look at tapes of his old interviews, or they're having yet another retrospective on MTV, it's just so goddam obvious. All the junkies can spot it from a crooked mile away. We all know why he fucking offed himself. We all know that we're only a personal tragedy away from doing it ourselves.

• • •

On Christmas Eve Andie and I head down to my mom's house. We stop on the way at a Christmas tree stand. A light covering of snow blankets everything, which makes the driving treacherous. This is the Deep South and there are no salt trucks, so everybody freaks and rushes the convenience stores and supermarkets on those rare occasions when the forecast calls for snow. But the trees look beautiful. There are naked lightbulbs strung across the length of the lot leading to a small wooden shack.

We call for the attendant but he is nowhere to be found. Andie says we should just take a tree but I don't want to do that. Stealing during Christmas is surely the highest possible form of sacrilege. So after twenty minutes standing with our chosen tree in the cold, I decide that we'll just leave him a sawbuck on the seat in the shack and call it even. The trees are marked at $20 but it's Christmas Eve and everybody else already has a tree so the absentee attendant's lucky he's even getting the $10.

Andie and I decorate while drinking a healthy portion of my mother's never-dwindled supply of red wine. We play Christmas songs on the massive surround-sound stereo—additional booty from Victor's settlement.

"You having a good time?" Andie asks as we dance like rich people in a ballroom.

"Yeah. I was just thinking about that—about how I haven't been this into Christmas since before my mom got remarried. There was like a five-year period after they hooked up when they didn't have money for presents until after the New Year. And when they did happen to have the money on time they'd always return the presents soon after Christmas was over, promising they would be bought back after the first of the year." They were never bought back, of course. We owned a TV, a stereo, a typewriter, and two different video-game consoles for approximately five days apiece thanks to this practice.

We continue dancing, pretending we know what we're doing. Burl Ives has a damn good Christmas voice.

"My dad always read us *The Night Before Christmas* every Christmas Eve," Andie says. "That was before he married Doris. She thought it was too cliché."

"Yeah, my mother would read us that one story, *The Best Christmas Pageant Ever.* That was always Jonas' favorite. I liked it, too. I loved that those little bastard kids thought the story said Jesus was wrapped in 'wadded up clothes.'"

Andie and I drink some wine, smoke a joint, and get the two dogs stoned by blowing smoke in their ears, as tradition dictates.

And then, even though it's only Christmas *Eve,* I give Andie her presents and she gives me mine because we aren't little kids anymore and we can open our presents any time we damn well please.

Andie opens her first gift and it's a couple of hair combs or some shit they had in a window at the mall. I thought it would be pretty funny because I read a story a few months ago about this couple that gives each other accessories to go with their most prized possessions. The catch is that neither can use the accessories because the guy sold his prized watch to buy his wife hair combs and she sold her ass-length hair to pay for a watch chain to present to her beloved husband.

At the revelation of this surprise ending, I thought how sweet it was that both of them had sacrificed their prized possessions for the benefit of the other . . . but then I started thinking about the fact that they'd probably never last more than a few years together on the long end of things. And even if they did last longer than that it would be a life together where both of them harbored secret resentments against each other. I mean, he sold this watch that he'd had for years and she did the same with her perfect hair and then they were both sitting there on Christmas morning holding useless objects, a watch chain and a couple of hair combs.

I realized it wasn't a sweet story at all. It was bullshit, a cosmic joke.

So my thinking, when I bought the hair combs for Andie, was that she'd see that it's possible to get hair combs without having to sell yourself to do it. Hair combs being a metaphor for everything you ever see that you ever want and don't know how to go about getting.

But Andie thinks the hair combs are just swell, really she does, though she has no recollection of that story even though I read it to her when we were both stone-cold sober and recovering from one binge or another. It's these little synapse lapses and general passings-in-the-night of this relationship that drive me batshit. Any time there is a seriously meaningful thing happening, she doesn't notice. And it goes the other way for me, as well. Half the time she's pissed at me for fucking around on her and the other half she's agitated by the fact that I don't remember the dates of significant times in our lives. She says that I pay no attention to the "moments." But it doesn't matter at this point because she likes the combs and she hasn't chopped all of her hair off to get me a goddam watch chain.

I open my present and it's a pair of Doc Martens boots, ten-hole, green. I've wanted a green pair of these forever and will now be the envy of every kid on my block. Docs are the shiny red Schwinn of my generation. Now my friends will have no choice but to love me or, falling short of that, look at me with quiet awe.

Andie opens her next present, a red velvet dress I bought for her at Victoria's Secret. Her eyes get wide with surprise as she unfolds the tissue paper and lets the dress unravel onto her lap. She had seen it back in the summer and tried it on and loved it so I even skipped on a couple bags of dope to make sure I could afford the three-figure price tag.

"Luke," she says, "this is the best present anyone ever gave me."

She looks more ravishing in that dress than I've ever seen her. She appears somehow more confident when she's wearing it, like she could have anyone she wanted. She pulls the dress up and we do it right there on my mother's eight-hundred-dollar Italian-upholstered chair and ottoman. Then we do it on the couch, the floor-length Persian rug, and on the kitchen counter. We sleep in Aaron's bed, and when we wake up at 9:30 Christmas day (I *still* can't sleep in on Christmas), it's only slightly disappointing that Santa has skipped me for the thirteenth consecutive year.

We bundle ourselves and trudge three miles through the cold and ice to the Waffle House for steak and eggs. I tip the waitress heavily and we hold hands on the way home.

The exterior of my mother's house looks truly magnificent on this winter morning. Maybe I've been wrong all this time about it being a bad move for Mom to obtain such a sprawling homestead. Maybe this is the real turning point for our family. Maybe this is where everything is going to change direction and we're all going to finally climb out of this hole, turn our backs on whatever curse that has hovered over our heads for as long as I can remember.

The sun has come out from behind December clouds and the front porch of the house is bathed in light. God is happy with us. God is smiling down.

TRANSMISSION 31:

getting to know your neighborhood gas station bathroom

February

We don't wait to get back to the house anymore before shooting up. We cop our dope and stop at the closest restroom on the way to the interstate.

The Crown station on the corner next to Burger King presented a unique problem. Some asshole was waiting to get in there and I couldn't open the baggie quick enough as he started banging on the door. I told him I had the shits, come back later, but he wouldn't stop banging. So I threw the door open, snarled at him, and walked out with a syringe full of dope in my jacket pocket. Then I made Andie drive so I could fix on the highway.

And that's how I got the bright idea to just start getting high right on the side of the road.

We drove up the 75 North on-ramp, where Andie pulled over. I slid the work in my vein and was flying moments later. Andie was taking all day to finish hers. Since I'm the most paranoid bastard ever I stumbled out of the car and opened the hood just in case a cop came by. Cops never fucking bother themselves with actual citizens in distress.

Andie's still got the dope in the spoon when the cop pulls up behind us.

"Put the spoon under the seat," I whisper.

"My dope'll spill."

"I don't give a fuck! There's a cop right behind us."

I get out of the car to try to intercept the cop before he sees what we're doing.

"Hi, Officer."

"Do you need any help?" she asks. A female cop. She suspects nothing, I can tell right away.

"My car does this sometimes when it gets too hot. We just have to sit around for twenty or thirty minutes and then it'll start again."

"Are you sure?" This is surely the best cop I've ever met. Not just angling to make a bust.

"Yeah. But I appreciate your stopping. I can't tell you how many times I've needed help and there was none to be found. You're a credit to your department." I laugh and the cop actually laughs a little, too. She climbs back in her cruiser and I wave as she drives off.

Andie's high by the time I get back in the car.

On my birthday, we put a floor down in a house on top of a mountain. But even with the view taken into consideration, I'm hating everything. My body is wracked with pain. I haven't had a bag of dope since the night before and I'm feeling shittier than usual because it's my birthday. This is the one day that everything is supposed to be perfect.

It wouldn't be that bad if I wasn't around Jonas and Lou. They both got high right in front of me this morning in the truck while I watched and salivated. So I'm dope-sick and neither of them will front me a bag. I already owe Lou more than two hundred bucks just for the smack he's fronted me this week. Jonas is my brother and all, but when he's got a habit going he is the most selfish prick on earth. I mean, it's my *birthday*, for God's sake, and both of them have an extra bag that I could be shooting right now, but neither of them will budge on it. Lou is probably justified in his refusal, seeing that I already owe him all this money, but Jonas is another story. We're brothers, for Christ's sake. Womb to tomb.

"See, dude," Chris says to me. "This is why it's always better to be an alcoholic. Cheaper that way. I can stay drunk for two weeks straight on the money you spend in two days on that shit."

"Chris, loan me twenty bucks, dude," I plead.

"I'll loan you twenty but I don't see what good it's going to do you up here," Chris says, pulling out his wallet.

I immediately turn to Lou. "Take me downtown. It's my fucking birthday, man. I need to get fixed."

"There's no way we're coming off this mountain until the job is finished. No way." It's easy to have resolve when it's not *your* birthday.

"Lou, I'm in pain over here and then I've gotta watch you two shoot up right the fuck in front of me? That's some bullshit."

"Maybe during lunch," Lou says.

"Jonas, give me a bag. I'll give you this twenty bucks right now for that one bag."

"I need the bag," Jonas says.

"After work you can get two fucking bags for twenty. Come on!"

They ignore me, turn away, and walk back into the house. I grab scraps of wood out of the trash can and hurl them as far as I can down the mountainside.

At lunch I watch Lou shoot up again after he finishes his goddam baloney sandwich. Then Jonas fixes his bag, and as he's getting his arm ready I beg him to give just half of it to me.

"You're not getting my fucking bag, Luke," he says, leisurely chewing the last bites of his lunch.

"You're both pieces of shit. I can't believe the selfishness of this fucking crew. You guys would sell out your own mothers if there was enough dope to be gained. Fuck you."

I head back inside and start working again despite the fact that it's only fifteen minutes into the lunch break. I have to do something or I'm going to strangle Jonas.

I grab a five-foot board and take a measurement on the wall for the last piece, the rip, to be dropped into place in the dining room. It's a typical table-saw cut. You set the fence at the correct inch mark, making sure you have deducted 5/8" to allow room for the wood to expand without buckling against the wall. I do the math in my head.

When I get outside to use the table saw, the three amigos are laughing. I ignore them and go directly to the saw.

The table saw is the loudest of our saws because its only use is for ripping boards, which basically means that you're cutting straight through the grain of the wood. It's one of the harshest screams in the world. You never get used to the sound. It's painful every time.

I decide not to use the fence because I'm feeling reckless. I take my pencil and, using my thumb and forefinger as a guide, move my hand down the side of the board, thereby creating a semi-straight line covering the length of it. No fence needed to keep the cut straight. And this way is faster, so I can cut more angrily.

I slam the board down on the saw and shove it into the screaming blade. It suddenly yanks me forward.

The tip of my right middle finger comes back ragged and bloody. Blood squirts everywhere. I call for Jonas and he comes. I still want that last bag of dope he's holding and now I have the pretext for it. I am missing a part of my body and it happened in a violent way, in the course of my vocational duties.

Jonas pulls the bag from his pocket and fixes the work for me. He offers to stick my vein with it but I tell him I'll do it. It is only now that I truly *deserve* to get high. Fuck birthdays. Being born doesn't mean shit. Being born, getting fucked up, and surviving, now that's worth something.

Laying floor for the rest of the day, I forget at times that my fingertip is gone. I just don't feel it. It is not there. None of me is here. My body is a little video-game simulation of myself and I am sitting somewhere comfortably controlling its movements. I am working harder than ever, trying to prove to them that I deserved that bag, that I was worth it.

I get home and it's the usual shit from Andie. She doesn't feel good. She needs to fix. I'm like, "Look, bitch, I don't feel good either. I cut myself on a fucking saw, OK? If anybody's getting high, it's me." The dope has worn off, leaving me irritable, the pain in my hand and arm no longer deferred.

Andie feigns interest in my injury, tells me her legs hurt so bad she can barely walk and standing up for six hours at the car wash didn't help either.

"You should try being bent over and on your knees all day," I tell her.

"So you don't have any money?"

I contemplate lying to her about the $20 Chris loaned me, but there's no way I could leave for an hour, go to the ghetto, get high, and then play it off in front of her. She's a bigger junkie than I am and it would never wash. Besides, she'd ruin my high with her constant complaining.

But then again . . . if I give her one of the bags then I won't get high myself. Neither of us will. We'll stay merely *unsick*, which is good enough if you've ever gone through a night of dope-sickness, but I want to be *high*, not merely normal.

She says, "You can pawn that ounce of silver your mom gave you." This pisses me off even more. But I have to offer her something. So I tell her that I'm going to hook up with Trizden, which is obviously total bullshit because I haven't seen him in months. But I figure she can't say a fucking word about it because she never talks to him.

"Ask Trizden if you can borrow twenty bucks," she says as I pour gasoline out of the can into the T-Bird's carburetor.

"I will."

I shoot the bags in the car at a stoplight. That's how fast I can fix. Two minutes. I contemplated waiting to fix until I got home and Andie went to sleep but decided to do it now because she'd be up half the night complaining about her body aches. The bags would call to me incessantly. There's no way I could wait until 1 or 2 a.m.

My finger throbs. I haven't yet taken off the duct-tape-and-toilet-paper bandage I made for it at work. But then, sitting at the light on the corner of North Avenue and Northside Drive, the pain is completely washed away. I hold my hand up and look at it as I push the plunger down on the syringe. I watch the pain disappear.

Every day is a good day that ends like that.

Of course, as soon as I get home Andie is on my ass. She asks for her bag and I tell her I didn't get any money from Trizden and then she starts throwing shit and saying that I don't care about her, that I never did, and that I used her for *sex*, of all things.

"Please leave me the fuck alone," I implore. "It's my fucking *birthday*, Andie. Can you please just give me one fucking minute of peace? Is it not enough that I pay for the majority of your habit? Huh? Is it? Isn't it?"

"Fuck you, asshole! I don't need you or your fucking money. I can get a ride with any guy I want."

I pick up a framed picture of us taken the day we went to the lake with that one slut friend of hers and wing it across the room so that it smashes into the wall and splinters in a thousand shards of glass and wood.

"I'm outta here!" I scream, emboldened by the double-bag of dope running through my veins, pumping rage through my every cell. As I walk to the door, Andie runs up behind me and throws her arms around my shoulders and *bites* me hard on the neck. I grab her hair and yank her to the floor.

"Leave me the fuck alone! Just let me leave."

I continue trudging toward the door, Andie wrapped around my legs and then, in a last desperate attempt at stalling me, she holds on to my wallet chain with all her weight and all I can hear then is the sound of our labored breathing and the tearing of my pocket as it gives way to her weight. I grab the wallet and yank hard and Andie yelps as the chain tears at her skin. She doesn't attempt to stop me again as I stand out at the car with the hood up, pouring gas into the carburetor.

Then I'm gone and staying with Splinter back at his transsexual aunt's house. We stay up until 2 a.m., planning our escape from all these overbearing women and their bullshit.

The next day we go to WoodCrest Apartments and apply for a two-bedroom. They say Splinter has to be gainfully employed so I ask Lou if he can put him on the crew. Lou sends Splinter to a friend who installs carpet and vinyl, a profession respectable in its own right but not nearly as prestigious as hardwood installation. We in the hardwood business like to think we do everything better, unlike the shoddy brick masons and flabby fucking drywallers and trim carpenters. And don't even get me started on plumbers and roofers. There is none of the attention to craft like that demonstrated by hardwood installers.

Within a day Splinter is employed doing carpet and vinyl and we have us our very own apartment. The bills in my name and everything.

TRANSMISSION 32:

pimpin' and hatin' life

April

Splinter and I have concluded that we have the ultimate apartment, I mean, this place is pimp. Not pimp in the bitch-slapping, fur-coat-wearing, '72 Cadillac–driving sense, but pimp in that it is just so fly, the perfect, consummate bachelor pad. Girls are in and out all the time.

And there's no problem with hookups. Anything—*anything*—we want in the way of drugs is available within a matter of minutes and a short car ride. And it's not like we live that much closer to the Bluff than when I was staying with Andie, but now that I'm out from under her everything seems so much easier. I am a singular unit, alone. I don't have to worry about anyone else. Oddly enough, this makes me all the more eager to be good to Andie. I actually go out of my way to call her every night after work, usually right after I've fixed.

That's not to say that I don't have other interests, though. Because now the entire world has opened up to me. But as a general rule, it's never as much fun scoring, in any sense of the word, if you're doing it stag. And the girls we scam on are the same fucking way. It's crazy. You'll be pouring on the compliments and thinking everything is all going *soooo* how you planned it, and then you turn around and the girls are walking, high for free, bong smoke following them out the door. We don't care, though. At least *I* don't. Any time with a girl, no matter how ultimately humiliating, is looked upon as beneficial to one's overall physical and mental well-being.

Splinter is my partner in all of this shit. Whether it's going downtown to some secretive rave location or scoring some crystallized skunk bud or dope in the Bluff, we are always together, always scamming. Then, last Saturday, the objects of our sincerest affections moved in right above us.

They are what we refer to as "Gap college girls," as in, they're in college and only shop at the Gap. Except for the occasional weed toke, they don't do drugs, and they date these stereotypical alpha males with Jeeps and crewcuts who wear t-shirts proclaiming row team insignias and mid-range designer brand names. But despite their crappy taste in men, these girls are what we consider the ultimate in untouchable, the *unapproachable*. They are these really spectacular *women* who are beautiful, out of our league, and—most important—know that they are.

Imagine our surprise then when a knock comes on our front door and there *both* the upstairs women stand, as intangible and gorgeous as ever. What's more, one is holding a bottle of white wine, glistening with condensation (the bottle, that is), with smiles on both of their impeccable faces.

Splinter and I can't believe what is about to happen. This is like a beer commercial come true. And it is about to happen to *us*.

"Hi. We just moved in above you guys last week? I'm Kristie and this is Jeannie."

"Oh my God," I think to myself. They have come with alcohol *and* their names end with that syrupy sweet *ee* sound. Our fool heads are moving up and down, surpassed in idiocy only by our stupid grins.

"So . . ." Jeannie continues after a moment of terrifying silence (our fool heads nodding and grinning), "we were just wondering if you guys might have a corkscrew."

We don't own a corkscrew.

Everything is about to go up in hellish, teeth-gnashing flames—unless . . .

It's amazing how well a pair of pliers and a screw can double for an actual corkscrew. I can't even remember how many times I've opened bottles of wine with my little Cro-Magnon man contraption.

"Wait right here," I say, taking the bottle from Kristie. She seems hesitant to let me disappear into the back bedroom with her wine (after all, nobody but those oil-massaging, mustache-having, bathrobe-wearing guys keeps a corkscrew in his bedroom), but she doesn't hold out for more than a second before I manage to wrest the alcohol from her hands.

The bottle secured on the bathroom counter, I slowly begin turning the screw. It's easy at first but gets progressively more difficult the deeper it is buried in the cork. I don't want to take any chances on prematurely attempting to pull out the screw. If it isn't deep enough the cork won't budge and all that will come out is the screw and a few splintered bits of cork. The process will have to start all over.

Finally, I have the screw buried nearly to the hilt. All that is needed now is a little brute force and the thing will come out like a shot. I pull hard. The cork doesn't budge. I pull again; still nothing. I put the bottle between my knees and give it all I have. The pliers suddenly shoot up, and in a flash I have punched myself in the mouth.

Blood is pouring from my two split lips. And what's even worse, the screw has prematurely ejected itself from the cork, which remains embedded as deeply as ever in the long neck of the emerald bottle.

Splinter pops his head in the door as I am spitting blood in the sink.

"What the fuck are you doing, dude?"

In my eagerness, I haven't noticed that I've already been holed away with the bottle for a full five minutes.

"The fucking screw-and-pliers trick didn't work!"

He stands there for a moment, looking at me. Incredulous.

"And the fact that you're spitting blood? Care to elaborate on that turn of events?"

"Stall 'em for two more minutes. I have to try again."

Splinter looks at me for a moment, sighs, heads back to his duty as I return to mine. Again I start screwing and again I pull and again I whack myself in the mouth. I look in the mirror and my lips are already swollen, the blood quickly congealing. The cork is a particled mess. It's all a big, disgraceful debacle, and now I have to go out there with those women standing in our Ultimate Bachelor Living Room with their blonde-streaked ponytails and suede miniskirts and tell them that I couldn't get their fucking bottle open.

"I thought I had a corkscrew but I couldn't find it," I mumble through one hand as the other flaccidly extends to return the wine.

Jeannie or Kristie, I don't know which one, accepts the shapely green glass bottle and stares mutely at what is left of the once-pristine cork. Mutilated.

Splinter looks at me like a crucified beggar and I wonder what he's been doing all this time to occupy the two beauties who will never again come a-calling. I am suddenly happier with the bloody mouth and egg-covered face. At least I haven't been trying to make small talk with supermodels all this time.

"Well . . ." Jeannie/Kristie stammers. "Thanks. Thanks, anyway."

They are so tall and inconceivable. Nothing can change that. Splinter and I stand there looking at the door, dumbfounded at our rapid turn of fortune. He looks at me as I pull a piece of crusted brown toilet paper from my upper lip. Then we laugh for a good long time. But it doesn't truly feel OK again until after I've taken a few tokes and a shot of bourbon. In the grand scheme of things, nothing ever feels right unless you're stupid, especially when confronted with the normal people on the doorstep, and almost in your life.

I nearly trip over Splinter when I walk in the door from work on Wednesday afternoon. He's smoking a cigarette, sprawled out on his back in front of the TV. We have two couches (Goodwill had a sale) and he never uses either of them. There is a forty-ounce bottle of beer and a saucer serving as a makeshift ashtray beside him.

"There's a fucking ashtray right there on the coffee table," I say, annoyed and pointing at the ashtray on the coffee table.

"Yeah, but I didn't feel like getting up and this plate was behind the faux plant in the corner," Splinter says.

"It's a *saucer*."

"Whatever."

I bring my trademark Gaze of Disdain from Splinter to the TV, and there on the news is a building with a hole in the side of it the size of fucking Utah.

"Holy shit," I say.

"Yeah, man, can you believe it? Somebody was pissed."

"Jesus."

"They're saying that they think this is some kind of retaliation."

"Fuck."

"Yeah."

We watch the screen silently for a few minutes. People shrieking and running around with blood all over them and little kids crying and grown-ups crying and describing how they barely escaped with their lives and all that. The building is still smoldering and they're saying that there are probably hundreds of people still trapped inside. Then Brokaw relates that there was a day-care center inside the building and none of the children have been recovered.

"You up for going downtown?" I ask.

"Hell, yes, dude. I'm fucking jonesing."

TRANSMISSION 33:

pendulum swings

May

I wake up and Alice is gone. She's one of those girls that sniff glue and huff Freon to get off. The kind of girls engaged (they never just have boyfriends, they're always engaged) to guys named Rusty or Smoky. The kind of girls named Dusty or Dakota or Daytona. The kind who wear way too much blue eye shadow because their moms always do and who have two or three kids by the time they're twenty-five and a mouth full of rotting teeth from years of drinking straight vodka and snorting speed with guys named Rusty and Smoky.

None of these facts mattered, though. I fucked all four of them. Like clockwork. Alice was the last of the four. They'd come to my bedroom one after the other for three nights in a row. The first night I had sex with one and then after we had fallen asleep her friend came in the room and woke me up climbing into bed with us. She was naked. It feels cheap just talking about it but it's not like I seduced any of them. They had to have told each other what was going on. Girls are always talking about shit like that with each other.

And yet, they kept coming. Like it was their turn or something. I buried my head in the pillow and threw my hips forward and pulled back again, then felt the burst, saw the flash of light, and she moved from under me and the one girl, Alice, she took my head in her lap and caressed me until I stopped shaking and then leaned down and kissed my mouth and forehead. That was pretty nice.

They all wanted to save me.

I asked Alice if she was seeing anybody.

She nodded.

"I'm actually engaged," she said.

The problem with doing anything you know you shouldn't be doing is that word gets around. I still don't know who told Andie about all the girls, but she sure as shit found out.

She comes barging in the door without even knocking and slaps the shit outta me. I grab her by the arm and throw her out the front door. I watch her stumble backward before the door swings shut again. I can hear her yelling at the top of her lungs that she hates me and then I go to the freezer, drink some more, move to my bedroom, turn up the stereo, walk in the bathroom, look at my red face and neck in the mirror.

When I get back outside, Andie's gone. I sit down on the cement by Splinter's feet. He swigs on his Crazy Horse.

I don't talk to Andie again until two days later. She tells me that she doesn't believe in Us anymore, that this was the last straw. I say that I understand, that she has every right to feel that way. I am indefensible. But she continues calling me every day, as soon as I get in from work. She cries and tells me she hates me for doing this to her, that I have crushed her and she can't see how to live anymore. I tell her that I've been using more dope than ever and she says that she has been doing the same. She tells me that she can find no consolation in anything but the dope.

This type of exchange becomes our primary means of communication and I come to rely on it. I rush down to the ghetto with Splinter after work and score my bags and then wait by the phone for Andie to call. I can't bring myself to call her because she deserves better than me calling her. She deserves to be rid of me. That's what I tell her when she asks why I never call her. I tell her I want her to regroup and move beyond me. I say these things because I feel like it is my duty to say these things.

And then, a week after the night we broke up for the last time, she doesn't call. Corey drops by to tell me that she has started seeing Hank. He says that she started hanging out with him when he mowed her lawn shortly after I moved out. And now he's living with her. He's moved in with her and Corey's pretty sure that they're fucking and I cannot *stand* this betrayal by either of them. You don't steal from your friends and you sure as shit don't fuck their exes.

I get on the phone and call Andie's house for the first time since she smacked me and I threw her out of my apartment. The voicemail picks up and she says on the message, "We aren't here right now. Leave a message and blah blah blah."

That's what she actually says: "Leave a message and blah blah blah."

I miss her so much.

I hang up and call back.

Again with the voicemail.

And then I'm struck by how she says, "We aren't here right now."

We.

We've been broken up a miserable goddam—month?—and

already she is including someone else in her fucking life. On *our* goddam answering machine. I call the message service to check her voicemail. She hasn't changed the password yet. I am privy to all her saved messages. There are three from Hank with his goddam whispery goddam voice telling her that he'll be home from work at so and so time. And saying shit like he can't wait to see her.

I have to get Sativa back.

I jump in the T-Bird, head to Andie's house wondering if I'll actually have the balls to do something heinous.

All I want is the cat, though. So fuck it. She can do whatever the fuck she wants with that traitorous piece of hillbilly shit. But I'll take the cat, thanks. The cat is mine.

Andie is just pulling up to the house in Hank's car as I get out of mine.

"You let Hank move in with you?"

"Yeah, I did," she says, turning her back to me to unlock the door.

"Why would you let one of my friends move in with you? Why? Can't you see how that is killing me?"

She turns around in the doorway and looks me up and down.

"Why should I care?"

I am momentarily dumbstruck.

"You look like shit," she says.

"So it's true that you don't love me anymore? You don't love me?"

"No, I don't." She sounds more sure of herself than she ever has. I am secretly proud of her for that. But it's this self-confidence, this self-assuredness that says she could pretty easily do without me in her life that is the most wounding of all. I feel like crying but I won't give her that.

"I came by to get Sativa," I say as stonily as possible.

"You can't have her."

"The fuck I can't. She's my cat."

Andie stares at me for a moment and then relents. It's easier to just give me the stupid cat and get me out of there before Hank comes outside.

"Wait here and I'll get her."

She walks down the hall and disappears around the corner. I try to see what the living room looks like now, if there is any evidence of Hank. Everything appears to be the same. One of my drawings is still tacked to the wall. I take comfort in that.

Andie reappears with an open-topped wicker basket. Sativa is lying inside with three kittens. She hands the basket to me.

"It's a package deal, you know."

"Shit. I forgot she was pregnant. When did she have them?"

"A few days ago."

"They're really cute." I smile at them and when I look at Andie she is smiling too.

"Thanks for this," I say, motioning with the basket of cats. Sativa is purring and looking at me with half-closed eyes while her kittens nurse. I needed this. Sativa will fix everything.

"You'd better go," Andie says.

"Tell Hank he's an ignorant, worthless dick."

"Tell yourself that you're a dick," Andie says.

"I already do." I head back to the car. "But at least that redneck fucktard'll be dead soon. Cancer-ridden fuck."

I place the basket with Sativa and her babies on the back seat.

Back at the apartment I shoot a bag of dope while sitting on the bed with the kittens mewing next to me. Splinter knocks on the door to ask if I'll take him downtown to get him one. I ignore him, pick up the phone and dial Andie. She answers.

"Please, Andie, please don't do this. Hank was my friend, for Christ's sake."

She says nothing. I hear the line click. I throw the phone across the room and it tears out the line connecting it to the wall and clatters to the floor behind the bed.

I grab my last bag of dope, fix and shoot it. I feel the warm envelope enclose me but that still isn't enough to quell this noise in my head. I am dying inside. The dope doesn't even work now.

I crack open a razor and tear off my shirt. I move over to the stereo, drop in some Mozart. Then I start cutting, hard. I can't feel anything at all. Like cutting paper.

I look in the mirror at the blood all over me. It flows freely and from many places. I run my hands around in it, smear it and watch it continue seeping from my chest. Sativa walks in and rubs against my legs. She stares up at me and meows while purring. It's a burbling meow, bubbly like a fountain.

Sativa's tongue prickles on my chest. She is cleaning me, *cleansing* me. I appreciate her for doing that. She cares. I collapse on the bed and lie there for a long time. I reach down and pick her up.

TRANSMISSION 34:

saved

June

Alex thought the cops were on to him so he packed all of his baggies full to the rim with smack and sold them at the regular ten-dollar price. That's like getting four for the price of one. Jonas copped seven of them and sold one each to me, Lou, and Splinter.

When Lou and I got back from the bank with the money to reimburse Jonas for his generous offering of overstuffed bags of dope, Splinter was lying on the couch with his eyes rolled back in his head, stiff as a board, a line of white fluid seeping from his mouth. The motherfucker. I'd even specified to him before I went out the door, I fucking specified, "Don't shoot that whole bag, Splinter."

"I won't, man," he'd said.

"I mean it, dude," I said. "Don't shoot that whole bag. You'll fucking die."

"I won't, Dad."

"I mean it," I said as we walked out the door.

"Splinter shot that whole bag," Jonas mumbled without looking up. He and Karen were sitting directly across from Splinter, staring at him.

Lou motioned for me to help him. Splinter's arms were stiff, locked and folded on his chest. He looked dead. He looked so fucking dead. Lou said we'd have to get his blood circulating or he *would* die, so I had to stop freaking out for a minute and help him drag Splinter around the room.

Splinter's body stayed rigid. He was still not moving. We tried everything. We smacked him hard in the face. We ran cold water over his head in the bathtub. Then there was no other choice but to call the ambulance. And they don't come out for social calls. They are there solely for clean up. Somebody was either going to jail or the hospital.

The paramedics showed up right after Lou left. He didn't want to have anything to do with an OD'd kid, he'd said. He has his business to think about.

Jonas and Karen told the paramedics that they came home and found him like that. They weren't even asked, they just offered up the information like that, the stupid fucks. I gave them both the evil eye because it was so obvious to everyone that they were stoned off their pathetic asses. The female paramedic asked if we could take a guess as to what happened.

"I have an idea," I said, cryptically.

Then her male counterpart said, real fucking private eye, "I think we've found the culprit." He was standing over the dining room table, holding up a syringe. It was one of the syringes Splinter ganked from the hospital the other day when he was in there for chest pains. He frequently goes to emergency rooms around the area complaining of phantom pains so as to possibly get painkillers prescribed. Junkies can never get enough syringes. They get dull after about five uses, and there's always someone coming over that wants to shoot but doesn't have a work and then you've got yet another person's blood in your shit. But the syringes Splinter got are made for elephants or something. We usually get 30-gauge, 1cc insulin syringes, which have a really fine point. When they're new they slide in like butter. The ones Splinter procured have to be at least 8-gauge. Even brand-new they feel like stabbing yourself with a fork tine.

The woman paramedic asked me if I knew what kind of drugs he was doing. I shook my head, tried to play dumb. Karen offered that he was probably using Heroin. The guy asked what the effects of Heroin are. Jonas and Karen fired off five or six different aspects of the high and I wanted to kick the living shit out of both of them.

"Alright," the woman said, standing up. "Jim, do you want to go out to the truck and get the bags?" Immediately I took this statement in the Vietnam sense, as in "body bags," and I started screaming at them to save him.

"You have to save him," I said. "That's what you people do, isn't it?"

"It's OK, it's OK," she assured me calmly. "'Bags' just means the oxygen bags we use to pump oxygen into an unconscious person's lungs. We're going to do everything we can to help your friend."

Jim the Paramedic had a cop with him when he came back with "the bags." The cop didn't say anything at first. He stood in the doorway and looked at Splinter with a disgusted look on his face.

And then, right when they were about to put the oxygen mask on him, Splinter sat up.

Just like that.

He sat up and looked around, still in a stupor from the massive dope hit. He pushed the mask away from his face and the cop asked him point-blank if he wanted to go to jail or the hospital. Splinter replied that he wanted to go to neither.

"You've got to go to one or the other," the cop said. "Once a call is made on an illegal substance problem, you have to go to the hospital or to jail."

Splinter looked at me with anger in his eyes, but I was so happy that he wasn't dead that I didn't care if he was angry or not.

He ended up in jail. It turns out that he had a quarter ounce of weed in his jeans pocket, so they pinned that on him, too.

When he called me collect from the county lockup he was livid and didn't care what my rationale was for calling 911.

"If *you'd* seen you . . ." I said.

He stayed in the can for a week before I could get together the $250 for bail. Now he says he's moving as soon as he can save the money because he has to get away from dope and he knows some hippies that are going up to NYC for a while to see if there's anything to protest up there.

"How smart is it to go to New York if you're trying to get away from dope?" I asked him.

"You're always such a pessimist, Luke," he said.

I walk to the bathroom to piss around 1 a.m. and something crunches under my foot. It's one of Sativa's kittens, the little gray male. Somehow he crawled out of the closet and now he's writhing on the floor and blood is coming out of his tiny mouth.

I know he's finished before I even pick him up, before Sativa begins her low cry of mourning. She looks up at me and I can see the despair in her cat eyes and I know that I have ruined yet another precious thing.

There's going to be bad luck following this one. You can't kill a cat without serious repercussions. They are God's chosen animals, is what my grandmother says. God gave us cats because they are the easiest to disregard. They are easy to take for granted, she says. He wanted us to have to approach Him, make a concerted effort, all that. And cats are just the same. They never come when they're called. They lie around and look at you and then, just when you are cursing them under your breath, you feel that swish along your leg and they are looking up at you and smiling. But this is only for your sake. Cats don't need you and neither does God. Both are self-sufficient. The good ones are at least willing to look in on us at times, clean the wounds and help them heal. Now vengeance is about to set in. I can feel the gray pallor settling down already, can see the signs as Sativa growls at me when I come to the closet to replenish her food.

Splinter helps me bury the kitten in the rocky dirt behind our back porch overlooking the woods and, farther down the embankment, the highway. The kitten is small enough that it only takes two, maybe three shovelfuls of dirt before the hole is deep enough for him to fit snugly. He looks comfortable there.

Splinter says a prayer, which is ridiculous, but he was always the more spiritual of the two of us. And maybe cats need the last rites as much as we do, though I highly doubt it because I can't imagine any other animal doing as much messed-up shit to themselves and everyone else around them as people do. We fuck ourselves and each other. That's us at our best, our most natural.

Alice comes back the next day. She looks hotter than ever, wearing a tight white t-shirt knotted at the stomach, torn fishnets, a black mini, and a pair of combat boots with the steel shining dully from behind the torn leather at the toe. She's brought a bottle of whiskey and is holding it up like a *Price Is Right* model, smiling. She asks if I have change for the taxi, because the fare alone was sixty bucks and she doesn't have anything for the tip. I give her a five and then we do shots. It's good that she brings whiskey because I've sworn off smack once again, this time determined to believe that Splinter's episode is the omen that means, finally, that the time has come to stop once and for all.

We get drunk that night, fuck, and the next morning she says she wants to shoot up.

"I don't do that anymore," I say.

"Not even with me?"

"I just don't . . ." She looks so sweet and sexy sitting there, looking at me like that. "Can you get some money?"

She reaches into her jeans pocket and pulls out an ATM card. We're high within the hour.

She pukes her guts out the whole night, and the next morning she's ready to go again.

"But you threw up all day yesterday."

"I like how you hold me when we do it."

"When we shoot up?"

"Yeah. And you're all peaceful and less worried about stuff."

"You're a precious girl, you know that?"

She whispers in my ear and plays with my dreads. We go back down to the Bluff.

We lie in bed most of the night, staring at the ceiling in the dark, lost in our stupors, a Portishead CD or something like it thumping quietly in the black of the room.

At some point between consciousnesses, the ceiling quakes and I am momentarily jerked from my half-sleep. I look at Alice and she is awake, too.

"What was that?" she whispers.

The ceiling rumbles again and we listen hard. A girl is yelling, followed by a deeper male voice. The ceiling moves again and then we hear crying.

"It's the Gap college girls. Somebody's kicking the shit out of one of them," I say.

We lie there in silence and listen to one of those all-American girls get her ass kicked by one of her all-American boyfriends. We are helpless to help, too fucked up to even comprehend talking to some cop on the other end of 911. I turn up the stereo and pull the covers over our heads. Alice lies in the crook of my arm and falls asleep. Andie and Hank can go rot for all I care.

TRANSMISSION 35:

an untidy suicide

July

Rick—my old man—the *real* one—calls when I get home from work. He says that he's been seeing a shrink (he calls the shrink his "analyst") and the shrink has told him that the reason he hates going to the dentist so much is because he was probably sexually abused as a child.

"How does the analyst know that?" I ask.

"We've been doing regression therapy, where he hypnotizes me and all these memories that have been buried for years come to the surface."

"And you remember being molested?"

"No, not when I'm awake. Like right now I couldn't tell you that I remember being molested. But my analyst says that when I'm in a trance I say some pretty strange shit."

"Like what?"

"Like that . . . look, I don't want to get into all the gory details. But the reason I called is that I've been doing a lot of praying lately and God has really put it on my heart to call you. I just needed to tell you that I love you. I want you to be OK, Luke. I want you to know that your life is just beginning, really, and that you have the power to make it as fulfilling as you can imagine it."

"Rick?"

"What?"

"You're acting really fucking weird. I'm not used to pep talks from the King of Gloom."

"King of Gloom? Whaddaya mean? We're always joking around about stuff. Are you saying our relationship is dark?"

This from a man who abandoned his wife and kids.

"I don't know, man. You call me up, tell me you've discovered that you were molested, then you say that God has told you to tell me that everything is just peachy. Seriously, your analyst said that's why you fear the dentist? Who the fuck ever heard of anything like that?"

"Use your imagination, Luke."

"I don't want to use my imagination."

"Yeah, well, I don't want you to use it, either. I just want you to be OK."

"I'm fine."

"OK. Good."

"If you'd call more often you might actually catch me at a bad time," I say. "I just had one a couple weeks ago. Several of them, in fact."

"Well, I told you months ago that I had an 800 number set up for the express purpose of you and Jonas being able to call me for free but I have yet to receive one call from either of you."

"That's great, Rick. You've got a free number set up for us so now all sense of responsibility is in our court. I get it. You've done your duty and now all is forgiven."

"I don't know what else to do for you, Luke. What else can I do?"

"I don't know. What else *can* you do? Why don't you go back to that shrink and ask him to hypnotize you and figure out why you'd ditch your kids for a slut."

"Hey, don't talk about Janice like that. She has been nothing but nice to you."

"When? When I was three and you kidnapped me and she sat me in front of *Sesame Street*? Do you even *know* who you're married to?"

This is the conversation I imagine having with him. It's the one I always imagine. In reality our conversation ends with me saying that that's some good advice, Rick. We never get beyond the surface shit, the hypno-revelations, the comedic anecdotes. I actually get off the phone with him on this occasion before he's even finished describing the hypnosis and its fruits. Because there's a knock on the door and it's Animal Mother and he's crying. He says that Michelle, as in Skinhead Michelle—Sinead from Dragon*Con—is dead.

She hung herself from a tree during a party. She excused herself to smoke a cigarette and then, after she'd been gone for a while, people started looking for her and found her hanging in the backyard with a chain from the tire swing wrapped around her neck. Animal Mother says that Michelle's eyes were still open and bulging out of her head and her face was purple and she looked like a monster. The funeral will be closed-casket.

Everybody Skinhead Michelle knew from high school shows up for the services, mainly suburban druggie kids wearing khaki slacks with button-down shirts and ties, the very kids Michelle's parents blame for her death. They haven't said as much but it's pretty obvious to all of us who are sober that they do. Which isn't many. Though I can say for myself, at least, that I declined to shoot up before this goddam funeral because Michelle deserves that much at least, to have her so-called friends clear-eyed as they remember her and send her officially from this world to the next.

After the preacher drones on for twenty minutes about her being in a better place, that her soul can finally be at peace, we drop flowers on her casket and then about twenty of us go to Waffle House to eat and remember the girl none of us really knew. Everybody claims to be completely taken by surprise, as though there were no warning signs. She seemed so happy and carefree, they all say.

Jonas says that her hands always looked incredibly *old*.

"Maybe she was old in spirit, you know, bro?" Jonas says. "Maybe she was ready to die."

"Whaddaya mean, her hands looked old?" I say.

"I mean, she had these hands that looked like an old woman's hands, like they were wrinkled before she was even old. Maybe she was old in *spirit* and her hands were the only manifestations of that oldness. Well, that and this early death."

"That makes no fucking sense. Is 'oldness' even a word? Are you high, Jonas?"

"Yeah. Wake up, Luke. Everybody here is high. It's like pouring a beer out for a dead homie, get it?"

"I think it's fucking pathetic. And I feel like it's my fault that your life consists solely of shooting dope, even when one of our friends has died."

"Hey, leave off him, Luke," Karen says. "Where do you come off acting like Mr. Holier-Than-Thou? Like you don't do the same shit we do."

"Fuck you, Karen."

"Don't tell my girlfriend 'fuck,'" Jonas says, Heroin anger rising in his voice.

"You're all pathetic," I say, attempting with some difficulty to keep my voice down. "Do you even remember what it feels like to have emotion, to feel like a human being? Because this is the first time I have in a long goddam time and that scares the shit out of me." I stand up and turn to leave, loosening my tie. Jonas stumbles outside after me.

"Do you really believe that, what you were saying in there?"

"Fuckin A."

"I feel like that sometimes, too," he says. "But the dope helps me, Luke. You know?"

"Yeah, I know, man. And I don't know what the answer is for that. I just know that I can't do this anymore."

"Me either," Jonas says. "I just know that I can't *not* do it, either."

I look at my brother. The skinny part of his tie is sticking out four inches below the fat part.

TRANSMISSION 36:

a new friend

August

The fucking car dies right after we get the dope. I turn the key but there is no response. It's mid-August in Atlanta and we're sitting bang in the middle of the Bluff. Sweat is rolling. The car's at the top of a hill, though, so at least there's that.

I decide to put it in neutral and let it roll, hoping that if it is in the act of doing what it does best, that it'll just start, you know, out of habit. But the T-Bird has an automatic transmission, so this plan of action is ultimately pointless, fruitless, hopeless, and in all other ways fucked. I hit the brakes at the bottom of the hill in front of the stop sign. And that's when the dealers, crackheads, and junkies—the locals—start coming out of the crevices. And that's when Alice starts freaking out.

I'm standing out there with the hood up, banging on anything that looks out of place with this ten-inch screwdriver that I keep in the trunk. It's the only tool I own, used mainly in flooring but coming in handy in other more desperate situations. I ask the crack-heads if they know anything about cars. I hear a few "motherfuck-ers" uttered, maybe a racial epithet or two. The police are a threat, too. At any minute a cruiser could drive past and we'd be fucked. White people have no reasonable explanation for being down here unless they're copping dope. The cops know this.

There was a time a while back when I was down here with Andie and we came a pubic hair's width away from getting busted. It was around 10:30 at night. I pulled up to the corner, where a guy I didn't know was leaning on a light pole. It was during one of the seasonal sweeps the cops made of the area, when all the streets are empty, so he was the only runner out at the time.

"Can you get me some boy?" I asked him with the window down. He didn't acknowledge me.

"Hey, man," I repeated. "Can you hook me up?"

He raised his chin until his eyes met mine from beneath his brimmed dreadcap. He was chewing a toothpick. Very slowly he cocked his head in the direction of a car parked down the block on the wrong side of the street.

"Are you fuckin' stupid, nigga?" he said, finally.

I peered hard at the dark car. And then it hit me. It was a cop.

I hit the gas and turned left down the intersecting street. Twenty seconds later the cop was behind me with his lights on. Now, there's a punk club about half a mile from the Bluff called the Lizard Lounge, so I told the cop that we were lost and trying to figure out how to get back to the club.

"That's the only reason I was talking to that guy, Officer," I said.

"Where's the fucking drugs?" he demanded.

"I don't do drugs, sir."

"Let me tell you something," he said, temporarily interrupting his search of my pockets. "If I find one fucking syringe cap, one fucking baggie top, anything, I'ma kick the living shit outta you, punk. Got it? And if that nasty hair of yours touches me one more time I'm gonna knock your fucking teeth out." He was very self-assured.

But what he didn't know is that I never hold works in the car anymore. It's too risky. We keep them in a little box under a dumpster behind the Lizard Lounge.

"We're just lost, sir," I reiterated. He didn't have shit on us. He nabbed us before we copped any dope. And after he grudgingly let us go we went to a different street and copped our dope anyway. Another junkie moment of triumph.

But this time is different. This time we have the dope on us. This time we can't just drive away. We're at everybody's mercy, the cops *and* the dealers.

"I can get this nigga over here to give you a jump for ten bucks," some asshole says to me, motioning to a house across the street. There's a partially dismantled '73 Cadillac in the front yard.

"I don't have ten bucks," I lie. "Why don't you see if he'll do it for five?"

"Nigga, you don't have ten bucks, you sit here all day. And you sure as shit don't wanna be down in this mothafucka after it get dark."

I lean in the window and tell Alice to give me a ten. She hands me the money. Her fingers leave sweat stains on the bill. He runs over and gets his uncle or cousin or whatever the fuck to drive his piece-of-shit Chrysler coupe over for the jumping process. The uncle charges two more dollars for the use of his jumper cables.

"Look at it like this," the uncle/cousin says as he pockets the two dollars. "It's that much less that you'll be putting up your arm, little brotha, and that's a good thing."

After five minutes he tells me to try to start the car. I turn the key. Nothing. He says he can't be doing this shit all day, that he'll let me try once more in five minutes and then he "got to be going."

"I gave you ten bucks, man."

"Ten bucks cover two charges," he says. These motherfuckers. Always trying to take you for everything. I try to start the car again and again nothing happens. The uncle packs up his cables and pulls back onto his front lawn, lets the screen door slam on his way back into his house. They have the TV turned up so loud in there that we can here the sound of canned laughter from across the street.

The crackheads and other menacing ghetto denizens come back and ask for everything ranging from "a dolla" to "a piece of that fine whitegirl ass." It's been over an hour and I'm seriously considering *snorting* the dope if it'll help relieve the stress of the situation. But that's sacrilege. A junkie—a true junkie—would never, ever snort, eat, or in any other way ingest Heroin other than mainline injecting. You might as well flush the bag down the toilet. I don't care if you have to somehow MacGyver a straw and a toilet plunger, you find a way to get the Heroin from the baggie straight into your vein.

I get back in the car with Alice. "Just imagine how good these bags are going to be when we get outta here," I tell her, as though that is going to make any difference to her. As far as she can see, we're never going to get out of here, and it's starting to look that way to me, too. It's already five o'clock. There're only a few more hours of light left.

We're sitting in the car trying to figure out our next move when, for no apparent reason, some nigger smashes out my car's right passenger-side window with a hammer. He runs off without even yelling anything antiwhite or antijunkie or anything remotely political. No motives are given. It is an act of unadulterated terrorism, pure and simple. And it works. Alice has glass in her hair and screams, terrified, for a good five minutes. That's right about when we meet this guy Paul.

He's very soft-spoken. He asks me if I can spare a few bucks.

I tell him I'll stick him with the screwdriver if he doesn't leave us alone.

"I don't mean no harm," he says. "Hey, I can get these guys over at this garage a couple blocks down to tow you out of here," he says, pointing down the street

"Why would you do that? I already gave my last ten bucks to this guy over here for a jump that didn't pan out."

"'Cause you seem like a nice guy and also 'cause I see your car down here all the time so I know that you'll do *me* a favor another day."

"You a dealer?"

"No, man. I'm a junkie. Like you." He holds out his arms so we can see the track marks. His tracks put our habits to shame. True junkie track marks. Years of injection mapped in scar tissue on the crooks of his arms like a river's tributaries. His eyes are true, full of sadness. I look at him and promise I will pay him back if he gets us out of here.

Twenty minutes later the tow truck pulls up.

"Don't take any wooden nickels," Paul says to me, rounding the corner out of sight.

The tow truck guy is a real dick. He says we owe him "big time." He drives us the two miles to the Lizard Lounge and drops the T-Bird in the parking lot. I promise to mail him a check for $25 as soon as I get home, which is total bullshit.

But that doesn't mean I'm not keeping my word with Junkie Paul. He's in the zone with us, part of the circle. He did me a solid and I will do him one in return. He will get at least two bags off me for his act of selflessness. It was an honorable thing he did, and honor is something found in the smallest of quantities when you're in this game. Everyone is out for himself. Everybody, from junkies to runners to dealers, is trying to somehow come out ahead. Paul's contribution doesn't slip by lightly. Paul is a goddam angel sent from above.

I run over to the dumpster and pull the box out from under it. The works are still inside, untouched. I fix my hit, then Alice's. We lean on each other in the front seat of the T-Bird, smoke a cigarette, feel the stress slip away. It doesn't matter that we don't have a way home. We made it through a blistering hot afternoon in the Bluff. We *must* be invincible.

Before walking to the Shell station to call a ride, I try the car one last time. It starts on the first key turn.

TRANSMISSION 37:

revelation

September

These are the things you notice with the sound off. Sometimes I like to pop in a porno and watch it silent. I know I won't be able to cum, what with the junk coursing through me, but that's not the point. The point is that the *Moonlight* Sonata is playing on the stereo, and as the piano tinkles and rises then converges, and I watch the expressions on the girls' faces on the screen as they get their orifices pounded for money, it occurs to me that porn stars are possibly the saddest people on the planet. In the slow-motion shots, where the camera is focused on the girl's face, she with the gritted teeth and the furrowed eyebrows, I can think of nothing better than to make love to a porn star.

They will never know the pleasure of pure lovemaking. They probably never have. Or maybe they did once and lost it and porn was their only recourse once they decided that love was irrevocably deleted from their lives. They are doing things with complete strangers that most of us will never do with spouses of thirty years.

But we are all doing what we have to do to get by, medicating to make it possible to live with ourselves. I wonder if porn stars ever contemplate offing themselves because their destitution is reenacted on a daily basis.

He's doing her from behind now, his hand squeezing the sensitive space between her hip and her thigh. He has her skin bunched there in his hand like he's manipulating one of those stress relief balls and she accepts the pain for a long time before she finally reaches back and makes him let go of her, all the while maintaining the illusion that she's enjoying the fuck. *These are the things you notice with the sound off.*

The piano crescendos. The girl closes her eyes while the faceless stud squirts thick into her mouth.

My mother asks me to go to church with her and for the first time in years I decide I'll give it a shot. My mother says I have so many problems because I don't try to keep "communion" with God. Church, for my mother, is like smack to a junkie. It used to be anyway. Then we got a TV and started listening to secular radio when I was twelve and now she only goes when there's some serious shit going down. She's vehement about getting her God fix then.

I leave Alice sleeping off a hangover and meet my mother at the church at 10:30 sharp. People can judge me all they want about my life choices, but at least I'm punctual.

Seeing all the clean-cut, well-rounded God followers milling about the church parking lot immediately makes me regret showing up. Standing there waiting for my mother to do some last-minute alterations of her makeup, I am underwhelmed by uptight white-bread assholes and their shiny cars and their spotless credit reports and their perfect orthodontia and their limp, patronizing handshakes. And their twice-monthly haircuts that are always the same. They all look alike, with their functional upbringings and their always-a-kind-word ethos. It makes you want to pop the shit out of one of 'em, just to see how kindly and faux-understanding they'd be then. That's what it makes you want to do.

I bring my church everywhere with me. I kneel at the crooks of my arms. And sometimes, when the hit is just right, I can feel the hand of God—maybe even hear His voice. I can't make out what it's saying, though. I am a prisoner in my cage of bone, my ear to the wall, trying to understand.

The service starts with a load of singing. The songs are some kind of nouveau gospel tripe. Then comes the earnest prayer, then more music, then money collecting, before the preacher finally takes the stage.

He doesn't speak in puritanical, Jonathan Edwards fire-and-brimstone metaphor and simile, which is what I always expect coming into these things. Hell, I probably decided to meet up here with my mom specifically because I thought that is what I'd be hearing.

But no, his is a message of Love. He implores the congregation of thousands to put aside their prejudgments of all who have fallen from God's favor. He cites that Bible verse where Jesus tells the people who want to stone the hooker to death to freely cast the first stone if any of them are without sin. "There are lost souls out in the world," the preacher says, "maybe in this very house of worship, who are without solace, who don't know where to turn, who have exhausted every possible avenue in search of an answer that will not come. They still wait for the miracle."

He continues on in this vein for a good forty-five minutes, and as he's admonishing the sorry fucks that make up his congregation I begin to feel sad or something. I can't help but cry.

My mother is rocking back and forth with her eyes closed with her arm around me. I lose track of time and the preacher's voice recedes to the background as I am overcome with emotion, relief flooding out of me. I want to run out of the church and head straight to the ghetto, find the pregnant woman who's always wandering around down there, pull her aside, tell her that we are not abandoned, only underused—that this is not the final act.

We are acknowledged, goddammit.

God has His eye on all of us.

When I get home Alice is watching TV with my grandmother's afghan wrapped around her. She looks like hell. All the shades are drawn and the apartment is like a fucking dungeon. Splinter comes out of the bathroom not looking much better.

This is the problem with having epiphanies, I've realized. In order to follow through on them you have to get everyone around you to make the same positive choices you have or else it won't add up to shit.

As Splinter rummages through the kitchen and Alice clicks through an endless litany of channels, I realize that I have to get rid of both of them.

I begin yanking open the blinds without answering Alice's imploration to make a run down to the Bluff.

"There's no fucking milk, Luke," Splinter whines, holding a bowl of cereal by his side like a six-gun. His boxer shorts have holes in them.

I ignore both of them. I'm above this now.

"I don't give a shit about the milk, Luke," Alice says. "I just want to go downtown. I *need* to go downtown."

Splinter drops his empty bowl on the counter and goes back in the bathroom, shuts the door. Alice throws the remote on the couch and closes the bedroom door behind her. The woman on the TV says she's gonna get revenge. If it's the last thing she does, she'll get that bitch, she says.

Sativa rubs against my legs, purring.

Bushwick the Lesbian comes out of Splinter's room, hacking up a lung as she heads to the bathroom. Bushwick attached herself to Splinter's jock at a bar downtown the night before and for some ungodly reason he brought her back here with him. Apparently Bushwick the Lesbo got wasted and decided she had a newfound hankering for dick. It's not that I have anything against lesbians or anything. I, like most red-blooded American males, like nothing better than fantasizing about two hot lesbians going at it. Not the butch kind, of course, with the mullets and the mustaches, but the porn industry–endorsed *lipstick lesbians*. Unfortunately for Splinter's pathetic ass, Bushwick is not of the lipstick persuasion. Though she does claim to have bagged Penthouse Pets on more than one occasion.

Bushwick comes out of the bathroom fully clothed, acts all gregarious, says she has to get something out of her car. She never comes back.

This is when it hits me.

I yank my wallet out of my pocket. It's all gone, all seven hundred bucks. She snuck into my room while I slept off the previous night's party and robbed us blind.

"Do you have any fucking clue where Bushwick lives?" I ask Splinter.

"Who the fuck is Bushwick?"

"The fucking lesbian! She stole the rent!"

"No, man. I have no clue. I don't even know her fucking name."

"How could you fucking bring someone like that into our house, man? I mean, what the fuck are we going to do?"

"Well, dude, I guess this'd be the best time to tell you that I'm leaving for New York in a week. I gave you my share of this month's rent because I felt like I owed it to you. But now that this shit's happened it feels like a sign."

"A sign? You're on the fucking lease! You're not doing me any favors by paying your share of the rent if you're just going to leave."

"I know, man, but I have to go where my heart leads me. There's a whole lot of shit happening up there and I've gotta be part of it. You only live once and all that shit."

"Well, what the fuck am I going to do, Splinter?"

"Fuck this place, Luke. Come with me."

"To New York? I can't live up there, man. I'll never stay clean if I live up there. And if you're smart you won't go either because we've both heard the stories about how easy it is to cop every drug in the universe in New York. A place like that will eat people like us alive."

"Maybe so, but at least we'll have fun getting eaten."

Later that night a couple of Splinter's hippie friends come over and we get stoned. Alice continues working on me to take her to the Bluff. It's on the third bowl-pack when I decide definitively that she has to go. I'll never get straight with her perfect ass always tempting me, her fucking voluptuous tits wagging in my face, her baby-talk begging for more of everything that feels good, her exquisite blow jobs, her nihilistic outlook on life.

The next day I take her to Little 5 Points and drop her off in front of the pizza place. I tell her to call me but she never does after that. Jonas tells me months later that he saw her in the ghetto giving head to some dealer for smack.

Splinter leaves for New York that same day with a hippie who goes by the name Laughing Horse. Seriously. I asked him what his name was and he said, "Laughing Horse."

These fucking people.

Not that "Splinter" is much better, but at least he's a noun without the extraneous action verb attached to it.

I get paid on Friday and hit the Bluff one more time with Jonas and Karen. It's somehow easier to do it this way, now that Splinter and Alice are gone and I don't have to feel responsible for them.

And I have a plan to save the apartment. So there's that to celebrate.

Trizden agrees to meet with me at the Smyrna Lanes bowling alley. He wanted it that way. We haven't spoken since the suicide. But now's not the time for pride or standing on principle. Now's not the time to hold grudges, to remind him that he ditched me just because I like getting fucked up.

We trade in our shoes and grab a pitcher of beer.

"Have you ever heard of Lord Byron?" I ask him between turns.

"Is that a new D & D thing?"

"Fuck no, man. I'm talking about the poet. The Romantic?"

He shakes his head, looks at me blankly.

"All right, fuck it, I'll tell you about him. Lord Byron was this guy who was born with a clubfoot and ended up being one of the greatest poets that ever lived. He was a legend in his own time. And not only that, but he was a goddam lord in the British House of Commons. And not only *that*, but he was infamous for his sexual exploits with literally thousands of women, all across Europe. He was so attractive, this guy, that even his nanny was infatuated with him when he was just seven or eight years old.

"But then, after having everything he ever desired—fame, fortune, women—he realized he was totally burned out, he had nothing left inside him."

"What the fuck are you talking about, man?"

"Just hear me out, alright? C'mon. For months you've treated me like a piece of shit. Like you don't know me, for Christ's sake. You don't even invite me over anymore. That's why we're at a goddam bowling alley, right? You can at least hear me out."

Animal Mother looks at the floor. I continue.

"The thing is, Byron realized that, at only thirty-two or thirty-three years old, he had lived a lifetime without really *helping* anyone, without any kind of self-sacrifice. He needed a cause to fight for. And that's the same point I'm at, Mother. I've squandered myself. And now I'm ready to fight. I've put myself in a hole and I need you to help me get out. I need you to help me turn my life around."

"How?"

"Well, see, this is the beautiful part. Byron went to Greece to help the people in their war for independence or something. He fought for them ferociously. Or so the legends say. And to this day he is still revered there, by the Greeks, as a national hero. He found a noble cause and fought for it. And now you are presented with that same opportunity."

"By doing what?"

"Damn it, man. I don't know how else to say it. Fuck. I need to borrow some money." I let him ruminate on that one for a minute while I take my turn. I get the dreaded seven-ten split on the first roll and miss completely with the spare.

"You're saying that by my loaning you money I'd be just like some fucking poet who saved Greece?"

"What? I'm not saying *you're* akin to Lord Fucking Byron just by lending me money. *I'm* the Lord Byron of this analogy. I don't know what else to do, Triz. I'm at my breaking point. I'm trying to stay off the dope and start living like I give a fuck but every time I try to get out, '*They pull me back in.*'"

"What the hell was that?"

"You know, from *Godfather III*, when Pacino is trying to make a break from the crime syndicate and shit?"

"Why you'd ever quote part three, the worst of the *Godfather* movies, is beyond me. Plus, your Pacino sucks."

"I need you to loan me money so I can make my fucking rent, man. So I can start my life over."

"How much?"

"$650."

"What? Holy shit, man."

"I promise you I'm good for it, Trizden. I swear. I'm turning over a new leaf and everything, dude."

"Fine. I can get it for you by next Friday."

"Yes, man. Yes."

Trizden stands up to take his roll. I drag hard on a cigarette. I feel dirty.

"What happened to the poet?" he asks after throwing his fourth consecutive strike.

"He died during the war. Of consumption. Drowned in his own fluids."

"That sucks. But—a national hero, huh? I guess that's not a bad way to go."

Animal Mother loans me the rent money. Two days later Andie shows up at the apartment and says she needs to talk. She says she wants me back, that I haven't called her in weeks and she can't stand to imagine that I would be out of her life forever.

Within twenty minutes we're screwing.

Then we go down to the Bluff and a mere two hours after Andie steps back into my world we're right back where we were in the first place.

Because that's what we do.

People like Andie can't be with people like me, no matter how good the intentions. We feed off each other. We are the ragged claws scuttling across the silent sea floor, picking the microbes off each other, barely sustaining life.

But I am a creature of habit. And I have nothing but the drudgery of day-to-day labor and an empty apartment filled with the memories of a thousand deferred possibilities. And I'm fond of Andie, to whatever degree one needs to be fond of someone to cohabitate with and sleep with her on a regular basis.

We are comfortable with each other.

And when everything else looks corrupted and void of possibility, you take the road you know best, even if the end it presents is the same one it has always given before.

TRANSMISSION 38:

scumbags always get away with everything

October

Last time, the excuse was that it was a beautiful autumn afternoon. This time it was O.J.

I got everybody to stop sawing and hammering on the latest floor install long enough to listen to the verdict being read on the radio.

Not Guilty.

I use this injustice as fuel for my fire. I go downtown with Andie and Jonas after work and get higher than I have in months. "This is for O.J.," I say.

"What the hell are you talking about?" Jonas mumbles between nods, his eyes all red-rimmed and angry.

"It doesn't matter how much we try to pull ourselves up by the bootstraps, you fucking idiots. Can't you see? We're going to be trapped down here forever because we have no marketable skills. We can't run or jump better than anybody else. We can't afford college. We can't act or sing. We can't do long division. We're the fucking plebes. We have no hopes other than what we find at the bottom of a bag of dope, the emptying of a syringe into a collapsing vein."

"That was inspirational," Andie says sarcastically.

I look to Jonas for his take but he's nodded out, as usual. The kid can't stay awake on dope. His whole life is spent either trying to cop dope or nodding off because of it. And for the in-between times he has his unrelenting anger to hold him over.

And I've got mine.

"Here's to O.J.," I say again, gasping, banging another bag of coke.

TRANSMISSION 39:

a short detour to paradise

November

Andie and I recently hooked up with a new contact down in the Bluff. His name is Quill. He's different from most of the go-betweens down there in that he has us take him to different dealers' houses and then asks for rides to the grocery store to pick up milk and shit like that. He's only twenty-two, but he's married and has three kids. His wife comes along sometimes when we go to pick up the dope. Her name is Meat.

Quill and Meat are cool. They seem to genuinely empathize with the plight of the junkie. They even gave us their hotel room phone number when they left their kids with Meat's mom so they could have a night off from the incessant stress of the drug-dealing ghetto life.

Andie and I sat in the Holiday Inn parking lot all night and shot coke until it felt like we couldn't breathe another breath and then I went over to the payphone and called Quill in room 509 and he brought me out some more cocaine as the sun came up.

On the way home, I sat at the stoplight at the entrance ramp to the freeway, the come-down bags of smack safely secured under the flat spare tire in the trunk, trying to see if I could fix my final coke shot in the time between the lights changing. As we merged onto the highway I pushed the least dull of our four works into my vein and began pushing the plunger down, could feel the rush hitting me again, but this time it was worse, like being body-slammed by a four-hundred-pound wrestler.

I don't know if it hit me harder because I was trying to pay attention to driving as well as rushing on my run, but first came the tunnel vision and then I started to die.

My chest heaved, trying to pull in another breath, my heart *thunk-thunking* so hard I could feel my pulse in my eyeballs and fingertips. I pulled the car over and leaned my head on the steering wheel long enough to try to find it in me to keep living. Andie freaked out and asked if I was OK and did I want her to drive.

By the time I regained some semblance of normalcy from the coke hit, it felt like I'd aged about twenty years.

These brushes with death have gotten more and more frequent since I started using again in earnest. That's why we're going to New York. I figure at least once in a lifetime a junkie must make the trip to Junkie Mecca. Now is our time. Now there's only One Thing.

We drive straight through from Atlanta to New York, just to hook up with Splinter and shoot dope. That's all. No higher reason or purpose.

Splinter gets the "bundle special" for us from a guy he knows over on Avenue C. Ten bags for the price of nine. He counts out four twenties and a ten, and the dealer hands Splinter a square stack of wax-paper-wrapped bags tied together with a small rubber band.

I can feel the adrenaline coming. It's a rush I've come to expect and appreciate nearly as much as the high itself. Andie squeezes my hand and I look at her and smile. She doesn't take her eyes off the bundle.

We brisk-walk the long three blocks back to Splinter's. Behind his building there's a little terrace with a stone picnic table. It's as good a place to fix as any. Splinter pulls kits from his coat pocket for each of us. Every kit contains a bottle cap, cotton ball, a little plastic flask of water, and a work, still factory-sealed in plastic. "These are brand-new, straight from the needle exchange," he says. It's a relief not to have to argue with Andie over who goes first. When there's only one work she's a total pain in the ass about it.

I pull a baggie from the bundle and toss it to Splinter. "I hooked you up *and* got you a deal, man. That should be worth at least three bags," he says. I toss him another. It's been nearly ten hours since Andie and I used our last rationed bags in the car on the way up. I don't feel like arguing.

Then it's a race to get fixed. I've got my method down to a science. I unwrap the wax paper, which is embossed with an ink stamp that says HITMAN, with a cross-hairs emblem over the word.

"What the fuck is 'hitman'?"

"A hitman," says Splinter, prepping his hit, "also known as an 'assassin,' is usually hired by someone to 'rub out 'or 'kill' another person."

"No shit, dude. Why does it say that on a bag of dope?"

"That's just the brand name the dealer puts on his shit to differentiate from the other dealers' shit. That way you can find out what the best stuff is that week and ask for it by name."

I pour my dope into the bottle cap and suck some water into the syringe.

"So Hitman is good?"

The dope turns a rich dark brown as it mixes with the water.

"It's so-so shit. The best stuff is Cardiac Arrest. It's so fuckin' pure. We'll hook up some of that in the morning."

I suck the skag into the work and in moments the needle is slipping into my right arm. I got my first "tattoo" on that vein. It's just a single dot of blue where I'd once inadvertantly sucked up the ink from the date stamp on the bottom of a soda can. When I shot the dope the ink left a permanent reminder. Now I use that dot as a target mark and know I'll be bang-on every time.

I push in the plunger and before I can depress it even halfway the wave of rush rolls over me, warm and thick. I pause, wait to see how far it will go, wait to make sure this won't be too much, that my heart can handle the rush, before I push the rest of the junk into my vein.

"Oh, Jesus. This is good shit."

I look over at Andie and she's lying on the walkway, the needle hanging from her arm. She doesn't take the same precautions I do. She always bangs the whole bag at once, no matter what. This is why I never OD. This is why Jonas, Splinter, and Andie have OD'd numerous times. Andie looks at me with half-closed eyes and smiles. I lay my head on her chest. The fourteen hours on the road, praying the car would last until we got here, have already been forgiven. New York City. Promised Land.

The next morning Splinter wakes me early and asks if I want to see the city. I tell him we want dope first. He says the best stuff should be on the corner by Tower Records within the hour.

"Is that the good shit? The best shit?"

"Cardiac Arrest or Murder One. The purest and least cut."

"Andie." I shake her awake. She groans and rolls over.

"You'll feel better soon." I jiggle the remaining dope bags in front of her nose. "We'll hit the rest of this bundle and then score some more."

We have hot vegetable soup and a hunk of French bread for breakfast, courtesy of the Catholic Church soup kitchen down the street from the apartment. It comes in a brown bag with a plastic spoon and a lidded Styrofoam bowl. We sit on a bench in the park and watch the heat rise from many a bum's soup bowl.

When we get back to Splinter's there are not one but two tickets under the T-Bird's windshield wiper.

"Sonofabitch!"

"I told you this city is a motherfucker to have a car in, man," Splinter says.

The T-Bird sits alone on the left side of the one-way street. Every other car is double-parked on the right side. You can see where the street cleaner navigated around my car. It has made two passes, one at 7 a.m., the other at 9. This explains the double ticketing. Andie says, "Fuck it. Let's shoot this dope."

So we do.

And after coming down a bit, we decide to walk.

We've got our hoods up and the wind is getting colder. Andie holds my hand and I realize that this is the first time she's touched me since we got to New York. We never fool around anymore, except for the kiss after we both get a good hit, when our heads are filled with clouds and our bodies are swimming in the Heroin womb. I squeeze her hand and she squeezes back and we look at each other and smile. This is our first vacation.

We wander uptown with no real destination in mind. A really

attractive girl, probably in her early twenties, runway model fashionista, nice handbag, all that, is standing under one of those roofed bus stops.

"Merry Christmas," I say to her, pulling out a cigarette. "You got a light?"

"Christmas is neither merry nor is it a holiday I celebrate," she snaps.

"Why, are you Jewish?"

"Not that it's any of your business, but yes, I am. Though I don't celebrate Chanukah either." She sneers, turns away from me.

Andie pulls on my sleeve to go but I still haven't gotten my light. And I know this chick smokes because she's got that pissed-off-at-the-world look and all of us in that boat are smokers.

"So can I get a light?"

She steps back, reaches into her shiny handbag, and pulls out a pink Bic.

"I wasn't going to steal your purse," Andie says.

She looks Andie up and down and deadpans, "Like you could."

"You're just pissed at the world, huh?" I say, taking a drag on the cigarette.

"What is it with you? I gave you a light, OK?"

"I just wanna know what makes you so pissed."

"What are you, fucking Freud? You don't even know me."

"You're a real New Yorker, aren't you?"

"So you're not from here? That explains the lack of common sense and the inability to know when to take a hint."

The Heroin is wearing off and so is my confidence. I resort to my joke. It's the only one I can ever remember.

"It's not me, it's you," I say. "Let me explain: A man walks into his shrink's office and says, 'Doc, I keep having these nightmares. One night I'll dream I'm a teepee, the next night I'll dream I'm a wigwam.

I'm a teepee. I'm a wigwam. I'm a teepee. I'm a wigwam.' The doc looks at him and says, 'The problem is, you're two tents.' Get it?"

"Blow it out your ass," she says, then disappears inside a cab.

We're sitting at Splinter's kitchen table taking monstrous shots of cocaine with Splinter's friend, I think his name is Damien. He has the master hookup at this bogus coffee shop that's really just a front for a major drug-dealing operation. We've already eaten the donuts that came with the stuff, the better to complete the illusion of coffee-shop legitimacy.

Andie's out on the patio puking. Everyone else is talking incessantly. Words piled on words, lost in a rush of give-me-more, I-can't-catch-my-breath.

I take my shot and I can't breathe. It's the most potent cocaine I've ever injected, like shooting a bag of ether, so light and full of air it makes you feel like it's sucking the very life out of you and replacing it with itself.

My face is numb and my guts churn but I don't want to run to the bathroom because I'm afraid I'll die in that little space, trying to get the bad stuff out.

I implore Splinter to fix me a hit of the Cardiac Arrest or 187. Every junkie worth his habit knows that cocaine is Heroin's evil twin, and when someone is lost in the shadows of the white stuff they can always turn to the H.

Splinter fixes the shot for me and I push the syringe into my arm with all the concentration and deliberation of a captain docking his ship. Splinter has saved me. The cocaine insanity leaves, the warm velvet of Heroin blanketing everything.

Damien has been unsuccessful in getting the needle to hit a vein. He's been trying for twenty minutes and his arms show it. Blood seeps from six separate entry wounds. This guy is at least 6'3" and has to weigh close to 250, but his veins are smaller than a baby's.

I offer to get him set up right. We use his belt this time. Nobody that's been doing this for any length of time bothers tying off like you see in the movies, but this guy has special issues that require drastic measures. I push the needle in at the crook of his elbow but his vein rolls away from me.

I pull the syringe out and watch a new blood bubble appear. The wounds are running in intersecting rivulets and he's starting to look like a suicide.

I push in again, trying to keep his vein in place with two fingers, but it's so deeply inlaid beneath the skin that it's impossible. The needle misses again but I tell him I've got it anyway. I push down on the plunger. He knows immediately that I was lying and fucked it up.

"You motherfucker, you skin-popped me!"

There's nothing worse than a skin-pop, when you miss the vein and shoot the dope into the surrounding soft tissue. This activity would get a "normal" person higher than hell, but for the experienced mainliner it's money down the drain, a wasted shot that makes you want to get high *for real* that much more. A mainline vein shot goes straight to the heart and then to the brain in a matter of seconds. Anything else—smoking, snorting, skin-popping—is far, far removed. We are fucking medical about this shit.

I flip the baggie of coke to Skin-Popper so he can try again and head outside to find Andie. She's sitting on the cement picnic bench, smoking and looking crazed. Even when she's not geeking she has the biggest eyes I've ever seen. Right about now they look like fucking portholes. Cocaine makes all the muscles in your face contort and pull back. Cokeheads always appear hyper-aware, but it's a façade. Our eyeballs are just more vulnerable to dust.

I lean down to kiss her and can taste the cocaine in her saliva. It numbs me further, if that's even possible. I realize that she's probably as high right now as she's ever been.

"Are you doing OK?"

"Yeah," she murmurs, sitting motionless, not meeting my kiss.

"I was worried about you," I say. "You were gone all of a sudden and I was about to die. Where were you?"

"I had to get some air before I passed out." She's staring at her shoes, or maybe it's the cracks in the concrete.

"We've got to quit doing this shit."

"What shit?"

"The fucking cocaine. It's so strong—it's evil. I can feel it taking me over."

"Alright," she says, stumbling to stand, "but let me take one more hit before you get all religious on me."

We come into the house and Splinter is doing his coke spiel, talking about the machine of capitalism being oiled by the blood of the workers, while Damien continues trying to score the money shot. Blood-soaked paper towels lie on the Formica table.

Andie dabs at his arm, waiting for her turn, then bangs herself again and turns pale, lays her head on the table. I'm still feeling the residual effects of my shot and am gritting my teeth, though the smack has helped greatly in cutting out the foregone anxiety. I ask Andie if she's OK and she drags her forehead slowly back and forth across the tabletop without looking up.

Splinter keeps talking, rabbiting on about the decay of society because of antidrug laws.

It's been nearly an hour and Splinter's still in the bathroom. I bang on the door and ask if he's OK but no answer comes back. And then we're all beating on the door but he still won't unlock it. So at the count of three the skin-popper—I think his name is Damien—and

I run our shoulders through the paper-thin door and there sits my best friend on the toilet like John Belushi or goddam Elvis.

The needle is still poking out of his vein and a small trickle of blood trails down his arm to a half-dollar-sized puddle on the floor beneath his wrist. His eyes are rolled back to the whites and his mouth is foaming.

After a few smacks in the face he stirs and his shirtsleeve flies up seemingly of its own accord to wipe away the spittle from his mouth. Then his eyes come back around. "What the fuck did you smack me for, asshole?" he growls. His speech is slurred and slow. He flails at us to back away from him.

"You almost died again, you retard. How long have you been doing this and you're still OD'ing? You'd better quit while you're ahead," I tell him.

But it doesn't matter. He probably likes the fact that he almost dies sometimes. A near-death experience every now and then holds much of the thrill of living like this. Because this isn't some kind of daisy-tripping mind warp we have going here. This is life and death. And every time the hit is a little too big and we can feel the life slipping from our grasp, one heartbeat at a time, it is cause for reevaluation of the self. You can't play with Death without looking him in the face while you're doing it. You can't walk away without knowing a little more clearly why you're here in the first place. Because once that initial shock wears away and you realize that Death is not necessarily as imminent as you thought—*that* is the best time to be a junkhead. You have the best possible high going and you *know* that, because you felt yourself nearly slip away—but somehow you held on. And *that* means you couldn't have gotten any higher without actually going away to that Other Place for good.

This is the constant tightrope walk, between life and death. We are always straddling that line, trying to get as close to the other side as possible without falling over the edge.

Splinter lumbers out of the bathroom just as some guy bursts through the front door, limping, a crazed look in his eye. He tells Splinter he just got a great score at Kmart and the old lady never realized that he was going through her purse as he stood behind her in the checkout line.

"She was looking straight ahead, the whole time. It was so goddam easy, man," he snorts, phlegm crackling down the back of his throat. "Mind if I fix here? Just got a brand-new kit." He drops into a chair at the table, pulls his bags out, and boils the liquid in a well-used spoon, its bottom black with soot. We need to score again.

When we return to the apartment, the unshaven guy is still sitting at the table where we left him. His breathing is sharp and heavy and it's obvious that he's high as fuck.

Empty baggies are scattered across the table. Splinter tells him that he needs to be leaving in the next few minutes because his girl will be getting home soon and she can't know about his junkie friends. The guy's arm suddenly shoots straight out in front of him, followed by his leg in mock karate action. He looks to be fighting imaginary forces of some kind, and yet he begins conversing with Splinter like nothing out of the ordinary is happening.

"Might I inquire as to the nature of what you've injected on this occasion, good sir?" I request. That's how I say it, too, because sometimes I like to make like we aren't lowlife junkheads at all, but rather connoisseurs of recreational pharmaceuticals, the wine tasters of the ghetto community. Talking like an uptight prick also helps take the pressure off in an unfamiliar situation. It's a bit like laughing while you fend off blows during that tender and critical moment when, say, your girlfriend catches you with your tongue accidentally inserted in another girl's mouth.

The karate guy says he always mixes it up: a little ketamine, a little Heroin, a little speed. I tried shooting speed months ago and found it far too painful to justify the high it delivered. It was like shooting fire, burned the whole way up the arm.

I ask the dude if he wouldn't mind if we join him for a little bit of the old in-out, in-out—the shooting-up kind. This with a terrible cockney accent.

We sit down at the table and I toss Splinter a bag. Andie and I get two each. This leaves little to last out the day and I have exactly $134 left. But I've got a trick up my sleeve. Tucked away safely in the trunk of the T-Bird is a brand-new DVD player—"the wave of the future in home entertainment"—lifted from a Kmart in Atlanta. We wrote a bum check for it just before we left, my brilliant idea of a backup plan in case anything went wrong up here in the Big Apple.

You always need a backup plan. That's straight-up Boy Scout shit. If worse comes to worst, we take the DVD player to our friendly neighborhood Kmart and they give us the four hundred bucks so that we will give back the merchandise we rightfully stole from them. We're Robin Hood, his merry band of men, and all the fucking peasants rolled into one.

Andie hands me my work and moments later we're banging away once again.

The karate guy's arm flies out and even when I'm high I can't get used to that shit.

The Kmart is on to us before we even get to the Returns Desk. The Jheri-curled black woman behind the counter looks us up and down with obvious disdain. We are clearly not the first people to approach her with an unopened box of merchandise looking for a no-receipt refund.

"Do you have a receipt?" the woman asks before I can even set the box on the counter.

"I already have one of these," I say, sticking to the script.

She stares at me, waiting.

"I got this DVD player for an early Christmas present and I don't need it. I already have one," I reiterate. She stares at me. "So I don't need this one."

She points to the sign that denounces all who would attempt to get something for nothing by approaching the desk without a receipt for "ANY" article worth more than ten dollars.

I'm tempted to ask for a manager, but by the looks of her I know she probably *is* the manager and this is a waste of everybody's time. I've never been too good at this part of the scam. And now, standing in front of this woman, with Andie next to me, I'm about to vomit.

For a moment I'm afraid that she's going to insist on keeping the DVD player, so I scoop it up without a word of argument and turn to leave. Andie chews her gum and gives the woman the finger. I wince, because I know that if the woman had any reservations about us being thieves and junkies before, she has none now.

"Look, we're in New York," I tell Andie, "and this town is always primed for the taking if you just know how. If they have fucking donut shops that sell cocaine I know there has to be somebody out here that'll want a top-of-the-line DVD player for a fraction of the store price."

"Yeah?" Andie asks. She reaches over to massage my crotch in that way that indicates she is starting to come around to my logic. "Well who do we ask?"

"I don't know . . . maybe I can ask my dad," I say. "He hasn't done shit for me ever, in my entire life, so he owes me. I'll just play the old guilt card and get him to wire us a couple hundred bucks."

"You always think of everything."

She nuzzles into my chest and I feel warm and hopeful. We're gonna make it out of here intact. I know it. My dad is going to make up for everything in one fell swoop: the missed birthdays, the letting my mother's new old man give me his fucked-up last name under the guise of "doing what's best for you and your brother." All of it can be wiped clean in this one expansive gesture of paternal concern. If he can bail me out just this one time.

He can do it—and he will. I'm certain.

I'm shaking as I thumb through the contents of my wallet: old receipts, stained photographs, an expired coupon, a resin-covered roach in a cigarette cellophane. I've kept the phone number since that day he materialized out of nowhere during my freshman year of high school.

As I pick up the phone to dial, I almost wish I hadn't found the number, that there was some other way out of this. I never return any of his phone calls or letters. His interest in me is cursory, at best.

He answers and immediately I am filled with regret, because he has an intonation of suffering in his voice. I know already that he isn't going to be able to do anything. Not now, not ever. But I'm already on the phone with him so I tell him anyway. I don't beg or plead, I just give it to him straight.

He dances around the subject a bit, asks me how I've been. He sounds so pathetic and needy. I almost tell him that I love him and all is forgiven. But I don't. Because I'm standing in Splinter's girlfriend's shoebox apartment asking for money from a guy I've met in person a grand total of twice and talked to on the phone possibly three more times than that.

And that's when I realize that I really do feel for this man. I want him to know he isn't hated. And that's when he gets to the point and tells me he "just doesn't have it." I contemplate giving him the speech I've had running through my head over the years, the "I've never asked you for anything and the one time I come to you for one fucking favor you shit on me" speech. But I don't. I'm welling up and I can't get another word out. This guy can't do anything for himself, let alone anyone else.

I hang up and stare at the pearl-colored plaster walls and reinsulate myself like I always do, square my jaw, try to nonchalantly wipe away any escaping salty discharge, breathe.

Andie comes up behind me and puts her arms around my waist and tries to sound all sexy, like she always does when she wants something.

"Is he gonna send you the money?"

"No." I try to sound as though it isn't a thing to be worried about one way or the other.

"Why not?"

"He doesn't have it."

"Well, what the fuck are we gonna do?"

I breathe in slow and exhale again, move back to normal.

"I've got a plan," I say. "Plan fucking B."

This is Plan B.

We're standing on the corner displaying our wares to myriad passersby. I'm holding the DVD player and Andie's got her favorite motorcycle boots and about ten of our CDs. The catch to this type of selling is that you can't set the stuff down on the sidewalk or the cops will take it from you on the grounds that it's stolen property. I don't know why the law says the shit's stolen if you're not actually holding it. According to Captain Spaz-o over at Splinter's apartment, if you want to sell merchandise on the street you have to have some kind of vendor's permit, so the loophole is that you can hold the stuff and sell it—but you can't set it on the ground.

New York is dark and I'm freezing even though I'm wearing four layers. Within twenty minutes Andie has sold all the CDs for two bucks a pop, and her boots for ten. That's three bags right there. I'm having no luck with the DVD player, though. Nobody's willing to part with two hundred bucks on the street. Then a man approaches me and says that he has "people" in a deli right down the block that would be interested if I'm willing to bargain. I follow him inside and there are three Italian-looking guys sitting at a table.

One is wearing a blue tracksuit and the other two are decked out in three-pieces. They tell me they'll pay $80, nothing more, and I say I'm only selling it to get home to Atlanta, that the gas alone is going to be $120. My T-Bird is a rudder away from being an actual seagoing vessel and only gets about seventeen miles per gallon on a good day. I know they can resell this DVD player, brand-new and still in the box, for three or four times what I'm asking. They wave me off and the tracksuit guy gets up and ushers me out of the store.

Andie's probably already back at the apartment and high by now and I'm still standing in the street with this bullshit DVD player. Just when I'm about to say fuck it and go back to the deli, a late-model Lincoln Continental pulls up and two Middle Eastern guys jump out. One says, in a thick accent, "How much you want? I give you a hundred dollars right now."

"Man, this is tip-top. Never used. I need one twenty just to get back to Atlanta. I'm not some crackhead. I'm just trying to get home."

"I give you a hundred, nothing more."

He hasn't even looked at what I'm holding.

"One twenty and it's yours, man. It's a Sony," I repeat, steeled in my resolve by his audacity. I'm tired and cold and ready to fuck somebody up if one more person tries to give me the high hat.

"You can get computers, too?"

"No, man, I can't get computers. I don't do this shit on a regular basis. I'm just trying to get home."

"You drive hard bargain. I give you one ten."

"Fine. Give me one ten."

He motions to his crony, who has been standing by the back passenger-side door of the Lincoln, and they speak for a moment in what I can only guess is Arabic, at which point the doorman whips out a thick wad of cash from his jacket pocket and tears me off five twenties and a ten. I hand him the DVD player and he puts it in the trunk. The guy I was bartering with pulls out a business card and reiterates his desire for black-market computers.

"Fine, man, just . . . yeah, I'll call you if I get any computers."

I finger the bills in my pocket on the way back to Splinter's. Already I feel warmer.

This is our last night in the Big Apple.

We try to ration the drugs because they have to last at least until we get back home. After that I can probably get Lou to loan me a little to help me through the rest of the week, though I know he's tired of always footing the bill for my habit because I never end up even with him. I'm always taking out of next week's check for this week's fix. And he has a habit at least twice as big as mine. He can't get rid of me, though, because he knows that when we're both soaring on the dope and firing on all cylinders, we can put down some mean flooring.

Splinter makes a special effort to be good to us. He makes me and Andie the best spaghetti I've eaten in forever, though none of us eat much because we're constipated from all the dope.

As we're leaving the next morning I hug Splinter and we hold the hug for a while before thump-thumping each other on the back. I recall the time we were tripping at his aunt/uncle's house. That night we made a blood pact to never do "needle drugs" because that's how his mom got AIDS and died. He never really knew her. We stayed up all night laughing at the absurd shit they'd play at three o'clock in the morning on the Lifetime channel. There was a show on about gap-toothed women and their careers. Everything was simpler then. You got stoned and drunk and dropped a few hits of LSD, watched shows about gap-toothed women and it was all fun and games.

Now it's your life all the time, the sum total, this trying to rationalize your bruised inner elbows and bloodstained shirts, this fetid cycle of needle abuse, this grand attempt at normal behavior, like we chose this life over going to shows and dating nice girls.

Halfway through Virginia we finish off the last bags of dope. A few hours more and we'll be sick as plague victims, with hundreds of miles to go. It's unbearably cold and the heater went out in my car long ago. We're shivering as we pass through North and then South Carolina. But now it has nothing to do with the weather. We're dope-sick. This is going to be the longest six hours of our lives, the innumerable miles dragging by in slow motion. We're sucking the loose snot back into our noses and down our throats, feeling the ache in our legs that twenty aspirin can't make a dent in, the slackness in our bowels that signals the shit that's been impacting in our colons for the last five days is about to make an untidy appearance.

We're broke by the time we hit northern Georgia. Andie has $2.78 in change, I have slightly less. I decide to do the old "pump and run," but with a twist. I fill the car up with gas, because there's no way we'll make it the last furlong without a full tank, and then go into the station and whip out the checkbook to write the check I know they won't accept because no gas station this side of goddam Brazil takes checks.

"But this is all I have," I reply.

"Well, you have to come up with something else, darlin', 'cause I ain't allowed to take nothin' but cash and credit."

"Look, I live in Atlanta and I'm coming back from my parents'

house up in New York where I stayed for Thanksgiving. I'm g
it. This is a good check."

I dislike lying to this woman because she's one of those motherly types who still applies makeup like she thinks she knows what looks good, but everyone else knows it looks like hell, and she really seems to regret turning me down. I want to give the gas back.

At least, that's what I tell her.

She says she'll need some collateral so she can be sure I'll eventually make good on the debt, so I hand her the pure silver dollar I've been carrying around for years since my mom gave it to me long ago. She winks at me and says she'll let it slide.

Then we're off again, back to our stomping grounds, where the reeking mess of everything is home. It seems like I've been doing this forever and I'm tired, so fucking tired. But I'm a rock star in this world and nobody and nothing can stop me: not the cops, not the dealers on the street trying to sell me flex, not my mom trying to feed me her holier-than-thou sermons, the "God doesn't like it when we treat our bodies like garbage cans," and "God has a plan for you and just let me lay hands on you," because when did any of that help her? She's married to a con-artist loser and I'm supposed to look to her for guidance?

I'll take my way, thanks. I'll take the hard road because this is my medicine and these are my people. We know what it means to survive, to breathe in when all that's left of the air is smog and all that's left of the rest of you are soulless shells, cicadas rigidly clinging to the dead trees of a society rotting from the inside out.

You did this to yourselves and you don't even know it. You can't even smell the stench of your own rotting compost, the decay of your soul.

But not me.

Every time I push that needle in and see the red plume of blood bloom in my syringe, I know where my solace lies.

TRANSMISSION 40:

business, good and bad

January

More people die in January than any other month. Famous January dead include James Joyce, Salvador Dali, Al Capone, and Henry VIII. My grandfather died in January. I guess it's as good a time to die as any if you've gotta do it anyway, because January doesn't have shit else going for it. The holidays are over, the weather is shitty and unbearably cold, and light only lingers for a few hours a day. Winter is a permanent psychic darkness that comes back around every year, and every year it feels like this time it's never going to go away. Plus, all you have to look forward to in January is fucking February.

So now I'm all paranoid, more so than usual anyway, because I've read this goddam article about people being more likely to die in January.

Pooky decided it would be a good idea to rip us off a few days ago, gave us six bags of flex and one bag of good shit for seventy bucks. He tried to play magician by letting me taste the good bag, then did the old bait and switch. He was long gone before we realized that he'd ripped us off.

In a situation like that, when there's no other money to be had and no other alternative, the dedicated smackhead will take out his anger and frustration on the next best target—in this case, the target was Pooky's brother.

I got him in the car with us and told him we had to run to the ATM. He willingly handed us the bags first. So the plan was to drive to the Citgo on Howell Mill Road, the one with the ATM, have him go in with us and then run out the opposite door to our waiting vehicle, leaving him with his dick in his hand.

But he wasn't stupid *enough*, because he insisted on waiting in the car.

So Andie and I walked in the Citgo trying to come up with a Plan B, left the car running and everything so as to maintain the ruse that we were trustworthy. But when we got back outside he'd turned the car off and was holding the keys, saying he wasn't getting back in—wasn't giving back the keys—until he had the money. With no other options, I told him we just checked our (nonexistent) bank account and realized we didn't have the money. He didn't say anything, just took off running with the fucking car keys. So I chased him down this alley and was almost on top of him when he turned and flashed a big-ass hunting knife at me, said he was gonna kill me for trying to play him.

"I just want the keys," I told him, palms up.

Pooky's brother lunged at me and we did the whole struggling-with-the-knife deal and then he had my hoodie pulled over my head and that's when I felt the cold blade graze my side. Then he just took off running again. So I chased after him again because he still had the goddam keys but I was bleeding and didn't have a shirt on and it was like ten degrees outside.

It was a superficial wound, though. The bleeding stopped on its own after a short time, although I ruined my favorite Jane's Addiction t-shirt using it as a compress to staunch the flow.

But we got the dope for free, so there's that. And here's the kicker: Andie had the spare set of keys in her purse the whole time.

Andie thinks we should find somewhere else to go until this whole thing settles down a little because what if Pooky and his brother come back swinging now that we've ripped them off? These kinds of things don't just go away. These kinds of things get bigger and bigger until they explode.

We're waiting for Alex in this empty lot on the corner where Pooky's tenement used to stand. Habitat for Humanity has been making an effort to reconstruct the neighborhood, so all the old abandoned buildings are disappearing and are being replaced by pastel-colored houses that these bleeding-heart construction workers throw up during their weekends off. All kinds of low-income families with small children are now moving into one of the most drug-infested neighborhoods in all of Atlanta.

You can't grow up around that shit and not start doing it yourself. If you look out your door and see crackheads banging pipes on the sidewalks and then watch the guy that sold them the crack driving down the block in a supped-up Cadillac with gold rims, are you going to straight-up join the fucking workforce after you drop out of high school?

Yeah, me neither. I'd rather have a shack on a hill somewhere than a "nice" house in a ghetto. I don't give a fuck what shade of turquoise it is.

While we're sitting there waiting for Alex to come back, this nigger I've never seen before strolls up with Pooky and his shithead brother in tow, looking like little kids who told on a sibling.

The fucking guy doesn't even say anything, he just taps on the window, smiling.

Now, I'm not too stupid most of the time, but for some reason, even though fucking Pooky and his brother are standing there, I think this smiley bastard is actually a nice guy. I mean, he's *smiling.*

Nobody smiles down here, even when they like you.

And when he taps on the window and smiles and everything, displays the gold and diamonds inlayed on his teeth, sets his forty-ounce on the roof of the T-Bird, I actually think he's some do-gooder dealer who's made Pooky and his fuckwad brother come out with him to apologize to one of his most consistent customers for ripping us off. Because any good businessman, drug dealer or not, knows that the way to maintain business is to always treat the customer with respect, never give him a shitty product, and he'll always come back for more. Of course, drug addicts come back for more anyway.

However, Pooky and his brother didn't tell this motherfucker about ripping me off. The way they told it, I took this nigger's dope and drove off without paying. There will be no apologies here. Violators will be prosecuted.

This fucking guy wants retribution.

I roll the window down before I realize this, though. Smiley stops smiling and leans in the window, quick and efficient, and puts his hand on the steering column. It immediately occurs to me that he's trying to get the keys, but the motherfucker didn't count on the fact that on a '68 Thunderbird, the ignition is under the dash. He'd have to practically climb in the car to reach the keys.

I put my hand across his face and shove as hard as I can. He stumbles back and the last thing I see before I can throw the car in Drive is Smiley reaching behind his back and I just know he's gonna start shooting. I yell at Andie to get down and I'm tearing down the street, trying to drive by memory because there's no way I'm getting the back of my head blown off. There's a crash on the back window and I don't peek over the dash until I have to make the turn onto the main road, where we'll be safe and out of the line of fire. Then, as I'm turning right onto Northside, the car feels like it's shoved aside like a toy. I push the gas pedal to the floor and pray.

We go to our hideout behind the Lizard Lounge to evaluate the damage. The back window has *not* been shot out. The crashing sound was Smiley's forty as it fell off the roof and shattered on the back window. There are still shards of beer bottle on the trunk. The worst damage was inflicted when we turned the corner and felt the car get shoved. Since I'd been ducking down I underestimated how far I had to pull out before turning and I caught the right side on a telephone pole. The pole caught my car at the seam where the two doors meet. Neither passenger-side door will open. And now that I've pissed off this dealer I can't take the T-Bird back down to the Bluff for a while.

But I'm not too worried about it. We white kids can walk around with impunity. We might get our asses kicked once in a while but at least we know we're not going to die without somebody paying. We have divine providence. We have precedent.

We know not what we do.

TRANSMISSION 41:

taking back what's mine

April

Jonas recently picked up a .38 revolver from some crackhead for $40. He brings it along. Just in case.

We pull down Washington Street but my man Alex is nowhere to be seen. So we go to the next corner and I order twenty bags of coke from a nigger I've never seen before, thinking nothing of it because there is always some new guy you've never seen before out here. Plus there's the added confidence of carrying a firearm.

Driving around the block I feel the overwhelming need to take a shit but make myself hold it in. I can usually convince myself that all the stressful stuff will be over in moments if I just sweat it out.

The new guy hands us the bags and I hand him the money. I open a baggie to taste the coke just as Jonas starts to pull away and it's pure. Pure baking soda. The motherfucker didn't even attempt cutting it or nothing.

"Fuck!"

"What is it?" Jonas says, the gun under his leg.

"That fucking guy just sold us twenty bags of flex."

"I told you this was a bad idea. We should never have tried to buy this much shit at once. That's when they fuck you. I just lost two hundred goddam dollars!"

"Drive around again," I say. "We're getting that fucking money back."

Jonas turns the car around and tears up the block, the tires squealing. The nigger is still standing there on the corner, brazen fuck that he is.

"Give me the gun and pull up right in front of this piece a shit."

Jonas skids to a halt and I've already got the window down and the new guy gives me this look like he doesn't have time for any of our bullshit.

"What you need, motherfucker?" he says with a jerk of the head.

"That shit you just gave me was fucking flex. I want my money back." I try to sound pissed and intimidating but I know I don't. I know I sound scared. I *am* scared.

"You better back up off me, bitch. I don't have your fucking money," he says.

I turn back to Jonas like, "Do you believe this?" But then Jonas gives me this look that makes it so much easier to go through with the plan.

I'm going to blow this piece of shit away.

As soon as he sees the heater the nigger puts his hands up and then he's not so tough. All of his friends take off as soon as the gun comes out. I'm sure some of them are going to be coming back with pistols of their own.

"Not so tough now, are you, you sorry fuck. Give me my fucking money." My breath looks like smoke in the cold morning air. I am on fire.

He doesn't say anything. He just stands there toad-faced.

"Give me my fucking money, motherfucker! I swear to God I'll kill you!" I cock the hammer for emphasis of this threat, just like in the movies. He starts rifling through his pants. Little baggies of coke and Heroin fall out of his pockets and hit the ground and then he's holding a wad of cash. He counts out two hundred dollars.

"Hand me the whole fucking thing! You tried to rip me off so now *I'm* gonna rip *you*."

He hands me everything. It's gotta be like five or six hundred bucks.

"You're gonna die, white boy," I hear him mutter.

"What did you say to me? You fuck! I come down here every fucking day and pay hard-earned fucking money to you assholes and all I ask in return is some real dope. I'm tired of this bullshit! You ever try some shit like that again with me and I'll kill you! Understand? Hand me those baggies!" I say, motioning to the pavement where the bags fell from his pockets.

"Let's go, man," Jonas says.

"Wait," I say. "This motherfucker's gonna give us *every*thing."

He looks around like he doesn't see the twenty or so baggies on the sidewalk at his feet.

"On the fucking ground! Hand me those fucking baggies, you fuck!"

He forks over the dope and Jonas hits the gas and then there are ten or fifteen black guys chasing after us. One of them actually hits the back window with a shoe just as we turn the corner.

This is huge. Pooky and that shit was one thing, but this takes it to an entirely different level. We just walked with somebody else's money, somebody else's dope. But fuck 'em. They had it coming. And by my count, I've got about twelve bags of Heroin and ten bags of coke to show for our troubles.

I pull my syringe out from underneath the carpet and am fixed in less than three minutes. We head back to the job and shoot coke all afternoon. The floor goes down in record time.

I get home and Andie looks ready to explode with happiness when she sees all that money and all the little baggies besides. We have to get another car now, and disguises or something.

TRANSMISSION 42:

jonas swallowed

May

I'm at the house maybe twenty minutes, the come-down already hitting me hard, when Jonas calls. He's panicking, says that something's wrong with Karen, that she took a dope hit and passed out, just like Splinter those times when he OD'd. I tell him to bring her over and I'll try to help but he says there's no time, he's too far away and and and . . .

". . . I think she's already dead, man. You've gotta help me. You've gotta help me! Karen!"

"Jonas, calm down. How close are you to the nearest hospital?"

"I don't know. Like five minutes."

"Go to the hospital with her, tell them you found her like that when you came home. They'll take care of her."

"I don't want to go to jail, man. I'm just a fucking kid, bro. Karen!"

"You won't go to jail. But if you don't take her now, *right* now, she might die, and I know you don't want that, right?"

"No," he whimpers.

"Take her to the hospital, and after they've got her checked in and everything, come by and pick me up and I'll go back with you."

"OK," he says, newly determined. "I'll see you soon."

"Do you have money?" I ask, planning for the future.

"A little."

"OK. Good luck."

An hour later Jonas bursts through the door with blood spilling from his mouth, all over his clothes and everything. I can't understand anything he's trying to say. He runs to the kitchen and turns on the water. He grabs a cup out of the cupboard and drops something in it. It looks like a piece of chewed-up gum slathered in blood. Jonas looks at me and opens his mouth.

And then I know what's in the cup. He's somehow bitten off his own tongue. I grab a bunch of paper towels and he puts them in his mouth. They are immediately soaked in blood.

"I've gotta call the ambulance, dude."

He shakes his head vehemently.

"You're gonna fucking bleed to death. What happened?"

He points at his mouth and gestures, as in, *Duh, I can't talk, dipshit.*

I grab a pad and he writes it out in ragged letters, says that he was too afraid to take Karen into the hospital, he didn't want to go to jail. So he left her passed out in front of a parked ambulance and took off. But on the way to my house he nodded off from the massive dope hit he'd taken with Karen, the one that had leveled her. When he woke up he had smashed into a car sitting at a stoplight and his tongue was sticking to the windshield, completely detached from the rest of him.

His note is a mess of scribbling and arrows and obviously hard to read, but that's the gist of it. He didn't know what to do so he just backed up and drove around the rear-ended vehicle, came the last mile or two to my house.

"Is Karen dead?"

He shakes his head and shrugs his shoulders, tears welling in his eyes.

"Somebody found her lying there right as I was leaving," he scribbles. "How am I going to talk for the rest of my life?"

I hand him another wad of paper towels. He spits the blood-soaked ones into the trash.

"There's probably a good chance that they can reattach it if you go to the hospital, man. I know you don't want to, but this is your health, your fucking life. Karen's going to be fine. But you have to fucking do what *you* gotta do. Right now."

Jonas looks out the kitchen window for a minute, then agrees.

The police are already in the driveway when we get outside. They see the blood on Jonas, ask him if he was just involved in a hit-and-run accident. He looks at me and then nods at the cops. They ask him why he ran. Jonas writes something on the pad and shows it to the cop. The cop frowns and shakes his head. I hand the cop the cup filled with ice and Jonas' tongue.

"That's the only reason he ran, Officer," I say. "He bit his tongue off and panicked. It could happen to anybody."

"Looks like you're gonna be doing a whole lotta writing for the rest of your life, man," the cop says to Jonas, like the cool motherfucker he isn't. As if wearing Ray-Bans and packing a pistol makes you automatically cool.

They escort Jonas to the station first and do all their fingerprinting and check-in bullshit before they finally take him to the hospital. By the time they get him in there his tongue is no longer on ice. It's rapidly decomposing at the bottom of a cup filled with lukewarm water.

TRANSMISSION 43:

a realization

June

Andie and I are taking a break from painting my mom's front porch for some quick cash, shooting coke in the bathroom, when I find out she's pregnant again. At first I think I'm experiencing some form of the expected coke-induced hallucinations, but when I put my hand on her belly I can see that, yes, it really *is* moving.

I yank her shirt up. She always wears baggy clothes.

She is blatantly, *obviously* pregnant.

"What the fuck is this?"

It occurs to me that I haven't seen her naked in months. We haven't even tried to screw since probably Valentine's Day, when everybody ends up screwing, even smackheads.

She starts to cry, just turns it on, like she's been expecting this moment to come and now here it is and how could she not expect it to come, really, because it's not like this sort of thing just goes away.

"I didn't know what to do," she sobs. "I didn't want to tell you when I found out because I was afraid you'd want me to get an abortion and I just couldn't go through that again, Luke. I couldn't do it, baby. I'm sorry."

"How long have you known?" I ask, gasping. The coke is really hitting me hard. And this revelation ain't helping any.

"I didn't know how to tell you."

"How far along are you?"

"Please don't yell at me," she sobs.

"How the fuck am I supposed to react? You've been pregnant for months and all this time we've been shooting every drug under the fucking sun. How am I supposed to react? When this kid is born it's going to be totally fucked up. How could you do that to our *child*?"

"I thought that if I kept getting high then maybe I'd have a miscarriage. But I couldn't go through the pain of another abortion, of knowing I'd killed *two* babies because you didn't want them."

And that's when it dawns on me.

This is the sign.

This is God's way of personally touching us. He's finally decided to step up and personally talk to us. This is the burning bush. This baby is the Red Sea parting, the clouds opening up, and the edict being handed down.

This is the miracle.

The next day I take Andie to Planned Parenthood and they run an ultrasound on her, set her up with a doctor. After all of their tests and questions they determine that the baby is four or five months along.

The clinic gives us the numbers of a few detox and drug treatment centers and within days Andie starts her methadone program in earnest. The people at the clinic said that since the baby is also addicted to opiates, she will have to stay on methadone until the baby is born.

The fact that she will be taking legally sanctioned opiates is excuse enough for me to continue using the illegal kind. It's all semantics, really. And since I no longer have gainful employment—just couldn't hack it anymore—I've gone on the shoplifting warpath. Every day I hit a different Home Depot or Wal-Mart or Target or Kroger, stealing blue jeans and copper pipe fittings and CDs and ball bearings and steaks and seafood and portable electronics and cartons of cigarettes, returning them without receipts for cash. It has never been easier than now. I am invulnerable. Nothing can get in my way.

Some days, when I'm feeling balls-on, I'll walk into a store and walk back out minutes later holding the merchandise right out in the open. It's not concealed under a trench coat or shoved down the pants. I just hold the stuff in my hands as though I was sent there by higher-ups and nobody need contact the police because I'm just doing my job, people.

Then it's straight to the store I ripped off the day before, where I walk in, plain as day, and get money for the stolen merchandise, with a "thank you" from the clerk tacked on top of it. I can do no wrong.

This is my final run here, and I am bound and determined to make the most of it. I even resort to asking strangers outside Wal-Marts and Home Depots if they'll make merchandise returns for me (all the major chains have a no-receipt return limit), saying I've lost my license. Inevitably the middle-aged men and women never ask for their share of the take and I thank them profusely before heading back out on the road, looking for more.

All the while Andie is taking her iron pills, keeping her doctor appointments, drinking her methadone at the clinic every morning at 9 a.m. sharp. On Sundays the clinic gives her a take-home dose, which she uses to fill three syringes. I help her slip all three into different veins, at which point we push in the plungers at the same time, thereby maximizing the potential of her actually feeling a rush. She says that it's a pretty fruitless process, that the rush is minimal and only lasts for a few minutes, but her need for the needle has not gone away. Needle lust is part of the romance of this thing.

There have been times, when there was no money and no way of getting to the Bluff, when Jonas and I have put needles in our arms just to have some semblance of a high and, believe it or not, even when we were only shooting water into our veins, there were moments when it felt like I was actually getting stoned. Just the suggestion of the possibility, the thought that somehow the water could transform into the narcotic—water into wine—was enough of a placebo to simulate a rush, if only for a minute. And then, in a possibly sick play on the water gun days with Corey, when we'd drive around and shoot pedestrians in the face with powerful jet streams of water before tearing off in a hail of burning rubber and cackling laughter, Jonas and I would fill syringes with our own blood and pull up to citizens waiting at crosswalks and squirt the blood on their white blouses and sport jackets, put the fear of God into them.

TRANSMISSION 44:

house of cards

July

He's sold our house for firewood.

When I get home from "work," Andie's standing in the front hall talking to her namesake, her dad, and he's telling us that he's sold our house to a fucking fire department so that they can use it to practice putting out fires.

"You pushed it to the breaking point, Andie. And now you're gonna bring a baby into this crap-hole. I need you to move on. You've caused nothing but trouble for this family. And the same goes for you, boy," he says to me. "I've given y'all one chance after another to straighten your act up and still it isn't enough. I didn't make you pay rent on this house and you treated it like your own personal dump. I haven't even been *in* the house and just in this hallway there's holes in the walls, the carpet is actually burned over there in the corner, there's plastic taped over the window where it's been busted out . . . you guys don't deserve this house. You don't really deserve anything."

He picks up a crumpled poster off the floor and tosses it aside.

"You can't just throw us out, Daddy," Andie says. "We're trying to clean up. For our baby. *Your* grandson. For once in our lives we're trying to do something right."

"I'm sorry, Andie, but it can't go on any longer. I'm done. Your grandmother's done. And if anyone gave you two custody of that baby, I'd be first in line to tell them why they messed up. Because the two of you are the worst thing that could happen to that child. That baby needs a loving, stable family. You don't have that to offer. And you're sure as hell not going to live here with it. For the past three years I've watched you destroy this house and do even worse to your bodies. It ends here."

"You've watched us, huh?" I have to interject now because this guy is about as full of shit as anyone has ever been. "That's funny, *Andrew,* because I've never seen you in this house, not one fucking time. Your office is less than two hundred feet down the road and you never came up here even once to see how your own daughter was doing. You don't invite her to your holiday family gatherings, you pretend she doesn't exist. How fucked up is that, man? She lives right in the middle of all your businesses, your homes, and all she warrants for contact on a yearly basis is an envelope filled with money every Christmas?"

He folds his arms and squints his eyes at me, moves the toothpick in his mouth from one side to the other. He's a much larger man than I am, could most likely kick my ass, but I'm done caring.

"Well, guess what?" I continue. "*It isn't enough.* People need people to tell them that they are there for them, that they are willing to hear what they have to say. I don't give a shit if you valiantly took custody of Andie when her mother proved herself a psycho, a parent is more than a source of money. You put her in this house and walked away, satisfied that you had accomplished your parental duties. But all she wanted was somebody to take some fucking interest in her life. Can't you understand that?"

Both Andie and I are crying now.

The elder Andrew says, "You have until Friday afternoon," and shuts the front door behind him.

TRANSMISSION 45:

flying kites is good for the soul

August

The Olympics are upon us now and the city is buzzing like never before. In a last ditch effort to clean up the streets, the city council decided it would be a good idea if they implemented a plan to scrape as many of the bums off the street as possible. So they put signs up all over the place saying they'd buy a one-way bus ticket for anyone to anywhere in the lower forty-eight states.

The plan was a resounding failure.

The bums here ain't stupid. There's gonna be more fucking money in this town for the next month than there has ever been. Hell, I'll bet there are some folks on the lower end of the job spectrum who have decided it'd be a wise career move to take some time off work simply so they can take up panhandling. There is a veritable assload of money to be made here. And that's not even including yanking cameras and handbags off the shoulders of unwary tourists.

But for junkies it's all little more than a pain in the ass. Half the Olympic venues are right in the area where we have to go to score. The traffic has been tied up every fucking day and cops are everywhere.

We are killing time until the baby comes. After Andie's dad kicked us to the curb so the fire department could burn down our house, we scrounged around for a while, lived in the T-Bird, stayed in a run-down hotel for a few nights until we ran into this kid Kevin who used to work at the car wash with Andie and who now dabbles in the big H.

None of the other junkheads have it like me and Andie. We've got *purpose* now. We know that just over the horizon we're gonna be out of this mess and in a way that makes it all easier. It makes it easier to relax, say "fuck it" about pretty much everything. You never know what you truly need in life until you're forced to fill a car with as much of your shit as you can carry. That's when the posters and crockery and knickknack collections fall by the wayside and you've got a trunk full of letters and clippings, old photographs, a few of your favorite books, whatever's left of the music collection that was unpawnable. A few pairs of jeans, a shirt or two. None of it really matters much. Only the child matters.

Kevin and I pick up Jonas from jail the day he's released. First thing we do is call Karen's mom for him. He doesn't like talking on the phone because nobody can understand what he's saying with only half a tongue. Karen's mother tells me that her daughter's in a treatment center in upstate New York and to tell my brother to never try to contact her again. I leave that part out when I give Jonas the rundown.

We stop by the Wal-Mart and actually pay for a couple of kites, then spend the rest of the afternoon with Andie standing in the old Peckerbrook soccer field holding on to the wind, feeling it try to pull us away.

"Ya know," Jonas says in his own brand of mangled dialect, "I couldn't talk for like a month after I got thrown in the can and it got me to thinking, what would it be like to be normal for days on end? I mean, 'cause I was living it in there, ya know? Those motherfuckers don't even let you smoke. Whether you like it or not, if you got a sentence, your ass is getting clean. You don't have a choice. But I thought to myself in there, if I did have a choice and stayed clean, how would that be? I just can't imagine it. Shit's fucking boring without having your mind a little fucked up."

"No shit."

"You can live a boring, bullshit-dull life with no bottomed-out lows," Jonas continues, "smooth sailing all along for the most part . . . or you can take the jump." He looks at me. "I can't stop taking the jump, Luke."

We stand next to each other, our kites in the distance. "I know what you mean, man. Like fucking Sisyphus, the Greek guy who was cursed to push a rock up a hill for all eternity because he betrayed Zeus. But when you really look around, stand back and see the big picture, all life is is pushing rocks up hills. Doctors, lawyers, bankers, judges, rock stars, electricians, construction workers, plumbers, fucking garbagemen. Eventually everything sucks if you do it long enough. There has to be something else to fill in the empty places."

"Yeah," Jonas says. "Remember back before Mom got married to Victor, when she used to take us out to Collier's meadow and we'd fly kites all the time? That's my favorite memory." The wind really picks up and I look across the field to where Andie stands full-bellied, her Hello Kitty kite dancing in the wind and her hair flowing, like in a shampoo commercial or something.

"Hey, don't worry, J. You're still searching for your rock, finding your path. And *then* the trick is figuring out a way to keep pushing your rock while flying the kite at the same time. You've gotta sneak off every now and then, take a piss behind a tree, flirt with a beautiful girl, feel your place in the world and be at peace with it.

"Like skipping out on work and flying a kite because it's Tuesday and tomorrow might be the end of the world."

We stand there flying the kites for the rest of the afternoon, just shooting the shit, watching the way the plastic kites, blue and yellow, turn and dive with a simple flick of the wrist. It's like nothing else.

It's the little things. I'm no fool.

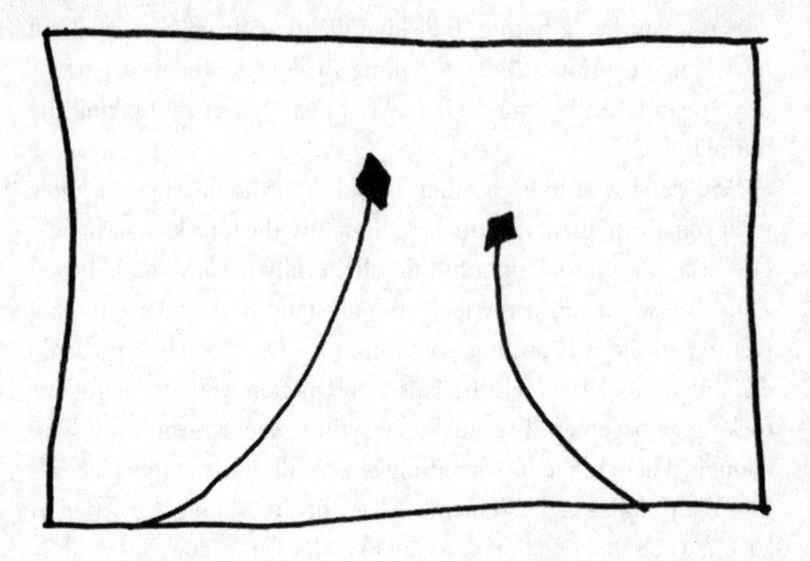

TRANSMISSION 46:

paper doll

September

We're driving down to this new ghetto Jonas discovered, ready to rip off the first unsuspecting nigger we find. Jonas tells me about one of the last times he went down to the Bluff with Karen.

"We didn't have a car, y'know," he says. "So we took MARTA down there, actually got off the bus right at the corner of Northside and North and walked the rest of the way."

"You walked around down there?"

"Yeah, man. What else were we gonna do? We didn't have any other way and we needed dope. We were sick as fuck. Plus we'd gone through all kinds of hell just getting the money, so there was no way I was turning back. Take a right here."

I turn into some projects and Jonas keeps talking. They are already running up to the car. The ghetto's the same everywhere. If you're white and you're down there, they know you're only there to score.

"Anyway, we find Alex and he sets us up right and we're walking away when that motherfucker Pooky comes up with four or five other niggers and they don't say shit to us, just start whaling on me."

"No shit."

"Yeah, man. I'm like 'FUCK!' So I grab Karen's hand and just start running and Pooky or one of them niggers grabs my hoodie and yanks me backward, drags me to the ground so hard the wind gets knocked out of me and I can feel myself blacking out and Karen's screaming and shit. It's really fucked up, right? Turn left here. And then, wouldn't you know it, out of nowhere comes Paul and he's got this massive fucking tree trunk of a staff or some shit and he just starts smacking these niggers off me like they were flies."

"Fuck yeah! Paul's my man!"

"He's good people. I mean—hold up. Pull up to this fucker."

I stop at the corner and Jonas tells the guy he wants seven boy and three girl.

"Circle the block, niggas," the guy says.

This is a huge heist. Brazen as fuck. We've got like three bucks on us, nothing. As I circle the block I can feel the urge to shit and puke coming up on me but having Jonas here, orchestrating this, has a calming effect on me. He makes it seem easy, just keeps talking.

"If Paul hadn't stomped them niggers, I don't know if we'da made it outta there that day. I was totally getting killed down there. . . . Alright look, there he is. Just pull up next to him and let me handle it. When I say 'Hit it' you fucking mash the gas as hard as you can and don't stop until you see the fucking highway, got it?"

I slowly come to a stop next to the guy and Jonas tells him he wants to taste it.

"You got some kind of fucking speech impediment?" the nigger says, laughing.

"I got half a fucking tongue. My stepfather cut it off with a pair of rusty scissors one night when he was drunk. You writing a fuckin' book?" Jonas says.

Possibly shaken by touching such a testy nerve with a self-consciously disabled junkie, the guy puts *all* the bags into his hand, if you can believe that. Easy as pie. I can't believe how fucking easy it is. In fact, I'm so stoked about the easiness of it that I just sit there when Jonas says 'Hit it,' and then the nigger's onto us and he's reaching in the window with both hands, grabbing Jonas around the throat with one hand, trying to wrench the bags out of his hand with the other.

That's when I hit it. But the guy doesn't let go and then I'm going twenty-five, thirty miles an hour and he's still holding on to the door frame with one hand and attempting to retrieve his soon-to-be-stolen bags with the other. These guys don't fuck around when it comes to getting ripped off. I can see his legs bouncing off the ground as he tries to hang on and Jonas is yelling at me not to stop. "Don't stop!" he screams. And then, right before we get to the next corner, Jonas yanks his hand back hard and the guy falls.

I keep driving. I'm going fifty when we turn the corner. I can see the dealer flipping down the street in the rearview, all haphazard and broken, a paper doll in a whirlwind. He won't be walking away from this transaction.

We make straight for the Lizard Lounge, shoot away the guilt.

TRANSMISSION 47:

i will

October

It's 2:30 in the morning when Andie wakes me and says that she's in severe pain, that the baby is flipping out inside her, that she's afraid he's going to die.

I call Animal Mother. I never paid him back that rent money, but fuck it, this is life and death. He's my friend. I need him. He will come.

I lay it all out, that this isn't just some kind of drug-addict scam. He's at the house in ten minutes and then we're speeding down the highway, making the twenty-mile journey to the hospital in twelve minutes. The nurses say we should have called earlier. They say Andie has gone into severe withdrawal because we couldn't get her to the clinic for three days straight (no gas) and now the baby is going into withdrawal. They give her some methadone and tell me all we can do now is wait and hope that the baby will calm down, that everything will get back to normal. That's what they say. They say that everything will get back to normal.

Animal Mother waits with me in the lobby until about 4 a.m. and then says he has to go, he has to work in a few hours. I check back in with Andie and the nurses say that the baby appears to have stabilized. I tell Andie I'm going to get a ride home with Mother and have Corey bring me back in the morning.

Mother loans me a twenty. I put ten in the gas tank and immediately head down to the Bluff.

It's like five o'clock in the morning and nobody's out. I wait.

I'm high when I see my baby for the first time.

Andie's no longer pregnant by the time I get back to the hospital. She's sleeping, knocked out by powerful tranquilizers. The nurse tells me she had to have an emergency C-section a couple of hours earlier because they couldn't get the baby's vital signs to stabilize again. Because of the traumatic nature of the delivery, the baby inhaled some of its own feces, a phenomenon known as meconium aspiration. Before they let me into the ICU, where my child now sleeps, they warn me that he doesn't look good, that he has tubes going down his nose and throat, that he has wires running from him to machines that monitor his vital signs to make sure he doesn't stop breathing, that he has tubes in his lungs to suck out the meconium he inhaled as he was being pulled out of Andie's belly.

"He's a boy?" I feel like crying but I don't.

"Yes. He's a very fragile, sick little boy," the nurse says. I don't know if she's being a bitch or what. I don't care. I just want to see my son.

I walk into the nursery preparing myself for the worst and as I pass all the tiny babies, row after row of them, I feel the full weight of my life and the choices I've made. Some of these kids are simply victims of their mothers' bodies' inability to maintain a full-term pregnancy, but most of them, I know, are in this darkened room because this is Atlanta, and it's a hell of a lot easier to get knocked up and stay on drugs than it is to do the right thing.

I am high when I see him for the first time. This is the ultimate failure.

I am worse than my parents ever were. At least they brought me into the world in one healthy piece. I fucked around and fucked around and now—look at this, my own flesh and blood, my own son. He is trapped in his body, doesn't know why any of this is happening to him, doesn't know why he can't scream, that the tubes running down his throat are cutting off the possibility of oxygen passing over his vocal cords.

In the hours that I sit there looking at my son with the sky-blue blinders over his little eyes, touching his tiny six-pound body as he quivers in discomfort, his red hair made redder by the burgundy hue of his scalp as he works himself into skin-reddening panic, I realize that this is it.

This will be the turning point, one way or the other.

I will not reside in limbo any longer. I will die or get better, but there will be no in-betweens. My son will know that his father tried *some*thing.

Because, my God, how beautiful he is, with his perfect fingers and toes, his tiny mouth, his seashell ears, his unmarked skin. He is everything I want to be. To try again. Start over with a clean slate.

He is the voice of God.

And when the nurse slowly, gently scoops him from the clear plastic bassinet, slides him into the crooks of my bruised arms, and I sit in that rocking chair listening to him breathe, feeling the warmth of his skin, watching his chest rise and fall with each breath, I know we have not been forsaken.

TRANSMISSION 48:

everything changes

November

Today we go to court to determine who gets custody of little Ben. Every day for a month we found a way to get up to the hospital to see him, called everyone we knew to get rides or gas money, and all of our friends were there for us when we truly needed them. Then, one afternoon after work (I now lay floor with this straight-edge guy), I went to the hospital and his crib was empty.

I panicked, started grabbing anyone who would listen to ask what happened to my boy. A nurse finally told me he'd been placed in state custody, would be living with a foster family until a court could decide if Andie and I were fit parents.

There's no question that *I'm* fit. I haven't shot dope since the day he was born. Except for today, my last hurrah. There are always final shots but this time I feel in my heart that it's real. I went cold turkey, endured all the sweating and aching and shitting and puking with unbendable resolve, a full week of that shit. But this time it was easier to do than it ever has been before because what the State doesn't understand is that Ben is my fuel. I hurt him, the most innocent and helpless of creatures, because of my selfishness and disregard for everything but the needle and now I must make it up to him. He has made it possible for me to do *any*thing. I will not be stopped. I have dedicated my life to my son, I have dedicated my everything to him. I will not be deterred.

This is something the State cannot begin to comprehend.

As a show of my determination, I cut off my dreads, one at a time, the night before the hearing. They will not be able to evaluate me based on my appearance. I will be well-spoken. I will appear as normal as anyone else, though maybe a little more sunken-cheeked and sallow.

Dreads or not, though, it doesn't matter. I'm not even given a chance to speak during the hearing save for replying in the affirmative when the judge asks me if the child is mine. The caseworker asks for full custody to be granted to the state until such time that it can be proven that we will be fit parents. Then five or six different caseworkers get on the stand and tell how, in their professional opinions, Andie and I are both fucked up and they tried to get us into treatment but we wouldn't go. I try to defend myself but the old bastard of a judge tells me that if I speak out of turn again he'll have me ejected from the courtroom.

We are demonized for twenty minutes or so until, with a bang of the gavel, full custody is granted to the state, with no visitation for the parents until such time that we have enrolled in long-term treatment centers and have successfully completed said treatment. Our state-appointed attorney tells us afterward that these kinds of cases are pretty much open-and-shut, that he didn't have much to work with because both Andie and I admitted to caseworkers that we struggled with Heroin addiction.

"But when do I get to see my son again?" I ask.

"The judge said that you have to be enrolled in a treatment center before he'll even entertain the idea of visitation."

"Where the fuck are we supposed to get the money for fucking treatment centers?" Andie asks.

"Please don't use that tone with me, ma'am. You got *yourself* into this predicament, not me," he says as he puts his yellow legal pad in his leather briefcase. "You'll just have to look in the phone book and see what's available."

It's all a scam. They knew it was going to be like this all along, and if not for the fact that my son had to be in intensive care that first month of his life, we *never* would have had a chance to see him.

Andie is in tears by the time we make it back to the car, the reality of the situation hitting her full force. But this isn't in the least bit complicated. I will not falter. Everything has changed.

But nobody gets that.

When I pull out the phonebook and start calling treatment centers, they all act like I'll just be another soup-minded junkie trying to reserve a temporary bed in their revolving-door in-patient addiction counseling services. Most of them won't even talk to me because I don't have insurance. But then I get in contact with a place named after a Catholic saint, located in downtown Atlanta. It's named after the patron saint of lost causes, the woman says.

Their waiting list is two months long. They say I will be given a piss test to make sure I'm clean when I first come in, otherwise I have to go through a detox first. I assure them that I am clean.

"Now that I have a child," I say, "I don't need drugs. I don't even want to get high. The compulsion has been lifted. I'm—"

"Sir, I don't want to sound jaded," the woman says, "but everybody that calls us says the same things you're saying. Just make sure you're here at 10 a.m. on January fourth, and we'll go from there."

"I will. Thank you so much for this chance. I won't let you down."

"Well, I hope not."

Andie's excitement over my securing a place in treatment is less than palpable. She's still out on a limb as to where she's going to go for her treatment and she's really upset about the fact that we'll be separated for so long.

She wants us to be a family.

But I'm not there anymore.

My head is shaved.

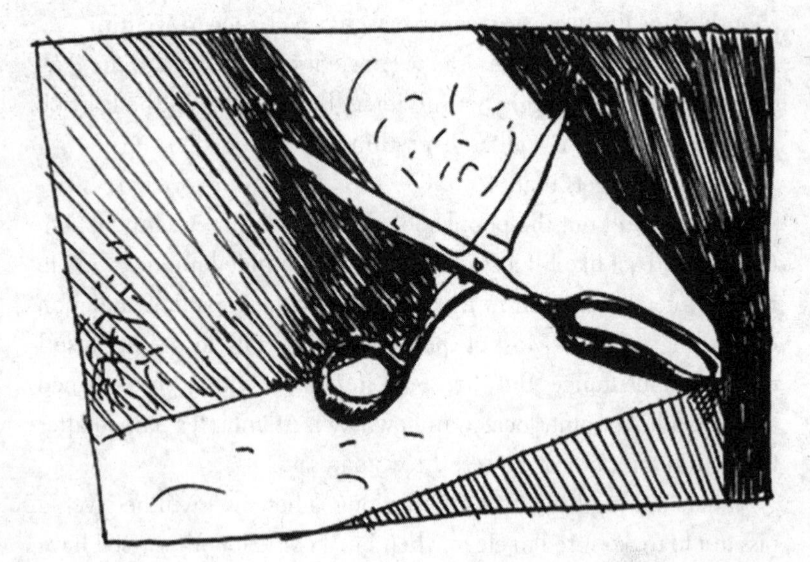

TRANSMISSION 49:

the first step

December

It's been three days since I got loaded and the pain is constant and so is the guilt. But I have to get high if it means breaking into one of these dealers' houses and taking the shit.

I'm contemplating crazy possibilities like that when I see Paul, or rather he sees me. I hear him calling me just as I'm turning off Proctor Street.

He breathlessly comes to the window, says he can get me a bag if I throw one in for him. I tell him I trust him and all, but that I have to taste the shit before I give out any money because this is the last of my cash and I have no way of getting more, and he says he'll take care of me, and when he comes back with the two bags and puts 'em in my hand I hit the gas. I don't know why I do it.

Paul runs after me for a long time, I can still see him in the rearview, running harder than he has in years, harder than when he was a teenager and had his whole life ahead of him and had energy for more than a fix, believed he could be the first black president or whatever it is poor black kids fantasize about, all that Horatio Alger bullshit that gets shoved down the poor kids' throats in school, all those Abe Lincoln and Frederick Douglass tales of rising above the bullshit and making something of ourselves.

But now Paul's in his forties and his heart's probably feeling like it's about to explode and his life's probably flashing before his eyes as he sees that this is what it amounts to, this is all everything added up to, this is his life, chasing some fucking lowlife junkie asshole he thought he could trust down the street, and now he's going to have to go back to that gold-toothed nigger in the run-down house and try to tell him that it wasn't him, it was this kid he thought he could trust and can't he just do him a solid just this once, let him have another bag for his trouble, for his *pain*.

I'm at the light and about to turn when Paul, way in the distance now, bends over and puts his hands on his knees. I can see him heaving. And then I can't do it. I can't carry on the junkie MO of everyone and everything being expendable except for the next hit.

I throw the car in reverse.

Paul's still bent over when I pull up beside him. He looks at me, his chest heaving.

"Why, man?" he asks, breathless.

"I don't know."

"Are you . . . tryin' to . . . git me killed?"

"No, Paul. No. You're my friend. I just—I didn't have the money to pay for both bags and I'm real sick, so the only way I knew I could get you to get me a bag was to take it from you. 'Cause all I have is ten bucks and I was afraid you wouldn't hook me up if I told you I only had enough cash for myself. I just need to get high, man."

That's when Paul starts crying. He starts fucking *weeping*. He's sobbing and his words are unintelligible, caught up in the back of his throat like they're being gargled.

I tell him to get in and we'll work this out. He opens the back door and slides in and for a minute I wonder if I should worry about him killing me from behind. But he's truly fucked up by this latest betrayal, which is somehow really endearing because betrayal is a junkie's stock-in-trade. We traffic in it. Nothing is sacred to us. The ripping off of our families, the wholesale theft of high-dollar electronics and everything else under the sun from every store that sells anything worth anything, the abandonment of our friends, the denial of everything we ever thought we cared about—all in the name of feeling better, pushing back the darkness of our inner psyches for just a few hours longer.

And then there's Paul. Paul weeping, his head in his hands.

I pull in behind the Lizard Lounge and park by the dumpster.

I get out of the car and reach under the dumpster for my kit but it's gone. I look around and find an old syringe from the last time I was here, when I decided that I was done for good and threw the work out the window and drove off, assured that that action of throwing the needle out the window would ensure the following through of my decision, my determination solidified by that one action. But no decision is final when you're a junkie. There's no final straw until you're dead. We keep coming back for more.

"Five fucking years, man," Paul says, between sobs. "I spent five fucking years in prison, from the time I was twenty-four until I was twenty-nine, and I couldn't think of nothin' other than the fact that when I got out I wanted to shoot up and get higher than I ever got. I didn't make no plans to rehabilitate myself. I didn't care about nothin' but gettin' high." He looks out the window, his eyes glazing over as he travels back to that place.

"And now, sitting here with you, man, I wish more than anything that I'd at least tried to imagine a different life for myself. 'Cause that would have been somethin', ya know? If I'd at least tried to clean up, get a job, maybe go back to my babies' mama and do right, that woulda been *some*thing. And now I'm runnin' down a fuckin' street at six o'clock in the morning, chasing down some kid and for what, man? So I can stay tight with some asshole who don't care about me one way or the other?"

"Don't say that, Paul. I do care about you. That's why I came back."

"Not you, man. I ain't talking about you. I'm talking about them drug slingas up in them houses. You think you the first person to rip me off? You think I ain't ever ripped a nigga off?" He smacks the top of my seat with his hand and a cloud of ancient dust rises from the upholstery.

"I realized a long time ago that the ones who burn the bridges, who take the stupid chances, are either tryin' to get clean, give themselves reason to try livin' again—or else they just don't give a fuck anymore, are ready to take whatever fate come their way 'cause a they careless actions. Me, I ain't neither a them. I'm caught in the fuckin' middle. I'm *still* tryin' to make this work. 'Cause I don't have no reason to get clean, got nothing to go back to, no job possibilities, don't know where my kids are. But at the same time—I ain't ready to die, neither, so I keep my shit clean as much as I can because I gotta somehow keep this shit goin' until I'm ready to give up on everything."

I finish fixing the first bag and hand the work to Paul over the seat back without turning around. There is a pause, a quiet settling over the car, and then his calloused fingers, rough as twigs, brush mine as he takes the syringe.

"Thank you, Dread."

We sit in silence for a moment while I fix the second bag. I use the same syringe. It doesn't matter anymore. If I'm gonna catch something I've got it already, because Jonas, Andie, Karen, and I have been sharing syringes for months.

The bag of dope is one of the best I've ever had. I don't know if it's because it's been so long since I shot up and was in so much discomfort before the welcome, familiar warmth enveloped me, drained the ache from my legs, but it feels like a final hit. I *want* this to be the final hit, here with Paul, one lost soul to the other, and then drive away from here without ever turning back.

I pass Paul a cigarette and we smoke in silence as it starts to drizzle outside.

TRANSMISSION 50:

every end is a beginning

January

Jonas is coming with me to sell the T-Bird. I figured I'd sell the car, fill up on dope for a few days, and walk into treatment with nothing but what I can hold in two arms. I won't look back. I'll be completely free of all connections to the past, my face toward the sun.

Alex set it up for us with these black guys that are into restoring old cars with the money they make slinging crack and dope. They don't like how the two passenger doors are all fucked up and use that as an excuse to give me next to nothing for my prize possession.

After fifteen minutes of haggling, the one nigger threatening to walk without my "piece of shit," we settle on nine bags of dope and a ride to the closest MARTA train station. I sign the title over to him and it's finished.

We kick the locked bathroom door open and shoot up while waiting for Kevin to arrive. It's basic junkie psychiatry. You can always get a junkie to do your bidding if you wave a big enough bag in his face.

Kevin drives us to Mom and Victor's house and I try my best to make my peace with them, even Victor, if for no other reason than the fact that Jonas is going to be living with him for God knows how long. He's run out of places to run to.

Animal Mother picks me up a couple of days before I'm due at the recovery center. I crash on his fold-out couch for ten hours straight, the deepest sleep I've had in ages.

The day before I go in I smoke a twenty-rock of crack and a dime bag of weed. Animal Mother refuses to go downtown, even if it's for one final hit, so I convince him to let me try the closest suburban ghetto to his apartment. There's no way to get another bag of boy so this will have to be my final hurrah. And it's good that way because final hits that are planned out, *known* to be final hits, are never actually final hits. There's always something else, some other "final hit" creeping up.

So in that way it's a good sign.

My last time shooting dope ends up being in a Baskin-Robbins bathroom, where Aaron, Adam, Jonas, and I go for ice cream in celebration of Aaron's thirteenth birthday. I give him my last two comic books for the occasion. They're in pristine condition, limited editions, so it's not like I'm stiffing him or something.

I watch him eating his sundae, all of us laughing about the good times, wonder what we would have been like, the four of us brothers, if we'd had a chance to actually grow up normal. How we might have fared together. How we could have gotten to know each other, trusted each other. I realize that I barely know my two youngest brothers. They are strangers to Jonas and me both. I wonder if they'll hold that against us one day. More guilt, more to pay penance for. Such as allowing Sativa to end up in the pound when we had nowhere else to put her. Like leading Andie to believe we would ever continue past the day I dropped her at her treatment center and kissed her eyelids as she cried for everything we'd been through. There's no way for us to ever go back to the way it was in the beginning. We've destroyed everything and all that's left for us is whatever life we can make on our own, trying to become better human beings, learning how to be parents, and most of all moving past the horrors we've inflicted on ourselves and each other. It's all over and all that's left is our little boy, my little Ben.

Animal Mother pulls up to the entrance of the rather stately looking treatment center. It was a prestigious hotel a long time ago is what the nameplate says next to the front door. A few guys stand beside the building holding AA manuals and smoking cigarettes. Mother and I hug, strong and steady, and he helps me grab the three duffel bags that contain everything I own.

I already have to piss even though I just went right before we left his apartment. Early this morning I drank a gallon of this nasty tea that cleans out your system because I can't have the crack and weed from last night showing up on the piss test. I've come too far to be turned away now.

I've got my copy of *Black Boy* in my back pocket, worse off than ever, the pages barely holding on, entire sections coming unglued, the spine held fast with duct tape. In my t-shirt pocket, carefully wrapped in a sheet of notebook paper, is the one picture I have of my son.

This is it. This is the moment.

My path awaits me. *Every*thing comes next. And as Mother pulls away and I drag on a cigarette, I remember it all. It all comes back to me in flashes and brilliant color. That was my life. This is my life now. I *need* to remember. Because I can never forget. Because every time it comes down and it seems like there will never be daylight again, I have to remind myself what I know to be true: we are born to be *re*born. No matter how many times we die, we are given another chance to meet our destinities. We just have to grab them.

We live again.

acknowledgments

I could not have written or seen this book published without the help of so many different people. My editor, Michael Signorelli, has an eye that has made *Futureproof* the book it was meant to be. Jenny Bent is not only a great friend but also the most incredible agent I've had the pleasure to meet and (finally!) work with. There are numerous persons whose contributions to the success of *Futureproof* are immeasurable: Ali O'Rourke (still my Only), my perfect Jake and Wrenn!, Brandon "The Terminator" Stickney, Berea College, Dr. Libby Jones, Dr. Richard Sears, the Skidmore Writers Workshop, Samantha Dunn, Dan Pope, Deena Neville, Christie Webb-Gibson, Black Arrow Studio and Press, Luca DiPierro, Nick and Isaac (finally true believers), Amelia Madison, Leah Pfeiffer, Ryan Scott, Billy Jacobs, Rose Koch, James Frey, Josh Kilmer-Purcell, Tony O'Neill, Brad Listi, Will Clarke, Kasey and Dolly Relford, April Sprinkle (yes, her real name and, no, she's not a porn star), Doug LaVigne, Christie Petersen, Ansley Fowler, Lefty Jones, Dakota LaCroix, Mike Smith, E. Nichols, and Atlanta's own *Creative Loafing.*

Finally, thank you to **The FutureProof 500**, the first supporters of *Futureproof*, who saw its potential and supported it from its inception. Thank you. You are truly the heroes of this story. Without your undying support it wouldn't have made it this far. Onward and upward!

WORD.

About the author

About the book

Read on

Insights,
Interviews
& More . . .

Meet Frank Daniels

Rachel Bradley

Frank Daniels was born in Philadelphia, Pennsylvania, and was moved up and down the East Coast from one house to another for the first fourteen years of his life before finally landing semi-permanently in ATLanta, Georgia. There he learned the value of (dysfunctional) friends over (more dysfunctional) family, the art of rebellion, and the quickest way to accumulate a hell of a lot of brain-numbing stories of urban adventure.

He briefly moved back to Pennsylvania in late 1997 before being accepted to college in Berea, Kentucky, where he and his future wife published two issues of the underground Xeroxed zine *Culture Vacuum*, which was accepted with mixed reviews by the college reading population. Daniels also made a point of writing inflammatory columns in the school paper, attacking both left- and right-wing extremist views, and was subsequently threatened not only with (grievous) bodily harm, but also with sexual harassment charges (for *writing a newspaper article critiquing a class's musical performance*—this was a LIBERAL arts school, after all). In 2002 he graduated magna cum laude and then moved to North Carolina with his wife and two children (shit happens fast in college—there's a time and a place for everything). There he attended UNC with the hopes of getting a master's degree. During the two semesters he was in grad school, he DJ'd at the college radio station (an extension of his tenure as a dance DJ while an undergrad). However, it soon became apparent to Daniels not only that Greensboro, North Carolina, sucks, but also that graduate school in general was not for him. At that time he took up writing in earnest, and the genesis for his first novel, *Futureproof*, was born.

In 2005 Daniels moved back to ATLanta after a seven-year absence. He spends most ▸

“It soon became apparent to Daniels not only that Greensboro, North Carolina, sucks, but also that graduate school in general was not for him.”

Everyone has a picture this terrible from his childhood, and mine was obviously no exception. I could rock the hell out of a butterfly-collared blue polyester suit in 1980. Note that even at such a tender and innocent age, I already had a highly developed oral fixation.

Meet Frank Daniels *(continued)*

days chewing bubble gum and kicking figurative ass. He admires graffiti *artists*, particularly Banksy and Doze Green. He's a luddite, though he does own a cell phone and a computer through which he communicates with other human beings and the occasional spambot, though he misses the days when people actually wrote each other letters. He's tired of finding only bills, unsolicited supermarket fliers, preapproved credit card offers, and fast food coupons in his mailbox. If only there were a way, Daniels muses, to have a junk-mail box just like on an e-mail account, except for real mail.

Daniels can be reached and happily communicated with at nfrankdaniels.com, myspace.com/nfrankdaniels, and nfrankdaniels@gmail.com. Just don't send any goddam junkmail.

I was twenty-one in this pic and had the world by the balls. Shortly thereafter the world grabbed its own handful and I was humbled. No, as it turns out, I wasn't the coolest motherfucker to walk the planet.

One for the Books: A Self-Publishing Stunner

THE STORY OF WRITING the story of *Futureproof* is, for me anyway, just as invigorating as the real-life events that greatly affected the topics focused on within its pages. As one might figure out after having finished the novel, *Futureproof* is loosely autobiographical. "Did all of this stuff really happen?" is the number-one question I get from everyone who has read the book. And by everyone, I mean the thousand-plus readers who have already beaten you guys to the punch. You see, *Futureproof* was originally just another of the tens or hundreds of thousands of self-published books that come out every year, mostly to fall on deaf ears.

My decision to self-publish this novel was based on a number of factors. Once the book was finished and I was ready to publish, I did some research and discovered a wealth of very successful authors who'd come before me who had started out by self-publishing, among them John Grisham, Will Clarke (now a good friend of mine), and, most notably, Walt Whitman, considered by many to be the greatest American poet. Armed with the knowledge of how hard it is for anyone to ▸

Yours truly resides on the right in this picture, with two of my younger brothers filling out the photograph. This picture was taken during the darkest days of my coming-of-age.

Tony O'Neill, Josh Kilmer-Purcell, and me at my first huge reading, in October of 2006, at the legendary New York literary bar KGB. All three of us are published by Harper Perennial.

find a publisher these days, especially for a novel (what with the memoir being all the rage and there being a swift and continuous decline in the number of active book readers), I decided, against the advice of many seasoned pros, to self-publish. I'd taken up many precious hours writing the book and editing and re-editing it, so there was no way in hell I was just going to let it fall to the bottom of countless slush piles. I formulated a plan. I would personally market the book to as many people as I possibly could via the Internet and its many avenues for self-promotion. I petitioned people, using primarily MySpace and Amazon, asking them to read the first fifty pages of the book and respond positively or negatively to what they'd read. The book would stand or fall on its own merits. The results were overwhelmingly positive.

“I'd taken up many precious hours writing the book and editing and re-editing it, so there was no way in hell I was just going to let it fall to the bottom of countless slush piles.”

Phase two of the plan was then put into action. I would publish the book via P.O.D. (print on demand). This would sate the thirst these hundreds of readers had expressed to read the rest of the book and would also provide hard numbers as to how many people would actually pay to read my writing. I began enlisting some of these readers to help me with artwork, cover design, layout, webpage development, et cetera. All of these people, who are recognized in the acknowledgments of this book, did this work completely pro bono. It was for them, just as writing and publishing *Futureproof* was for me, a labor of love. They all wanted to be a part of something they saw as immensely promising. So, on February 6, 2006, *Futureproof* was published via lulu.com. I had my fair share of connections to other already established writers by this point and was able to include blurbs from James Frey, Samantha Dunn, Josh Kilmer-Purcell, and others on the cover of the book.

If there's one thing I've learned during the long process of writing and publishing a book, it is that you *must* get connected to others who are already on the "inside" of the complex organism that is book publishing. I'm convinced that, in this age of so much media and information and distraction, William Shakespeare himself would have had his work turned down for publication had he not the know-how when it came to enlisting an army of word-of-mouth virus spreaders and a particular penchant for reaching out to those writers and industry insiders way out of his league as far as exposure and clout goes. So if nothing else, though I'm no Shakespeare by any stretch of the imagination, I was rewarded on an almost daily basis by readers from all corners of the globe telling me how this book had positively affected their lives. And none of that would have happened if not for the ▸

"If there's one thing I've learned during the long process of writing and publishing a book, it is that you *must* get connected to others who are already on the 'inside' of the complex organism that is book publishing."

One for the Books ***(continued)***

viral marketing I took up, using such tools as Malcolm Gladwell's incredible book *The Tipping Point*, which scientifically breaks down how cultural "viruses" occur. To sum it up in far too few words, the trick lies in hitting a few specific types of people who then enthusiastically express their excitement for this little-known cultural artifact—the excitement of coming in on the ground floor. And make no mistake, that kind of viral spread is now possible on a global scale. I've had soldiers from Iraq and Afghanistan contact me, having had friends or relatives send them the book.

But luck cannot be overlooked. Soon after *Futureproof* came out, I petitioned the person who was then the most prominent reviewer of "the most deserving" books published via P.O.D. Her name was POD Girl, an anonymous mainstream "midlist" author who took it upon herself to sift through literally hundreds of authors' P.O.D. manuscripts and then review those she thought most deserving. She gave *Futureproof* an "A" rating and, not three weeks later, *Entertainment Weekly* ran a small piece about what she was doing, including in the piece small blurbs along with pictures of the book covers of the last five books she'd reviewed. *Futureproof* was right in the middle of those five books, and somehow, unbelievably, my novel ended up in the August 11, 2006, issue of the magazine. I was doing everything right, the sales kept coming, as did the e-mails gushing praise. The one thing that wasn't coming, however, was the book deal that all of this was meant to culminate with. I once again decided to take matters into my own hands. I collected as much money as possible and embarked on an eight-city book tour along the East Coast, a round trip of more than 2,500 miles. The results of the tour were fair to middling, but the experience was incredible. A full account of this book tour can be found in my blog archives, in the October 2006 section. Yet even after a great turnout in New York City, which was the most important reading of the whole tour, as well as promotion in the influential *Time Out New York*, still I had no book deal.

By the end of summer the next year, I was ready to throw in the towel. I was burned out, and my family was exhausted by my never-ending push to have all this legwork finally pay off with a book deal. By this time I had completed the follow-up to *Futureproof* and decided that I was going to put this first novel on the back burner and turn my focus solely to finding a publisher for my second novel. The idea was that if I could find a publisher for the second, much edgier and experimental novel, then perhaps *Futureproof* would be published later, after building on the success of the second novel. I geared myself up for another run at the powers that be with this new book. And that's when it finally broke. My excellent editor at Harper Perennial, Michael Signorelli, contacted me (via MySpace!) and told me that they were interested in publishing *Futureproof*. Just like that, it happened. You push and push and push, and then when you stop pushing, you realize that the door said "Pull" all along. So here we are now. I have an amazing agent at one of the biggest and most respected agencies in the business. I have an amazing team behind me at Harper. I've met even more incredible authors. I'm finally on the other side of the fence. The lion's share of work still lies ahead, true, what with getting a much larger audience to take ▶

“By this time I had completed the follow-up to *Futureproof* and decided that I was going to put this first novel on the back burner and turn my focus solely to finding a publisher for my second novel.”

One for the Books ***(continued)***

notice, to somehow lift *Futureproof* above the litany of other books all vying for attention in a glutted industry. But sometimes you have to stop pulling your hair out and start believing in miracles. And busting your ass to lay the groundwork for those miracles to happen.

Excerpt: The Next Book

The following is an excerpt from the next book in the Futureproof *storyline, tentatively titled* Gravity Eats the Dawn. *Enjoy.*

THERE ARE 27 OF US slumped in folding chairs forming a ragged circle, in the center of which stands a man with a clipboard who is yelling at us with the cadence and ferocity of a Marine Corps drill instructor. *Only 1 maybe 2 of you in this room is going to succeed where so many others have failed*, says the guy with the clipboard to all of us pathetic fucks staring up at him from our circled metal folding chairs. *Addiction has stolen all of your lives this treatment center is here to help you get them back but make no mistake you will be doing all of the work we are only here to show you the way you will have to do the work. There will be no other options. Stand up.* We look at him. *STAND UP*. We stand and wonder if this is the part where we have to strip down and guys in surgical masks and hospital scrubs throw some of that delousing shit on us while they hose us down with piping cold water. *This is the beginning of your new life. In order for this life to become a life without drugs and prison and ruined families and relationships and friendships and lost jobs—you're going to have to make* ▸

Aside from two or three pictures I've taken of my children, this is my favorite photograph I've ever taken. It features prominently in the next book.

Excerpt: The Next Book *(continued)*

changes. These changes include who you hang out with where you hang out. There can be no more weekends at the bar with your buddies. There should never be a single instance this early in your journey to recovery that you ever *hang around these old people and places. They will only bring temptation and make it all the more likely that you will end up right back here again or worse in jail or a grave. These are the facts. You will only succeed if you follow the path that has been proven to work—the* only *path that has been proven to work. If you make yourself open and available to that path you will succeed but most of you are still too caught up in your own shit to let go enough to allow someone to help you, to allow someone to show you the way.* He speaks to us like an evangelical preacher leading his sheep he is mesmerizing. *Now—there are 27 of you in this room some of you are here because you want to be others are here because you have to be but it makes no difference whether you want to or have to only 2 of you are going to last only 2 of you are going to see this the whole way through regardless of what—a wife, a family, a court order—is on the line. Look at each other.* We glance at one another without making eye contact stare at the floor look again. *Which of you is it going to be which of you has the guts to take your life back? Sit down if you think you have what it takes.* One guy sits down almost immediately and then it's contagious and all of us start sitting down in bunches until nobody is standing except the guy with the clipboard. *Most of you are liars 2 of you are not time will sort out who is who.*

“There are 27 of you in this room. . . . Only 2 of you are going to last.”

I was in this Treatment Center/Rehab environment for 7 months and I've now been out for close to 6. So far I've been one of the few who've stayed clean I don't know who the other guy might be from my original intake group that stayed clean but all that matters is I'm one of 'em I'm one of the 2 people who is no goddam liar.

Back right after I started Rehab my brother Jonas and his dumbass girlfriend showed up at the door of the Center on visitation day and asked me to walk down to the IHOP for a cup of coffee and a stack of pancakes. I immediately accepted the invite because the cunt posing as a nurse that ran the menu/chowline at the Treatment Center was this sadistic robot-bitch that wouldn't let us have any sugar for stuff like coffee or salt for stuff like instant mashed potatoes. She explained through her human faceplate that this was for our own good we needed to cleanse our bodies of all impurities even sugar and salt but you could tell she reveled in the complete power of her position and even Bobby who runs the goddam place came just short of admitting that she was the cunt she really was. I could tell as soon as we started walking toward the IHOP that my brother and his dumbass girlfriend were higher than hell but I was worried about Jonas and was also just happy to get out of the Rehab for an hour so I kept walking anyway. Like now, they were living on the street and I figured this was a safe outing there was no way I could get into a hairy situation just by walking to the IHOP whether they were high or not. So I went. We sat in a booth and I watched his dumbass girlfriend nod off repeatedly as I tried to maintain Jonas's attention long enough for us to exchange more than 2 subsequent sentences in a row. He couldnt have been more fucked up I mean he had to have shot up right before he materialized at the Treatment Center. ***What the hell have you*** ▶

“I could tell as soon as we started walking toward the IHOP that my brother and his dumbass girlfriend were higher than hell but I was . . . just happy to get out of the Rehab for an hour.”

been doing? Are you even trying to get into a place? A Detox? Or are you happy living like a complete bum? *Dude, we just got fucked over royally*, he said, completely ignoring me. *We went down to the Goodwill over there on Howell Mill and bought this fucking awesome down comforter for 10 bucks and then we left it in this abandoned car we've been sleeping in then we went and copped a few bags and when we got back to the fucking car the fucking blanket was gone some fucking crackhead took it or something. We're fucking freezing.* He scratched his nose a bunch it looked like it was about to bleed from all the scratching I mean it was nonstop. I ordered some pancakes with strawberries and whipped cream and was eating those pancakes really enjoying them, staring at Jonas with his pin-dot pupils and his dumbass of a girlfriend with her nodded-out head slumped against his shoulder and thanking the Almighty that I was out of that racket I mean if Jonas and his dumbass girlfriend weren't the best goddam deterrent ever then nothing ever would be.

Then Jonas asked me if I wanted some.

Before I could say anything he slid a little green baggie across the table toward me. It was filled almost to the top with white Heroin. It was a huge bag. ***Do you have a work?*** I asked him. He furtively slid a syringe across the table as if it was an envelope filled with payoff cash from a mobster to a cop or something. I slid out of the booth and skulked back to the toilet. It wasn't until I'd slapped the deadbolt shut and placed the work and the baggie on the corner of the sink that I really gave some thought to what was happening to what I was about to do it wasn't even me doing it it was like watching someone else doing it. I stared in the mirror for a good long time and watched the bees buzzing in the glass hive and weighed out my options. I thought about how I could cover up this one last indiscretion, could shoot the Dope then head directly back to my room at the Center and feign sleep until the next morning when the physical manifestations of the high would have worn off. Then I thought about how I'd justify it if I were found out how I'd convince the state to give me another chance to prove myself worthy of my son. I stood in the IHOP bathroom. Kept staring in the mirror. The bees went about their work. Then I punched myself hard in the mouth my bottom teeth cutting my lip, went back out to the booth and tossed the bag and the work to my brother told him he was a cunt for doing that bullshit scooped up my still steaming plate of pancakes and in one motion turned and walked out the door ignoring the confused waitress as she explained that the plates were not part of the to-go deal, smiling to myself for a whole range of reasons. Saw Jonas' face pasted to the other side of the window in the same booth where I'd just conquered the world. I couldn't believe I'd just beaten the demon and he couldn't either.